Lead White

First published in 2017 by
Liberties Press
1 Terenure Place | Terenure | Dublin 6W | Ireland
Tel: +353 (0) 86 853 8793
www.libertiespress.com

Distributed in the UK by
Turnaround Publisher Services
Unit 3 | Olympia Trading Estate | Coburg Road | London N22 6TZ
T: +44 (0) 20 8829 3000 | E: orders@turnaround-uk.com

Distributed in the United States by
Casemate IPM | 1950 Lawrence Road | Havertown | Pennsylvania
19083 | USA
T: (610) 853 9131 | E: casemate@casematepublishers.com

2 4 6 8 10 9 7 5 3 1
A CIP record for this title is available from the British Library.
Cover design by Roudy Design
Printed in Dublin by Sprint Print

Lead White

Ronan Lyons

lead white / led white /

noun

a poisonous pigment used in painting, notable for its covering power and tough, flexible film-forming properties.

Contents

About the Author

A graduate of Trinity College, Dublin, Ronan Lyons has worked as a staff journalist with The Economist Group, covering eastern Europe, Russia and the former Soviet republics. He also is a founding director of The Molesworth Gallery, now one of Ireland's leading contemporary art galleries. Ronan lives in Dublin with his wife, Teresa, their three children, Rory, Oscar and Flora, and their dog, Fred.

Author's Note

This book is a tribute to all of the people I've met working in the art world and to the talent and bloody-minded dedication that sustains them, often for little financial reward. If some of the characters' opinions and the actions they inspire can seem a little cynical about contemporary art, they rarely represent my own point of view, no more than Thomas Harris ever, himself, wanted to eat a man's liver with some 'fava beans and a nice chianti'.

The book does take aim at the absurd sums of money swilling about at the very high-end of the contemporary art market in London, Basel, New York and Miami and, for this, I make no apology. Frankly, anyone who tells you this most rarefied end of the market isn't insane probably has something to sell - or is in palpitant denial on the value of a piece they've just bought.

I'd like to thank all of my early readers, in particular Aengus Kelly, PJ Lynch and Blaise Smith, for encouraging me to stick with it. The inspirational group of people I met at Curtis Brown Creative deserve a mention too, as do the Arts Council of Ireland, who supported the book in its early stages with a Travel and Training Award, and Richard Scrivener of the Creative Rights Agency in London, who worked so hard to get the book published. Thanks as well to Liberties Press, who signed it up, to my delight, in January of 2016.

I should also thank my family and friends for putting up with me but, above all, I should thank Teresa, who never once questioned my devotion of so much time and effort to a project that was unlikely to contribute to our mortgage repayments any time soon. To have a partner so gracious, kind, funny and intelligent makes life a lot easier.

Prologue

A burst of fluorescent light in a white cube, and a red mist, a blood mist, a fine spray across gesso walls. Crimson lake spurting, splashing, dripping like a Pollock, and burnt umber smeared across a polished concrete floor, and a knife – a palette knife? – scraping raw sienna across a wall towards handprints, either side of a torso.

The bloody after-image of a scream.

The corpse lay beneath, blood sluicing from a partially-severed head. The knife slashed through clothes, through gristle, nerve, tendon and muscle. The work was exact in every anatomical detail, apart from the face: a crude, blood-sodden maquette of pummelled cartilage and shredded skin. And the hands: unresolved, no fingertips, just bloodied stumps.

Synapses crackle.

His optical nerve shorted.

Reality flickered in and out of focus.

He heard blood coursing – his own – and muffled speech.

'I . . .'

'What?'

'I . . . it.'

Hands motioned beside him, fingers splayed, and his own unthinking voice: 'What did you say?'

'I love it,' the voice repeated.

'What are you talking about?'

'The work.'

His breath came in short, fitful gusts. 'The work?'

'Yah, the work. The installation, the fabricated murder scene. I love it. It's site-specific, totally uncommercial. Why was there no press release? When is the *vernissage*?'

'The what?'

'Forgive me, I'm not in Basel now. When is the private viewing, the opening?'

Hugh's gaze fixed on the gaping neck wound. 'The opening?'

'Yah, the opening.'

He turned to the man by his side – Diedrich Weiss, noted critic and curator – then back to the scene in the gallery. His breathing steadied. His brain rebooted, made sense of what his eyes could see, of what the other man's eyes could see. And if he'd learnt one thing over the past few months, it was that what the eyes see is malleable, a supple clay in the right hands.

'Of course,' Hugh said, a tremor still in his voice, 'the opening. What was I thinking? We haven't fixed a date yet. The artist is still ironing out some technical issues. Trying out various fake-blood recipes. You know, for their . . . viscosity.'

Diedrich nodded gravely. 'Yah, *natürlich*, the viscosity. I can see the pooled blood around the head hasn't clotted, or rather, it hasn't congealed – which is the desired effect, I take it?'

Hugh paused, then nodded in turn. 'Yes, this has just happened. We – the viewer – have just happened upon it. That's the artist's intention.'

'And who is the artist?'

'It's the work of . . . an emerging Russian talent.'

Hands clapped gleefully. 'Russian! I should have guessed. Post-Soviet art is so visceral. Unshackled from the chains of ideology but unburdened by Western bourgeois mores. I must say, this makes Hirst's musings on our mortality look like kindergarten stuff.' He turned to Hugh. 'Waxwork, I presume?'

Hugh paused a moment – *waxwork*? – then fixed his eyes on the German. 'Yes, of course . . . waxwork.'

'It is gloriously gruesome,' Diedrich said, turning back to the scene before them. 'The head almost hacked away. The fingertips removed.' As he leaned closer, the giddiness wavered and his upper lip gave a slight quiver of revulsion. 'Goodness, even the teeth have been pulled out.' A pliers lay in a bloody pool – mixed with what looked like vomit – next to a toothless orifice where the mouth should have been.

Diedrich rubbed his chin. 'I'm beginning to see how the body has been depersonalised. It's the everyman.'

'In a Paul Smith,' Hugh said, as much to himself as Diedrich, who looked confused.

'The suit, it's a Paul Smith,' Hugh said again. The jacket flapped open on one side with a label clearly visible, as was the Cleverley's moniker on the soles of the shoes.

'Ah, the suit, the attire of the successful man. Perhaps the artist is posing a question here: 'Is this capitalism's sacrificial lamb?' He nudged Hugh. 'Or perhaps it's the dealer, no?'

Hugh shuddered. 'Jesus, it could have been.'

Diedrich placed a hand on Hugh's shoulder and fixed him in the eye. 'But seriously, I'm co-curating the Yokohama Triennial next year, and I want this artist on the programme. No ifs, no buts, no schedule clashes. Let's diarise now.'

He edged closer to the work as a fly landed on the stump of spinal cord protruding above the neck.

'It might be best to stay back,' Hugh said.

'Yah, of course, very *güte*,' Diedrich said jovially. 'One mustn't tamper with the crime scene.' His eyes settled on the bloodied gallery walls. 'Bravo! Such a multifaceted work.'

'Why not come back and have a proper look when it's fully installed? I forgot we had the . . . technicians in today.'

'Yah, of course.' Diedrich surveyed the space one last time. 'This is *wunderbar*. It's a desecration of the gallery as cultural temple. It's the gallery as mausoleum. It's the deposition of relational aesthetics by the alter-modernists.' He puckered his lips – as if cramp had set in – before concluding: 'The piece just works on so many levels.'

'Yeah,' Hugh said, ushering the critic towards the exit and glancing back over his shoulder. 'There's certainly a lot here to dissect.'

Part 1

Four months earlier

CHAPTER 1

Gild It and They Will Come

'This man called by looking for you,' the message said. 'A big chap. Rude too. Bit of a bolts-through-the-neck job, actually.' There followed an awkward pause. 'Anyhooo, the intern told him where you'd gone. Sorreee!'

The message was from Vicky, his gallery manager. Hugh hung up and slipped the phone in his pocket just as the taxi pulled up at the kerbside in Whitechapel.

'That it, sport?' the driver asked, pointing at the hundreds of light-bulbs fixed onto plywood and hung above the entrance of a building across the street.

Hugh sighed. 'It might very well be.'

He paid the driver and stepped out onto the pavement. A canvas of low cloud with a fine craquelure of sunlight gave the halo of bulbs over the gallery doors an unintentionally gothic quality. They spelled out the title of the exhibition opening that evening – *con Temporary art?* – billed as a showcase of twelve up-and-coming young artists.

Hugh mulled it over and, in the spirit of blind optimism that had sustained him for the past year, decided that Neck-Bolts was unlikely to pursue him across central London at half six on a Thursday evening. He crossed the street and rounded a knot of smokers on the pavement outside the gallery. A porter held the plate-glass door open and he walked straight into the main exhibition space. Scanning the crowd for Craig Charlton, his gaze settled on the far corner, where there was a commotion, a shimmer of flashbulbs and a clearing around the artist, who stood next to his work.

Charlton was the main attraction. No surprises there. He'd caused a minor stir in the national press with his latest body of work: the dung of various animals, gilded and mounted on granite plinths. A story about him in the *Telegraph* was headlined CRAIG *CHARLATAN*?.

The *Daily Mail* ran with STATE-FUNDED GALLERY MAKES A SPLASH WITH *PLOP* ART.

Charlton even earned the sobriquet of THE TURD MAN OF BRITISH ART from the *Sun*.

None of this was the kind of publicity that London's art aficionados could resist, and so here they all were, like flies around shit – eighteen-carat gilded shit, according to the exhibition catalogue.

Hugh's attendance was more a case of needs must. He'd always had reservations over bodily discharges as artistic media, but Charlton was just the type of artist he needed to sign up if he was to trade his way out of his debts – get Neck-Bolts off his back. The artist wasn't represented by a blue-chip London gallery and, word was, the Tate was buying some pieces from this show; having work in the Tate's collection meant artists could at least double their prices, sometimes add a zero.

So, steeling himself, Hugh took a glass of champagne from the bar next to the entrance and eased his way into the crowd. There was a din of clinking, chattering, forced laughter, corks popping, extravagantly insincere greetings. All around him artists preened and talked about money, while the moneyed swooned and talked about art. Dealers and art consultants oiled the space in between. Hugh could also spot the rubber-neckers – well-heeled ones, granted – drawn here by the no-doubt-spurious tweet that Brad Pitt was coming, likely emanating from the gallery's PR company.

In a way, the PR people had their work cut out. The space wasn't the pristine white box that all artists aspire to nowadays. It was a converted Victorian industrial space run by the city council, with lots of rough edges: a colonnade running along one end with a mezzanine above it, and three enormous sash windows at the other – which meant the light in the space varied according to the time of day. There were oak floor-boards as well, instead of the polished stone or concrete floor that was *de rigueur* in most newer spaces. But the gallery had a reputation for showing cutting-edge work and had helped establish the careers of some of the bigger beasts of the art world. Its openings were also a fixture on the city's social calendar and were lavishly sponsored by a phalanx of banks and companies lining up to give a cultural sheen to their corporate branding.

At the very least, this meant that the canapés were half-decent. Hugh had skipped lunch and was taking full advantage. He bit into a pleasing confection of cranberries and smoked duck and studied Charlton's demeanour from across the room. There were plenty of other people there he knew, none of whom he could risk being drawn into conversation with, just in case Neck-Bolts did stalk him across the city. He only had time for Charlton and the waitresss who hovered around him with a near-empty tray of canapés, most of which he had eaten. He took the last one and ate it whole.

'I bring you more,' she said, winking at him and slipping past the two couples alongside.

The couples looked forlornly at the tray before turning back towards Charlton. 'Any idea how much Craig's shifting his stools for?' the one still wearing his shades snorted into a champagne flute. Hugh had already clocked them as artists, even before he overheard their conversation. The grungy dress and the frantic quaffing of the free bubbly were a dead giveaway.

The artists paid little attention to the work on the wall behind them. Simple line drawings of fornicating office workers vied for notice with a huge, garishly-coloured painting of Pokémon-like creatures, playing croquet and shooting clay pigeons – think Manga comics meets *Country Life*. Further along the wall, a pink neon sign smugly declared: *You can't afford this work of art.*

'Throwing down the gauntlet with most of this crowd,' Hugh muttered to himself.

He moved through the crowd towards the centre of the gallery, where a gruesome scene from a Hieronymus Bosch painting was re-enacted with Lego figures on a ten-foot-long white plinth. A porter hovered over the piece, keeping a wary eye on the small boy next to it who hadn't quite grasped that it was a work of art and not left there for him to play with. The boy was clearly used to getting his own way and shrugged off the porter, scuttling around to the other side of the plinth with his

Filipino nanny in a rather sluggish pursuit. She seemed more interested in her phone than her infant charge.

Hugh smiled at the boy and corralled him back towards the nanny. Straightening his back, he gazed blankly at the Lego apocalypse, then back towards the entrance, the smile fading as he did so.

The competition had arrived.

Alexandra Friedman sauntered into the room, her beatific smile holding fast. Friedman was more than just an art dealer. She was a high priestess for devotees of contemporary art, her gallery a shimmering white temple – although one where merchants and money-changers were always welcome. She paused now and then to minister to some rapt collectors or simpering artists, vainly hoping they too might be anointed.

Friedman was unlikely to be troubled by Hugh's presence. There were too many has-beens or never-likely-to-have-beens in his stable of artists. His sales pitch was always a little off-key; his taste in art a little too erratic; his clients a little too gauche. He didn't even look like a typical contemporary-art apparatchik. He was big and athletic, and still lined out on a rugby field every Sunday morning, determined to eke out a few more seasons before turning forty.

If Friedman did make it to Charlton first, Hugh's gamble on sticking around would have been in vain. Playing it cool wasn't an option. He pressed through the crush of suits around Charlton, bumping into him, feigning surprise.

'Craig! Great to see you again. Congrats on the show.'

Charlton gagged a little on his canapé. 'Hello, Hugh,' he spluttered. 'Didn't think this was your scene.'

'Nonsense. For my money, this is the most important show in London at the moment.'

Charlton was slight and twitchy – nothing like the shameless self-publicist portrayed in the papers. The tweed cap he wore hid a scutch of receding hair. Beneath its peak, his eyes flitted about like bluebottles in a jar. He was anxious, no doubt, that Hugh's presence would deter other dealers from approaching him.

They'd met before at another opening, though at the time the artist scored much lower in the 'Hierarchy of People to Schmooze' that every dealer employs, a crass but effective calculus of social opportunism.

Hugh divided the world into two basic classes of people: the ones he needed something from, and the ones who needed something from him. A couple of shrewd publicity stunts and a high-profile exhibition had leapfrogged Charlton from the second group to the first.

But Hugh wasn't alone in revising his attitude to Charlton. The suit next to them drained his champagne flute and placed it on the tray of a passing waiter. The Mandarin collar on his jacket and the pelt of ash-blond hair extending below his earlobes marked him out from the corporate crowd. He stuck out a hand, pitched at an angle on the acute side of camp. '*Güten abend*. Deidrich Weiss. Have we met?'

'Hugh Rhattigan from the Lead White Gallery.'

'Ah yes. A nice *little* gallery.'

Hugh bristled. 'I wouldn't call us little. We've got three thousand square feet in St James's.'

'Really? Perhaps I am mixing you up with another gallery. Golly, it is difficult to keep up. There are so many galleries; so many artists.' Weiss plucked another glass of champagne from a convoy of waiters that was snaking by before fanning out across the room. 'Have you met Larry Cockburn, CEO of the Optimus hedge fund, and one of the exhibition sponsors?'

Hugh hadn't copped who it was until then. A large, tanned hand was held out to him, this one spirit-level straight. Its owner was tall, only an inch shy of Hugh, and perfectly groomed, looking like he'd just stepped out of a Rolex ad. The hand wrapped itself around Hugh's. It was the hand that wrote the cheques for one of the biggest private modern-art collections in the world. Hugh almost curtsied.

'So, you own a gallery?' Cockburn asked, the voice a mellow baritone, the accent a languid Virginian drawl.

'I do. For my sins.'

'What kinda work you show?'

'Contemporary artists, mainly. We also handle a couple of estates.'

'Anyone I've heard of?' Cockburn glanced over Hugh's shoulder towards the exit as he spoke.

'We represent Jacob Gertz and Matthew Lomas.'

Heads shook. No flickers of recognition.

'Lomas has just shown at the Middlesbrough Institute of Modern Art.'

More head-shaking. The din grew louder.

'We also have work in stock by Sean Scully and Henry Moore.'

'Ah, those I *have* heard of,' Cockburn said, to the evident relief of all four of them. 'I believe we have several of each. Are you familiar with our collection?' He was clearly concerned that Hugh might not be. It had been assembled by consultants – among them Weiss – at vast expense.

'Funnily enough, I've just seen some of the work you have on loan at the Irish Museum of Modern Art, when I was home on a visit. Very impressive.'

'Ah, you're Irish,' Cockburn said, brightening. 'I thought I recognised the accent. I'm a big fan of your country … wonderful golf courses.' His voice trailed off, his eyes flitting towards the exit again. 'Well, it's been a pleasure, Hugh, but I see my driver is here. I'd love to go on your mailing list, though.'

'Of course,' Hugh said. 'I'll have you put on straightaway.'

As it happens, Cockburn had been on the list for the previous four years. That meant about fifteen invitations and ten catalogues a year might as well have gone straight into the gallery's recycling bin instead of in the post.

Cockburn put his glass down on a plinth next to what looked like a gilded cow-pat, then shook Charlton's hand while gripping his forearm and telling him what an 'interesting experience' it had been. He gave a perfunctory nod to Weiss and turned towards the exit, heading straight for Alexandra Friedman, who was standing nearby, talking to a freelance curator Hugh owed money to.

'So,' Weiss bellowed to regain Hugh's attention – he'd helped himself to another canapé, with a pastry flake from the last one still attached to his upper lip – 'I am curious to hear the *trade* view of Craig's work?'

Hugh had little option other than to be civil. 'Well, I suppose the most obvious reading is that it's an anti-consumerist statement.' As he spoke, he watched Cockburn greet Friedman with a galling familiarity.

Weiss dithered, arranging his thoughts, his tongue retrieving the pastry flake with a gecko-like flick. 'I think the work very cleverly subverts the idea of the value we place on material possessions.' He paused to sip his champagne. 'If I have a curatorial mission statement, it's to give a platform to artists who challenge conventional wisdom. Craig is just the type of artist I want to support. His work is so . . . . well . . . you know . . . challenging.'

Hugh glanced at Charlton, who was nibbling on a pastry puff. He might have had time to engage in glib, half-intellectual art criticism with a professional windbag like Weiss, but Hugh certainly didn't. The gooseberry had to go.

'Tell me Deidrich, have you spoken to the critic from the *Independent*, over there by the Lego apocalypse?'

'*Wirklich?*' Weiss stood on the tips of his toes, scoping the room like a meerkat.

'Short chap. Shoulder-length grey hair. Dark-rimmed glasses.'

'Perhaps I should go and speak to him?'

'Definitely,' Hugh said. 'Share your insights on the work with him.'

No sooner had Weiss turned his back on them, than Charlton picked up the glass Cockburn had left on the plinth. He looked around for a waiter to give it to. Not finding one, he held on to it, smiling nervously at Hugh.

Alone at last.

Charlton's body language spoke of discomfort. If they'd been sitting on a sofa, he'd have moved to the far end and perched on the edge, clutching a cushion. Hugh would be edging closer, a rose gripped between his teeth.

'So Craig, have you thought about your next move?'

'A holiday,' he answered, sidestepping the question. 'It's been pretty hectic for the past couple of months getting ready for this.'

'Of course. I can imagine. Where are you off to?'

'Sri Lanka. There are some great surfing spots there I want to visit.'

'Isn't there a war on?'

'Not in the part I'm going to. Anyhow, after five years surviving as an artist in this town, I feel quite battle-hardened.'

'Is it really that bad?'

'You tell me.'

Hugh shrugged. This wasn't a constructive line of conversation. 'I suppose I'm really more interested in your longer-term plans. You know I've always been an admirer of your work.'

'Have you?'

'Absolutely, ever since your masters show at the Royal College of Art.'

'Really? I don't remember seeing you there.'

'I missed the opening. I'm usually in Basel in mid-June.' Not at Art Basel, the most prestigious art fair in Continental Europe, but at one of its satellite fairs. Naturally, Hugh didn't make this clear, but Charlton probably knew it anyway.

'Listen, Craig, I'll cut to the chase here. We'd love to have you come on board with us.'

Charlton waved at an artist friend standing nearby who was holding a bottle of Moët & Chandon triumphantly above the crowd. 'To be honest,' he said, 'I'm considering a couple of offers at the moment.'

'That doesn't surprise me. If you did decide to go with us, though, we could offer you a signing-on fee. We could also guarantee to place your work in some important public collections.'

Charlton was barely listening to Hugh as he raised both champagne flutes in the air, his own and Cockburn's. The message: he had two drinks on the go, and wasn't this a great lig. Hugh ground his teeth: *you can take the artist out of art college* . . . .

He glared at the buffoon with the bottle, who came over all sheepish and lowered it. When he did, a familiar face by the main entrance came into view. The polished veneer of the professional salesman, already covered in a fine filigree of cracks, began to flake away. Neck-Bolts, aka Harry Sykes, *had* stalked him across the city. Harry Sykes was Hugh's relationship manager with his principal creditor – and the relationship was going through a tricky patch. Hugh had been avoiding Harry for weeks now, hoping against hope that his luck would turn. But it wasn't to be that evening.

He turned back to Charlton, now being embraced like a penitent sinner by Alexandra Friedman, who'd finally negotiated her way through the crowd. 'Let's talk soon, Craig.' He turned then to Friedman, palm raised. 'Alex, great to see you. Here to admire Craig's work as well, are we?' Friedman didn't answer; she just smiled serenely and adjusted the folds of her long black velvet dress.

'Are you leaving us, Hugh?' she asked.

'Got to go, I'm afraid. Having dinner with a client.'

'Such a pity,' she said, still smiling.

Hugh slipped in behind an eight-foot-high glass case – containing a waxwork of a man in a pinstriped suit, wearing a safari helmet and armed with a blunderbuss – and tried to devise a strategy.

Maybe the blunderbuss was loaded?

Not a good plan.

Maybe he hadn't been spotted? But like Hugh, Harry Sykes was a head taller than most of the people around him. His totemic face glowered over the throng close to the main entrance, looking as incongruous as some of the exhibits. A few of the artists here strove to add a sinister element to their work. Harry Sykes *was* sinister.

Hugh craned his neck around the side of the glass case. Harry stared right at him, then barrelled into the crowd.

CHAPTER 2

Emergency Exit Only

Harry Sykes was an old-school henchman, who seemed a little lost in the ever more multi-ethnic criminal underworld Hugh had somehow strayed into; a Disunited Nations of vice, brutality and general scumbaggery; a grown-up Benetton poster, with guns. All of it rich anecdotal fodder for the dinner parties he was invited to – less often of late, admittedly – were he ever reckless enough to draw on it.

Hugh peeked from behind the column and felt his chest tighten. Harry was homing in on him, almost lifting one size-zero woman out of his way, pausing briefly, surprised by how light she was. Harry was ex-infantry and built like the barracks armoury: an Easter Island statue in a trenchcoat. He drew curious glances from some in his path eager to engage bohemian types, who, if they'd seen in their own neighbourhoods, would react to by pressing the central locking button on their black Range Rovers. Hod-like hands rested on their shoulders and eased them aside.

Some of the men in his way, City types who spent an hour a day in the gym, bristled and flexed at his gruff directness. Harry cowed them with one of his don't-even-think-about-it-mate expressions. They might've been toned, their bodies might've been hard, in many cases even their hearts, but they weren't *hard* in the sense that Harry was. What made him hard was not that he'd killed a man with his bare hands, which of course he had, or bitten a man's nose off in a fight (twice), or poured the contents of a boiling chip pan over another (his brother-in-law). What made him hard was that he did none of these things in anger. Harry did them for a living. He was hardened to acts of extreme cruelty by their very mundanity.

Hugh retreated further under the colonnade, almost backing onto a pile of rubble entangled in sheets and blankets. On the wall beside it, a video projector cast footage of Palestinian houses on the West Bank being bulldozed by the Israeli army. He appraised the work and dismissed it in the time it took him to adjust his footing. There was little more tedious – or less saleable – than political art.

When he turned back to the crowd, a petite woman in her early thirties with a pinched, freckled face held her hand out for him to shake it. Her blue raincoat and insistent manner were familiar, although he couldn't quite remember from where. He could recall a more general classification: she fell into the category of people who needed something from him.

'Clarissa Booth,' she said, allowing her hand to linger in his a moment too long. 'We met at an exhibition opening in your wonderful gallery. I promised I'd show you some of my work the next time we met.'

'Clarissa, of course, good to see you again.'

'I hope I haven't caught you at a bad time.'

Before Hugh could answer, a portfolio was produced with blown-up photos inserted into transparent plastic sleeves. Scrubby, expressionist nudes rolled on top of one another as she flicked through the pages.

'Apologies for the quality of the reproductions. They need to be seen in the flesh, so to speak, although they're not framed yet. Oh, and the halogen lights in the studio do put a slightly pink cast on them. Photographing paintings is so tricky, don't you find?'

'Absolutely.' Hugh lapsed into the reflexive patter of a conversation he'd had many times before.

'The work is really about the objectification of women's bodies in popular culture,' she said

'Yes . . . objectification. Of course . . . I see.'

Hugh glanced left, then right. He could make for the exit, although negotiating a path through the crowd without being drawn into a conversation again would be difficult. It was too late in any case. Like a monstrous grey cloud floating in front of the sun, Harry loomed alongside them, cutting into the beam from the video projector. Ghostly bulldoz-ers floated across his chest while head-scarfed women flailed helplessly as their homes collapsed into rubble. He looked down, appalled at the drama unfolding on his trenchcoat. As he stepped to one side, almost tripping over the rubble on the floor, the bulldozers flitted onto the wall behind him and continued their grim work. His larder of politeness, sparse at the best of times, was stripped bare by now.

'What's all this then, a *fackin* jumble sale?' he said.

'And you are?' said Clarissa, turning the pages of her portfolio – a little quicker each time.

'Andy bleeding Warhol, now piss off. I need to have a word with Rhattigan.'

'I beg your pardon.' She paused on a painting of a woman Hugh's old Jesuit headmaster would have deemed to be 'interfering with her-self'. As Harry's gaze dropped from Clarissa to the painting, he nodded approvingly.

Hugh closed the portfolio. 'We'll finish this conversation some other time, Clarissa. Why not call into the gallery some day next week?'

'I'll be there on Monday at ten. Tell your friend he needs to work on his manners.'

'Believe me, he's worse when you get to know him.'

There was no response from Harry, other than a glimmer of offence in a slightly furrowed brow and a protrusion of his chin. Clarissa slipped off into the crowd, fumbling with her bag and her work.

'All right, Rhattigan?'

'I was until you arrived.'

'Did I interrupt? Was you about to pull?'

'No, she's an artist.'

'Why was she showing you those dirty pictures then? Was they of herself, or are her friends into it too?'

'Into what?'

'Taking their clothes off and making dirty pictures?'

'She's an artist. She paints nudes.'

'Nudes, dirty pictures, that's what I said.'

'You've just dismissed a vast swathe of Western classical art as *dirty* pictures.'

'You said it, mate, not me.'

Hugh sighed, his eyes still flitting left and right. 'Can I help you with anything, Harry? There are people here I need to speak to.'

'You arty types are mad for it, aren't you?'

'Mad for what?'

'You know.'

'No I don't.'

'Yes you do, you filthy sod!'

'Really, I don't have time for this.'

Harry's expression darkened. 'You're right, you don't. You've got an appointment to keep.'

'I don't have an appointment.'

'I've just made one for you.'

'With who?'

'The boss.'

'I told you, there are people here I need to speak to.'

'Does you owe them money too?'

'Can't this wait until some other time? Tell Douglas I'll call him in the morning.'

''Cause if you do, they'll have to get in the queue.'

'In the morning, I said.'

'And hope they're not chasing up a stiff for their money.'

Alexandra Friedman floated by, with a couple of wealthy clients in tow. She gave Hugh a plastic smile, which dissolved into a look of bewilderment when her gaze drifted on to Harry. Hugh responded with a plastic smile of his own, Harry with a leaden scowl.

Hugh turned his back on Friedman and said through gritted teeth, 'Maybe we should have this conversation outside.'

'After you, mate,' Harry said, extending his arm in a gesture of mock chivalry.

Hoping to slip out quietly, Hugh made for the double metal doors beside them bearing an 'Emergency Exit Only' sign. He pushed down on the bars but couldn't budge them. Harry shoved him aside and in the same motion pushed on the bars. The doors swung open, setting off an alarm, more cloying bleat than siren. Light gushed in, washing away the image from the video projector.

They stepped outside into an alleyway bathed in shallow early-evening sunlight. Harry jutted a finger and tipped his head in the direction of Cannon Street, his black brogues crunching on broken alcopop bottles as he set off. Without breaking his stride, he stepped out onto the road, an open hand to stop the traffic morphing into a raised thumb when the drivers yielded, not out of courtesy but rather because the only alternative was to run him over.

Hugh's jaw slackened and a long exhalation deflated his chest. Life had been like a slow-motion train-wreck for the past couple of months. It was almost a relief that Douglas Virgo had hit the play button again.

The car was parked outside a laundrette in the bus lane opposite, emergency lights blinking. It was a 1962 silver Bentley Continental, a long swooping beast of a car with a snarling radiator grill and four leering headlamps. A proper Englishman's car, Virgo had once crowed to Hugh, not one of those Swedish cars that hector you to put your seatbelt on, or an off-roader – a Chelsea tractor – useful only if your wheels got stuck in a gravel driveway.

'Get in the car,' Harry said, directing him towards the back.

'What's the magic word?'

'Abraka-fuckin-dabra. Now get in.'

Hugh opened the door and sank into a red hide seat. His nostrils were singed by aftershave, presumably the driver's, who turned and gazed at him. He was lean – built like a welterweight – and would have a hunted look to anyone who hadn't just been hunted by him. His pale blue eyes gauged Hugh's size and condition.

A tremor went through the car as Harry's twenty-odd grizzled stones hit the front passenger seat. Without a word the driver tugged on the dash-mounted gearstick and launched into a three-point turn, spinning the steering wheel with the ball of his open palm. Hugh lurched back and forth, looking in vain for a seatbelt, then clutched instead on the overhead handgrip.

The car gunned the hundred yards to a crossroads, stealing through the orange light and on to Commercial Road before pulling up at a line of traffic. The driver tilted his head back, though not far enough to meet Hugh's eye.

'You the bloke who is owning gallery, are you?' he said, in a heavily accented voice, Russian perhaps.

'I am.'

'You an artist?'

'No, I represent artists.'

'Oh,' he said, pausing. 'My girlfriend paints. How you say? *Obstruct?*'

'Abstract.'

'Yes, abstract. Not old-fashioned shit.'

'Right.'

'She not selling them, though. Only *geeving* as presents.'

The conversation waned when the lights turned and the line of traffic crept through the junction.

'How much you take?' the driver began again abruptly, this time catching Hugh's eye in the rear-view mirror.

'Sorry?'

'How much you taking when selling paintings? Twenty percent?'

'The gallery's usual commission is fifty percent.'

'Fifteen, not bad.' He nodded his approval in a histrionically un-British way.

'No, fifty – five zero,' Hugh said, mouthing the words carefully.

The driver inhaled sharply. '*Feefty focking* percent. I thought we was the crooks.'

Harry heaved his shoulders in an arc, meeting Hugh's gaze full on. 'Fifty percent. You thieving swine.'

'It's not cheap running a gallery in the West End,' Hugh said. 'And I pay for art fairs, catalogues, advertising, mailings, private views. I've got staff too, you know.'

'Fifty percent,' Harry said again. 'Pavel, my son, we are in the wrong business.'

'I think we open gallery, *Arry*. Make crazy money.'

'Do *fack*-all work.'

After a moment's reflection, Harry added: 'Pity we're not queer, though.'

'Ah,' said Pavel, the kopek dropping. 'He big faggot.'

'Not that it's any of your business,' Hugh cut in, 'but I'm married – to a woman. Well . . . separated, actually.'

There was another pause before Pavel asked: 'Wife no liked you shagging men?'

The two cropped, tonsured heads in front bobbed in amusement. At least they seem to enjoy their work, Hugh thought — which was more than he could say.

CHAPTER 3

Nearer, My God, to Thee

They drove along Aspen Way towards the Docklands, the city's entrails stretching from Tower Bridge down to Woolwich. It was a part of London Hugh steered clear of, unless he was lunching with a client at Canary Wharf or catching a flight home to Dublin from City Airport. Mostly, he just found it ugly, but today it seemed full of menace as well. A pillow of dark cloud smothered the Royal Victoria Dock from the east. Across a slate-grey Thames, the Dome sat like a giant slumbering insect that would lay waste to the Greenwich Peninsula if disturbed. Above them, the whining of a jet bound for the airport drowned out the rumble of the Bentley's four-litre engine.

Hugh's forehead began to ache. Champagne never agreed with him – bit of an occupational hazard. He took a pack of paracetamol from the inside pocket of his jacket, and popped the last two blisters onto his hand. He could really use something stronger. Maybe some of those downers Virgo sold to strung-out cokeheads in the City to take the edge off their morning-after jitters. Most of them had bought the coke from Virgo as well. Not that they knew – or cared, for that matter.

The paracetamol stuck to Hugh's tongue, which was still chalky from the champagne. He swallowed hard but the tablets lodged in his gullet and seemed to swell to the size of pound coins. He sat up, pushed his shoulders back and gave a slight tremor. He wound down the window a couple of inches and let the cool evening air gush over his face, then gagged a little when a battered old Transit van pulled out from the

19

slip-road in front of them and belched thick exhaust fumes over the Bentley.

As the fumes cleared, he caught his reflection in the chrome wing mirror. He was handsome, so he'd been told, if a little dishevelled – what had begun many years ago as an affectation had become habit. But the shadows under his eyes and the first flecks of grey at his temples were wrought by more recent stresses.

He'd told Harry and Pavel that he was separated but strictly speaking that wasn't true, not since that morning, at any rate, when the final divorce decree had arrived in the post. He'd read it with a numbed regret, a sense that he'd been a remote spectator for the last year of the marriage, unable or unwilling to save it. There'd been no real acrimony, just a creeping realisation that the marriage had failed – a failure, mercifully, not compounded by having children.

Sitting at the kitchen table of his flat in Camden, his gaze had drifted from Rebecca's signature on the last page of the divorce papers to his credit-card statement, lying like a lead slab on the table in front of him, and from there to the mood-jarring verdure of the beech trees outside his window, stretching over Albert Street, glistening after an early-summer sun shower. The numbness slowly gave way to a gnawing guilt. He knew he'd behaved badly. And the worst of it was that he'd never even said sorry.

She filed on the grounds of 'unreasonable behaviour' – which was about right. She'd had enough of the drinking, the erratic hours, and the questionable company he was keeping, although she barely knew the half of it. She'd also wearied of his chaotic finances, of Hugh shovelling everything he earned back into his money-pit of a business.

He'd always been cavalier with money – reckless, she would have said. He spent it when he had it and – over the past few years – had borrowed it and spent it when he hadn't. But even she acknowledged that bad luck had played its part. Hugh had opened his gallery on 15 September 2008, the day Lehman Brothers was declared bankrupt. The opening party felt more like a wake for the boom years than a celebration. The small crowd that came brought their condolences but not their chequebooks. One wag, while quaffing the free bubbly, even suggested that Hugh ought to have hired a string quartet to play 'Nearer, my God, to thee' as the ship went down on its maiden voyage.

Little had improved in the almost four years since. The very high end of the art market stumbled after the financial crash but quickly found its stride again. Meanwhile, Hugh got caught in the squeezed middle and never shook himself free. When Rebecca asked him to close the gallery and look for his old job back, he refused. When she pressed him, he withdrew, and towards the end he avoided her altogether.

It already seemed like another lifetime – someone else's lifetime.

He'd moved out six months earlier, taking little other than his share of the mortgage and the shreds of the promise he'd once shown. Rebecca was the sister of a teammate at the London Irish Amateurs, where Hugh had played rugby since moving to London fifteen years earlier. She reminded him near the end how eligible he had seemed when they'd first met: shabbily handsome, with a wry charm and a blossoming career at the auction house, Frith's, where he'd worked in the Modern British department before opening his own gallery. There were kinks in his personality – an irreverently independent mind and a rashness that early on she'd only ever seen on a rugby field. But Rebecca seemed to feel that these were kinks she could straighten out. That was her biggest mistake.

She wasted little time in getting on with her life. Within two months of Hugh leaving, she'd put their house on the market and moved in with the head of corporate finance at a Swiss investment bank in the City who, as it happens, she'd met at an opening in Hugh's gallery. Bastard hadn't even bought anything. Hugh had since heard from her brother that they'd got a Portuguese water dog – to fetch the sticks thrown by the child they were expecting.

Hugh's solicitor suggested he counter-file on grounds of adultery, given that the new relationship overlapped with the old one. But Hugh let it go. In fact, he didn't respond at all to the divorce petition, which meant, after twenty-one days, that he agreed with it. He certainly didn't try to talk her out of it, not that there would have been much point.

As he held his own gaze in the Bentley's wing mirror, heading east across the city, he was resigned, almost stoical. He wouldn't talk his way out of this either.

It wasn't that Douglas Virgo was the only person he owed money to: his club of creditors had become less exclusive by the day. It was just that, with the others, he'd consoled himself with the thought that his problems had become theirs. The bank and his landlords had a vested interest in giving him a chance to redeem himself. They wouldn't get their money if they forced him out of business. Smaller creditors would send a plaintive invoice with OVERDUE stamped on it in red ink, or a stern letter from a debt-collection agency. They would badger him or his solicitor, whose fee he hadn't paid for two years, but he could always drip-feed them some cash or string them along with his gladly-pay-you-Tuesday routine, which was second nature by now. This was hardly a source of pride to him, but the alternative – allowing the business to tank – would crush whatever vestige of pride he had left.

He wasn't sure why, but until now he hadn't fretted so much over the money he owed Virgo. It hadn't seemed like such a pressing problem. Maybe it was because Virgo had been such a hands-off investor. Or maybe it was because Hugh thought he had the measure of him. The gallery had been a diversion, not so much a trip as a gentle little spin for Virgo's ego.

Douglas Virgo: patron of the arts, pillar of low society, the Lord Sainsbury of the criminal class. He wasn't much different to any other benefactor of the arts. A life devoted to making truckloads of cash was somehow validated by giving a little back to something with a higher purpose. You get to bask in the reflective kudos of the arts without braving the penury and personality disorders that often came with it.

Virgo's vanity was tickled by putting money into a gallery, and he seemed embarrassed, or maybe just too distracted, to ask for it back. Come to think of it, by Virgo's standards, it wasn't even all that much: a few hundred grand, give or take. And it wasn't as though Hugh's casual approach to servicing his debt would undermine Virgo's fearsome reputation on 'the street' – or whatever vernacular it was he used to describe London's criminal underworld.

The reason had seemed obvious to Hugh: the art world and the underworld didn't overlap.

CHAPTER 4

Good Lord, the Attitude

Aside from Felix Lazaar, that is. He was Virgo's *entrée* into the art-collecting fraternity, and Hugh's into the criminal.

'My reputation is my collateral,' Lazaar had said the first time they shook hands, six years before, when Hugh was still working at Frith's. There was a wretched artfulness about the line, just like the man who coined it. It was a dagger in the heart of desperate creditors. A 'fuck you' and a 'how dare you impugn my integrity' in the same breath.

An art dealer, an antique dealer, and a naturalised crook, Felix Lazaar used the words 'reputation' and 'integrity' as freely as he spent the money he owed to his many unrequited creditors. Hugh knew him to see from auction viewings: the man who scratched, tapped, tugged and sniffed on furniture, paintings, clocks and statuary, held Meissen teacups up to the light, chaperoned by a skittish porter, and nodded in agreement with his own appraisal. During auctions, he stood at the back of the saleroom, arms folded, head bowed, bidding with a furtive twitch of a rolled-up catalogue.

Lazaar was part of the 'Ring', a cabal of dealers who didn't bid against one another in the auction rooms. One of the Ring would buy the lot, then they adjourned to a local hostelry or a hotel room, where they re-auctioned the piece and divided up the difference between the hammer price and their own 'knock-out' auction price among themselves. Everyone was happy, except for the original vendor. And the auctioneers. Oh, and the person who eventually got fleeced in an antique shop or a gallery. It was against the law, but then it was difficult to prove what they were up to, even though they'd been doing it under the noses of the auction houses for years.

Hugh had no direct dealings with the Ring, so Lazaar's sudden interest in him caught him off guard. He was having a lunchtime sharpener in the Golden Lion on King Street on the afternoon of a porcelain sale, mulling over plans to get out of Frith's and open his own gallery. Lazaar sat in conclave with the other dealers in the Ring, under the bowed window, dappled in light from the stained-glass partition that wrapped around them. He caught Hugh's eye from across the bar and raised his gin and tonic by way of a greeting. Hugh looked over his shoulder to see if the greeting was directed at someone behind him but saw only his own reflection in the etched mirrors. He nodded back, then slouched a little so that his face was screened by a bank of hand-pumps. He watched them through the gaps, though, as they flicked through the sale catalogue, discussing each lot.

They were all men, the youngest in his mid-forties, the oldest in his mid-seventies. Lazaar was one of the elders of the group: not the alpha male, but he had the status age bestowed on anyone in such a precarious business, which was under constant assault from recession, shifting tastes, Habitat. There were booming voices, guffawing and pontificating, fading into a conspiratorial murmur, no doubt when money was being discussed. Their scent drifted across the bar, laden with cologne, body odour, cigar smoke and stale pheromones.

They ordered another round, chatting up the barmaid.

'Where are you from, my dear?' asked Lazaar.

'From a Spain,' she said, with practised curtness.

'I guessed as much. Where in Spain?' He wrapped his arm around her waist, lest she try to escape. His broken-veined cheeks flushed with excitement, setting off his burgundy cravat.

'Granada.'

'Ah Granada, the Alhambra, the magical red fortress. How marvellous for you. An interesting fact about the Alhambra . . . '

Hugh drained his glass and slipped out while Lazaar and his chums leered at their Spanish conquest.

He thought no more of Lazaar's greeting in the Golden Lion until the following week. He was sitting outside Franco's on Ryder Street, cigarette in one hand, espresso in the other. The mid-afternoon lull was broken by a futile growl of acceleration from a black Lamborghini that burst from a parking space before pulling up sharply at St James's Street. Hugh twisted in his seat to admire the car, and turned back to find a bridling Lazaar standing by his table.

'Ignorant so and so,' he said, in a strangulated Home Counties drawl.

Hugh gazed back towards St James's. 'Nice car, all the same.'

Lazaar sat down opposite him. 'Mind if I join you?' he asked, already shuffling his chair under the table.

His navy blazer was embroidered on the breast with the moniker of a sailing club in Kent. He usually wore a golf-club tie or some other emblem of status, like a tag in a cow's ear telling you its pedigree. Deck shoes, chinos and a white cashmere scarf completed the look. He had unerringly lush hair for a man of his age – early sixties – even if it did only cover half of his head.

He set down an Avery's bag on the chair next to Hugh. The bag was bulging with a parcel of bubble-wrap and brown tape.

'Hugh, isn't it, from Frith's? Recognised you from your photo in the ModBrit catalogues.'

These smiling mugshots gave a false impression of warmth and charm, the degree of which in reality depended on your net worth. Hugh's knowing frown jarred a little with the other photos. There was a surfeit of fresh-faced, female Oxbridge graduates, attractive in a bland sort of way. The men were older, bespectacled and balding, their names double-barrelled – with at least one 'von' something-or-other thrown in for good measure. Their expressions were singularly smarmy.

Hugh nodded at Lazaar. He didn't like having his afternoon coffee disturbed. Every moment of the day he would wrest back from his employers was precious. Lazaar either didn't notice or didn't care. He caught the attention of the barista through the window and simulated sipping from the cup of tea he wanted to order. He then placed hands that seemed too big for his short, stocky arms flat on the linen tablecloth.

'How's business?' he asked.

Hugh shrugged. 'So so. There's no shortage of buyers. The problem is persuading people to sell when they think they might get a better price if they hold off for a year or two.'

'A word of advice, old man: you might lure a few more sellers into the market if you drop your fees, especially those weasel charges you add at the end for insurance, shipping, pictures in the catalogue, answering the bloody phone, and so on and so forth.'

This was a perennial gripe for dealers who bought and sold at auction. It might even have been true. It was just hard to take seriously from someone who – over a long and disreputable career – had probably pulled more strokes than Sir Steve Redgrave.

The dealer would usually blame Hugh for the practices of his employers, and he feared Lazaar was about to do likewise. He shaped as if to leave before professional ennui completely incapacitated him for the afternoon. He placed his cup on its saucer, and checked the time on his phone.

'I really have to be going,' he said.

He really should have left.

'What's the hurry? I'm sure Frith's won't go belly-up if you have another coffee. Take a look at the letterhead: it's been around since 1790. I might be able to push some business your way, anyhow, from a client of mine. A big collector. *High* net worth.'

Hugh sank back into his chair. 'Go on,' he said, wearily.

'I've placed some super-smart pieces with him. Aubusson carpets; Garrard silverware, a Louis XV ormolu clock. Even a giltwood console table made for the Duke of Urbino.' The latter was pronounced with a Latin flourish, as was the habit of middle-class English men of a certain age who often had no real facility with languages.

Lazaar leaned back in a vain attempt to catch the waiter's eye. His puffed-out cheeks deflated, sending a gust of cigar-heavy breath across the table. 'Service in this city has gone to the bloody dogs.'

Hugh recoiled a little, then shifted in his chair. 'You were saying: you have a client?'

'My very best client. Only buys top-notch stuff. Has a jolly good eye, although I must confess I've trained it well. He's not a damned tyre-kicker either.'

Hugh gave a wry smile. Tyre-kickers, he knew the sort all too well. They'd grill him at the private view, ask for a condition report, show up at the auction and take a front-row seat, only for their bidding paddle to go flaccid as soon as the piece hit the lower estimate. They were the bane of every auctioneer's life. One of them, at any rate.

'That all sounds great,' Hugh said, 'but I sell paintings, not antiques.'

'I know. That's what I need to talk to you about. I've also been sourcing paintings for him for the past couple of years. He's already built up a fine collection. He has three Turners, a couple of Constables, a Gainsborough, and seven or eight pre-Raphaelites – a particularly nice Rossetti of the Annunciation.'

Lazaar paused to make sure he'd piqued Hugh's interest, then added, almost as an afterthought: 'He also has a rather ghoulish collection of Walter Sickert sketches of the London Ripper's handiwork.' The latter revealed a taste for the macabre that Hugh failed to pick up on at the time.

A waiter finally appeared from behind one of the miniature conifers in black earthenware pots, three of which stood like sentinels under the awning in front of the restaurant.

'Are you ready to order, sir?'

'Been ready for the past ten minutes,' Lazaar said. 'I'll have the finger sandwiches, and a pot of Earl Grey. And some of those biscotti thingies. My friend here will have another coffee.' He stared at the waiter for a moment. 'Aren't you going to write that down?'

Sighing, the waiter made a show of pulling a notebook from his apron and writing down the order, before going back inside.

Lazaar shook his head. 'Good lord, the *attitude*. Now, where was I?'

'Your client.'

'Ah yes, my client. Like I was saying, he already has a fine collection. The problem is, the clock stops around 1940. That's where you come in, given that the ModBrits are your area of expertise. We've decided to plunge deeper into the twentieth century and buy some postwar work. We're thinking David Hockney, Henry Moore, Anthony Caro. All British, all blue-chip. Nothing too contemporary; certainly none of that gutter art that seems to be the in thing, like that Tracey Emin – or Tracey *Enema*, as I like to call her – with her unmade bed and soiled prophylactics. Or that German artist who uses menstrual blood in her paintings and who, it turns out, is actually a lesbian. All so terribly with it!'

Hugh smiled. 'Each to their own, Felix.'

'But it's not art.'

'Nobody has a veto over what's art and what isn't. And maybe you shouldn't tar all contemporary artists with the same brush.'

'A *brush*? Most of those charlatans wouldn't know which end of a brush to use.'

Hugh had little interest in preaching to the unconvertible. 'Fine, let's stick with the names you mentioned. Our next modern British auction is in three weeks. There should be a lot of work in it that will interest your client. Tell him to give me a call.'

A finger wagged. 'No can do, old boy. Everything goes through me for now. He's quite a private sort. Doesn't like to draw too much attention to himself.'

'Does he have a name?'

Lazaar paused, his fingers steepled in front of his face. 'I'm sure we can trust one another,' he said. 'His name is Virgo. Douglas Virgo.'

'Doesn't ring any bells, but if he's as serious as you say he is, I'll give you the heads-up on any major works that come our way.'

'That's super-smart. Look forward to doing business with you.' Another pause. Lazaar's eyes fixed on the table. 'There is also the rather delicate matter of payment.'

Hugh turned wary again. 'We generally only offer an introductory fee to agents for vendors, not buyers. I suppose I can always speak to my boss – depending on the volume of business this Virgo chap does with us. You must have your own arrangement with him anyhow?'

'No, no, you misunderstand me,' Lazaar said coyly. 'It's more a question of *how* he pays, not *who* he pays. There tends to be quite a lot of third-party cheques, you see – all from reputable sources, of course. Mostly big City firms. Banks, legals, a couple of oil companies. There's also the occasional cash sum. I'm not sure if Frith's would be amenable? Always useful for paying staff bonuses, you know.'

Somehow, the revelation that Lazaar's client might not be entirely above board didn't surprise Hugh. Although it didn't unnerve him either.

'That's a little above my pay-grade,' he said. 'I'll have to discuss it with my boss.'

A spasm of panic shot across Lazaar's face. 'All hypothetical, of course. No need to use any names' – he stammered – 'my name, no need to use my name.'

'Don't worry, *old boy,* heart of valour and all that.'

The espresso arrived. Hugh took one sip. Not too hot. He downed the rest like a whiskey shot and bade farewell. Ambling back to his office, he mulled over his encounter with Lazaar, unsure if his bosses at Frith's would go for it.

He needn't have had any doubts. Money talks in this city, and Hugh's bosses were all ears. They would take cash payments up to 50k. Anything above that would have to be cleared through a bank account – a proviso that seemed more practical than ethical. They were also happy to take third-party cheques from firms in the City, even though they knew full well that the work was being bought by somebody else. In fact, they had no moral qualms at all about taking in four or five million quid a year from such a shady client. But they wanted no direct dealings with him. Everything had to go through Hugh. They asked no questions about who Virgo was or how he earned his living.

They didn't need to meet him. The money spoke for itself.

Money talks. It was one of Virgo's favourite sayings.

You just have to listen carefully.

CHAPTER 5

The Rocky and Bullwinkle Show

There was silence in the Bentley, broken only by the occasional rumble of phlegm from Pavel, who rolled down his window and gobbed on the street as they passed Butcher Row.

Twenty-five years after the City set up its outpost at Canary Wharf, the rest of the Docklands still seemed a work in progress to Hugh. New hotels stood next to crumbling warehouses, as if they'd only just been bombed in the Blitz. A block of apartments, mottled with red, green and blue balconies, bore a giant banner: 'Available July 1st'. It overlooked a canal basin where two yachts floated like dead goldfish in a bowl. Opposite it was a scrap-metal yard, across the road a warren of council flats. There was little else to cut the requiem of browns and greys other than the odd patch of graffiti.

Pavel turned up the radio. The DJ gave a big shout-out to Bianca in Stepney from all the posse at Point Blank FM. Music pulsed from the speakers under the back window.

'Turn that drivel off,' Harry barked, reaching for the tuning knob. 'It sounds like my old dear's washing machine.'

'Maybe you should buy old dear new washing machine,' Pavel said, looking unduly pleased with his riposte.

'Or maybe I should just get her a Russian bird to do the washing. The ones that aren't hookers, all seem to be cleaners.'

The tone was even. Calculated.

Pavel slapped the steering wheel with both hands and fixed his gaze on Harry. 'You are offensive, man,' he said, wrestling with his temper – which already had him in a half-nelson. 'I told you, I don't have work with racialists. My country is great one. We could blow this *sheet-hole* in million tiny pieces.'

Harry warmed to his task, a craftsman setting to work on Pavel's malleable temper. 'I know – superpower, Russian empire, Peter the Fucking Great. Don't start, mate. That's all ancient history. Nowadays, you're a nation of cleaners, skanks, crooks and peasants. *And* you've never won the World Cup.'

Pavel's voice became shriller. 'You are nasty little England man. Why this country so great? It is USA's pet doggie. Open your *focking* eyes, man.'

Harry shrugged, unmoved by Pavel's jibes. 'That's David Cameron you're talking about mate, not Britain. That slimy bastard doesn't represent me.'

As he spoke, he twisted the tuning knob, skipping over a newsreader, some Beethoven and some Indian drum 'n' bass that drew a 'fuckin 'ell' from him. The dial settled on the familiar opening bars of 'It's Not Unusual'.

'That's more like it,' he said. 'Tom Jones. Proper music.'

'*Tomasz* who?' Pavel asked.

'Tom Jones, you half-wit.'

Hugh could see the wounded expression in the rear-view mirror. Pavel mumbled something in Russian, then came over all peevish. 'Music for *babushki,*' he said, without taking his eyes off the road.

Harry was smiling now. 'Music for *baboons*. What the fuck you on about?'

'*Babushkas*. Old ladies,' Hugh said, regretting his intervention as soon as the words left his mouth.

Harry looked over his shoulder, the smile wilting. 'Who are you, Magnus fuckin' Magnussen? Shut the fuck up.'

Turning back to Pavel: 'Tom Jones was making great tunes while your lot were still only listening to music they could march to.'

This time, there was no response. Without shifting out of fourth gear, Pavel accelerated through the lights as they turned red and swung the car from Victoria Dock Road onto Connaught Bridge.

On the quayside, a row of cranes stood to attention, a guard of honour for cargo ships that would never return. A Royal Navy frigate and a giant private yacht with the name *Anna Karenina* written on the side in Roman and Cyrillic letters took the salute instead. The yacht was no doubt parked up while its Russian-oligarch owner did a spot of shopping in the West End. Clothes, jewellery, a Francis Bacon, a couple of hotels, maybe even a football club. But Pavel didn't seem to notice the yacht, his gaze still fixed on the road.

*

In the cab on the way home that evening, Rebecca had also sat with her eyes fixed on the road – in a thousand-yard stare – with her hair scraped back, her lips pursed and her Burberry trench buttoned up the neck. On her lap she clutched a Fendi handbag, the one Hugh had got for her birthday. He'd put his name down on a waiting list for it and bought it on his credit card – but had yet to pay it off.

'You're not actually in business with that man, are you?' She'd just met Virgo at an exhibition opening. It was their first and only encounter.

'It's complicated,' Hugh said.

'Either you are or you aren't.'

Hugh looked at her, considered taking her hand, then thought better of it. 'What exactly did he say?'

'He asked me if I was your missus, then winked at that creature with him . . .'

'That'd be Harry,' Hugh said coyly.

'Telling me it was nice to meet Hugh's other sleeping partner, and looking on gleefully while I squirmed.'

'It's just a temporary arrangement,' Hugh said. 'Virgo's put up some working capital, that's all, to tide the business over.'

She sighed, then turned to him, the line of her mouth softening and a faint ember of fondness flickering in her eyes. 'I want things to work out for us, I really do – just not if you carry on like this.' Then she looked to the front again, as flinty as before. 'You can't make your own set of rules for living, Hugh, without breaking everyone else's.'

She may have been right, but what she couldn't have realised at the time was, there are different sets of rules for different sets of people, and that Hugh would end up breaking *all* of them.

*

He was jolted back to the present when Pavel turned sharply to the left and plunged the car into the underground car park of a new office block by the King George V Docks. His eyes adjusted to his surroundings: a dimly lit concrete tomb. Grey walls were intersected by wires and pipes and hung with primary yellow and red signs: *Danger. Hard hats must be worn. No unauthorised personnel. Strictly no parking.* Pavel pulled up under this last one, by the stairwell doors. He sprung from the car and opened the back door for Hugh, while Harry hoisted himself out from the other side.

They climbed the stairs in procession, Pavel in front, Harry to the rear, the condemned man in between. Doors were wedged open at every second return. Hugh could see a scattering of construction workers, languidly fitting out the building before its intended occupants – whoever they might be – could move in. It would suit Virgo perfectly in the meantime. He seemed to occupy those in-between spaces that had either just been built or were just about to be torn down, neatly mirroring his business, which grew in that netherworld between the criminal and the respectable. A weed with roots in each.

After eight flights of stairs, they emerged onto a large open-plan area with glass walls on three sides. Harry breathed heavily and muttered about 'using the *facking* lift'. Pavel dragged his hand along a window-pane, his fingers leaving four parallel lines in the thin film of white dust that coated it. Hugh stepped onto an overhanging window-ledge and gazed down into the vast concrete pit below that had a mesh of heavy steel bars sat at the bottom to gird its concrete foundations.

He tasted Harry's breath – the curry, the bile – before he heard him speak. 'They'll never find you down there, mate,' he said. By the time Hugh turned around, Harry was trailing Pavel across the empty floor. Turning back to the window, he was startled by a pane of thick green glass, arcing towards him and then veering off towards a neighbouring block.

Harry was right. A lot could go unnoticed here, or just get ignored. These were identikit buildings, functional boxes finished off with the latest architectural fad – some wood cladding or a floating panel of concrete. Architecture by numbers. Their very blandness made them a perfect workplace for Virgo: unremarkable, impersonal, soulless like mass-produced cars, built by Poles and Romanians who took little pride in the buildings and showed even less interest in any occupants.

They set off across a rough concrete floor. Silhouetted on the far side, Virgo sat with his legs crossed on a mahogany desk. He wore an open-necked shirt and a charcoal suit. A paunch rippled over his belt buckle. His hair remained taut, though, stretched over his skull like vulcanised rubber. He gazed at his iPhone as if he'd just seen one for the first time, a finger hovering accusingly over the screen. When he heard the men approaching, he flipped his legs off the desk and rolled forwards in his chair. His face resolved into a perma-tanned sneer.

'Rocky and Bullwinkle found you then, did they?'

CHAPTER 6

The Girlfriend Experience

'*Fineeshed?*'

'Yah, I'm all done.' He was still panting. There was a stale odour of cigar and brandy on his breath.

Ana lay on her back on a king-size bed. Beneath her was a quilted cream bedspread embroidered with a fine gold *fleur de lis,* just like the curtains. The two sash windows were open. There was a murmur of traffic seven or eight floors below, on Park Lane.

'Can you get off me then, please?' She was tired and a little raw. He was her third trick that night, all from the same Dutch bank.

He raised himself up on both arms, like a mantis. 'You have a bad attitude,' he slurred, his mouth listing into a smirk.

Ana turned her gaze to the brass lamp on the bedside locker. 'Please get off me. Maybe then we have chat.'

He slouched to one side so he could look her in the eye. 'What *eesh* your problem? I'm the paying customer here. Maybe you should take some pride in your work. I told the woman outside I wanted the girlfriend experience, not the . . . ' he paused, swaying a little, then steadying himself, 'not the miserable-bitch experience.'

Ana returned his gaze this time, without flinching. 'Yes, but if I was your girlfriend, I would turn into miserable *beech*, so that is what I give you.'

He recoiled, then keeled to one side and flopped down on his back with a dull thud. He couldn't resist another swipe at her, though: the chinks in Ana's bravado were all too obvious. 'Oh yah, you're very clever,' he said, stretching his long spindly body, '*for a whore.*'

It was too easy. She rolled away from him, thumped her fists down on the bed and thundered across the room. '*Peeg* of a man,' she said, catching the light-switch of the en suite with a right hook and slamming the door behind her. She sat on the edge of the bath, avoiding her reflection in the mirror that ran the full length of the wall opposite her. It straddled a marble counter with two sinks recessed into it. His and hers.

After a moment she raised her head, pulled her long chestnut brown hair – one side of it matted with semen – away from her face and studied herself in the mirror. Dark rings cradled the pale blue eyes that stared accusingly back at her. Three months, that's how long she'd been doing this, and she wasn't sure how much longer she could last. Getting drunk beforehand didn't help. Some of the other girls took whatever the agency laid on: Es and coke as liveners, so they could act like they were keen, then prescription drugs like rohypnol and temazepam to come down again. Sometimes they even took the horse tranquilliser, ketamine – 'special K', they called it – after a particularly long night. But Ana decided from the outset not to dull her senses, not to drug herself to the point where having sex with men for money became tolerable. As long as it still hurt, still made her feel nauseous, she would stop as soon as she'd saved enough money.

There was a stirring in the bedroom. She could hear the trick getting dressed, zipping up his trousers, whistling *La primavera* – 'Spring' from Vivaldi's *Four Seasons* – which they played over and over in the lobby of the hotel. These places all had an air of refinement, but like the *faux*-rosewood veneer on the furniture, or the canvas prints on the walls framed and varnished to look like real oil paintings, it all seemed fake to Ana.

A Blackberry chirped, and the trick took the call. He spoke in Dutch but the tone was warm, intimate, the way you would talk to a wife or girlfriend.

Ana turned the bath-taps on and waited for him to leave. She had no desire to see or speak to him again. It wasn't just that he was particularly obnoxious. From her very first night, she had refused to engage them – the punters, the *tricks,* to use her boss's vernacular – in post-coital small talk. Some wanted to salve their consciences; others paid for sex so routinely that they behaved as casually with a prostitute as they would having their hair cut or picking up their dry cleaning. Ana never indulged them, though, in part because she knew it was a charade, another roleplay, just as fucked-up as GFE, the dominatrix, the kinky secretary or the naughty schoolgirl; but also because she felt that if she withheld her personality, she could at least preserve a part of herself. Keep it off the market.

She could still hear the trick talking above the rumbling of the taps. The pitch of his voice had changed, as though he was talking to a child. Papa seemed so sweet. Sickly sweet. Was he talking to a little girl? Maybe that's a roleplay she could do. 'Tonight, *meester*, you like I be your daughter? No extra charge.' A wry smile formed briefly on her lips before wilting at the thought of her own father, of how ashamed he would be if he could see her now, of how he would mask his feelings with a fatalistic shrug and wonder why anyone should be surprised.

With a deep breath, she suppressed a swell of emotion and sought out distractions in the space around her. Her eyes flitted from the brass taps to the sandstone floor tiles, scored with mineral deposits and fossilised shells, then from the dado rail to the marble counter and the dried flowers in a crystal vase illuminated by a spotlight in the ceiling, as though it was set up for a still-life study. With an almost involuntary movement, her left hand traced out its form. It was strange, but for the first time in months she felt the urge to sketch, to revive that part of her brain that mapped the world around her and rendered it on paper or canvas – almost as though she were in control of it.

It was hardly the time or the place, though. She was cowering in a hotel bathroom. She had no paper to sketch on. No paints or pencils. No pastel or charcoal crayons. She'd left it all behind her when she moved out of Kolya's apartment. All she had was the lipstick, eye-liner and mascara in her handbag.

CHAPTER 7

Two Hundred Windows and Not One of Them Opens

Hugh stood in front of the desk, his eyes moving warily from Virgo to Harry to Pavel. The Russian returned Hugh's gaze, then rolled his shoulders and jutted his head forward, as though resisting the urge to punch someone.

Virgo turned to Harry. 'What time do you call this, then?'

'He weren't at his own gallery, boss. He was at some poncy fuckin' shindig in Whitechapel.'

'Did I ask you where he was?'

Harry didn't answer. Instead, he slapped Pavel on the back of the head, gathered in the folds of his enormous trenchcoat and sat in one of three chairs off to the side of the desk. Pavel slouched in another, rubbing his head, muttering something in Russian and pulling his phone from his pocket.

Virgo gestured to Hugh to take a seat opposite him.

'How do you like my new office?'

'It's a little out of the way,' Hugh said, slipping into the chair and then shifting uneasily at the recurring thought of how much could go unnoticed or just be ignored there. 'I don't know how you find these places.'

'Apparently, I own this one. It wouldn't have been my choice, but my accountant seemed to think it was a good idea. I have to say though,

Parkhurst had more charm about it. You know this place has two hundred windows and not one of them opens?'

Hugh wiped away the sweat beading on his temples. 'It is a little airless, now that you mention it.'

'And why the hell is all the glass green?'

Neither of them bothered trying to answer.

Virgo gazed out onto the building site opposite. 'Did you see that glass-and-steel canopy out the front?'

'Can't say I did. It all went by in a bit of a blur. Your driver doesn't like to drop below fourth gear.'

A silent shrug from Virgo said, *What do you expect from a hired thug?*

'The architect told me he was inspired by the tall ships that used to moor here.' He paused, as if to allow them time to reflect on what he'd just said.

'Architects say lots of things, Douglas.'

'Almost as full of it as art dealers, I'd say.'

Hugh gave a palsied smile, unnoticed by Virgo, whose eyes remained fixed on a neighbouring building. 'I used to work out of one of the old redbrick warehouses in the lot next door before that block of apartments got built. *Waterside living from as little as six hundred thousand pounds,* the brochure said. Waterside living? Fuck me, it ain't exactly Venice, is it?'

Hugh wasn't taken in by Virgo's cor-blimey-guvnor routine, which he turned on and off as it suited. The patter never chimed with his expression, which rarely betrayed very much. He spoke like he was mouthing someone else's words.

Not so Hugh, who felt like his face was a stage for a melodrama, every thought acted out by a burlesque actor. He leaned forward in his chair, unfolding his arms and placing a hand on each knee, shaping as if to leave. 'Listen, Douglas, is there something you need to discuss with me? I did have plans for this evening.'

'Working, were you?'

'I was running the eye over an artist we're interested in showing.'

'Who's that then?'

'Craig Charlton.'

'Didn't I read about him? Lacquered turds?'

'Gilded, actually.'

'Obviously,' Virgo said. 'What was I thinking? Are they his own, or does he employ a studio assistant?'

'They're animal, as it happens.'

Virgo rolled his eyes. 'And you're gonna exhibit him, are you?'

'We're in discussions. It's difficult work, though.'

'Difficult?' Virgo snorted. '*Real* art, that must be difficult, but the stuff you've ended up selling . . . a five-year-old could make half of it.'

Hugh settled back into his chair. 'Look, Douglas, you can sneer all you like, but this guy is hot. The Tate are buying the work and he's being tipped for the Turner shortlist. A rake of top galleries want to sign him up. He's just the kind of artist I need.' Hugh sounded like he was trying to convince himself as much as Virgo. 'Anyhow, judging a work of art on the skill of the artist is a rather quaint, old-fashioned idea.'

'Fuck it then, I'm quaint,' Virgo said, straining to look effete. 'Fetch the tea trolley will you, Pavel? Don't forget the doilies.'

Pavel sat up, putting his phone into his pocket.

Hugh looked at Pavel, shook his head, then looked back at Virgo. 'Originality and conceptual rigour count for far more nowadays, but that's not to say good contemporary art doesn't draw on work from the past in one form or another.'

'So this Charlton chap's not the first to make art out of bodily discharges, then?'

'Not at all,' Hugh said, babbling now. 'The Dadaists experimented with all sorts of materials, including their own . . . you know . . . as did the Viennese actionists. And in the early sixties, the Italian artist Piero Manzoni filled ninety cans with his own . . . well, excrement, for want of a better word, labelled each *Merda d'Artista* and priced them by weight, based on the market value of gold. One of them sold at auction a couple of years ago for eighty grand.'

Virgo glanced at Harry. His expression said, *Can you believe this bloke?*

But Hugh wasn't done. 'Then, about fifteen years ago, the Northern Irish artist Eamon McLinchy had an exhibition at the Chicago MCA exploring the mythology of the dirty protests in the Maze prison in the 1970s. *Shit Happens!* was the title, if memory serves. I could go on.'

'I'm sure you could,' Virgo said.

'There's Gilbert & George's *Naked Shit* series. And of course Chris Offili uses elephant dung in his paintings. And there was *Piss Christ* by Andres Serrano. Really, all I'm – '

This time Virgo cut him off. 'So you reckon I could buy one of Rembrandt's turds? Or maybe one of Vermeer's? You can't beat the Old Masters.'

'All I'm saying,' Hugh said, ignoring Virgo's tinder-dry aside, 'is that Charlton's work is not as outrageous as it might first seem. Even the idea of gilding unusual objects is tried and tested. Sylvie Fleurie has gold-plated shopping trolleys, and Paola Pivi even gilded a jet fighter. The alchemy in Charlton's case is putting the two together.'

Virgo's tone hardened. 'Or maybe one of Hockney's?'

This time Hugh winced, his stream of verbal effluvia ebbing away.

The Hockney.

Fuck it.

Hugh had bought a David Hockney painting at auction for Virgo for two hundred grand. He would occasionally act as a proxy bidder for clients at auction who didn't want to alert rival bidders, or the auction house, to their interest. In Virgo's case, it was more the Inland Revenue and the CID who needed to be kept in the dark.

'Listen, Douglas. About that Hockney. I'll have it collected for you this week.'

'Oh yeah, about the Hockney. To be honest, I've changed my mind. I think I'll have my money back instead.'

'I don't have your money, Douglas. I paid for the painting with it. Just haven't got around to collecting it yet. Been up to my oxters.'

'And here was me thinking you were an idle bastard.' Virgo flipped his legs onto the floor, his elbows coming to rest on the desk. 'The funny thing is, I sent Harry into Frith's to collect it yesterday. Some chap took him aside and told him it was never paid for. The old boy seemed a bit miffed.'

Hugh said nothing, but a spasm of unease rose into his throat from the pit of his stomach. He hadn't expected this. They viewed auctions together but Virgo always left the business end of things to Hugh. For Virgo to have gone directly to the auction house, he must really have run out of patience. Virgo was calling time.

At first, only the drone of power tools seeped through the silence. Then Pavel's phone stirred into life. A low bleat was followed by a volley of percussion. House, garage, dub-step, hip-hop? It was some class of electronic dance music. Looking around him at first to confirm that no else was talking, Pavel answered it. He spoke in Russian, although Hugh could make out the odd word. 'Da, *galleria* . . . *Piatdesat* percent! . . . *Niet* . . . *Da* baby, *da*. . . . McDonalds? . . . Kebab?'

Virgo snapped.

'Switch that fuckin' thing off, will you? Make yourself useful. Go and wax the car.' He turned back to Hugh. 'Can't get the staff these days. All the local lads have got themselves proper jobs, or else they're on the scratcher. These foreign hounds are hungrier, keener, but they've no fuckin' manners.'

Pavel stood up, flicked his shoulders back and checked that his scrotum was still where it should be. He gangsta-strutted towards the stairwell doors, muttering something in Russian again. This time Hugh couldn't decipher anything, but it wouldn't have taken a linguist to figure out that the words were laced with obscenities.

Shaking his head, Virgo pulled a pack of Marlboros from his trouser pocket. He flipped them open and placed a cigarette between pale, dry lips. Hugh's chest and stomach tightened. He hadn't smoked in six months – partly to eke out another couple of seasons playing rugby, but also out of a resolution not to become a sad, dishevelled bachelor, reeking of stale tobacco. His resolve was crumbling now, though. If Virgo offered him a smoke, he'd take it.

Virgo took an engraved silver lighter from the other pocket, opening it with a ching, like a knife being sharpened. He lit up and drew long and hard, before blowing a sinew of smoke across the desk. The Marlboros went back into his pocket.

'Now, where were we? Ah yes, you were about to ramble aimlessly about my money?'

'OK, so I'm juggling a few commitments at the moment.' Hugh said it without much conviction, but at least managed to rally some kind of excuse.

'You mean you've fucked over some other people as well?'

'I wouldn't put it like that, no.'

'How would you put it?'

42

'I'm a little overstretched, that's all. I've pumped so much money into the gallery.'

'You've pumped so much of *my* money into the gallery.'

The Hockney was just one of Hugh's problems. Having tapped up the bank for all he could, Hugh borrowed another eight hundred grand from Virgo to buy the leasehold and pay a grotesquely overpriced firm of architects to remodel it.

'You're not my *only* creditor.' As he spoke, Hugh realised what a feeble defence it was, especially given that Virgo was the only one given to casual sadism.

'I'm not stupid enough to think I am,' Virgo said, 'although I am starting to feel like a bit of a fuckin' mug. So let's cut to the chase here, Rhattigan. Exactly how much do you owe?'

'Rounding down, about two million?'

'Rounding down from what?'

Hugh gnawed on his lower lip. 'Eh . . . four million.'

Virgo threw his arms in the air and turned to Harry. 'Christ! He's a walking debt mountain.'

'He's Kiliman-fuckin-jaro,' Harry said.

'I'm in an expensive business,' Hugh said, ignoring the wingman.

Virgo shifted in his chair. 'Looks like I am as well.'

Hugh sat forward, hands open, his body language flagging in advance that he was about to offer Virgo a deal. 'Listen, I could give you a great price on a Henry Moore, a lovely reclining figure in Travertine marble, from the mid-seventies.'

'Do you own it? 'Cause if you do, I'll 'ave it anyway.'

'I don't own it, no. It belongs to a client who wants to sell it discreetly. Messy divorce. Wife's lawyers are cleaning him out.'

'What's in it for me, then?'

'I'll waive my commission.'

'Much as I'd like to help your client weasel his way out of paying off his missus, I'm not interested. Anyhow, I haven't brought you here to buy anything from you. You're here to discuss how you can help me with some of my own cashflow problems.'

Cashflow? He used the word as though he was running Debenhams.

'You always seem to have plenty of cash, Douglas.'

'True, but my cashflow problems differ from yours in that I've got too much – unlike you, who's got fuck all.'

That much Hugh grudgingly conceded.

'In the grand scheme of things, you're not one of my bigger problems. If you were, I'd be using your kneecaps as drinks coasters by now. My biggest problem is that I've become a victim of my own success.'

Hugh couldn't help wondering how many other victims of his success there were, buried in shallow graves all around Greater London.

Virgo flicked some ash onto the floor. 'I can deal with the villains who stray onto my manor. But violence isn't such an elegant solution to the axe-man or the Old Bill asking questions about how I earn my money. That's what I need to talk to you about.'

'I really don't see how I can be of any use,' Hugh said, almost with an air of resignation. 'I'll get your money. Just give me a couple of weeks.'

'It's too late for that. I've written off the money and, to be honest, was about to write you off too when my accountant explained how distressed loans get converted into equity in companies that go bandaloo. It was then we decided to take a controlling interest in your gallery. Here's Luca now, late as per fuckin' usual. He'll go over the finer details.'

Hugh looked anxiously over his shoulder, as a chair was dragged along the concrete floor and parked between him and Virgo's desk.

CHAPTER 8

Crunching Numbers, Not Bones

Luca Ambrosini put a briefcase on the bare concrete floor, undid the buttons of a Harris tweed jacket and folded his willowy frame awkwardly into the chair. Luca was Virgo's accountant, although he'd long ago been struck off for defrauding another client. In the meantime, he'd done a seven-year stretch for de-flowering a fifteen-year-old schoolgirl. The best that could be said of him was that he'd never worn his disgrace lightly, although whether this was because of remorse or self-pity, Hugh couldn't be sure.

'Ah, Luca, good of you to come,' Virgo said, tapping his cigarette on the ashtray on the desk. 'What is this, a fucking gentleman's club? I said six o'clock.'

'Sorry I'm late, Douglas.' Luca's voice was reedy, with an Australian lilt still intact after half a lifetime spent in England. 'I had an appointment in the West End.'

Harry looked up from his black brogues. 'Bringing your girlfriend to see *Shrek,* were you?'

Virgo's mouth coiled into a smile. Luca didn't respond, almost seeming to expect the jibe. He blew vainly at the pall of smoke that hung above the desk. The smoke glowed spectre-like from the low evening sun that streamed in from the windows behind. 'It's a little smoky in here,' he said, waving a hand in front of his face. The palm and fingers looked soft, pink, almost nubile. 'Can't we open a window?'

Virgo wafted his cigarette in an arc. 'You can try, but apparently windows that open are extra.'

'I'm sure there's a designated smoking area downstairs.'

Virgo blew more smoke across the desk. 'I'm fine here, thanks all the same.'

Luca always maintained the calm exterior you often see in people professing a deep religious faith – that sham, brittle serenity that events were always conspiring against. In Luca's case, the veneer owed more to pharmacology than religion, but the effect was similar. One perk of working for Virgo was a steady supply of any illicit substance that took your fancy and Luca had a weakness for the barbiturates Virgo peddled to strung-out City boys.

Luca could hardly have been blamed for popping a few pills before meeting two weapons-grade bullies like Virgo and Harry. They gave most people a hard time but seemed to treat Luca with particular scorn. And being 'a filthy fuckin' nonce', as Harry was wont to call him, meant ceding the moral high ground even to them – not a stigma many were likely to endure.

The fact that Luca never answered back was only partly due to artificial sedation. It also showed how badly he needed the work. The employment opportunities for convicted sex offenders were limited, however much he protested his innocence with the hardly novel defence that 'she told him she was seventeen'. A back-to-work scheme administered by the parole board offered him a placement in a lightbulb factory for three months after he left prison, but any other efforts to find work came to nothing. Needless to say, KPMG didn't return his call.

Even if he hadn't been so desperate for a job, what would be the point in standing up to Virgo or Harry? He seemed to lack his tormentors' venom. There was a gentleness about him that somehow made his penchant for underage girls even more disturbing. He was also physically slight, despite being just shy of six foot. His wiry frame meant that no matter how expensively tailored his clothes were, they still never seemed to fit him properly. Add to this the fact that any physical confrontation would mean taking on Harry, who made the Klitschko brothers look wispish, and Luca's rationale became clearer.

In the coterie of sadists and sleazebags that surrounded Virgo, there was a clear division of labour. Everyone seemed to know their place and accept it unquestioningly. And why wouldn't they? The pay was excellent, even by London's bloated standards. True, the benefits were structured differently to other firms. The health plan consisted of staying on the right side of Virgo to avoid being maimed or, if you crossed him on a bad day, buried under two hundred tons of concrete on a Docklands building site. The travel benefits included couriering cash to Dubai or the Caymans or cruising around London in one of the boss's vintage cars on all manner of nefarious errands. There was little need for a pension plan, as the life expectancy was short.

Problems with any of the above were dealt with by the HR department, i.e. Harry. Virgo could be faulted for many things, but a lack of organisational skills wasn't one of them.

So Luca understood his role with crystal clarity: he crunched numbers, not bones. Aside from his five-year sabbatical in Belmarsh Prison sex offenders' wing, Luca had been Virgo's bagman since being struck off as a legitimate accountant. In particular, it was his mastery of the financial alchemy of making dirty money clean that kept him in the fold. There were the staples: a couple of bars and clubs around London, and more recently property investments, like the place they were in now. There were also some beachfront properties in Cape Town, even a share in a syndicate that owned ten thousand hectares of virgin rainforest in Venezuela.

Then there was the more complicated stuff that Hugh had heard referred to but never explained. Money was churned through accounts in Switzerland and the British Virgin Islands. Companies registered in Panama that Virgo controlled through a web of crossholdings were bled of money before being liquidated. There were share options in shell property investment trusts that were cashed in before the credit bubble burst. 'That was a genius fuckin' wheeze,' according to Virgo.

He openly admitted to Hugh once that without Luca's financial conjuring, he would still be running his business empire out of Parkhurst. 'Luca might be a filthy bastard,' he said, 'but the man is the Harry Houdini of tax evasion, the David Copperfield of blink-and-you-miss-it accounting.'

And for his next trick, could he have a volunteer from the audience?
Luca turned to Hugh with an almost apologetic air.

'Good to see you again, mate. You're looking fit. Been working out?'

'Not unless you count the eight flights of stairs we just climbed.'

'Lift's not working yet,' he said. 'It's not exactly the Dorchester here, is it? Probably not what you're used to.'

'He's a tea caddy, ain't he? Probably born on a fuckin' building site.' Virgo turned to Harry as the most likely to indulge him with a laugh. Harry guffawed dutifully.

Luca ignored them, and kept his eyes fixed on Hugh. 'How's business?' he asked.

'Business-like.' The tone was abrupt. Hugh had no intention of making this easy. They all knew that if business had been going well, he wouldn't be sitting there.

'I've had a look at your accounts,' Luca said, pulling a manila folder from his briefcase. 'Your turnover seems to be growing steadily but your costs have grown even quicker. The temptation when you enter a booming market late is to try and buy market share. It doesn't always work. All the money you're spending on rent, staff, art fairs, publishing books, entertaining and whatever else, is wiping out the gallery's revenue. Bigger turnover just seems to mean bigger losses. Let's face it, that white box you have in St James's is a bit of a black hole when it comes to money.'

He had a point, it was just somehow even more humiliating coming from Luca. Having his second skin of self-denial peeled away by those hands was a new low.

'The contemporary-art business is a tough one to crack,' Hugh said, by way of resistance that owed more to pride than reason. 'It was bound to take time. Rome wasn't built in a day, you know.'

Virgo flicked his cigarette butt across the floor. 'Julius fuckin' Caesar didn't owe me money, though, did he? We've heard all of your feeble excuses. Don't wanna to hear 'em again. Simple as.'

'It's been four years, and the debts are mounting,' Luca said, his voice calm, unlike his boss's. 'We think it's time for a change of direction.'

'I just need a little patience. It'll come good.'

'Douglas is not a patient man.' Luca gave Hugh a knowing look.

'I'll speak to the bank about extending my overdraft.'

Virgo twitched, shifted in his chair.

'You're already massively overdrawn,' Luca said. 'No bank will extend your limit even further while the business is still losing money. Anyhow, we have other plans. Did Douglas mention we have a proposition that could help to straighten out your finances?'

A crooked plan to straighten out his finances. 'He mentioned something about taking a stake in a gallery. I'd be happy to offer any advice I can give. Maybe I could even offset some of my debt as a kind of mentoring fee.'

'You're a cheeky bastard, aren't you?' Virgo said, shaking his head.

'We would like you to work more closely with us,' Luca said, 'and I suppose it is sort of a mentoring role we have in mind. We've been keeping a close eye on your gallery, and on the art market generally, and we think we've spotted an opportunity.'

'Thinking of packing it all in and becoming an artist, are you?' Hugh asked.

'In a way, yes. Although not just one artist, several artists.'

'I'm not following you.'

'Yeah, get to the fuckin' point, will you, Luca.' Luca's even tone had clearly begun to rile Virgo.

'We'd like you to front a gallery for us,' Luca said, unruffled, the barbiturates still working nicely. 'We plan to wind down the gallery you have now and open a new one with a whole new group of artists.'

'It's taken me long enough to assemble the artists I have.'

'You'll have to dump them.'

'Sorry?'

'And dig up a crop of new ones.'

'Where?'

'You'll have to invent them.'

The conversation was taking a ridiculous turn, but Hugh was happy to pursue it rather than talk about the money he owed Virgo.

'I can't just manufacture a whole new group of artists.'

'Why not?' Luca asked. 'Fake works of art have been around as long as there's been an art market, so why not fake artists?'

'Because there's a financial incentive to fake works of art by important artists, not to fake the artists themselves. If anything, there are too many artists out there, far more than could ever earn a living at it. Do you know, there'll be more fine-art graduates in the US this year than there were people living in Florence at the time of the Renaissance?'

'Perfect. That means nobody will pay too much attention to ten or twelve new ones. The gallery you'll be fronting for us will be a conduit for funds from Douglas's main business. You do know what that is, don't you?'

'A florist? A Montessori? To be honest, I've tried not to think too hard about it.'

Luca smiled. *He* was patronising Hugh.

'We deal with lots of people who like to look the other way over where the money comes from. Plausible deniability, isn't that what the Americans call it?'

CHAPTER 9

The Sherbet Dip

Hugh always made a point of knowing the business of his clients, although he feigned ignorance or indifference. Dealers, artists, critics, even curators, draw a veil between commerce and art, as though the two aren't bound together like Humbert and Lolita: commerce besotted but corrupting; the art world coquettish but all the while submissive. For their part, collectors like to keep their interest in art separate from their working lives, sometimes out of caginess but more often because they regard how they earn their living as of little interest to people working in the arts, whom they mistakenly believe to be above workaday commerce.

To his credit, Virgo either wasn't aware of – or had no interest in – the niceties observed by other clients of Hugh's. As he got to know Hugh better, not only was he quite happy to let him know how he earned his living, he liked to stretch him on a rack of middle-class discomfort by describing his business to him in lurid detail.

Hugh got a potted life story from Virgo over dinner one evening shortly before he opened the Lead White. That wasn't why Hugh had suggested they meet – he'd long ago adopted the see-no-evil, hear-no-evil attitude of his former employers towards Virgo. The fact was, he needed money and knew Virgo had lots of it. He'd extracted as much as he could from the bank, which had stopped just short of asking for a charge over his vital organs as collateral. A personal guarantee was asked for and given, and his house was remortgaged to the hilt.

But this still left him about eight hundred grand short. Enter Virgo, who met the two criteria needed for an investor. He was *minted*, to borrow from his own vernacular. He also had that keen interest in art which meant putting money into a gallery wouldn't be a purely financial investment but would also have other, less tangible rewards, like owning a racehorse or a football club. Be it as a status symbol or a plaything, Hugh didn't much care, so long as he got the money.

The plan was to spend a couple of hours viewing the Royal Academy summer exhibition before crossing over the street for a spot of dinner at the Wolseley. Hugh reckoned he could soften Virgo up with the academy's annual open-submission show, where almost everyone saw something they liked. He might even ask Virgo to pick out some younger artists they could approach to exhibit at the gallery – make him feel like it wasn't just the money Hugh was after. Tell him what a great eye he had, suggest he make more use of it.

It was almost half six when Hugh's phone gave a tinny rattle on the perforated metal table where it sat next to his espresso. It was a message from Virgo: 'There in 5'. By then, Virgo was already an hour and a half late. Hugh had looked around the exhibition on his own and was sitting under a parasol in the courtyard of Burlington House, trying in vain to enjoy the early-evening sunshine. He gazed at the distended shadows flitting over the sandstone paving in front of him, his mind brimming over with sums. Rent, key money, architects' fees, builders, decorators, *lighting consultant.*

Christ, did he really need a lighting consultant?

More to the point, did he really need Virgo's money?

The crowds were still filing in and out of the grand Palladian entrance that led to the gallery rooms, most of them tourists ticking off another item on their cultural to-do list. Some stopped to admire the three sculptures of dinosaurs by Jake and Dinos Chapman in the centre of the courtyard. They looked like giant origami models, made from sheet-metal instead of paper.

A group of Italian students arranged themselves under the belly of the long, rangy dinosaur – a brachiosaurus? – before one of them broke ranks and walked over to Hugh, holding a camera in her outstretched hand.

'Would you, please?' she said.

'Of course,' Hugh said, easing himself out of his chair. He framed the shot carefully, taking the opportunity to admire the girl who had handed him the camera on its digital screen.

'Say *fromaggio*.' Hugh cringed a little as he said it.

As the camera gurgled out that sampled sound of a shutter opening and closing, Virgo strolled into the frame, talking on his mobile. Realising that a camera was pointing at him, he held his hand up reflexively. 'Have to go, gettin' smudged up here.' He listened for a moment to the reply. 'Very funny. Better not be the fuckin' *Standard*.'

The Italian girl came over to retrieve her camera, glaring at Virgo, her fine features rearranged into an inimically Latin expression of *What's your problem?* Hugh gave an apologetic shrug and sat back down at his table. Her indignation was wasted on Virgo, who didn't lift his eyes from his phone. He read over a text message and then answered it, before flicking the phone shut.

'Sorry I'm late,' he said eventually. 'I had a meet with my solicitors. Can't believe I pay those bastards by the hour to waste *my* time.'

He sat down opposite Hugh, tugged on the sleeves of his Paul Smith jacket and brushed some fluff off a lapel, before catching the eye of the waitress. 'Get us a pot of tea, love, would you?'

His eyes tracked the waitress as she made her way inside, before he turned back to Hugh. 'Looked around, have you, then?'

'Afraid so.'

'Did I miss much?'

'Not really.' Hugh saw little point in talking up the exhibition, as his scheme for the afternoon had already unravelled.

'Just as well. I've seen enough art for one day. I was in your old stomping ground earlier, looking at the British watercolours sale. I was thinking of bidding on one of the Turners.'

'I thought you were buying more twentieth-century work?'

'I was, but you know me – old school at heart. They wheeled out one of their experts for me. Strange bloke. Plump, tense, couldn't decide whether to brown-nose me or look down his nose at me. Can't remember his name. It was double-barrelled, though.'

'Doesn't really narrow it down much in that place. What did the expert have to say for himself, then?'

'I think he was a tad pissed off over the crowds viewing the contemporary sale upstairs. Downstairs, it was just me and a couple of old birds in tweeds, up from the Shires for the day.'

'They sound like sellers, not buyers, to be honest.'

'You think so? Anyhow, he seemed to think Turner was more collectible than the contemporary stuff because his work had already stood the test of time, unlike the YBAs, who he said were just a flash in the pan.' He meant the Young British Artists – Damien Hirst, Tracey Emin, the Chapman brothers, Gavin Turk et al – who had burst on to the London art scene in the early nineties and had since taken possession of it like a gang of unruly teenagers showing up at your house and finally, after a long and arduous stand-off, taking you aside to tell you that it just wasn't working: *We think you should move out.*

Virgo dissolved two lumps of sugar on a spoon, partially submerged in his black tea. 'He even reckoned Turner was more radical in his day than Hirst. He told me how Turner, in his late sixties, had himself tied to the bridge of a steamboat in a storm to better understand "nature's ferment" – his words obviously, not mine. It was for one of his most famous paintings, apparently.'

Hugh had heard this yarn lots of times, had even spun it himself on occasion. He also knew it was more than likely apocryphal. 'That'd be *Steamboat off a Harbour's Mouth,*' he said.

'That's the one. This chap said artists just aren't as vocational any more: now they're obsessed with money and celebrity, like everyone else. Said Hirst was more likely to be seen sunning himself on a yacht in the Adriatic. Can't help agreeing with the man.'

'So what would you have Hirst do?'

'I dunno, maybe I'd drop him into a tank of live sharks, give him a better understanding of one of his most famous works.'

'What is it you object to?' Hugh asked. 'Hirst's work, or his celebrity and wealth – because to me they're separate things.'

'I object to everything about him. He's a fraud. A northern chav: the worst kind. And how many versions of the same works can he do? He's been copying himself badly for years.'

Virgo did have a point. Whenever a *catalogue raisonné* is produced of Hirst's work – a monograph on the artist with a list of all of the work he has ever produced – it will be very long, but very repetitive. He has churned out over a thousand of his spot paintings, a similar number of spin paintings, as well as multiple versions of his medical cabinets chock-full of pills, and his collages of dead butterflies stuck down on gloss paint. Even his most famous work, *The Physical Impossibility of Death in the Mind of Someone Living* – the shark in a tank of formaldehyde – has more than one version, and not just because the original began to decay.

But very few successful artists haven't had their potboilers – that work with a familiar style and subject that collectors will always want to own. All professional artists, by definition, need to commodify their work for sale, and what better way to do it than have a signature work or style that they can sell with relative ease, ideally freeing them to take risks with newer, more innovative work. The danger is that they become slaves to the market, which for some successful artists becomes a rapacious beast that must be fed. The problem is compounded by collectors only coveting the type of work an artist becomes known for, one that can easily be identified, preferably at some distance, like a giant label they can hang on their walls.

Hugh opted to let the discussion lie there, reasoning that he hadn't arranged to meet Virgo to defend contemporary art against the brickbats that rained down on it from time to time. In any case, they were both getting hungry.

They strolled across Piccadilly, which was still disgorging the last of the peak-time traffic, and in through the baroque entrance of one of London's more fashionable eateries. In the couple of years since it had opened, Hugh had really taken a shine to the Wolseley. There was a Habsburgian excess about the place: the soaring, vaulted ceiling, perched on marble columns; the grandiose bar, decked in brass and mirrors; the starched-linen tablecloths; the punctilious staff who stopped just short of clicking their heels when they presented themselves at your table. Even the menu would've had Franz Ferdinand twiddling his handlebar moustache. Lobster, bratwurst, goulash, Wiener schnitzel, oysters, caviar and whatever you're having yourself, Empress Elisabeth. The belt-loosening gluttony of it all.

It was just so gloriously fucking decadent.

And Hugh had a seat at one of the best tables in the house.

They were shown there by a lithe young waiter with dark hair, oiled and combed to one side. Two menus were handed over with a flourish, and the candle in the centre of the table was lit with a Zippo the waiter had in the breast pocket of his waistcoat. Virgo fidgeted in his seat for a moment before announcing that he needed to 'use the little boys' room'. Hugh badly needed a drink but the waiter flitted to a nearby table before taking orders for aperitifs, deciding to wait until Virgo returned.

Virgo was never easy company. He was sharp-witted but aggressive, with a volcanic temper. And Hugh was never quite sure what might cause an eruption. One thing was certain, though: booze and drugs didn't help. Hence the ominous feeling Hugh had about the trip to 'the little boys' room' as Virgo rarely left home without a couple of ounces of high-quality coke flake in his pockets. Virgo excused his habit on the grounds that 'when you run the sweetshop, you tend to develop a sweet tooth'.

Hugh caught the waiter's eye and was about to order a gin and tonic when Virgo came striding back across the cavernous dining room, slaloming between tables, eyes like silver chargers.

'Fuck it, let's have a bottle of Bollie,' he said, before Hugh had a chance to order his G&T. Hugh nodded to the waiter, who turned and headed straight for the bar. Virgo stayed standing, scoping the restaurant, his face locked in a maniacal grin. He was clearly having one of those sugar rushes you only get from nose-candy. This was shaping up to be a long night.

He dropped into his chair and gripped the table in front of him. 'All go in here tonight, ain't it?' he said, turning to the couple at the next table, who couldn't have helped but notice him. They were well-groomed professionals in their early thirties: black suits and designer spectacles. Chinese, more than likely.

'Is that *your* bird?' Virgo asked.

'I suppose you could call her that,' the man answered. The tone was curt but polite, the accent neutral.

'She's lovely. You're a very lucky man, or should I say a *rucky* man. You're a *velly rucky* man.' He mouthed each word slowly for effect.

The couple smiled politely but knew better than to engage him in conversation. Virgo's eyes remained fixed on the woman, until Hugh broke his lustful reverie.

'Here's the champagne now,' he said.

'About fuckin' time,' Virgo said, clicking his fingers and pointing at the couple. 'And two glasses for Mr and Mrs Moto, here.'

They tried to decline the offer, but Hugh smiled apologetically and suggested that they accept, even if they had no intention of drinking it. Meanwhile, Virgo glowered at the elderly couple on the other side who'd been tut-tutting him since he got back to the table.

Hugh had done coke the odd time but it had never appealed – cigarettes and alcohol being his preferred poisons. He'd had ample opportunity to observe its effects, though, given that London had been in the grip of a blizzard of white powder for most of his time there. It may have been the purity of what Virgo had taken – he kept the best for himself and didn't cut it with novocaine, glucose, baby laxative and whatever else dealers used to bulk up what they sold – but it seemed to have a confessional effect on him. By the time the froth had settled on the first glasses of champagne, he was already midway through act one, scene one, of *Douglas Virgo, The unexpurgated life and times of a total [and utterly misunderstood] cunt*. It was a bravura performance.

He was born in Bethnal Green, in modest if not impoverished cir-cumstances. Things seemed to spiral downwards from there. 'My sister and I didn't have a father,' he said, without any hint of self-pity. 'We had a pet fuckin' beer monster who slept on the couch downstairs. If he wasn't pissed by lunchtime, he was probably up in court that day. Because he never beat us, the neighbours called him a *harmless* drunk. I almost despised him more for that.'

Virgo emptied his glass, after which his head and shoulders went into a brief spasm. 'The old dear kept us going with a part-time cleaning job down the local comprehensive. Christ knows why she never kicked him out. Think she actually felt sorry for the bastard. That's why, as soon as I had the cash, I bought him a flat in Hoxton, gave him twenty grand and told him to fuck off out of it.'

He raised his empty glass in the air and waved it from side to side, like a distress signal. Then he resumed his life story, telling it without remorse or regret, and with the moral certitude of someone who'd written his own code of ethics and treated other people according to its tenets, regardless of whether or not he'd bothered to explain them first. He interrupted himself only to shovel food into his mouth, drink wine and order more.

He'd left school at sixteen and begun working for a scrap-metal merchant. It was there that he realised he had a knack for trading, a skill that was soon to be in even greater demand a mile or two down the road, when Margaret Thatcher's government deregulated the financial markets. The subsequent explosion in the size and scope of what the City did was dubbed the Big Bang at the time, by someone who seemed to believe it was an event on a par with the birth of the universe. That may have been a tad hyperbolic, but it certainly changed the course of Virgo's life. Within five years he'd travelled down the Hackney Road, onto Old Street, and in the back entrance of a City investment bank, where he'd landed a job as a post-room clerk.

'I felt like the butcher's dog,' he said, with a note of condescension at his own callowness. He didn't stay callow for long, though. He was hungry and razor-sharp; his employers soon realised that his skills would be better deployed ten storeys above, on the trading floor. Within another couple of years they'd moved him up there, and unleashed him on the international equity markets.

The butcher's dog stole into the abattoir. He was one of the original 'barrow-boy stockbrokers', and thrived in the brief flowering of meritocracy in the City of London in the 1980s. For a while at least, social class was no longer an obstacle to a career. Being working class almost became a boon. Before the shutters came down again after the 1987 stock market crash, the only employment criterion was how much profit you would yield for the firm, however squeamish they were in the oak-panelled boardrooms about the school you'd gone to. And no matter how conspicuous your consumption or lurid your lifestyle, the important thing was that you made yourself rich, and your employers even richer.

But for Virgo, the fat salary and morbidly obese bonus weren't enough. He built up a lucrative sideline brokering with drug dealers and pimps to feed the chronic pang of his colleagues and their clients for recreational depravity. 'They don't shout about it,' he said, 'but firms in the City offer more than dinner at the Ivy and trips to Wimbledon as corporate entertainment. If you're getting five million quid in fees, another fifty grand on some racier R&R is a modest overhead.'

He said it like it stood to reason. As if the business couldn't be done otherwise.

'I came unstuck when a tabloid hack got wind of an especially sordid little shindig I arranged in the presidential suite of a West End hotel.'

This time, it was Hugh who refilled the wine-glasses and waved the empty bottle in the air. Virgo barely paused for breath.

'You should've seen the place, it was *seething*. I laid on a whole troupe of hookers, male and female, more bugle than the Glen Miller orchestra, and enough smarties to keep Damien Hirst in art supplies till he retires. I'm telling you, mate, if it came in a jar and rattled, I fuckin' had it. Uppers, downers, screamers, laughers' – he reeled them off, tapping the fingers of his left hand with the thumb of his right. 'But even I didn't think they'd get *so* out of control.'

Virgo's attempt to absolve himself of blame by pleading naivety rang a little hollow to Hugh.

'At first it was just the noise. There was a baying sound from one of the bedrooms, where two sets of Brazilian twins were going to work like a Formula One pit crew on our CEO, Jeremy Jiggins. I don't think he had as much fun again until he got his knighthood.'

Hugh laughed, but Virgo's expression didn't alter, the delivery tinder-dry as ever.

'You might have thought some responsible citizen would call the law, but not in this town. Someone decided to call a red-top instead. The reporter pitched up around midnight with a photographer. He slipped the concierge a monkey and got a key to the suite. He couldn't believe his luck when he opened the door. It was tabloid fuckin' heaven. Right there on the floor in the hallway, some bloke – no idea who he was, but he looked like he did it for a living – was about to perform a sherbet dip on this bird, as it happens a board member of a blue-chip merchant bank and, if memory serves, a special government adviser on financial-market regulation.'

'Hang on, back up a little,' Hugh said.' Forgive my sheltered upbringing, but what on earth is a sherbet dip? I take it you're not referring to the powdered sweet.'

'Well, not that type of sweet. Now let me think.' He paused to glug on the brandy he'd just ordered. 'How was it the *Daily Mail* described a sherbet dip at the time? Something like "covering the male appendage in cocaine before penetration, not unlike Delia Smith dusting a piece of fish in flour before frying".'

'I should have guessed,' Hugh said.

'That wasn't the end of it, though. The reporter had clocked the commotion in the main bedroom. There was some bloke out on the window-ledge singing at the top of his voice with three or four others trying to talk him back inside. Did I mention we were on the eighth floor? His name was Mr Park if memory serves me.'

Virgo glanced again at the Chinese couple next to them, who both had their faces screened with their hands.

'We'd just signed off on a $400 million bond issue we's arranged for a South Korean car company. Mr Park was the company's chief financial officer. I'm not sure what he'd taken, but he seemed to get a mite more caned than anyone else.

'The hotel's night manager must have heard the racket as well, because he was in the room desperately trying to avoid a PR disaster for his employers by having a guest scraped off the pavement eight floors below. In the end, Mr Park refused to come back inside until the manager joined him in a chorus of "I should have known better" by Jim Diamond. He was really fuckin' mashed.'

Virgo leaned back in his chair, holding aloft a cigar in one hand and a brandy in the other, and burst into song: '*Ah shuh a know berra, den to rie to wan as bewrifur as yew*'.

His voice was a strangled, toneless mongrel of cockney and a comically generic South-East Asian accent. Hugh cast another apologetic glance at the couple next to them.

'Apparently,' Virgo said, 'this Korean bloke had just broken up with his mistress after she'd found out he'd been unfaithful to her with *her* sister.' He shook his head despairingly.

'What a wanker,' Hugh said.

Virgo paused for a moment's reflection, and to drag on his cigar, before adding, 'Not a bad singer, though.'

There was a stirring at the table next to them. The Chinese couple had left.

'Anyhow, that was the end of my career in finance.' Virgo said this without a hint of regret. 'When the reporter phoned the bank for a comment, they denied all knowledge of my antics, before sacking me and reporting me to the police. Then they closed ranks. The bastards.'

It seems that the old class divides re-emerged: a praetorian guard of public-school old boys formed around senior management, leaving Virgo on the outside with a bowl of cocaine and an address book that read like Pablo Escobar's Christmas-card list cum hit-list – delete as appropriate. He was sentenced to eight years in prison, commuted to six years for good behaviour. As a parting shot, he arranged for the soon-to-be *Sir* Jeremy Jiggins to enjoy the services of another hooker before she paid an urgently needed visit to an STD clinic.

'I learned that night never to underestimate people's appetite for debauchery,' Virgo said. 'Especially rich people's. In the short term it cost me, but longer term it turned out to be a very lucrative lesson.'

The Old Bill suspected Virgo's employers knew what he was up to but couldn't – or wouldn't – pin anything on them. 'I knew I'd been rumped, he said, 'by dodgy handshakes, old-school ties, years of political donations, but I still kept schtum. Did a Colditz number on them.'

'How do you mean?'

'Name, rank and serial number.'

Hugh gave an uneasy smile, not sure if he really wanted to know so much about the delinquent morals of some of the most powerful people in London. He was struck, though, by the absence of any bitterness on Virgo's part – at least of the self-destructive kind. Virgo was pragmatic, methodical even, in exploiting his connections, and the debt he felt was owed to him.

He did 'his bird' and was a model prisoner who made full use of the prison library. He read *The Communist Manifesto, The Wealth of Nations, The Origin of Species* – always going for original texts, so he could form his own opinions, however unpalatable they ended up being. He read Plato's *Republic,* taking a particular shine to one of its characters, the sophist Thrasymachus, and his dictum on justice, which Virgo felt compelled to share with the priggish old couple at the next table who'd been casting disapproving glances at them all evening. 'Of course you do realise,' he announced to them, as they tucked into their *petits fours,* 'that justice is merely an illusion fostered by the strong to facilitate their oppression of the weak.' The couple looked predictably appalled, not just by the substance of what he'd said, but also by the fact that he'd spoken to them at all – and gestured to a waiter to bring them the bill.

Virgo read prison memoirs like *The Gulag Archipelago, Borstal Boy,* even *Mein Kampf,* which he abandoned midway through because 'the bloke was barking'. He also read anything he could lay his hands on about Jack the Ripper, especially any book supporting the theory that the Whitechapel murders were never properly investigated because of a conspiracy by the establishment to protect one of its own. The most likely culprit in Virgo's mind was Prince Albert Victor, Queen Victoria's grandson, who, he claimed, committed the murders having been driven mad by syphilis.

'Now *that* is barking,' Hugh said, a tad too dismissively.

There was a flicker of menace in Virgo's hooded brown eyes. 'And what the fuck would you know?' he said. 'It's all out there. You just have to go and dig it up.'

Hugh let it lie, knowing better than to rile his dinner companion. Not that Virgo dwelt on the subject in any case, as he was already pressing on with his own prison memoir. When not in his cell reading, he survived the daily trials of prison life with the aid of his own in-house security in the form of Harry, who was doing an eight-year stretch for GBH on the same wing.

'I first noticed Harry when some West Indian lag was giving him a ribbing, calling him a Little Englander and what have you – ironic, really, since Harry was born in the colonies as well. His father was a colonel in the Royal Rhodesia Regiment. The family had a bit of money, but the old man lost most of it investing in some hooky property deal in Kenya. Then he drank the rest. Harry never knew his mother: she died when he was still wet and wild. A woman who worked as a nanny for the family took him in, back in England. She couldn't cope with him, though. He was a bit of a handful, was our Harry. Spent his teens in and out of Borstals and approved schools.'

Virgo shook his head with a wistful, almost paternal smile.

'Anyhow, he knocked ten types of shit out this bloke in the yard later that day. People knew better than to pick a row with him after that, so I stuck him on the payroll. I couldn't have hacked it on the island without a basher on a lead. They don't call it the Hate Factory for nothing. The place was full of antsy cunts, usually with a couple of mackerels by their sides, always giving the screws grief and getting it back twice over. But I kept my head down, got Harry on the case only when one of them was practically begging to have his head trod on.'

Virgo emerged from prison unscathed, self-improved even, and set about realising the business plan he had carefully drafted while inside.

He would reap the rewards of his circumspection in the dock at the Old Bailey, of his 'Colditz' routine in the basement cells of Paddington Green Police Station. He would establish himself as the prime provider of all manner of nefarious services for London's investment banks and large corporations. The fact that he already had so much incriminating material on so many high-profile people in the City meant that they had little to lose in continuing their dealings with him. They also paid him such vast sums of money that there was little incentive for him to extract more through extortion or blackmail.

The Square Mile and the Docklands became *his* manor. He offered upmarket sleaze with professional integrity, a transparent pricing structure, and utter discretion. Over time, he diversified into the role of an all-round fixer. Graft, money laundering, blackmail, the occasional contract hit. Whatever needed sorting, Virgo was their go-to guy.

'It's all about customer service,' he said. 'Building long-term relationships. Exploiting synergies.' Hugh couldn't tell if he was being ironic or not. He'd clearly read a management textbook as well while he was inside. But the business-guru gloss, already a little flaky, fell away like a snake's moulted skin when Virgo mentioned 'leverage', as Hugh just had a vision of Harry hitting someone over the head with a crowbar.

He knew better than to share the image with Virgo, who was now expounding on how 'the customer is king'.

'You have to understand their needs,' he said, 'sometimes even spot their needs before they do. That's how you win them over.' Mind you, the vast archive he'd built up of compromising photos and video footage of a rake of CEOs in FTSE 100 companies had also been useful in 'cementing relationships'.

It was cunning like this that gave Virgo the edge over the competition – which, apparently, was legion. 'The Square Mile is such a dirty great honey pot that all manner of villains want to get their paws into it,' he said. 'In fairness, the local crims know better than to trespass. The occasional upstart comes down from Birmingham on the M1 – the only good thing ever to come out the place, as far as I'm concerned. But most of them are just Keystone crooks, *dis*organised criminals, easily dealt with.'

The IRA tried to get a piece of the action. They were ruthless but disciplined, and even commanded a degree of professional respect from

Virgo. Harry ran a few out of town. It brought back fond memories of his time as a squaddie, kicking in front doors on the Falls Road: *Paddy-bashing,* he called it. More recently, the Chinese Triads had staked a claim, and the Jamaican Yardies were forever sniffing about.

But the real threat came from the Russians. They first pitched up in London in the early nineties, and soon acquired a reputation for plumbing new depths of viciousness. They had a particular penchant for knives, and were caught out early on bringing knives to gunfights – a mistake they quickly rectified. They still brought the knives, but disabled their victims first with a couple of shots – back then with an old Red Army Baikal pistol. Then they finished them off with sixteen-inch blades that wouldn't have looked out of place in a Samurai movie.

One in particular stepped out from the pack – Vladimir Nemirovsky – although Virgo seemed to prefer his colloquial name. 'Vlad the Inhaler', they called him, though not to his face. Chronic asthma, by all accounts. Got the name when he was shown on the giant screen at Stamford Bridge dragging on his inhaler when everyone else in the directors' box was celebrating a Chelsea goal.

'But I wouldn't underestimate him. Bloke's got access to serious working capital. Whoever's bankrolling his business is well fuckin' minted. I have my suspicions: when oil and commodity prices go through the roof, the Ruskies are always cashed up.

'Anyhow, that kind of wedge gets Vlad facetime with the Colombians. He's buying product direct and in bulk. Hammers down the price so he can retail it as low as I can. Thing is, he has a rep for cutting it half-in-half with baby laxative that he buys by the container-load – in Indonesia, from what my sources tell me. I never tire of telling my clients that if you have a nose-up care of Vlad, you should expect to spend the next day on the khazi.'

Virgo shook his head ruefully, as though Vlad was giving the trade a bad name. 'He even deals with the Taliban' – evidently a bridge too far. 'I don't do business with those psychotic ragheads. In fact, I don't touch horse at all. Got to have some standards.'

'It's all organic fair trade for you, is it?'

Virgo bristled with professional pride. 'Look, I like to think of meself as a progressive villain. I don't deal smack on council estates. I'm not some Shylock loaning money to single mothers on benefits. If some desk-jockey pulling in a couple of mill a year has a nosebleed on his loin of venison, why should I care? You want me to drive him down to Harley Street, have that deviated septum looked at?'

He looked across the restaurant, talking to himself as much as to Hugh. 'No, these people do it to themselves. If they didn't buy from me, they'd get it somewhere else.'

'What about the women?'

Virgo turned back to Hugh, his eyes drawing a bead. 'What about them? They don't work for me. They work for agencies I let on to my manor. They're not trafficked, though. Not slapped about. They do it 'cause they want to.'

'Oh please, spare me the happy-hooker fairytale.'

'I weren't gonna give it to you.'

Virgo's elbows rested on the white-linen tablecloth. The napkin he wiped his brow with was like a curtain coming down on the life-and-times monologue. Now they were talking about Hugh. 'Holier than thou, are you? Why'd you ask to meet me today?'

'No particular reason,' Hugh said, without much conviction.

'I figured you wanted money.'

'No, what made you think that?'

'I stopped by your new gallery on my way to the Royal Academy this evening. Had a word with your builder. Paid him off. Your architect too, and some of the other contractors hangin' about. I cleared your overdraft as well.'

Hugh's jaw slackened. 'How . . . ?'

'Don't ask. Suffice to say, anyone's powers of persuasion can be sharpened with a chequebook and some inch-thick wads of cash. I reckon you're a sound investment anyway, *and* I need someone new to handle my collection for me.'

'What about Felix Lazaar?'

'Lazaar?' Virgo said with a derisive laugh. 'I'll be *sacking* that bastard, when I find him.'

CHAPTER 10

Vanishing Point

Virgo legs perched on the edge of the desk, crossed at the ankles. The last of the evening sun gave an added lustre to his stippled brogues, with their Cleverley's label on the sole. They were bespoke, of course – like most of what he wore – made from eighteenth-century reindeer hide salvaged from a Danish brigantine that sank off the coast of Plymouth. The thick black mud of Plymouth sound protected the leather from the salt water. Hugh remembered Virgo telling him about them, how he'd had to call in a *favour* to get a pair. There was so much demand that the makers had even said no to Michael Heseltine. Virgo was particularly pleased about that.

He didn't look pleased now, though. His face was blank. He inspected some dirt under his fingernails. When his gaze shifted back to Luca, his expression didn't change.

Luca leaned forward in his chair, palms pressed together between his knees, doing his best to ignore the brooding presence opposite him. Hugh couldn't help thinking what a professional Luca was. The guy was all business, like he was here to sell life insurance.

Shite. Maybe he was.

'The way it is,' Luca said, his tone matter-of-fact, 'we provide professional services to companies, that cost them a lot of money.'

He made quote-marks in the air as he said 'professional'.

'The problem is, these services are too sensitive to declare.'

'I can see how that might be awkward,' Hugh said.

'I don't just mean Douglas's core business – and I'm guessing you know what that is. Our clients also have other expenses we can help them with, that can't be filed in the annual accounts. I'm talking about incentive payments, performance bonuses. All off-balance-sheet. Others might call them bribes – graft, payola. I'm not sure what you'd call them in Ireland.'

'I think we just call them political donations.'

Luca shrugged. *Whatever.*

'You remember Enron, don't you?'

'I do. "The smartest guys in the room".'

'For a while they were, back when they knew how to get business done. Which palms to grease. They'd build a private power plant in a developing country – India, say, or Latin America – and set aside 10 percent of the project cost for the "education budget" – basically a slush fund to pay off everybody from national politicians down to local officials. The problem with Enron was that just about everybody knew what they were at. There was a lack of subtlety there. In the end, it was their undoing. They got found out closer to home, but they could have tripped up anywhere.'

Luca crossed his legs and laid both hands on top. 'Most of the companies we deal with have a little more finesse. They know how to oil the wheels of commerce without sending the whole locomotive careering off the tracks. Say you work for a bank in the City and you want to arrange the $200 million export financing of the cocoa crop for a small west African country. Do you win the deal with the most competitive tender?'

Hugh was looking at Harry, whose eyelids had begun to droop. 'I have no idea,' he said, turning back to Luca.

'No, you win by paying off the right people. That's why that official in the farming ministry on $5,000 dollars a year, drives a $50,000 Beamer.'

There was a snort from Harry when his head drooped onto his shoulder, then jerked upright. His eyes closed again as his chin settled back on the lapel of his overcoat.

Hugh glanced nervously at him, then at Virgo, who rolled his eyes, then back to Luca. 'Is that so?' he said.

'I'm afraid it is. That's just how the business gets done. It happens time and time again. State bond issues. Privatisations. Project financings for roads, bridges, airports. Drilling licences for oil and gas wells. State contracts for big pharma companies. Licences for new drugs, or permits for testing them. Graft is a fixed cost. There's no getting around it.'

'Well, I suppose that's Johnny Foreigner for you.'

'Not just foreigners,' Luca said, ignoring the sarcastic tone. 'The gorging starts a little closer to home. There are gannets everywhere, mouths agape. Even in this country.' He gestured to the wall of windows behind Virgo, towards the Canary Wharf tower, a red light blinking on the steepled roof, and beyond that to the Square Mile, the Gherkin, the NatWest Tower and the Stock Exchange. Beacons of commerce. Icons of wealth and power, cast in concrete, steel and glass.

'Look at the banks here. Ever wondered why they've been left alone to make money, no meddling government looking over their shoulders. Nobody asking how exactly they made such vast profits? As though it would be rude to ask. The government and the regulator just saying, "That all seems jolly complicated. Gosh, you guys are brainy. We'll just leave you to it, then, shall we?" Why so cavalier when we all know now how much was at stake? Ever wondered?'

'Can't say I have,' Hugh said.

Luca rubbed a thumb and two fingers together. 'Money. Quite a lot of it, actually. That kind of light-touch regulation hasn't come cheap. And it'll cost them even more now to buy off the people who want to rein them in. Some of the payments are above-board. Political donations, the odd charitable gift to a minister's pet cause, or a seat on the board for a permanent secretary when he retires. But most of these people can't wait that long. They want their jam today.'

Hugh nodded, still not sure where the conversation was headed, but sensing that the hook was being sharpened.

'The thing is, all of these expenses create an accounting problem.' Luca's voice was calm, almost pastoral. 'How do these companies show the money in their books, make it look legitimate? They're always looking for new ways. Mix it up a little. Not make it too obvious. That's the problem we can play a modest part in solving.'

'When you say "we" . . . ?'

Luca nodded. 'Yes, that includes you, mate.'

Fuck. Now they were *mates*.

'You know what I do for Douglas and his clients?' Luca asked.

Hugh shrugged.

'I'm the laundry man. I take money with all sorts of stubborn stains on it and give it back. Cleaned and pressed. You can do this down a back street and hope nobody comes snooping around, or you can do it in the open, in a bustling market, with so much money swilling around that telling the clean from the dirty is nigh-on impossible. Personally, I've always found that the bustling market offers the best cover. When a business is awash with money, establishing the source can be more difficult, while dirty money getting flushed through the system is far less likely to be spotted.'

Luca's opened his palms towards Hugh. 'So I look at the contemporary-art market. Worth billions. The so-called banking crisis barely winded it. The Damien Hirst sale at Sotheby's a couple of days after Lehman's collapsed still turned over a hundred million. High-end prices are pretty much back where they were.'

'I'm not seeing much of it,' Hugh said, 'but you're right, there's still an awful lot of business being done – at the high end.'

Luca nodded. 'For us, though, the real beauty of the art market is that our clients are already massive players in it. You don't need me to tell you how corporate art collections have grown over the past thirty years. Did I read somewhere that about a third of all high-end art sales are now to corporate collectors?'

'That sounds about right. A third might even be on the low side.'

Luca was nodding again. 'For someone in my line of work, there's an opportunity here. This is virgin pasture.'

Hugh glanced at Harry, sure that Luca's use of the word 'virgin' would draw an acerbic comment, but he was still dozing. Virgo sat side-on, gazing out of the window. He seemed content now for Luca to do the talking, even though Hugh had a feeling that whatever scheme they were about to embroil him in had Virgo's stamp all over it.

Luca did collect art – British watercolours, mainly. When Hugh first heard this, William Russell Flint's work came to mind: paintings of louche women in all sorts of erotic poses. But apparently they're not his bag at all. Luca collects the portraits that were popular at the end of the nineteenth century of tender, chaste young maidens. These were studies in vestal purity: portraits of graceful, doe–eyed girls on the cusp of womanhood. The kind of work men on the sex-offenders register really shouldn't be allowed to buy.

Luca leaned back in his chair, palms still open. 'So I'm looking at this market worth billions of pounds a year, where, as far as I can see, there's no policing, no regulation, no oversight of any sort. I mean, who can really make sense of the art market? The prices just seem . . . ' – he paused, puffed his cheeks out, searching for the right word – 'so *random*. It's as though establishing the value of a work is an art-form in itself.'

Hugh was about to argue the point when Luca cut back in.

'There's no Art Standards Authority, or a regulator capping prices. The Fraud Squad or Her Majesty's Customs & Excise don't have teams of officers in black polo-necks and tortoise-shell spectacles nibbling canapés at exhibition openings and asking awkward questions about the prices of the works on display. The woodentops like to work at football matches, but I doubt there'd be many volunteers for private views on Cork Street.'

He laid a hand on his chest. 'I'm an accountant. My speciality is finding blind spots in the system. You have a blind spot here that starts at the point of sale and spreads through a whole industry. Like a cataract.'

'Come on, Luca, you're exaggerating. OK, so some prices can seem a little inconsistent, but generally speaking, the cream rises to the top.'

'That might be true, but from what I can see, so does quite a lot of dross. Aesthetically speaking, I mean.'

'One man's cream is another man's dross. And who says prices are random? There are lots of things that determine prices. Like whether or not critics take the work seriously.'

'I'm sure you can always find somebody to say something nice about the work.'

Virgo stirred, flipping his legs off the desk and turning to face them. 'Bollocks. You tellin' me there aren't a load of bent, low-rent critics out there who are happy to earn a few quid on the side?'

'A couple.' Hugh had their numbers in his mobile, but left it at that. 'There's also the collections they're in. Who's buying the work? Major corporate collectors, maybe, or influential private buyers like Charles Saatchi or Robert Orca – although they can be fickle – or, better still, a museum.'

'Don't worry, mate,' Luca said, 'the corporate collections will look after themselves, and we'll leave every other gallery in London to woo Saatchi and Orca. As for museums, do you mean the Tate, say, or the Guggenheim?'

'You're setting the bar pretty high there. There are lots of smaller regional museums that buy work or accept donations.'

'So you just give them a piece.'

'Sort of.'

'*We* could do that, if we have to, although it shouldn't be necessary.'

'I don't know where you're going with this,' Hugh said, getting agitated. 'You buy Victorian watercolours, Luca, and Douglas has always been a sceptic about the contemporary market. Neither of you really know the scene. There's good and there's bad work out there. Original and old-hat.'

'Great, then maybe you can explain how the market works to me, 'cause I've been looking through some auction catalogues and I'm a little confused.'

He pulled a glossy Sotheby's catalogue from his bag: *Selected Works from the Lehman Brothers Corporate Art Collection.* Hugh had viewed the sale. The collection was light on major pieces by blue-chip names, but it still made for decent carrion for the vultures who'd survived and prospered since Lehmans bit the dust.

Luca flicked through the catalogue. 'Sure, some of these artists, even I've heard of. The likes of Gerhard Richter, Sean Scully, Damien Hirst, Andy Warhol. Even Richard Prince and John Baldessari – although I didn't realise they'd become *so* expensive. But there are so many artists in here selling for tens of thousands, hundreds of thousands, even millions, that very few people will have heard of.'

'Such as.'

'Let's start with one of top-priced works in the sale, Julie something-or-other. How do you pronounce that? M-e-h-r-e-t-u. Born 1970. *Untitled 1*. A pencil-and-ink drawing with some squiggly lines painted on top. Estimated $600,000 to $800,000.'

He pulled out a folded-up sheet of results he had tucked in at the back of the catalogue, opened it out and ran his finger down the side. 'Strewth! Sold for over a million.'

Hugh leaned over and looked at the illustration. 'Fair enough. She's not a household name, but she's highly thought of and that's a signature work.'

Luca was reading from the catalogue again, this time from the blurb on the facing page. 'Apparently, this is . . . *a dynamically iconic painting from the artist's intricate and energetic* . . . em . . . *ooovra*? How are you pronouncing that?'

He gave Hugh a quizzical look but didn't wait for an answer. 'I quite like this painting, and I can see some work has gone into it, but why is an artist barely out of her thirties selling work for that kind of money when even I can see that it's similar to what Kandinsky was doing in the 1920s.'

'It's not that simple, Luca.'

'The problem is, it's in your interests to make it seem complicated.'

By Luca's standards, that was cutting.

He began leafing through the catalogue again. Virgo reached across the desk and snatched it from him. 'Gimme that fuckin' thing. We'll be here all night.' He flipped the catalogue over and back. 'Who's that, then?' he asked, pointing at the image on the front cover, of multi-coloured stripes, running crossways and diagonally.

'That's a Mark Grotjahn. American artist. Lives and works in LA.'

Virgo looked at the title page, found the lot number and flicked through the catalogue until he came to the work. 'Mark Grot . . . whatever the fuck his name is. *Born 1968. Oil on canvas, $600,000 to $800,000. Untitled*. Again. Fuck me, for that kind of money you'd think these artists would at least give the work a name. Basically, what we have here are different-coloured stripes. I know these bilge-merchants are going to tell me otherwise, but that's what I'm looking at.'

He skimmed the text, shaking his head, before reading aloud. '*The kadeidoscopic creation that is the present work is flamboyant and electric yet deliberately enigmatic at the same time*.' He did his best la-di-da accent, straight out of a Monty Python sketch.

'*The essence of Grot*' . . . I can't fuckin' pronounce that . . . *the essence of the work lies in its own polarities. It is at once infinite and banal, rational and absurd, methodical and chaotic. A graphic exploration of illusionist space*.' He looked at the full-page illustration – 'Christ, who writes this stuff?' – and held it up for Hugh to see, then read again from the facing page. '*His genius lies in his revolutionary use of perspective and geometric manipulations of space.*'

His eyes fixed on Hugh. 'Are they seriously telling us this is original? How can that possibly be new?'

Hugh paused: he was reaching. 'Well, for starters, the stripes converge on three different places. I suppose it has more than one vanishing point.'

'That's original, is it?'

'Not really, no. There's very little original that can be done with a canvas and some oil paints.' Hugh held his hands up. 'I mean, you're right, it's basically op-art.'

Luca nodded, with a look that said, *OK, we're making progress here.* 'Op is short for "optical", right? It started in the sixties with people like Bridget Riley?'

'Actually, it goes back even further, to Josef Albers in the 1950s, and before that to the Bauhaus in the 1930s. But I suppose Albers is the main guy. He wrote a book, *Interaction of Colour*, that a lot of the work draws on.'

'So unless you've studied the book, you can't do the art?' Luca asked.

'Well no, there are no hard-and-fast rules. And breaking rules is part of being an artist.'

'It stands to reason, I suppose. You don't need to be a Rembrandt to paint some stripes on a canvas.'

'No, and you don't need a PhD in art history to look at them, but it can still be done well or done badly.'

'Fair enough,' Luca said, and looked back to Virgo, who was leafing through the catalogue, shaking his head, muttering obscenities. He stopped about halfway through. 'Abstract expressionists,' he said, and left the words hanging there.

'Abstract expressionists *what*? Is that a question?'

'Sort of. There are artists in here younger than me still doing it. Splashes of paint on a canvas. Drip paintings, for fuck's sake. I'm no art historian, but didn't Jackson Pollock come up with that wheeze sixty years ago?'

'Wheeze? Steady on. That's one of the key figures in Modernism you're talking about.'

Hugh paused, regrouped, then tried a different tack – the one he might take with a client. 'Maybe you just need to approach the work in a new way, Douglas. An abstract painting has different registers, like a piece of music, and one of them is emotional. It may resonate with some people in a way it doesn't for either of you.'

He leaned back in his chair, hands gesturing as he spoke: he was moving through the gears now. 'The work doesn't have to be labelled, put in a box marked "op-art" or "expressionist". Sometimes you just have to trust the artist's intuition. Try and feel what the artist felt when he made the work. In a way, what you take from the work depends on what you bring to it.'

Luca's gaze dropped to the bare concrete floor; Virgo's stayed on Hugh. 'Are you finished?' he said.

'Not quite. Maybe you should hear me out.' There was an edge to Hugh's voice that surprised even him. 'All I'm really saying is that you're only reading the work on one level. There are the formal problems you have with any work of art: the materials used, the technique; and with a painting, the composition and the palette. Then there's the concept that underpins the work, drawing on art history and the world around us – physical, social, political. Last but not least, there's the emotional frequency of the work, which the artist is a cipher for, knowingly or not.'

Virgo didn't seem to be paying much attention. He had the catalogue resting on the edge of the desk as he leafed through it. 'I'm hearing you,' he said, 'and I like what I'm hearing. That's the kind of drivel we need you for. Cover our arses. Give the gallery an air of authenticity. We'll need pukka bullshit. Eighteen-carat gilded bullshit, like your friend might make, the *turdsmith*, what's-his-face?'

'Craig Charlton.'

'That's the one. And I mean that as a compliment. When it's just between us though, leave it out. Especially all that twaddle about artists being emotional ciphers, as though they don't have to explain their work. If someone's gonna charge me a couple of hundred grand for some pigment on a canvas, they better fuckin' know what they were doing. And are you seriously telling me that the people who buy this stuff – hedge-fund managers and the like – really get it in the way you're saying they should? The work in this catalogue came from Lehman's, for fuck's sake – the greediest bastards on the planet. All they ever cared about was wonga, and how to make truckloads of it as quickly as they could.

'No, the one thing the people who buy this stuff have in common is not some artistic sensibility that the rest of us stunted, pig-ignorant yahoos were born without. What they have in common is money, dirty great piles of cashish. So much that whatever they can't gorge on or shovel up their hooters, they collect stuff with – cars, boats, planes, houses. And art. The art they're told is fashionable. The art their chums are buying – or the people they'd like to be their chums. Ideally, art with a bit of upside. Share certificates they can frame and stick on their walls. Might even be an exhibition in that. Take a note, Luca.'

Virgo was flicking through the catalogue again. He looked like he was starting to enjoy himself. 'All of these photographs,' he said. 'C-prints, lambda prints. What are they?'

Hugh sighed. 'C stands for "chromogenic". Technically, a C-print is just an ordinary photographic print, like you pick up from Boots, say. A lambda print is the digital version.'

'Not expensive to make, then.'

'It depends. A lot of the time, artists just print them on ordinary photographic paper, but they can be printed onto plexiglas or stuck down on aluminium as dibonds. Depending on the quality or the size, you could get them made from fifty quid to a grand.'

'So all of these photographers, then. Rodney Graham. Who he?'

'He's a Canadian artist. Shows with the Lisson Gallery in London.'

Virgo was reading aloud again, half to himself. 'Born 1949. *Welsh Oaks (No. 6)*. Estimated $70,000 to $90,000. Sold for . . . ' – he scrolled through the results sheet that was wedged in at the back of the catalogue – 'sold for 160k.'

He was shaking his head, smiling at the same time. 'It's a bog-standard photo of a tree, right, black and white an' all, only he's turned it upside down. Fuckin' genius.' He was looking at Hugh again, his eyes mocking. 'I take it that's the gimmick, right, and not just a mistake by the printer.'

Hugh winced. 'I don't think the artist would call it a gimmick.'

'Course he wouldn't.' Flicking through some more pages, Virgo said, 'Here's a photo of a busy street-crossing in Tokyo – a C-print. Thomas Struth. Estimated $20,000 to $30,000. It's big, I'll give you that much:

about six by eight feet. But it's basically just a photo of the street, unless I'm missing something.' Scrolling through the results again, his jaw dropped when he found the lot-number. 'Sold for 55k. That's fuckin' criminal, that is. And I ought to know.'

Hugh leaned over the desk to take a look. 'Now, Douglas, there's more to it than just a photo of the street,' he said defensively. 'Look at the way the perspective is elevated, like he's six or eight feet above the crowd.'

Virgo shrugged. 'He's got a stepladder. So does Bob the fuckin' Builder.'

'The work is about atomisation. About dislocation in an urban environment. Loneliness in a crowd.'

Virgo pulled a face like he'd just got a bad smell.

'What these artists are doing is deliberate, considered,' Hugh said, a note of desperation creeping in. 'It might seem random to a novice, untrained eye.'

'Convincing a novice, untrained eye will do just fine,' Luca said, trying to sound reasonable. 'And I don't think we'll really have to worry about the *trained* eye either because, you have to admit, there is a touch of the emperor's new clothes about a lot of this work. Nobody on the scene *wants* to point out the obvious.'

Here we go. Hugh wondered when they'd get around to this. 'Luca, that old chestnut about the emperor's new clothes has to be the most hackneyed, most redundant criticism of contemporary art. As if the entire market was just one almighty act of collective denial.'

Virgo slapped the catalogue down on the desk. 'Yeah, Luca, the emperor doesn't *just* have no clothes. As well as being stark-bollock naked, His Eminence is also doing a pole-dance with a leering mob of rich cunts – we're talking flash lemon here – desperately trying to shove bundles of cash up his arse.'

'That's not quite what I had in mind, Douglas.'

'Still an' all, it's a lovely image. Might work as a performance piece. We could document the work it in a series of lambda prints on plexiglas' – his did his hoity-toity accent again. 'Charge twenty grand each. No, fuck it, make that forty grand. Wouldn't want to arouse suspicion by making them too cheap.'

He leaned back in his chair with his hands knitted together behind his head. 'This could turn into a right giggle.'

A fluorescent light flickered over his head, then off to the right and left of him, with a rattle and a *ching*. The grey, rough-hewn concrete floor, which was shrouded in a dusky pall, unfurled itself around them again on all sides. Reflected in the wall of windows behind Virgo, the rods of fluorescent light stretched out over Victoria Dock until they touched the concrete floor at the vanishing point.

The vanishing point.

Christ, all of sudden everything's a work of fucking art. The Dadaists have a lot to answer for. It's almost a hundred years since Marcel Duchamp exhibited a urinal as a work of art, signed with the name 'R. Mutt'. At first he was pilloried, but he ended up being celebrated for it. So much so that a couple of before, a panel of five hundred experts (including Hugh) had declared the urinal to be the most influential artwork of the twentieth century.

Did Virgo know this? He probably did. He always seemed to know a lot more than he let on.

CHAPTER 11

The Artful Dodger

On the stroke of 9PM, Jack switched off the digital projector. A painted ember of the image remained on the canvas, like an exposure on a sheet of photographic paper. Jack picked up a luke-warm mug of chamomile tea and settled into the armchair in the corner of the studio. He appraised his day's work with all the detachment of a man who'd just put up a shelf.

The fine detailing on the bowl had taken three hours but was worth the effort; the green of the apples was a little too acidic, and needed to be brought down a tone or two; the porcelain figurine was too painterly, not as tight as the rest of work, but would only take a half an hour to sharpen up; the pattern of the tablecloth just needed to be resolved around the edges of the canvas.

Not a bad day's work, considering he'd only got up at midday. Of course, the projector did make things quicker and easier. There was no need to square up a preparatory drawing, fiddle with the perspective or replace spoiled fruit as the inevitable corrections dragged out the process.

The likely buyer would no doubt marvel at how the painting *could almost be a photograph.* Jack did feel a twinge of guilt over this little deception, over supplanting so much time and effort with the flick of a switch. Just a twinge, mind you. The painting still took more skill than any other artist his age he knew of could muster, especially working as quickly as Jack did, wet on wet. Anyhow, he didn't subscribe to the academic painting diktat of doing everything from life, of squaring up his subject from a smaller drawing or just plain eyeballing it. He salved his conscience with the thought of the Old Masters, who painted over an image projected with a lens or a convex mirror. He reckoned deceit had been a part of the art business ever since it became just that: a business. Not that this lessens the achievements of Vermeer or Caravaggio or any of the other great masters. It's just that what the artist or dealer sold wasn't always what the patron cum collector thought he was buying.

The collectors in this case were the clients of Campion Fine Arts, the gallery in Hampstead where Jack sold his work; the dealer was its owner, Julian Campion. The no-nonsense philosophy of Campion on selling art had a perverse appeal: he told Jack once that they were mere confectioners, selling treats and fancies to the wealthy. Unfortunately, this was one of the rare occasions when Campion stopped to talk to Jack. Usually when Jack called by the gallery, Campion was just leaving, harrumphing his way to the front door, his mink-collared cashmere coat – which could very well have had a selection of wristwatches and ladies nylons attached to the inside breast – swishing in his wake. The more brusque Campion was, the more money he owed Jack. At the very least, there were no rambling excuses. Campion was far more shameless than that.

Felix Lazaar, on the other hand, whom Jack would much rather be making work for, always paid in full, cash on delivery. Jack's increasingly rare skill-set, allied to his ethical broad-mindedness, was far too lucrative to Lazaar to risk pissing him off.

But there's been no word from Lazaar for three months, and even that was only a voicemail: 'I'll be laying anchor off-coast for a while, old boy. Keep out of mischief.' As to where Lazaar had lain anchor, Jack was clueless, though he couldn't help worrying that the old shyster had gone down with his ship and might end up taking Jack with him.

Jack Hastings was a twenty-eight-year-old graduate of Silversmith's College of Art in Camberwell. He'd been awarded a third in a year when no student failed. The only other student to get a third hadn't even bothered to show up for the exams. In truth, Jack had never fit in at Silversmith's. He'd been accepted for the fine-art degree course on the basis of a portfolio of drawings of male torsos with the outline of a head sketched in, and the faces left blank. He had no other reason for choosing this subject, other than liking male torsos, but the selection panel seemed to think there was some conceptual subtext to the work, and offered him a place.

Jack had a feeling they'd made a mistake on the first day, when the college's director, Christopher Bell, delivered not so much an introductory lecture as a mission statement. The students were told that fifty years ago Silversmith's would only have instructed them '*up* to the wrist: in the craft of making art in commodity form – paintings and sculpture. Nowadays, we like to think we instruct our students *down* to the wrist: in the practice of making art with your minds, not with your hands.'

There followed a torrent of jargon from which Jack salvaged the occasional piece of flotsam. This was the era of post-skills and post-studio art, of site-specific interventions and relational aesthetics – whatever the hell that meant. 'You are here to remake yourself, as much as to make art,' Bell declared. 'In many respects, *you* are the work of art to be created.' He scrawled four words on an overhead projector: 'The id as muse.' 'You're here to explore the self as the object of its own reflective consciousness, the alter-ego as the progenitor of the art of the ego.'

With this opening spiel from the college's director, Jack became tangled up in a briar of art-speak that he never quite found a way through. Nor did many of his classmates, as far as he could see, although quite a few did latch on to the phrase 'the art of the ego' as the starting point for the work they would make or, more often, just talk about making.

For one thing was clear, in this brave new world of post-skills and post-studio art, students would be allowed ample time for self-examination – or navel-gazing, depending on your point of view. His tutor assured Jack that this was an essential part of the art-college experience. It was how the student artist found his or her voice. 'But what about life drawing?' he asked. 'Not on the curriculum in fine art,' he was told. 'Try the animation department: they still offer it.'

And so Jack ghosted through art college, drawing now and then in the animation department, or wiling away afternoons in the fashion department – where most of the best-looking men were enrolled – tie-dying canvasses and stealing lustful glances at the fey and ever-so-stylish wannabe Alexander McQueens who flounced around the place.

He was rarely seen over in fine art unless there was a crit in the offing. The crit is a seminar where student artists present their work to other students for collective critique. Crits at Silversmith's had acquired an almost mythical status, as had the man who oversaw them, Martin Finch, himself an artist, although he rarely made any work and hadn't sold anything since the mid-1990s, when he had submitted a crude drawing of a ship (that he'd stuffed inside a bottle) to a charity auction.

Most students were in awe of Finch. He had a monkish demeanour. He wore grey crew-neck jumpers and John Lennon spectacles. His utterances were sparse and ambiguous, his presence so minimal that he was barely there at all. Far more tangible was his influence on the student body – or psyche, to be more precise. He was a provocateur with the poise of an oracle. He was a mullah to the art-world jihadis, bent on crushing infidels – designers, painters, pretenders, mere illustrators – whose work had no conceptual rigour.

But Jack wasn't so enthralled. He realised Finch's cerebral calm was just a veneer that was easily scuffed. He sat on the margins of the class, sketching Finch and the other students. It was a useful way of sharpening up his life-drawing skills, but it also rankled Finch and his acolytes. As did his baiting of the student artists presenting their work. Finch saw the crit as a conceptual foundry where half-formed ideas were moulded and forged, patinated and polished for presentation to the world. If the idea was eventually rejected, then that was part of the process. 'Art comes out of failure' was his motto. Student artists were encouraged to talk about their work even when they had little to say, or there was little to be said. Waffle went unchecked; feeble ramblings were buttressed with jargon, camouflaged in art-speak. In many ways, it was the perfect preparation for a career in contemporary art. It built up a tolerance for the background stench of bullshit that permeates the scene.

But Jack just couldn't suppress his sense of smell. The odour was far too pungent.

Matters came to head in a third-year crit, when one of Jack's classmates screened a video she'd made of a vase of flowers on a window-sill being bombarded with multi-coloured paint balls. She began her pitch confidently: 'Central to my practice is the role of chance as the creative partner of intention'. Finch and the rest of the class nodded in approval.

All bar Jack, that is. 'Bollocks,' he grunted, Tourettes-like – before realising he'd said it aloud rather than just thinking it.

The presenting student never recovered her composure, which must have been tenuous enough to begin with. There followed a tearful intellectual breakdown, punctuated by half-remembered snatches of her prepared blurb. Finch was apoplectic. He said nothing, but the bulging veins in his temples spoke for themselves.

The next day, Jack was summoned to a meeting with Finch in the college director's office. Christopher Bell opened the door for Jack in the uniform of the visual-arts professional: grey shirt buttoned up to the neck, and a charcoal linen suit. Finch was already there, sitting with his back to the door. He didn't acknowledge Jack.

'Have a seat, Jack,' Bell said, gesturing to the empty chair next to Finch, before taking a seat himself behind a desk which was empty save for an iMac and a copy of *Art Forum* magazine. 'This is just a clear-the-air meeting, an unofficial chat,' he said jauntily. 'So don't worry, we won't be issuing any formal warnings – not today, at any rate.'

Jack smiled thinly. If there was one thing Jack and Finch had in common, it was a disdain for Christopher Bell. He was a careerist, an intellectual whore who would have subscribed to whatever the prevailing ideology was in the art world. Had he been a member of the *Academié des Beaux-Arts* in the 1860s he would no doubt have been among the most vocal in banishing the Impressionists to the *Salon des Refusés*.

Bell turned to Finch. 'Martin, you have some issues with Jack's behaviour in . . . '

'He's uneducable,' Finch cut in tersely, looking only at Bell, and speaking with a revealing speed and precision.

Jack's leg dangled over the arm of his chair. 'Is that even a word?'

Finch ignored him. 'He seems to be suffering from this strain of artistic autism one finds quite a lot in this country. Conventional autistics have difficulty reading other people's emotions or facial expressions. *He* seems unable to interpret any work of art that isn't *skills-based*.' He spat out the words like a bilious reflux.

Even Bell seemed taken aback, not just by Finch's strident tone but also by the length of the outburst. By Finch's standards, that was an epic monologue.

Bell held his hands over the desk, palms facing down like a blanket to smother a flame. He looked anxiously from Finch to the errant student.

'Our major concern here, Jack, is the tone of your contributions to crits. You've been upsetting your classmates.' The hands came together, the fingers and thumb of his left hand braced against those of the right. 'What we want to foster at Silversmith's is a spirit of *criticality* rather than criticism. By all means shed light on a dialectic in another student's work, but let's refrain from more forthright judgments.'

His head tilted to one side. 'I propose we start over with a blank canvas or . . . . ' – he turned to Finch, reassuringly – 'with, em . . . a clean slate.'

Bell proposed a truce – a tacit understanding that Jack would be awarded his degree if he stopped disrupting crits or, better still, stayed away altogether. Jack didn't think he could sit through another of Finch's bilge-fests in any case, so it seemed like a mutually agreeable arrangement.

But he still had to make a body of work for his degree show. He looked around at what his classmates were making and realised that Finch was right: Jack just didn't *get* it. To his eye, the work all seemed so self-indulgent, so fatuous. The randomness was uniform. The lack of convention was conventional.

In the end, he did the most radical thing he could think of. He maxed out his student credit card, and bought all the how-to books on painting he could find. He scoured artists' memoirs for advice on technique, for those tricks of the trade that in the past artists learned at art college or as apprentices in the studio of a master. He discovered a slew of books by forgers that were full of insights into the methods used by the Old Masters. Eric Hebborn's *Art Forger's Handbook* was a revelation.

For his graduate show, he made three paintings: a still life, a landscape and a portrait. He air-dried six willow panels in his father's shed over the winter. As they dried, one of them buckled and two of them cracked. He discarded these and set to work on the other three. He made his own gesso with warm rabbit glue and chalk whiting, and applied six fine coats. Then he sealed the panels with a layer of gelatine size and a ground of burnt-umber and yellow-ochre oil paints – Old Holland of course, the best you could get, short of grinding your own pigment. Preparatory sketches were squared up onto the wooden panels before he spent a month working on each painting. He even made the frames himself from willow, which he carved, gessoed, ebonised, gilded and waxed.

He hung the paintings in the booth he was assigned with an air of defiant trepidation; stuck a note on the wall next to them saying that they were made using the same materials and techniques as the seventeenth-century Dutch masters – his way of saying there was nothing faddish about the work. To emphasise the point, the buyer would be offered a four-hundred-year warranty. He expected scorn but a little part of him fantasised that the sceptics would be overcome by the sheer virtuosity of the work. Every artist believes that they could be *the one*.

The opening drew the usual crowd of college staff, friends and family of the artists, plus the ever-growing cohort of collectors eager to snap up work at bargain prices by the next Hirst or Emin. One of his examiners called him 'a talented mimic' but lamented that this wasn't a school of mim-icry. The collectors just seemed a little confused: they looked around the otherwise empty booth, then looked at the paintings from the side, even underneath, wondering what the trick was. Some of the parents and grand-parents of the other students discreetly, almost guiltily, admired the work. 'Did you paint that yourself, dear?' one old lady in a twinset asked him.

Jack just nodded, with a rictus smile.

After four days standing in his booth, it was clear that no one who mattered was impressed by his work, or even all that interested in it. In the weeks that followed, he began to wonder if he should just go with the flow, and try to make more original work, even if only for the sake of it. But he had went straight from the first flush of enthusiasm to a weary self-doubt, with no serious attempt made to realise them.

After a couple of months, he did start painting again – sloppier ver-sions of the work in his degree show – to sell through Campion Fine Arts. The choice of gallery was accidental. He met Campion's significant other, a Moroccan chap named Faisal, in the toilets of the Black Cap pub in Camden. After a quick fumble they got chatting, and Faisal decided that Jack was just the type of artist who did very well in his boyfriend's gallery. If nothing else, it would pay the rent.

He was two years out of college before he had his epiphany. He real-ised that if he was no more than a talented mimic, then why not pursue his talent for mimicry to its logical end: forgery?

He chose a minor painting by the eighteenth-century Italian master, Giovanni Battista Piranesi, and did a preparatory drawing for it, having concluded that forging a painting was too ambitious: he tried, but his attempts at ageing the work never quite came off. Then he had to decide what to draw. A compositional sketch, dashed off with the freedom and economy of style of a master, would be too difficult to replicate, even for an artist of Jack's calibre, so he settled instead on a study for a detail.

His medium was natural chalk – black argellite and red chalk – which were still readily available online or from a decent art-supplies shop. They were exactly the same in their chemical structure as those used by the Old Masters. The modern-day synthetic variety would never have fooled an expert.

Finding the right paper was trickier. After 1800, most paper was machine-made, and was useless for his purposes: he had to source some paper that Piranesi might actually have used. His plan was to sit through as many auctions of Old Master prints and drawings as he could, maybe get to know some of the dealers, find out what they were buying.

Eventually, he found what he was looking for. A bound folio of etchings by a very minor Italian master, but a contemporary of Piranesi, came up for sale. The work was second-rate but was ideal for his purposes, as it was still in its original bindings, with endpapers, and blank sheets between each etching. Perfect for producing his ersatz Old Master on.

But no matter the relatively poor quality of the folio, it was still beyond Jack's limited means. So after the sale, he approached the dealer who had bought it, and asked him if he intended to take it apart and sell each etching separately.

'What if I am?' the dealer said.

'I'd like to buy the blank sheets.'

Caginess gave way to an avuncular smile. 'Nice to see the torch being handed down.'

'Not sure what you mean,' Jack said, wide-eyed. 'I've just graduated from Silversmith's. It's for a project I'm working on using antiquarian paper to make papier maché models of key works by Jeff Koons. I got a grant for it.'

The dealer looked disappointed but still handed him his card. 'Call around tomorrow afternoon with three hundred pounds. Cash.'

The deal was done. After a few rehearsals on some cheap paper he bought in the local art-supplies shop, he set to work in chalk on the eighteenth-century paper. He needed to work quickly if the drawing was to emulate the freehand of a master. He used Piranesi's distinctive style of cross-hatching, added some *pentimenti* – visible corrections to the line – and a few random smudges. When he'd finished, he even surprised himself with the quality of the work. It was worthy of the master himself – on an off-day, at any rate.

The next step was to have the work authenticated by an expert. He reckoned an auction house was his best bet, given the vested interest they'd have in declaring it genuine and selling it in one of their Old Master sales. The expert he brought it to at Frith's was impressed. He said it wasn't right, of course, but that it was very well done. 'You can tell it's a later drawing done on period paper by the chalk lines running over onto the inside edges of the worm-holes in the paper.'

Drat. Foiled at the first attempt. The expert looked at Jack knowingly, as though he suspected him as the forger. Jack didn't hang about. He slipped the drawing back into a folder and scuttled out the door, straight to the bus-stop and back to Finchley, where he spent the rest of the day waiting for a knock on the door. He knew there was an art police: the contemporary-art Gestapo, distrusting of anyone under thirty who could draw. They'd lock him up if they could. But was there a Forgery Squad, who'd bash down his door with a hooky Rodin? Go through his studio with a magnifying glass and an ultraviolet light?

Fuck. Maybe he should find a new flat. Or stop drinking so much coffee – made him too edgy. Stick to herbal teas.

When he'd calmed down, it dawned on him that he was expending a lot of energy needlessly trying to replicate the virtuoso naturalism of the Old Masters, to sell into a market that was flat, if not in decline. Wouldn't it be easier, he realised, to forge the work of a contemporary artist, whose work required a little less technical accomplishment, but where the market was insatiable?

Canvasses from the sixties, seventies and eighties were cheap and plentiful at auction. It was just a matter of removing whatever daubing was already on them, sometimes with a fine sander but more often with a solvent of alcohol or acetone. He tested a corner of the canvas using turpentine to dilute the solvent if it began eating into the primer on the canvas – which he decided to leave intact, so that the painting would look the same from behind as it did before he went to work on it.

He drew up a shortlist of successful contemporary artists whose work would be easy to copy, and set about researching their early exhibiting careers. He realised that artists airbrushed their CVs as they moved up through the highly stratified art world, and that less prestigious galleries were excised from their exhibition history as their stars began to rise. This was useful knowledge, as not only did he need a twenty-, thirty- or forty-year-old canvas, but he also needed the label that galleries place on the backs of works they exhibit to help establish provenance later on. He couldn't afford to buy work even by the lesser artists that the top galleries now exhibited, but he could afford to buy work by the lesser artists that showed in the galleries where the artists he would copy started off. He settled on the work of Sean Scully, who had carved out a hugely lucrative career (his work went from thirty thousand to a million quid) painting stripes, with three- and six-inch household brushes. Scully restricted his palette to no more than three or four colours: greys, yellows, ochres, earthy reds.

Jack carefully removed the labels, which were generally printed in colour with spaces left for the cataloguing details of the painting to be handwritten or typed on by one of the gallery staff. He scanned them in on a drum scanner and Photoshopped the resulting JPEG, erasing the added text. He printed out the doctored label on adhesive-backed paper and inserted the new cataloguing details, either on an old typewriter he bought in a flea market in Camden or by forging the handwriting on the original label. He smudged and scratched it a little – which, combined with the sepia tint preserved by the drum scanner, left a label which looked as authentic as the original.

The actual painting was straightforward enough. He discarded early efforts for their overwrought precision – they didn't have the almost rustic quality of the artist he was copying – but it didn't take him long to produce a small group to choose from.

Then he had to decide on where to offer them for sale. He couldn't risk going back to an auction house, so he decided to try a dealer. He flicked through a few issues of *Modern Painters* and *Art Forum*, for the ads mainly, then did some more research online. Places like the Lisson, Alexandra Friedman or Hauser & Wirth were just too well-known, too intimidating, so he settled on the Lead White, which had a fancy new space but wasn't quite so blue-chip. It also made it clear on its website that it kept a stock of twentieth-century moderns and contemporary work by artists it didn't represent, so it must have been in the market to buy work.

He pulled up outside the gallery in a minicab just after midday. He pushed on the plate-glass door, wedged it open with his foot, rested one painting against the wall just inside and reached outside for the other. A friendly girl walked over to offer him some help.

'Are you the owner?' he said, slightly flustered. 'I was wondering if you might take a look at these for me.'

'No, I'm Vicky, the gallery manager,' she said, holding the door. 'That's the owner, Hugh Rhattigan, over there.'

She pointed to a big man on the main gallery floor with an even bigger voice – Irish accent – in a crumpled cream linen suit with shirt-tails sticking out. One hand nestled inside a thicket of hair. He was handsome – shabbily so. Seemed to be cultivating the look of a burst mattress. He also had a slightly startled air, like he'd just been hit over the head with a . . . what was it they called them in Ireland . . . a hurling?

He was talking to a much shorter man in a monikered blazer and a white cravat with a theatrical Home Counties accent, bordering on the camp. This blazered gent had a lush mane of grey-blond hair that stretched down to the nape of his neck but was set back three inches from his forehead, as though it had been foiled in making a quick escape.

Rhattigan looked over towards Vicky with a plaintive, please-rescue-me look. Vicky answered the distress signal. 'Could you excuse Hugh for a moment, please, Felix?' she said, with cheerful poise. 'There's someone here who wants to speak to him.'

Rhattigan marched distractedly into the gallery's reception area, hand still pinning his hair back, looking warily at Jack, then at Vicky, with a face that seemed to say *Is this the best you could do?*

'This gentleman has some paintings he'd like to show you,' Vicky said, folding her arms and stepping back to enjoy the spectacle.

The dealer's eyes rolled before they settled on the work. He stared blankly at them for a moment, nodded in approval, then leaned over and checked the labels on the back. His nostrils flared ever so slightly – a definite 'tell', in poker parlance. He said he liked them, and asked how Jack had come by them. It was a question Jack had been expecting and had prepped an answer for, but when the time came he stuttered, equivocated. 'Er, my uncle – *bachelor* uncle, that is – bought them.'

'And he wants to sell them?'

'Well, not exactly. He's dying . . . dead . . . . I mean, he's dead. He *was* dying; now he's dead.'

Rhattigan's face relaxed into a smile. The smile was intelligent, insightful, if a little rueful. Then he looked back at the paintings. 'This one looks a bit early for such a minimal palette. We could ask the artist, but he's produced so many works in a similar style that he mightn't remember it. I'd really have to check with the gallery that put the label on the back, see if they have a stock number for it.'

Jack's brow creased with doubt.

Rhattigan smiled again. 'Or else you could just take them around the corner to Friths on Bond Street. They might do well for you at auction? This artist's work is in big demand.'

'That's what I'll do, then,' Jack said, with self-incriminating haste. 'Sounds like a plan.'

He gathered up the two paintings and nodded at Vicky, who held the glass door open for him. 'Well, thanks for the advice,' he said. 'It's great to have some professionals run an eye over them.'

He stepped out onto St James's and looked behind, to see Rhattigan and the man in the blazer exchanging a few words, before the shorter man pushed open the door and followed Jack out onto the street.

A short arm with a large, nodular hand was extended. 'Felix Lazaar. Don't believe we've had the pleasure.' His eyes were fixed on the paintings.

'I'm Jack,' came the wary reply. The older man's hand was like a vice. Jack could feel the blood draining from his fingers.

'Fancy a spot of lunch, old boy?' Lazaar said, fixing Jack in the eye this time. 'You look like you could use a square meal.'

And so began a highly fruitful business relationship (as opposed to Jack's dealings with Julian Campion – fruitful only in terms of the subject matter that was requested over and over, with the occasional vase of flowers and assorted crockery thrown in for good measure).

For the previous few years, Jack had been producing about two forgeries a month for Lazaar, all for shady clients, about whom Jack was content to know nothing other than pseudonyms, like 'the Russian' and 'Mr V'. That was until the commissions dried up: he hadn't heard from Lazaar for three months.

He slurped on his mug of chamomile tea and picked up his phone off the shelf beside him. It was dead, so he fumbled around on the floor for the charger and plugged it in. There were three missed calls and three new messages. He put it on loudspeaker and dialled into his mailbox. The first was from Campion, asking how the still life was coming along and reminding Jack that he'd promised to visit the home of a client who wanted a portrait amended to show off a nose-job and some breast implants.

The second was a message from Lazaar. 'Hello . . . hello . . . .' There was the sound of rustling, fumbling, more buttons being pressed, some cursing. Then nothing.

The third was another message from Lazaar. 'Jack, Lazaar here. Been trying to call you. How goes it on the Western Front? Staying out of trouble, I hope. Listen, I have some more commissions for you. The Russian wants a Howard Hodgkin. Not my bag, but the client is always right. Nothing too big. Let's be extra-discreet on this one, stay well below radar cover. Something medium-sized, nice and colourful. Five k to you, plus expenses, like last time. He also wants an Auerbach. Impastos are tricky, I know: you'll have to dry it out somehow. Another 5k should sharpen your wits.'

Jack set the phone down on the arm of the chair and rubbed his hands. Finally, a job to get him out of bed before midday.

He settled back into his armchair, drained his mug and mulled over the details. He'd start with the easier one. Hodgkin showed at the Gagosian Gallery, and Jack had an archive of three or four jpegs of back labels from there that Felix had sourced for him. His itinerary for the next day could go like this: the Gagosian first, then maybe swing by Thomas Heneage Art Books on Duke Street, buy any new monographs or *catalogues raisonnés* on the artist. Then hop on the Tube to Tate Britain.

He would also need a suitable piece of wood to paint on. Hodgkin favoured wooden panels, often salvaged. He looked at the oak chest of drawers in the corner of the studio. It was Edwardian, bought for fifty quid in a house-clearance sale. The top was caked in paint, a fixative for an array of half-drunk mugs of tea and murky jars sprouting brush-handles of various lengths and thicknesses. He stood up, set his mug down amid the detritus, moved the canvasses that were leaning against the front of the chest and pulled out the bottom drawer: the top one had already been scavenged for an earlier Hodgkin knock-off. He kicked out the base and put it up on his easel.

That should do nicely.

CHAPTER 12

From the French Word *Mort*

In the cold white light, Luca and Virgo's sallow complexions looked bleached, washed out. The dozing Harry's was pink, with blotches of red shaving rash leeching above his collar. Hugh could see his own reflection in the floor-to-ceiling windows that arced around them. The fluorescent lights and the green glass gave him a ghoulish pallor. He looked like his own ghost.

He shifted in his chair to stop the tremor in his leg. Metal scraped on the concrete floor. He did his best to tune back in to Luca, who was giving a lecture on money-laundering: what it actually meant, popular misconceptions, the do's and don'ts. He was almost scholarly about it, like some sort of professor of bent accounting.

'Even the term "money-laundering" is confusing,' he said, 'because it doesn't just cover dirty money that needs to be cleaned: it also includes clean money that becomes criminal. It's more a sort of alchemy, if you will, or transubstantiation. Speaking as one Catholic boy to another.'

Hugh smiled thinly. Luca's clumsy attempts at bonding still grated, even though this was the least of Hugh's problems.

Luca and Virgo had it all worked out. Hugh was the lead stooge in their latest scheme. They weren't pitching the scheme to him; they were briefing him on it. His cooperation was a given. Virgo was calling in the collateral on his money and Hugh *was* the collateral. The best he could hope to do was pick holes in the plan. Point out the logical flaws. That meant staying calm. Concentrating.

But Hugh was too edgy to focus on Luca's reedy voice. The urge to look over his shoulder was triggered again and again by a faulty fluorescent light behind him and to the right, flickering on and off, making him think that someone was moving about there, bearing down on him. He felt like he'd cast himself in some kind of arthouse thriller. Or a Bill Viola video – that one where the artist sits in a chair in a dimly lit room and is struck viciously from behind by a silhouetted figure who emerges from the shadows at random intervals.

The light flickered again, and this time gave a static crackle. Hugh jerked his head to the side again, reflexively. *Christ, it was annoying*. Maybe one of the workmen would come to fix it. But the drone of power-tools had faded. Gone, too, the guttural shouts from the floors above and below, which Hugh had found reassuring. If he could hear the workmen's shouts, he reasoned, they might hear his.

He took a deep breath, fixed his gaze on Luca, watched the lips move, synced the lips with the lilting voice. 'Classic money-laundering,' Luca said. 'Cleans up dirty money. It establishes a legitimate source for the proceeds of crime. If you're smart, you'll declare the money and pay whatever tax is due on it. Lower down the food-chain, small cash businesses are your vehicle of choice. Flower shops that sell every last tulip. Greasy spoons that can't flip enough burgers. Cleaning contractors that are buffing and polishing every other floor in south London. That's according to your books, of course. It doesn't matter if your business is idle most of the time in reality. As far as Her Majesty's Customs & Excise are concerned, you should be getting the best-in-show rosette at the small-firms association annual do, a pat on the head and a call to keep up the hard work. *You* are the bedrock of the British economy.'

Luca crossed his legs gingerly and adjusted the pristine crease in his slacks. Somehow, his effete manner jarred a little with his cool exposition of how to run a criminal enterprise.

'Now that's all well and good if you're a small-time dealer shifting five grand's worth of product a week. All cash. But we're dealing with much larger sums, and with people who want to pay by cheque or bank transfer.'

'Ideally, they'd like a fuckin' VAT receipt,' Virgo piped up.

Luca frowned. 'What Douglas is saying is that they expect us to treat them like any other supplier. We just need to figure out what it is we supply.'

He kept saying 'we'. Hugh placed one hand on his knee to quell the tremor, and the other at the side of his face to screen the faulty light-fitting from his peripheral vision.

If Luca noticed how edgy Hugh was, he didn't let on. 'The second type of money-laundering involves *hiding* from the taxman money that might even have been earned legitimately, freeing it up to use for all sorts of nefarious purposes.' The sums here seemed larger, the schemes more elaborate, involving shell companies, offshore accounts, investment trusts. Hugh's attention flickered in and out like the dodgy light, but he picked out terms like 'smurfing' – breaking larger sums up to make them less detectable – and 'layering' – carrying out multiple transfers of money, to put as many transactions as possible between the ultimate recipient and its original source.

Luca reckoned the beauty of their scheme to use a gallery as a front was that it could do both types of money-laundering: clean up some of Virgo's ill-gotten spoils and act as a corporate sluice for some of the payments London's captains of industry and finance would rather not have to explain in their end-of-year accounts.

Virgo even had a space lined up for the gallery – a four-storey Victorian building in Shoreditch that he owned through one of his shady holding companies. 'It's not exactly Cork Street,' Luca admitted, 'but it's an up-and-coming area. It's as plausible a location for a gallery as Hoxton was before the White Cube set up there.'

Hugh sighed. 'And exactly how much money are you planning to funnel through it?'

'The gallery will be perfect for payments of 10 to 300k. I've been looking at the accounts filed by some of the top galleries in London, and I reckon we could spin about ten million through the books in year one without drawing any attention to ourselves.'

Virgo did his Cheshire-cat grin. 'In one end, soiled and grubby; out the other, clean as a whistle.'

'You're forgetting that I already have a gallery,' Hugh said, looking anxiously from Virgo to Luca, 'with real artists and real clients. Granted, not enough of the latter at the moment, but I'm working on that. So I'd really prefer it if you just bought some work by the artists I already represent.'

'We don't propose to pay any money to the gallery's artists, because they won't exist,' Luca said. 'Douglas will be putting money through the business and paying himself – be it as the gallery owner or the artist. We'll just set up accounts for the fake artists in the UK and abroad – accounts that we'll control. The London art market is so diverse, so globalised, that no one will bat an eyelid. When our clients need us to redirect the money to someone else, we'll cream off our commission and use the rest to pay for whatever it is they need to pay for. Of course, we'll have to provide our clients with a piece of art to take away. That's where *you* come in.'

'I just crank out the work, then?' Hugh said, shaking his head. 'Having already conjured up a whole new group of artists out of thin air. Won't that look suspicious?'

'We've done our homework, Hugh. There are thousands of artists being shown and sold in London by hundreds of galleries. Not to mention the auction houses.' He pointed at the Lehman's catalogue on the desk. 'But even at the higher end, a lot of the work isn't particularly original. And a lot of it didn't take very long to make. The artists aren't well known outside of a very rarefied circle. Surely we can produce this kind of stuff and pass it off as real art.' He made quote-marks in the air when he said 'real'. 'Let's face it, the people we have to convince – the taxman, say, or, worst-case scenario, Criminal Intel – will be as baffled by the contemporary-art market as the rest of us. That's in the unlikely event that we ever get investigated. So the work doesn't need to be brilliant, by whatever standards it is you apply. It just needs to be plausible.'

'*Plausible*,' Hugh said, edginess giving way to frustration. 'There's that word again. What about integrity, credibility? And do you really think suspicions won't be aroused?'

Virgo drew hard on a freshly lit cigarette and tossed his lighter down on the desk. 'Do me a favour. If that artist you were talking about – Craig what's-his-face – can sell shit on a stick, we can run a gallery with fake artists and not draw too much attention to ourselves.'

Luca coughed into a delicately clenched fist. 'You have to admit, Hugh, Douglas has a point. And all-new-artists isn't necessarily a problem. What was that you said about there being more fine-art graduates in the US each year than there were people living in Florence at the time of the Renaissance?'

Hugh slouched in his seat and rubbed his eyes. The truth was, he'd become so cynical about the contemporary-art scene that he was now arguing with himself as much as with Virgo and Luca – and losing on all counts. He could also have told them that it wasn't just the US that was seeing a glut of new artists. There were three times as many fine-art graduates in the UK today than there had been in 1980. He had his own theories as to why that was. Most of these young artists were the cosseted children of the post-industrial middle classes, who saw earning a living through self-expression as a right, not a privilege. The question of whether or not they had anything worthwhile to express was an afterthought.

Or maybe all they had to express was an overweening ambition. They wanted to be famous as much, if not more, than they wanted to be artists. Seventeen-year-olds saw the celebrity and wealth of artists like Damien Hirst, Jeff Koons and Takashi Murakami and decided they would like to go to art college, maybe do a bit a drawing while they were there – although it wouldn't be compulsory. The self-analysis and self-denial of Generation X had been consigned to the past. This was Generation *X-Factor*. They saw themselves through the prism of popular culture rather than stepping outside and observing it. Somewhere along the line, the Royal Academy and *Fame Academy* had got mangled into one.

Luca was also right about the concentration of artists in London, the city where they all want to make it – the fledgling artists from British art colleges and the best of the rest from around the world. From Moscow to Madras, Shanghai to Sao Paulo, artists, dealers and collectors had converged on London, which vied only with New York as the capital of the global art market.

With so many artists clamouring for attention, subtlety was the first casualty. There was the hard-core conceptual stuff that government grants and a handful of wealthy patrons paid for, ranging from the wilfully arcane to work with a shrill shock-value that *might* get it noticed. Then there was the stuff that most collectors went for: work that was lairy and easily commodified, with a conceptual hook that owed as much to the advertising industry as to art history; work that presented itself so slickly that it slipped from your mind minutes after you'd seen it.

Hugh already knew what Luca and Virgo had just figured out. With so many artists making so much art – brash and bland in equal measure – and with oh-so-much money swilling about, a lot could go unnoticed. In spite of himself, the kernel of logic in their scheme had formed itself in Hugh's mind long before this evening. It had been growing there for years, like some kind of intellectual tumour.

'Had you heard of all of the artists in this sale?' Luca said, pointing at the Lehman's catalogue again.

'Not all of them, no. Like you just said, there's a lot of artists out there.'

'If even *you* haven't heard of some of the artists in a high-profile sale like this, who'll bat an eyelid at ten or twelve new ones?' Luca didn't wait for an answer. 'If we tried to pass them off as real and actually *sell* their work, then it could get messy – although I reckon we could get away with it. But our clients are in on it. One of them actually suggested it to us.'

'And what are your clients supposed to do with the work?'

'Don't worry. It's not as though they'll be hanging it in the board-room. Maybe in the back office. But to be honest, most of the work will probably just go straight into storage, along with the thousands of other pieces they've hoarded.'

Luca picked his briefcase up off the floor. 'Like most good plans, it's really quite simple. You organise the work and front the gallery. Douglas gets a paper-trail for some of his business. Our clients get a paper-trail for some of the less orthodox areas of their business.'

He stood up. With a slight tremor, his long, bony fingers closed one button on his tweed jacket. 'Now if you'll excuse me, I have an early flight to catch in the morning.'

That was that. Luca had laid out the plan, and Hugh was laid bare. Like the space they were in. Exposed. All the trappings gone. All the layers that covered up the bare walls and concrete were peeled away, leaving only a hollow core that could be done up, fitted out, *fitted up* to the owner's taste.

Luca made it sound so simple, so *plausible*. Achingly plausible. Not just because the contemporary-art market could be so absurd, but because of Hugh's own failure to accept the fact, and work to its diktats. Maybe that was really why his gallery was foundering.

He looked up at Luca. 'Where am I supposed to source the work?' he asked, the tone jaded.

'We'll leave that up to you.'

'We wouldn't want to compromise your artistic integrity,' Virgo said, smirking through a plume of smoke.

'I do have one suggestion,' Luca said. 'I met a Russian girl the other night who's done some work for our clients. She studied at some Academy of Fine Arts in Moscow. Let's just say it wasn't her art she came here to prostitute, but she's looking for a new challenge.'

With his head in his hands, Hugh stared blankly at the concrete floor. He noticed a rust-coloured stain around his feet, covered in a film of dust. Luca was still talking as it dawned on him that he was looking at a bloodstain.

'And maybe you've come across some talented forger?' Luca was saying. 'If they're already bent, then they won't take much persuading.'

'Yeah, sure,' Hugh said, without looking up.

The stain radiated out on either side of his chair. He followed one of its spurs out to the tip and saw a tooth, caked in dust but still recognisably a tooth – a molar with yellow roots and a white crown. It must have belonged to the last poor sod who couldn't pay up on demand. No doubt it was the first instalment on a revised payment schedule. *Amortisation*, wasn't that what bankers called it? The paying down of an outstanding sum. From the French word *mort*.

Hugh looked up, first at Virgo, who was taking a long, self-satisfied toke on his cigarette, then at Harry, a lumpen mass of bone, muscle and gristle, who even managed to look menacing while asleep. Then back at Luca.

'Looks like we're going into business together then, doesn't it?' he said.

Luca smiled. 'I was sure you'd see our point of view.'

CHAPTER 13

Don't Grow Cabbages Then, Uncle

The door opened, and the trick stepped out into the sitting room of the hotel suite, leaving it ajar. There was a raucous greeting from his Dutch workmates.

'Go on my *shun*!' one of them shouted.

Ana slipped from the bathroom and made her way over to the door. She could hear him griping to her boss.

'I said I wanted a fresh one. I think *that* one has been around the bull-ring too many times.' There were groans and laughter from the other men. 'It wasn't a girlfriend experience, man, that was a . . . a *wife* experience.'

More groans, more laughter.

Ana peeked out from behind the door. Minus the people, the room was like something from an interiors magazine: swagged curtains, gilt-wood mirrors, a ceiling rose, a smattering of chintzy occasional furniture. The scene on the two gold damask sofas, though, was like something from a different kind of magazine: two naked Dutch bankers, with 'Mindy' from Thailand doing a reverse cowgirl on one and 'Bianca' from Rio a sixty-nine on the other. Between the two sofas was a hairy Dutch rump, its owner bent over the rosewood coffee table, recharging with a line of coke. On the floor beside him, a half-empty packet of Viagra thwarted the best efforts of the girls to sate his priapic urges.

Ana closed the door and flicked the latchkey.

She walked over to a velvet-upholstered chaise longue, flanked by more swagged curtains gathered up in a gold braided cord. (The décor was a stab at late Baroque that looked, aptly enough, like a brothel in a Toulouse-Lautrec painting.) She picked up her handbag and sifted through its contents – mascara, eyeliner, lipstick, perfume, a compact, a packet of Durex – till she found her phone. She flicked it open and scrolled through the call-log, looking for the number of the creepy Australian man she'd met the other night, Luca something-or-other, the one who'd somehow got her number and called her the next day, the one her boss was so nervous around and refused to accept any money from, the one who took such a keen interest when Ana broke her cardinal rule and told him something about herself: that she'd trained as an artist. 'But that doesn't mean I *am* one,' she'd said, qualifying not just because she'd revealed something about herself but also because calling herself an artist sounded so self-aggrandising, given what she was doing – what she'd just done.

He wondered if she'd ever considered taking up art again, for a living this time. He said a position had become available in his firm. He said it would pay well. He didn't seem to care that she had no work permit. In fact, he seemed to regard that as an advantage.

'It has to be better than what you're doing now,' he said.

She saved the number and put the phone back in her bag. She took out the condoms – fruit-flavoured – and dropped them in the wastepaper basket. Then she double-checked that the bedroom door was locked and made her way back into the en suite. Letting the dressing gown slip from her shoulders, she climbed into the bath. The water felt balming, if not entirely cleansing.

'It has to be better than what you're doing now,' she mumbled to herself. 'Just not any easier.'

Only a year before, Anastasia Ivanovna Zaitseva had been a full-time student, in her second year at the Moscow Academy of Fine Arts. She'd been a mere four or five years older than the other students in her class, but they'd seemed callow to her all the same, childish even, there to have fun as much as to learn. Ana was struck by how much about being an artist they'd still had to learn. For her part, the longer she'd spent there, the more she'd realised how much she already knew.

She could draw long before she stepped through the mock-Renaissance portico of the Academy's lyceum on Krymski Street. From the age of twelve, her father saw to it that she had the same classical training any artist apprenticed to an Old Master would have had. Drawing every day, always from life, studying anatomy, making her own gesso ground with chalk whiting and rabbit glue, squaring up a preparatory drawing onto canvas. Everything short of picking up a brush, which she was forbidden from doing until her sixteenth birthday. Her father insisted that she be able to draw first. 'If you can't draw,' he would say, 'you're not an artist.'

Her apprenticeship may only have begun when she was twelve, but she couldn't ever remember *not* wanting to be an artist. One of her earliest memories was of sitting in the hallway outside the room in the apartment her father used as a studio, watching dust-motes dance in the light that seeped out underneath the door. To Ana, the door was a portal to another world, a world where colour, form and light could be manipulated, modulated, as easily as the picture on a television set could be adjusted by twisting its dials.

Mostly she sat and waited, listening to him whistle along to Shostakovich's *Gadfly*, playing on his pride and joy, the Phillips record-player he'd bought from a gap-toothed Moldovan market trader outside Kievskaya Station. Every couple of weeks, however, she and her mother would be ushered in, to admire a finished painting. Her mother would issue the standard platitudes – 'Wonderful light', 'Beautiful flesh tones', 'A museum piece, Ivan' – but Ana could barely look at the new work, so engrossed was she by the multi-coloured array of half-finished canvases and discarded palettes; by the watercolour studies pinned to the walls; by the artist's mannequin with the floral-print fabric draped over one shoulder; by the wooden box overflowing with pastel crayons, which had the same allure to Ana as a box of boiled sweets would have to another child.

She even loved the smell of oil-paint and turpentine that her mother found so overpowering. The fumes had leeched into the floorboards and plaster walls, so that the residents of the neighbouring apartments would complain endlessly. Her father dismissed them as philistines, although his sense of smell was dulled by the unfiltered *papirova* cigarettes he chain-smoked while he worked.

There was a battered oak cabinet running along one wall of the studio, with doors ajar, drawers half-open, a giant box of tricks, ransacked and plundered by its owner day in, day out. Its shelves groaned with art books; with tin cans stuffed with brushes – sable, squirrel and hoghair; with jars of pigment – flake white, chrome yellow, raw sienna, red ochre, vermilion, burnt umber, ultramarine and ivory black. All of his materials had been painstakingly assembled over many years in return for favours to senior Party officials, mostly flattering portraits of them or their families.

Her father always worked within the system. Until the Soviet Union was dissolved, he was an 'official artist', drawing a wage from the state. He was also a member of the Party-sanctioned Moscow Union of Artists, which gave him status and a like-minded social circle. He was almost fifty when Ana was born and already had a large body of 'official work' to his name, all in the socialist-realist style: paintings of workers in the field – collectivised, of course; of grandiose state-building projects; of cosmonauts and space rockets, tanks and missiles. All of them a tired glorification of the dictatorship of the proletariat that had long since grown cynical about its supposed empowerment.

His unofficial work was more understated: interiors, still lives, portraits of Ana and her mother. It was always a source of wonder to Ana that such a big, barrel-chested man could do the most intricate, delicate drawings.

The relative comfort and privilege of Ana's early years collapsed along with the economy. Her father was forced to retire on a modest pension, which was quickly consumed by inflation. Whatever work he did produce to sell became deeply unfashionable among the only Russians with the money to buy it. What he'd called the Cerberus of modern art – abstraction, expressionism, conceptualism – which had been caged for seventy years by the Ministry of Culture, overwhelmed him and artists of his ilk. The clique of New Russians, who seized control of so much of Russia's wealth under the cloak of free-market capitalism, sought out the work of more modern artists, who had variously been suppressed, even imprisoned, in Soviet times as non-conformists, or just ignored, thereby excluding them from official patronage.

The belated recognition of this group was a bitter pill for Ana's father. 'Tricksters, swindlers, homosexuals,' he called them. 'Bring back the bulldozers!' he would say, referring to the infamous exhibition in Moscow in 1974, when a group of avant-garde artists had commandeered a vacant lot and put on a show of their work, only to have it torn down by an angry mob. The KGB claimed the mob had gathered spontaneously, that the work had affronted their pure proletarian sensibilities, untainted by decadent Western ideas about *art*. The KGB, however, couldn't explain how this spontaneous 'mob' had had the collective presence of mind to bring three bulldozers and a water-cannon with them.

Ana had many arguments with her father over the merits of the work of the non-conformists. As long as an artist was sincere, she would always keep an open mind, but her father seemed to construe this open-mindedness as almost a personal betrayal of him.

The more bitter he became, the more his health declined, as though his mind was cannibalising his body. He spent his last ten years eking out a living by selling pastiche scenes of Moscow to Western tourists on Arbatskaya Square. To supplement this meagre income, he drove around the city's yawning, slush-rimmed streets in the evenings in his ramshackle old Volga, picking up fares wherever he could. The economy was in ruins for all but a few, like a derelict factory with a half-full oil-tank to be siphoned off, and some lead left to be stripped from the roof. The rest of the populace scraped a living any way they could. Almost every car without a Western marque became an unlicensed taxi once an arm was stuck out to hail it. Moscow degenerated into a city of taxi-drivers, haggling with passengers over the fare, then griping to them about a venal, corrupt government and the tiny cabal of robber barons it had enriched.

'Only in Russia do we leave the goats in charge of the cabbages,' her father would tell his captive passengers.

Ana and her mother had heard the line a hundred times.

Kolya only heard it once. 'Don't grow cabbages then, uncle', was his answer.

Ana met Kolya while she was working as a barmaid in the Baltschug Kempinsky Hotel, one of those glittering gemstones of New Russian bling that flecked Moscow like diamonds in a coal seam. The bar served a hundred varieties of vodka but the end result was always the same: drunken men leching after women half their age. Ana put up with it because the generous tips she earned there had paid for her enrolment at the academy.

Kolya sat at the bar one evening while the four thickset men in dark suits he had came in with sat at a table in the far corner, working their way methodically through the bar's vodka menu. The station where Ana collected her rounds of drink was right beside him. She knew he was watching her. He ran the ignition card to his Mercedes through his fingers like a card-sharp, his eyes trailing her around the bar.

He was handsome: tall and lean, with grey-blue eyes and jutting, angular cheekbones that had a scar running parallel on the left side, like a *pentimento* on an Old Master drawing – the rough undersketching before the artist settled on the final line.

They got chatting. He told her he traded commodities. He said deal-making beat working for a living any day. But the scar wasn't the kind of injury he'd picked up trading commodities. When she asked, he said he'd got it in a fight while doing his national service on the Chechen border. She didn't believe him at the time, and knew now he was lying.

In truth, she was more curious than infatuated – to begin with, at any rate. He was the antithesis of her father in every way. He clearly had money and the trappings that came with it. He was in tune with the New Russia. He seemed adaptable, ambitious.

'Grasping,' her father said, the first and only time they met.

Ana was midway through her second year at the academy when Kolya announced that he was moving to London. She had no other reason to stay in Moscow: she buried both her parents within six months of each other, both of them ravaged by cancer. The unfiltered cigarettes had finally choked the life out of her father; her mother seemed to follow him, not from a broken heart but more in the spirit of dutiful obedience that had marked their relationship. As for the Academy, she didn't think twice about dropping out. It was full of spoilt rich kids who made more shapes than art.

Maybe the decision was rash. However she felt about Kolya, she knew the relationship couldn't last. He was remote, always walking a fine line between mysterious and shifty; the only intimacy they shared was sexual – pleasurable and all as it was. But she liked the idea of living in a different country, so she said she would come with him. He just shrugged and said, 'If you like.'

She thought she could set herself up in a studio, maybe find a gallery in London to exhibit her work. At least that was the plan. It was just that she had never painted anything she felt was good enough to show.

She could draw – that much she knew. (Her life-drawing tutor at the academy had told her after six months that he had nothing left to teach her.) But what use was the means of expression if she had nothing to express? Or nothing of interest, at any rate. The successful young artists she'd seen in London didn't just rely on technique; many had dispensed with it altogether. They delved into art history, psychology, anthropology, literature, physics, economics, with a conviction that what they were doing was worthwhile.

Ana had spent enough time around artists to know that she lacked something – not ability so much as the core of egocentricity that most of the artists she knew had; that kernel of self-belief buried deep within them that meant they could spend months, years even, making a body of work, unwavering in their conviction that people would want to look at it when they were done. It was the one thing they had in common, more so even than talent. It wasn't that they were all *egotistical* – most of them were perfectly nice people. But they still had the artist's ego, usually locked up in a cage at home, even in the face of others who carried theirs around on their shoulders, spitting and snarling at the world.

So Ana never actually showed her work to anyone, even Kolya. Not that he had any real interest in it. She saw less and less of him. All she really knew about what he did was that he worked for a man named Vladimir Nemirovsky.

Their relationship, as far as they had one, ended six months after the move to London. He came home late one evening with a tattoo of an eagle emblazoned on his chest, and stars tattooed on his knees, which apparently meant he would never again kneel before anyone. He told her he was a *vor*.

'Kolya,' she said, 'don't tell me you're mixed up with those psychotic Boy Scouts.'

'Don't call me "Kolya" any more,' he said impassively. 'Call me "Nikolai".'

Then he told her he couldn't have a girlfriend any more. 'It would be bad for me,' he said, *'and for you.'*

It seemed that Nemirovsky was the London boss, or overlord, or whatever the nomenclature was of the *vor v zakonye* – 'thieves-in-law' – part criminal gang, part cult of amorality. It dated back as far as the vast archipelago of gulags created under Peter the Great and revived on an even greater scale by Stalin. A hard core of inmates organised themselves into the *vor* and developed a strict code of behaviour, like never paying taxes or working in a legitimate job, and never serving in the army or co-operating with the police or the state – unless it was to dupe them. They were forbidden from having a wife or even a girlfriend: any attachment that could compromise their commitment to organised criminality.

'I'm in London illegally,' Ana said. 'What I am I supposed to do?' Looking back, she must have seemed so pathetic to him. So weak. He told her she could keep the apartment, that he would pay the rent. He also gave her an envelope full of money, but Ana left it in the letterbox of the apartment when she moved out later that night.

She did keep the card he gave her, though, of a woman who might be able to get her a *job*. She thought now that it was his way of making a clean break.

This woman, Melanie, told Ana that a girl like her could make three thousand pounds a week with the right agency. Melanie was expensively dressed – in a Dolce et Gabana suit and Manola Blahnik heels – but she still had a slightly ragged, used look, like she'd spent twenty years turning tricks before moving into management.

Three thousand a week was a lot of money. Ana thought that if she could last six months, maybe even a year, she could save enough to open her own business back home, even buy an apartment. She wouldn't be a victim. Nobody was forcing her to do it, other than herself.

But she couldn't force herself any more. She couldn't numb herself with temazepam, rohypnol or ketamine. She couldn't chase the dragon like Nawinda (professional name 'Mindy'). The agency had put them in an apartment together, and she'd seen the works in her room, smelled the sweet, vinegary odour of the smack.

That was her way of coping, not Ana's.

She would call Luca Ambrosini in the morning.

Part 2

'But the Devil whoops, as he whooped of old:
"It's clever, but is it Art?"'
Rudyard Kipling, *The Conundrum of the Workshops*

CHAPTER 14

The Monkey and the Organ-Grinder

The Bentley coasted up to the pavement outside Liverpool Street Station, prompting a Jeremy Clarkson-style *nice* from two pinstriped suits nearby, toking their mid-morning cigarettes. Hugh felt like asking them if they wanted to get in instead.

He discarded the dregs of his coffee and stepped up to the kerbside. Riding shotgun in the front passenger seat, Harry rolled down the window. 'Don't just fuckin' stand there,' he said, with a stout thumb directing Hugh towards the back of the car.

Hugh's hand lingered on the burnished chrome door handle. He'd mulled his options over. His first thought was to get out of London, but with no money and no prospects, he wouldn't get very far. He'd also have had Virgo's hounds on his scent, and they'd have done more than politely ask for their boss's money back when they found him. No, this wasn't a fight-or-flight dilemma. Go along with the scheme for now, he'd reasoned, and he might survive to fight another day.

In the meantime, he was resigned to fronting a gallery for Virgo. When Hugh closed down his space in St James's – after Luca wound up his old company for him – the London art world hardly went into a tailspin. Everyone knew that his gallery was foundering, that his artists weren't on the money. Galleries come and go. Some find a voice, and an audience to go with it. Some find their own distinctive pitch among the artistic sirens blaring out around them, but the Lead White's plaintive bleat was not drawing enough collectors into its embrace. Frankly, few gave a shit when it closed down. And Virgo reckoned even fewer would notice what Hugh did next.

He opened the door and slumped into the red-hide seat next to Virgo, who folded away his *FT*. His mouth curdled into a sardonic grin. 'Ready to go to work then, are we?'

'Champing at the bit, Douglas.'

'*Champing at the bit*,' Virgo said, the grin holding fast. 'He's a card, ain't he?'

'A proper fuckin' comedian,' Harry said, leering over his shoulder. 'Does he tap-dance as well?'

'Only if I tell him to.'

Harry turned his leer on Hugh. 'Looks like the organ-grinder's got a new monkey then, don't it?'

Hugh managed a thin smile. Just about.

As Pavel pulled the car out into the slow-moving traffic, Hugh watched the two pinstriped suits mash their cigarettes into the pavement with their black Chelsea boots and march back towards the twenty-storey glass tower next to the station. Driving past them down Bishopsgate, more new office blocks were spreading along the street, away from the City, like folds of fat on an obese man billowing along a couch. Liverpool Street once marked the outer reaches of the City, but it had lately been swallowed up, as the financial district engulfed it and moved beyond towards Spitalfields, Shoreditch and Whitechapel.

After half a mile, they hit Shoreditch High Street, and took a sharp left down a side-street. Its proximity to the City had transformed Shoreditch from a wasteland of abandoned light-industrial spaces – colonised by artists and students – into what estate agents would now call 'an upscale bohemian enclave', even if it was only bohemians with a trust fund who could afford to move into the area.

Shoreditch had yet to be fully purged of its older denizens, though. It remained a curious hybrid of tattoo parlours and chi-chi boutiques, of greasy spoons and Parisian-style bistros. They drove by the Bricklayer's Arms, which sat opposite a swanky jeweller's *atelier*. A few doors down, a gastro-pub offered a special of sea bass with a herb crust. Across the street, a white-eyed tramp with matted hair and a crust of filth and sun-chapped skin, peered out from above a wheelie-bin, as a stream of his piss trickled out below.

They passed under a vaulted railway bridge; the brick wall on one side was painted red, with the word 'SCARY' blocked-in in black and white letters. As street art went, it was poor, but it ran close enough to the bone to add to Hugh's grinding unease.

Pavel pulled the car in a hundred yards further on. The building looked a little dour from the pavement. Stone-faced to the first floor, there were three big sash windows facing onto the street, with smoked glass, and a bricked arch to one side. Anyone with an interest in vernacular London architecture might have looked up at the ornamental pilasters, the corbels and the stone parapet that divided the ground floor from the two floors above, both of which were clad in London stock brick and capped by a decorative frieze, but Prince Charles didn't gander around Shoreditch very often.

The entrance to the gallery was through the arch, in a courtyard at the back. There was one sheepish little fascia sign: 'LW2' etched into a stainless-steel plate with a glass pane floating over it. The gallery wasn't set up for passing trade.

At a stretch, the courtyard had a grungy chic, but inside, the building was sleek and modern; the previous tenants were a firm of architects who'd spent a fortune refitting it before outgrowing the space (on the back of two commissions to design venues for the Olympics). A reception hall ran the width of the building, with open double doors halfway along leading to the gallery space. The gallery covered the rest of the ground floor. The supporting walls were replaced with five exposed steel girders running across the twenty-foot-high ceiling. The walls were sheer white; the floor was polished concrete. It looked the part.

Virgo had so many buildings, he couldn't think what to do with them. Some were no more than sinkholes for the vast sums he was earning. Finding a use for them was at best an afterthought, sometimes just a tiresome distraction from raking in the cash to buy more. But even Hugh had to admit that this one made for a decent art gallery. The space was perfect: the kind of sterile white box artists fixated on. The location may have been leftfield – down a side street, in an area that was up-and-coming but still hadn't quite arrived for the indecently rich clients high-end galleries courted. That said, the location was no more implausible than the White Cube setting up shop in Hoxton Square. Maybe Virgo *had* thought this through.

There were four Polish painters (of the decorating variety) in the gallery: two cleaning up; two adding some finishing touches. There were also two surly electricians, fitting a ring of boxed-off fluorescent lighting around the ceiling.

While Harry and Pavel loitered in reception, Virgo paced up and down the gallery, talking on his phone, his eyes flitting about, watching the workmen. He put them on edge, strutting like a prize cockerel, all flicks and juts and icy glares. Finally, he held the phone to his chest and told them to '*Fack* off out of it' before returning to his call. 'It won't be you who gets his collar felt if things go tits up,' he barked into the phone, 'so I'll need to see more of an upside. Kapisch?' He hung up, looked at Hugh and said: 'Cunt.'

'Sorry?'

'No, not you. Different cunt. One of your new clients.' He scraped his black brogue over a dried splash of paint on the floor and rolled his eyes before fixing them back on Hugh. 'This little venture could work out very nicely – for both of us. Just do as you're told, keep your head down, and we'll keep you out of the boneyard. For now, at any rate. We might even see about writing off some of that money you owe me.'

Hugh said or did nothing to signal gratitude; Virgo likewise to signal he expected any. 'You get hold of that forger you was talking 'bout?' he asked instead.

'Yeah, I managed to track him down.'

'On the jungle telegraph now then, are we? We'll make a villain of you yet.'

'I got hold of him on Facebook, as it happens.'

'Fuckin' 'ell. Why not just put an ad in the paper?'

'He's not the kind of guy who's in the phonebook, or who reads the paper for that matter. I only met him the once. Knew his name, that he lived in London, had a rough idea of his age. That narrowed it down to six guys named Jack Hastings. And don't worry: the one we wanted was the cagiest of the lot.'

'But we'll still have to brief him on the importance of keeping his mouth shut,' Virgo said. He put an arm around Hugh, ushering him out of the gallery and sweeping his free hand in front of them. 'You're both in my circle of trust now,' he said. 'That has its advantages. Step outside of it, though, and I'll happily use your innards for a heavy impasto work on the walls of this place.'

Pop psychology *and* painting technique in the same breath: Hugh was reminded yet again what a credit Virgo was to Britain's prison libraries.

Hugh followed Virgo up the stairs. Harry trailed behind. The first and second floors were empty, save for a few pieces of abandoned office furniture. The stairwell narrowed as they climbed towards the top floor of the building: a converted loft, with skylights and exposed oak joists. Virgo had earmarked it for a studio. It was, to be fair, the kind of workspace most artists would sell their mothers for, or at the very least the *Portrait of My Mother* they'd given her for Christmas.

There was a slender woman standing with her back to them. She was looking through the window at the gable-front of the building, across the rooftops, back towards the City.

She turned when she heard them coming, and clutched at a leather portfolio resting against the wall beside her. Even silhouetted against the window, her steely-blue eyes had a luminescence, a pale fire that looked like it might scorch anyone she fixed her gaze on. She pushed a lock of hazel hair behind her ear and straightened her back. Her body language said *I'm here for the interview.*

'This is . . . ' Virgo paused and turned to her. 'What's your name again?'

'Ana,' she said. 'Anastasia.'

'Well, Ana, Luca tells me you're an artist who took a career break to blow off rich bankers. Had enough of turning tricks, have we?'

She hesitated, but held Virgo's gaze. She seemed taken aback, either by his east London argot or his abrupt manner. 'It was not good job for me,' she said at last.

'Well, let's hope this one works out a little better.' His eyes ran up and down her, before he turned back to Hugh. 'Her English isn't much cop, is it? Just tell her to keep schtum. If she breaths a fuckin' word to anyone, it'll be you who gets it in the neck. Tellin' you, mate, Tipperary'll never have seemed so far away.'

When Virgo made for the stairs, Harry stepped into the space vacated by his boss. He leaned into Hugh – eyes deadpan, skin like blood-flecked sandpaper – and burst into a chorus of *It's a Long Way to Tipperary* in a passable tenor voice. His breath was bilious, with high notes of last night's lager. He had the face and physique of a grotesquely tumescent Harry Secombe.

Hugh held his gaze, straightened his back, faced him down the way he would an opposing lock in a line-out on the rugby field. Harry gave a malignant smile. 'That'a boy,' he said. 'Keep it up, and I'll have my turn yet.'

When Virgo and Harry had left, Hugh turned to Ana, who was opening her portfolio on the long trestle table in the centre of the room. She must have seen Harry's performance, but didn't let on.

'I'm Hugh,' he said, extending his hand. He felt old, although at thirty-seven he couldn't have been more than ten years her senior.

She shook hands warily. Hugh noted the film of faded freckles floating over pale skin and the grey shadows beneath her eyes. He was careful not to allow his hand to linger too long in hers. 'So you're an artist,' he said, doing his best to sound businesslike.

'I study at Moscow Academy of Fine Arts, but not graduate. My father was artist. He teach me as well.'

'Have you exhibited much?'

'No, I do other things. I make mistakes.' She held Hugh's gaze so that he looked away first. 'Is allowed?'

'Oh, it's allowed,' he said, smiling. 'It's practically compulsory around here.'

Her expression softened. 'You don't look like English *mafiya*.'

'First of all, I'm Irish,' Hugh said, feigning indignation. 'I'm not a gangster, either – at least not by choice. I'm an art dealer. There is a distinction – although some artists would beg to differ.'

Ana's eyes took on a quizzical squint. 'You owe this man Virgo money?'

'And then some,' Hugh said, trying to sound casual, but not quite succeeding. 'That was my mistake. And what about you? How did you end up working as a . . . ?' His voice trailed off.

'Is OK, you can say it: a prostitute. Is best not say "call girl", "escort" or "courtesan", like agencies say. They want women to think is glamorous. Men to think is not sleaze.'

'How long did you do it for?'

'Three months. Is long enough for me. Anyhow, I was very bad prostitute.'

Involuntarily, Hugh arched an eyebrow.

Ana frowned. 'Not *bad* like in sad male fantasies, just not very good. I was not friendly to johns. Not looking in their eyes. Not kissing them.' She puckered her lips as she said it, seeming to sense that Hugh was more embarrassed than she was.

He clasped his hands, then rubbed them together, his gaze shifting uneasily to the open portfolio. 'So, Ana, you've brought some of your work with you?'

'I'm bringing some drawings only. Pencil, charcoal. I'm throwing away all my paintings.'

'Right,' Hugh said, a sceptical note creeping in.

On top was a pencil drawing of a man, about the same age as Ana, handsome but with a scar running down his left cheek. The scepticism was quickly dispelled. Hugh could see straight away not just how talented she was but also that she had trained. There was an academic rigour to the drawing, almost like that of an Old Master, that he hadn't seen in an artist her age in a long time. The work was beautiful, however unfashionable it might have been.

Underneath, was another drawing of the same man. This one showing his naked, muscled torso as well. 'A friend of yours?' Hugh asked.

'Not any more,' Ana said – without meeting his eye this time.

He leafed through more of the drawings, some charcoal, some pencil – each as good as the last. 'These are wonderful,' he said. 'You're very gifted. Clearly a much better artist than you were a . . . .' He winced as his voice trailed off again.

Ana rolled her eyes. 'A prostitute. I said is OK, you can say it. Just don't *keep* saying it. Anyhow, now you want that I prostitute my art. What does that make you? Some kind of art *peemp*?' There was a mischievous glint in her eye, like she already had the measure of him.

Hugh gave an apologetic shrug. 'I'm afraid I crossed that bridge a long time ago.'

CHAPTER 15

The Fox and the Glove-Puppet

Hugh hadn't even been sure if Jack would show up, but there he was, in the CCTV monitor, glancing first at the camera, then over his shoulder, as if he was being followed. He wore navy jeans and a skinny yellow T-shirt, with da Vinci's *Vitruvian Man* printed on the front. His hands rested on a leather satchel slung across his chest. He was striving for poised, but only managed shifty.

Hugh buzzed him in and sat, arms crossed, on the desk in reception. He had to suppress a smile as Jack sidled warily towards him, eyes pinballing around the entrance lobby to the gallery.

Hugh extended a hand. 'Good to see you again.'

Jack fixed a sideways squint on the hand but didn't offer his in return.

Hugh clucked, and slipped the hand in his pocket instead. 'Sorry if I put the frighteners on you.'

After a terse exchange on Facebook, Jack had only agreed to meet when Hugh asked if Felix Lazaar was keeping him busy – the insinuation being that he knew all about Jack's *interpretations* of other artists' work. Lazaar had often asked Hugh to hawk Jack's forgeries to the Lead White's clients. At the time, Hugh wasn't in the business of selling fakes, and brushed Lazaar off.

'I've been getting jittery anyway,' Jack said. 'So where is he?'

'Who?'

'Lazaar. Have you heard from him?'

'Decamped to Tangiers, the last I heard. A favoured haunt of reprobate Englishmen. Hope he doesn't owe you any money.'

116

'He paid me for the last couple of commissions – a Howard Hodgkin and a Frank Auerbach – but that was two months ago.' He paused, mumbling to himself as much as Hugh: 'The Auerbach was a tricky one. Impastos are a bitch to dry out.' Then he met Hugh's eye again. 'In fairness to Felix, he always pays me. Keeping his golden goose in corn, he calls it. I'm not sure he ever pays anyone else, though.'

'From what I can see, he generally has a posse of angry creditors on his trail.' Spend an hour in Lazaar's company, and if he wasn't declining calls on his mobile, he was fobbing off the muffled fulminations of the creditors whose calls he did accept.

Jack inched forwards and glanced into the gallery. 'He's not involved in this place, is he?'

'Are you mad? What's being planned for here makes your arrangement with Felix look like a cottage industry. Once I've told you the details, though, you're involved, whether you like it or not. It will pay well, but speak out of turn and . . .' Hugh held back. Now it was him who looked shifty. 'Speak out of turn, and things could get very unpleasant – for both of us.' Threats didn't trip easily off his tongue – other people's threats, especially – but Jack seemed no more ruffled by the warning than he had been to begin with.

'Will I go on?' Hugh asked.

Jack gave an impassive, if-you-must shrug. It was only when Hugh began explaining the scheme that Jack's eyes brightened, and his grin widened. It felt like coaxing a fox out its den with a rabbit glove-puppet – a crude one at that – but it seemed to be working. 'I know you're versatile,' he said. 'Felix reckoned you could turn your hand to any style, any school of painting. But you'll have to work quickly here as well. You won't have time to labour over any pieces. We might have to pass off slapdash as "an expressive brushstroke". That said, I have plenty of ideas for shortcuts we can take without compromising too much on the finished work.'

Jack was still grinning, caginess giving way to a skittish excitement. 'Christ, Felix would love this all the same. It's like taking those fake Hermes handbags out of the flea-market and onto the high street.'

Hugh allowed himself a smile before turning serious again. 'But we won't be telling Felix about it, will we? Him or anyone else.'

CHAPTER 16

Maybach? Bacharach? Auerbach!

Vladimir Nemirovsky sipped on a thirty-year-old Lagavulin, wrinkled his nose and putted, spraying spittle and whiskey down the side of his tumbler. Scotch still tasted like fermented goat-piss, no matter how much the bottle had set him back. Give him a shot of cheap vodka any day, even the nasty bootleg grog he used to run back in the old country – nasty enough to give you jaundice for a hangover.

He sat behind the desk in his 'study' – not his word, what the property locator who'd found the house for him had called it. Draped across his lap was the *FT*'s 'How to Spend It' magazine. He'd been poring over a special feature on Islay single malts – brow furrowed, lips grappling with words on the page – when there was a knock on the open door. He looked up to see Kolya standing in the doorwell, with a painting propped against each leg. They were two of Vlad's latest acquisitions from Felix Lazaar. One was a Howard what's-his-face: a blue swirl and a yellow swirl on a piece of old timber. The other was a Frank . . . This one he knew . . . A Frank . . . Maybach . . . or was it Bacharach? It was a portrait, anyhow, of a man, some kind of mangled, fucked-up man, like a Chechen war vet who'd taken a shrapnel wound to the face and had then gone ten rounds with the Klitschko brothers.

Kolya flipped the paintings around, resting one against each knee. 'These were still in the boot of the Merc. Where do you want them?'

'Somewhere they'll be seen. Just not in here. And Kolya?' (He wanted to be called Nikolai, but Vlad preferred the diminutive. Kept him in his box.)

'Yes, boss?'

'Take it easy. They don't look like much, but I had to shift five keys to pay for them.'

Kolya said nothing. He just held up his hands reassuringly, then manoeuvred himself between the paintings and eased them out the door, making a show of being careful. Kolya was a smart kid; he could do the maths. Five keys meant Vlad had paid a hundred grand for the pair. Lazaar said they would retail for five hundred but that he had a client who needed to move them on discreetly. Vlad didn't ask why someone would sell them for so little. Messy divorce, bankruptcy, shit for brains, whatever. Not his problem.

His only problem was what to do with all the money he was making, because business was good. He was shipping more product into the UK by the week. Sourcing the submarine for the Colombians was a stroke of genius. It was a decommissioned Soviet sub, a diesel-propelled Piranha class. The crazy dago bastards wanted a nuclear one but Vlad just laughed at them. The last thing he needed was the Calí cartel tapping him up for fuel rods as well as cash. That said, the arms broker was keen. He said it was like selling a computer printer and then making twice as much again on the consumables. 'That's ink cartridges,' he added, by way of explanation, like Vlad was some kind of cretinous shitwad with a keen interest in office supplies.

They met in a suite at the Connaught, the broker pitching his wares through a plume of Cohiba smoke that snagged in Vlad's chest till the coughing and wheezing began. Everyone looked away promptly – except the broker, who only averted his eyes when one of Vlad's bodyguards intervened. The broker's eyes then made a doleful arc as the fifty-dollar cigar was snatched from his mouth and tossed through the open window out into the Mayfair traffic.

'No, thanking you,' Vlad said, catching his breath. 'The Piranha will do just fine. As for terms, how about I pay you half of price you ask and agree not to stare into your weasel eyes while I sawing your *focking* head off?'

It turned out to be a good day's business. He hadn't sawn the broker's head off – not yet, at least. If there's one thing you learn about in prison, it's delayed gratification. But he did buy the Piranha. With a crew of six, it could make two crossings a month, carrying half a container-load of product from French Guyana to the southwest coast of Ireland. The hull had a titanium shell that made it almost undetectable to sonar. Anyhow, the coastguard and Customs weren't even looking for subs. They were looking for cargo vessels or searching random containers, hoping they'd get lucky. The odds were better in the rigged lotteries Vlad ran for the shit-kicking *sovoks* back home.

The Piranha was servicing the mass market, but Vlad was also cultivating the higher end, not just because the margins were juicier, but also because it kept the FSB off his back. They might have rebranded the KGB, but the FSB was still as rotten, ruthless and inept as its Soviet forebear. His handler there was keen that Vlad muscle in on high-end vice and drug-dealing. Russia's spooks finally woke up to the trick they missed in not having any *kompromat* on Dominique Strauss-Kahn when he was boss of the IMF, and a potential president of France. The FSB thought it could have managed his colourful private life more efficiently.

Vlad was making decent progress on fixing the oversight. He already had the chairman of a City bank and a Tory grandee on a lead. Literally, in the latter case – attached to a black leather studded collar, mewling like a whipped pup.

Vlad gave a shudder as the scene flashed before his mind's eye. Honestly, you play back these high-definition videos on a sixty-inch plasma screen, and it's hard to get the images out of your head, no matter how many horrible things you've seen, and Vlad had seen quite a few – been responsible for even more.

These rich, powerful studs are as greedy as they are weak, as horny as they are dumb. Think about it. You're the kind of man who can set up a cocaine-fuelled orgy for a Cabinet minister, the chairman of the IMF, a US property mogul with political ambitions or the boss of one of the biggest banks in London, and they think you can be trusted? Arrogant fools. Can't see beyond their pharmacologically enhanced cocks.

Now the pre-*glasnost* communists, the old guard – not Gorbachev and his turd-fondling lackeys – they knew how to have a good time *and* keep control. They'd live like kings but would send you to a *gulag* if you broke wind without filling in a form first. That's how you run a country. Methodical tyranny, fronted by a cadre of stone-faced bureaucrats.

Nobody could be bothered taking on the system. Resignation trumped dissent every time.

The capitalist *nomenklatura,* on the other hand, are just as venal and grasping as the Soviet elite ever were, but they leave themselves open to coercion. They have to maintain a front of social responsibility, of moral integrity, of obeying the laws that apply to the lumpen proles. Maintaining that front means placing their trust in the people around them – and that trust can be abused. Which is why the FSB is so keen for Vlad to muscle in on the action. 'Drawing strength from the weakness of others,' is how his handler put it.

But to expand this part of his business, to *grow* it, as they say in the *FT*, Vlad would have to dispose of the local competition, and one man in particular: Douglas Virgo. He was a lackey to the rich and powerful, he did their bidding, cleaned up their messes, never fucked them over.

Virgo was *in* the system. Think of this way: some smart-ass Yankee journalist described Goldman Sachs as 'a giant vampire squid wrapped around the face of humanity'. The same could be said of most of the banks and corporations in this town. But Virgo, he was like a parasitic worm in the vampire squid. That seemed to Vlad like a very snug place to be.

It was just a matter of time before they faced each other down. They'd had skirmishes – 'handbags', Virgo would call it – but no bloodletting. That would come. Vlad had the means; he just needed an excuse.

The means came from a credit line Vlad had with one of his ex-pat compatriots, one of the New Russians who'd colonised London's more exclusive boroughs. Vlad had made himself useful, provided security, eliminated rivals and nuisance journos: clean, professional hits, not like those clowns who took out Alexander Litvinenko with the polonium 210. The Marx Brothers could've made a better fist of that job.

Vlad had never felt comfortable with the non-criminal classes, but he did feel a certain kinship with the New Russians. They were a different breed to the local swells. They'd retained something of the Soviet elite they seamlessly replaced – that callous disregard for what the plebs thought of them. They swapped the high-walled *dachas* on the outskirts of Moscow for security-gated enclaves in Kensington, the Zil limousines with black-tinted glass for Beamers and Mercs with black-tinted glass.

Otherwise, it was *bizness* as usual: fortunes grabbed, opponents crushed or just ignored. And they didn't even need to send the *refusniks* to the *gulag* any more. They just left them behind in Russia and moved to London or the Côte d'Azur.

This affinity Vlad felt meant it wasn't all business with the New Russians. He was making inroads socially as well: the director's box at Chelsea, openings at the White Cube, the private dining room at Sketch. True, he got rebuffed now and then. That business on the first tee at Wentworth was a setback. He'd forgotten to clean his pitching wedge after he'd last used it. It was just some dried blood. And an earlobe. But these fucking golf commissars – strutting around in plaid strides and white, tasselled shoes, looking like the two-bit Georgian pimps he used to run back in Moscow – they get antsy if you don't replace a divot. The club captain made some snide comment about 'his ilk' and 'the greasy pole'. Vlad lost it, said he was a Russian, not a Polack. Told him to go fuck himself, repeatedly, with his golf umbrella.

Not his finest moment.

He squirmed as he took another slug from his tumbler.

He hadn't played golf since, but there are other ways to gain respect: the whiskeys the fine dining, the swanky address, the flash motors, the yacht, and above all – for reasons he can't quite grasp – a big, fuck-off collection of modern art.

Which is why he'd been dealing with Felix Lazaar. He needed some art with cachet but he didn't like galleries, asking him what line of business he was in, looking down their noses at him. Skinny bitches, clopping around in four-inch Jimmy Choos, yawning while he spoke to them. 'I'm afraid that one's reserved. . . . Oh no, we couldn't possibly sell you that, there's a waiting list for that artist.'

A waiting list? A queue? To get screwed?

The queues back in Soviet times drove him to crime, but at least the prices were controlled, even if you still couldn't get what you needed. He'd queued for five hours once for a tin of *kholodets* – jellied pork – before he realised there was a quicker way to get what he needed.

Vlad reckoned it was the same with art: you go around the system, not through it. Fuck the galleries, and the auction houses. They just look at the car you roll up in and make up the price on the spot. Or else they decide whether or not you're one of the capitalist *nomenklatura*. Why would he pay their bullshit prices for a service like that?

Lazaar respected his privacy; sold him what he needed, at a reasonable price; would even take cash. As for the art, well, it was what it was. He would never understand it, but how could so many people be wrong?

Vlad just played along; Lazaar didn't tell him what to buy, like he was some kind of peasant *mudak*, or even try to explain the work to him. He just gave Vlad some books on modern art, told him to pick out a few names. Vlad never got around to reading them, but he checked out the pictures. He didn't want to seem like a total clod, so he chose work that looked like it could've been painted with a mop, and told Lazaar to get some for him. The funny thing was, Lazaar even complimented him on what a good eye he had. The man would crawl up Vlad's ass for a rusty kopek.

He gave a little snort, drained his tumbler and grimaced, just as his phone burst into a chorus of *Please Release Me, Let Me Go.* (The ringtone was an ex-con's note-to-self not to get caught again.) He answered to the yacht dealer who'd been hard-selling him a ninety-footer.

'I told you, I not want a fucking dinghy,' Vlad was saying as Kolya strode back into the study, his hand held out in front of him, with something small and black pinched between thumb and index finger, eyes fixed on it. Kolya's other hand was by his side holding the portrait by Frank . . . kraut name, definitely kraut. Amer . . . Auer . . . *Auerbach*, that was it!

Kolya put the painting down on a button-back leather armchair and leaned over the desk. 'How old is that painting you asked me to hang, boss?'

Vlad put a hand over the receiver – 'I'm on the phone here, man' – then sighed, said, 'Forty years or so. Why?'

'Look, the paint is still wet.'

'It couldn't be.'

'I just moved it like you told me, and look.' He held a knob of black paint – dry at the tip, but soft at the base – under the anglepoise desk-lamp. The still-tacky paint glistened in the light. 'This came off when I brushed against it.'

Vlad hung up, threw his magazine down on the desk and squinted at the treacly underside of the paint. By the time he looked up at Kolya, his eyes were bulging and he could feel his face flushing with blood. 'Are you saying that bastard kike sold me a fake?'

Kolya backed away, shrugging, like he knew there was no right answer to the question.

Vlad felt a tightening in his chest, then a burning sensation, like a cloud of hornets swarming in his lungs, up his windpipe and out through his mouth. He began to wheeze and splutter, suppressing a cough.

He gestured to Kolya to leave, then summoned him back. 'Wait,' he said, gasping. 'Find Lazaar and whoever painted . . . the Elephant Man's ugly cousin here, and . . . . ' – more coughing, spluttering – 'bring them to me.'

As he spoke, he pulled open a desk drawer, rifled through it, picked up a loaded Smith & Wesson mag by mistake, tossed it on the floor, then grabbed his inhaler. Wrapping his lips around the mouthpiece and drawing hard on it, he saw Kolya, in the hallway, glancing over his shoulder. Their eyes met for an instant before Kolya looked away sharply, wincing and ducking out of sight.

Within seconds, the inhaler worked its magic, its tranquillising effect aided by thoughts of revenge. The forger meant nothing to him: two bullets in the forehead would take care of it. But Lazaar would get the special treatment. When he found him, he'd cover his hymie balls in liver pâté (back in the day, he'd used *kholodets,* but that was hard to source in London). Then he'd put them in a cage – still attached to Lazaar – with a half-starved mink. From his previous observations, he'd learned that the mink regarded the foreskin as something of a delicacy. That pleasure would sadly have to be foregone on this occasion.

Another minor disappointment.

A business rival told him once that life was a process of managing disappointment. They were pretty much his last words. Fond memories. (Thoughts of past acts of revenge also had a tranquillising effect.)

Feeling calmer already, he poured himself another slug of whiskey. As he sipped on it, physical and mental balance almost restored, he had a minor epiphany. It occurred to him that Ventolin actually improved a heavily-peated Scotch.

CHAPTER 17

Figure Painting

Hugh set a box down on the trestle table in the loft-cum-studio. The table buckled slightly under the weight. The box was full of contemporary art catalogues from the main auction houses: Sotheby's, Frith's, Christie's, Phillips de Pury.

'These are just for starters,' he said, glancing from Jack to Ana. She edged towards the table, craning to see what was in the box. She was tentative – like someone on her first day of a proper job. Hugh already felt bad about her being dragged into Virgo's latest wheeze, even though she said she was there by choice.

The introduction was brief. Ana was friendly but watchful; Jack was just watchful. He sat by the window in a battered old school desk that had somehow found its way into the loft. An image of the younger Jack flashed into Hugh's mind: a caustic nerd winning over his classmates with deft but nasty caricatures of his teachers.

Hugh pulled out an inch-thick catalogue. 'This is a supposedly cheaper afternoon sale. It grossed forty million quid. The evening sales take in two to four hundred mill. There are lots of very good artists in here but there are also lots of mediocre, journeymen – and women – artists selling for five- and six-figure sums, artists few people will have heard of. They're not quite the marquee names you've been so . . . *inspired* by, Jack, but it's a part of the market that's grown in line with the number of very rich people who buy their work – the reviled 1 percent that had the Occupy protesters tearing out their dreadlocks.

'You especially, Jack, know how easy it is to copy some of these artists, but that's not all we have in mind. We'll be manufacturing the artists as well as the art. For starters, we could produce variations on themes or motifs that other artists have used, to synthesise them into plausible works of art. There's a rake of young abstract painters who've been burning up the sale rooms in the past few years — artists three or four years out of college selling for half a million quid. It's not their bad painters — although some critics have labelled the work 'Zombie Formalism', even 'Crapstraction' — it's just that their prices have been hiked to insane levels for work that's fairly generic. So the work we make doesn't need to be original. It just needs to look like something a corporate collector *might* hang in their offices.'

Hugh glanced from Jack to Ana. Neither spoke, so he carried on.

'I've written biogs and CVs for twelve artists so far. We'll have two Chinese artists: one emerging young talent and one sadly deceased painter that we've just rediscovered and whose estate we'll represent. There's a Serbian, a Peruvian, an Indian and a Welsh artist in there as well. We'll also be rediscovering an East German artist — a contemporary of Georg Baselitz, Gerhard Richter and Sigmar Polke. Good pedigree. He'll have taken a blowtorch to his oil paintings to the point where they began to bubble, char, even burn away altogether. We'll be reworking a job-lot of abstract paintings I bought for six hundred quid at a small auction house in Dorset.'

Jack was nodding, rubbing his hands; Ana was more reticent. She'd pulled another catalogue from the box and was leafing through it. As her eyes flitted from Hugh to the catalogue, her brow furrowed. Whether in confusion or consternation, Hugh couldn't be sure.

'We can also mix it up with some forgeries,' he said, still watching Ana as he pulled out a Christie's evening sale catalogue. 'There are a few prime candidates whose work we should be able to start churning out straight away. Lucio Fontana springs to mind — canvases painted one colour and slashed a few times with a blade. Medium-sized pieces make more than half a million quid.

'The Japanese artist On Kawara's day paintings — just that day's date painted on a plain background — are also ripe for a decent pirating. Kawara has painted over two thousand of them and they've made 300k at auction, so spinning a dozen more through the gallery at, say, eighty grand a pop doesn't seem so outrageous. They're all documented in a catalogue raisonné, but given that there are so many of them, I reckon the risk is minimal to zero. Most of the work that leaves here will be going into corporate collections – and more than likely straight into storage. No one will ever see it again. Well, maybe just the charred remains when it gets torched – less artfully this time – in an insurance scam.'

Jack smirked; Ana's features had settled on perplexed.

'Only joking,' Hugh said. 'Although nothing would surprise me.'

Ana looked warily from Jack to Hugh, then held her hand up like she was asking for permission to speak. Hugh signalled that the floor was hers.

'Sorry if I not understand,' she said, 'but maybe someone will see that work is not real?'

Hugh nodded. 'That was my first thought as well, but the banks and companies buying the work will be handling everything in-house. The work won't be vetted by any experts and, the fact is, for every supposed expert who rates a piece of contemporary art, there's another out there who dismisses it.'

'But they still think work is real. That artist is sincere.'

'Sorry?' Jack cut in, cupping a hand to his ear as though he'd misheard.

Ana looked sheepish. 'Sincere? Is right word? That artist is telling truth.'

Jack bridled, pointing at the box of catalogues. 'Some of these artists are sincere but deluded; some are just outright charlatans. Most punters can't tell the difference, and the ones that can don't give a toss either way. They're just speculators. Or social climbers.'

Ana shifted her gaze to Hugh. 'And what do you think?'

He puffed his cheeks out, his hand slipping like a garden prong into a tangle of hair. 'I think it's time we got to work.'

Ana pressed him, a smile teasing the corners of her mouth. 'You think like your *mafiya* boss now?'

That made him bristle. 'It might sound glib, but I think truth in art, like beauty, is in the eye of the beholder. It's like looking in a mirror. Everyone who looks in it sees something different. And even how people see themselves in a mirror isn't always clear-cut: from dysmorphics to narcissists, what people see depends on what they bring to it. It's the same for a work of art. Sometimes, what you see depends on what your level of understanding: like the difference between a Joycean scholar reading *Ulysses* and someone new to the work reading it without a glossary. For others, it depends on their relationship to the piece: for dealers and auction specialists, on whether or not they're trying to sell it; for the artists, on what they want to see; for collectors, on what they're *told* to see.'

Jack cleared his throat. 'Christ, it's like being back in art college.'

Hugh gave a wry smile. 'Where was that, the Royal College of Forgers?'

'I did my Masters there,' Jack said, absently, eyes still fixed on Ana, before turning back to Hugh. 'Are you sure Heidi here is cut out for this gig? I mean, for Christ's sake, *sincere?*'

'You're a forger, aren't you? Isn't imitation the *sincerest* form of flattery?'

'Very funny,' Jack said waspishly. 'Hilarious, in fact. Is this the level of workplace banter I'll be subjected to?'

Ana looked at Hugh, eyebrows at a quizzical cant. The expression said *what's his problem?* 'Maybe I not right for this job,' she said, sighing. 'My work is, how you say, in old-fashion?'

'Look,' Hugh said, 'this isn't an art-school crit. Let's leave art philosophy out of it and keep it practical instead. I thought you could start with some figurative work, anyhow. Here are some catalogues, with work by Jean-Michel Basquiat. I also brought along a monograph on him. He's an interesting artist – some would say a unique talent – a figure painter who never worried about likeness; who often made several paintings a day. The work has a naive, almost childlike quality, but still sells for vast sums. The drawings go for tens or hundreds of thousands. The paintings have made $15 million. He might be a good starting point for you. See if you can paint as loosely as him. Work in some motifs of your own. Change the palette.'

'It can be your first *sellout* show,' Jack said, smiling thinly.

Ana took the catalogues, ignoring Jack and muttering something in Russian. 'Figure painting?' she said after a lull. 'Is that a portrait, or do you mean a money figure? *Five figure, six figure, seven figure?*' She hunched her shoulders, sounding tentative again. 'Maybe you mix up money and art too much. When did it become just business for you?'

Hugh gazed blankly through the gable window, before turning to her with a shrug. 'Maybe it was when I racked up my first million quid in debt.'

CHAPTER 18

Closed Circuit

Jack placed his hands face-down on the desk. The cuticles and nails were encrusted with paint: vermilion and cobalt blue. There was a fine tracery of greys and blacks inlaid on the creases in the skin. The outside edge of the index finger on his right hand, where he gripped his brush, was paint-chapped and beginning to crack. It stung when he made a fist.

His gaze shifted to the CCTV monitor on the desk, showing him sitting alone in the reception area of the gallery at a walnut-veneer, Art Nouveau desk that jarred a little with the austere surroundings. Opposite him, the gallery entrance emitted a cold white light and faint echoey buzz, like a fridge with the door left ajar.

The monitor blinked. The image jumped to the pavement outside on Rivington Street. Table staff from one of Shoreditch's trendy eateries idled by on a cigarette break, while a pert-buttocked gym-bunny scurried around them on her way back to the office after a lunchtime workout. The gallery façade was drably anonymous and drew little interest from them or any other passersby.

Another blink, and the screen cut to the exhibition space. There were twenty paintings on the walls, all of them monochrome save for a few murky shapes. They were as unashamedly stark as the gallery itself. The exhibition was Hugh's idea, the execution Jack's. He'd taken a blowtorch to the abstract paintings Hugh bought in Dorset and felt, at the very least, that he'd improved on them. It had been trickier than it looked: he'd had to retouch where the paint came away altogether and put a layer of matt varnish on the heavily charred bits, to add some lustre. That said, he'd still managed to pull the show together in three days.

They mulled over some titles – *Trace, Remnant, After Image* – something that would look good stencilled on the wall in reception. In the end, they went with *Vestige*. It was written in italics, waist-high on the wall opposite the desk where he sat.

Jack was no front-of-shop man but Hugh had asked him to keep an eye on the gallery for the afternoon when he was summoned away at short notice by that Herman Munster lookalike Harry and his brooding sidekick Pavel. Harry was the one who'd threatened to put Jack's right hand in a vice if he stepped out of line. There was little doubting the intent behind the warning, but Jack was less scared than he ought to have been. It might have been some kind of twisted psychological displacement, but he was too busy checking out Pavel: a short, taut flick-knife of a man, but very cute, in a rough-trade kind of way. Jack had since had impure thoughts about Pavel – involving a forcible entry at gunpoint. He did of course realise it would be prudent to keep these thoughts to himself. Pavel looked like he'd maim any man whose gaze lingered on him a shade too long. Jack still checked him out again, though, as Pavel held the door open for Hugh and Harry before following them out into the street.

When they'd left, Jack threw his feet up on the desk and meshed his fingers behind his head. He was glad of the break from the studio; he'd made more work in the past two weeks than he had in the previous two years. His rate of output had more in common with the building's original purpose as a light-industrial space than a studio or a gallery. As well as the show on view, he'd also made work for eight of the artists the gallery would be *representing,* to illustrate on its website.

He'd added the finishing flourishes to a series of passable Canaletto copies that Hugh had commissioned and shipped over from China. Jack replaced the two patron saints of Venice on the granite columns at the waterfront of the Piazzetta di San Marco with Mario and Luigi of Nintendo fame, and had brightened up a Grand Canal scene with a McDonald's, a KFC and a Domino's Pizza sign. The shimmering reflection of the latter in the water was an especially nice passage of painting.

Just that morning, he'd finished off a large abstract work on a six-foot-square sheet of marine ply: uniformly blue, in thick gloss paint, overlaid with an irregular octagonal shape formed from yellow string and panel pins. When the paint had dried, he put the sheet flat on the studio floor, built a timber mould around it and poured over a centimeter-thick layer of transparent resin. It hadn't set yet but already looked the part. Hugh was impressed, said he could even picture it in the lobby of a Goldman Sachs office. He wrote a blurb about it for the website, saying 'the poised sparseness of the work invites meditation, even reverie, and that its evasion of definitive meaning is a rebuke of scientific determinism'.

That impressed Jack. Vintage bullshit.

When Hugh first pitched the idea to him of working here, Jack went into a reverie of his own. It wasn't just the perfect job-spec – he would be the artist in residence of the criminal underworld, the Artful Dodger of the London gallery scene – but Hugh was also offering a retainer of five grand a month, plus the occasional cash bonus. This at a time when Jack was hardly overwhelmed with career options, other than knocking out pastiche still-lives for the Julian Campion Gallery in Hampstead and then getting stiffed for the cash when they sold. Or lounging about in the ragged, paint-flecked armchair in his studio wondering when Felix Lazaar would pick up the phone with another commission.

As for going out on his own as a forger, Jack didn't have the mettle for a solo career in deception, the effrontery to eyeball a mark while he conned him. He needed a dealer, a gallerist, a fence, a grifter – whatever it is you call someone who sells forgeries – or most contemporary art, as far as he could see.

Hugh fitted the bill perfectly. He was charming, knowledgeable and good-looking, although he never acted like he knew it. He also had an aptitude for generating throwaway ideas, any one of which some artists would eke an entire career from.

Hugh was even making work himself; he'd been out and about with a large-format digital camera. The images weren't bad, although modern cameras made it look easy. He'd taken pictures of derelict buildings and graveyards: he'd made a whole series of prints of Highgate Cemetery at various times of day. He photographed Karl Marx's grave, along with the one facing it – apparently that of philosopher and biologist Herbert Spencer. *Marx & Spencer*, he'd called the photograph.

He'd also commissioned a taxidermist to make some work, paid him a flat fee and made him sign a waiver over any creative rights to the work, the same way Jeff Koons's studio assistants, who actually make his work, cannot claim authorship of it. There was one of a fox cavorting paw-in-paw with a hare, of a cat reading to a mouse nestling in its belly, and of a lamb snarling with the teeth of jackal.

As for Ana, well, if Jack was the Artful Dodger of the London gallery scene, she was the Oliver Twist. She was too naïve: her instinct was to give every artist the benefit of the doubt, no matter how artless or vacuous their work was. Nor was she pulling her weight in the studio. She'd made some abstract paintings, under careful direction, but had yet to make a start on the expressive figurative work Hugh had asked her to try, aping the primitive style of Jean-Michel Basquiat.

Jack had left her up in the studio, idling.

At least Jack had earned an afternoon doing likewise. He pulled out his phone, logged out of Grindr, logged into Facebook. He sighed, skimming through the usual guff. He'd been asked to like an artist's page, one of his old classmates at art college and current flavour of the month, Craig Charlton, who was showing at Alexandra Friedman's gallery – that art-world shaman, uber-luvvie, designer-black witch.

And as for Craig *Charlatan* – Jack could feel the bile rising, a vein throbbing in his temple – he was to be equally despised. Even at art college, he'd had that galling combination of a meagre talent spread thinly over a colossal ego. For his degree show he'd mounted a pig's head on a stake and encircled it with five screens playing looped footage from rolling news channels. He got a First for it.

Now he was gilding and mounting turds.

Plop art.

Jack gave a snort of derision just as the buzzer went. He declined the request to like Charlton's page. Then he looked at the CCTV monitor, at the view of the main entrance to the gallery, and did a double-take. The buzzer sounded again. He sat bolt upright, eyes still fixed on the monitor.

'Holy fuck,' he said.

CHAPTER 19

Cicatrise

Ana stood over the pile of books: a monograph on Jean-Michel Basquiat and some auction catalogues with PostIt notes marking the illustrations of his work. Before going downstairs, Jack had told her to stop 'procrastinating' and get on with making some work of her own. She'd guessed the word's meaning but still pulled out her phone to look it up. No doubt Jack would tell her to look up 'irony' as well while she was at it.

Steeling herself, she put down the phone and picked up the monograph. She'd read it the day Hugh gave it to her and knew Basquiat's story well: a graffiti artist plucked from obscurity in his early twenties by a New York dealer. His brief career was as iridescent as his work, his star burning too brightly, before exploding like a supernova. He was dead from a heroin overdose by the age of twenty-seven, the same age Ana was. It seemed the money and the fame meant nothing to him.

Flicking through the illustrations, the work was like that of a gifted child, with a startling lack of convention in line or colour, uninhibited by any attempt at the anatomical correctness drummed into Ana by her father. There was a rawness to the work: the paint came from a spray-can; the crayon was applied so roughly that the paper puckered either side of the line.

She put the book down and picked up a Sotheby's sale catalogue. She found a Basquiat illustration: *Orange Sports Figure*. It was a roughly drawn, almost cartoonish face, in oil crayons and spray-paint. Jack would call it crude, then scoff at the estimate of $2 to 3 million.

Ana liked the work, although its appeal dimmed the more she read of the catalogue note. The writer said the work was 'an unmitigated masterpiece of unrivalled pictorial invention'. She looked blankly at the work, sighed, then thumbed on to another Basquiat in the same sale: a simple line drawing of a slingshot stuck down on a white-painted board. It was naive, almost like a cave painting. The catalogue note said the work was 'emblematic of a significatory realignment within the vernacular of contemporary painting'.

She needed the dictionary on her phone to decipher that one. When she did, even she could see that the writer did the work no favours by overselling it so much.

She looked again at the drawing. It couldn't have taken long to make – a matter of seconds, so simple was its execution. That's what Jack would tell her, at any rate, as though that was all she needed to know. But Ana could never judge a piece of art solely on how long it had taken to make. Every artwork is, or should be, the culmination of a lifetime's experience. All of the emotion and knowledge distilled into it made it more than the sum of the time it took to make and the materials used: a drawing more than a series of lines on paper; a painting more than an arrangement of pigment on canvas or board; an installation more than an assemblage of random objects.

Reducing an artwork to its constituent parts was as anathema to her as the mentality of the men who came to her as a prostitute, betraying the same coldness, as though a part of their brain was turned off.

By his logic, Jack was just a sack of carbon and water.

Quite a lot of acid as well.

She closed the catalogue and put it back on the table. She picked up a sheet of Arches paper and pinned it to an easel with two bulldog clips. Then she began a pencil drawing of her father's face from memory. It took her ten minutes to get a decent likeness. She switched to a cobalt-blue Conté crayon, scribbling furiously, following the contours of the face, with spaces left for the eyes, nose and mouth. She added shading in red ochre, then accelerated to almost a scouring motion, using patches of colour to give definition to a new head. Slowly, her father's face receded and a new face emerged through the colour-mottled, shape-shifting death-throes of the drawing underneath.

She stopped after half an hour as a bead of sweat dropped from her brow onto the drawing. She squeezed some black paint onto a palette, picked up a stubby, hog-hair brush and scrawled terms from the *Gray's Anatomy* textbook onto the drawing. The book was first published for medical students but had also become a reference work for high-minded academic artists. Her father had made her copy its illustrations as a child.

The chin in the drawing had regressed into a haze of yellows and pinks: she traced a line from where it should be to the edge of the paper and wrote 'mandible', did the same from the bridge of the nose and wrote 'inferior nasal concha', the same from the eyebrow and scribbled 'supraorbital foramen'.

She set the drawing aside and began another of her father, this time in profile, mouth open, ready for a visceral scream of colour. She continued in the same vein with drawings of her mother and then of Kolya, to the point where the scar on his left cheek was the subject of the drawing and his face merely the backdrop it was set against. She scrawled 'cicatrise' and 'scarface' across the top.

She carried on until, by early evening, work lay scattered around the studio, on the desks, draped over an easel, on the floor – scuffed, dog-eared, stood-on. She gathered it up, untroubled, as the pastel scuffed even more and edges of the paper tore. She rolled it up and bundled it into a green recycling bag in the corner of the studio.

She felt drained but calm. She'd often wondered how art therapy worked. Now she knew.

CHAPTER 20

All Hail the Anti-Hirst

Jack clocked who it was straight off. Anyone with an interest in contemporary art would have – financial or aesthetic. Robert Orca was rarely photographed but when he was, the same jaded green eyes would settle on the camera, challenging the viewer to a staring contest, Orca safe in the knowledge that he'd gone a thousand bouts undefeated. The eyes nestled over sallow jowls and under a tussock of backcombed white hair. A corpulent torso sloped away below, clad in a loose-fitting charcoal suit and a grey grandfather shirt buttoned up the neck.

'Holy fuck,' Jack repeated, his voice echoing around the empty lobby. 'What's *he* doing here?'

He picked up his phone, put it down, then picked it up again. He ran his fingers through his hair, biting on his lower lip. The buzzer sounded for a third time. Jack turned to the intercom on the wall. 'I didn't sign up for this,' he muttered, before pressing down on the button lit up with a key symbol.

After the static rattle came the clunk of the door opening. There was a dramatic pause before Orca emerged into the lobby at a pace that could best be described as stately. His eyes scrolled regally about him before settling on the paint-flecked hands on the desk – which Jack promptly withdrew into a ball on his lap. When their eyes finally met, Jack couldn't be sure if Orca was smiling or stifling a yawn.

Jack opened his mouth to speak but Orca quelled him with a raised palm, then pointed towards the entrance to the gallery. 'In here?' he asked.

The voice was deeper than Jack expected, but then he'd never heard him speak before; Orca didn't do interviews.

'Yes,' Jack said, 'it's an exhibition by . . .' His voice trailed off as Orca turned and walked into the gallery.

Still visible from behind the desk, Orca stopped in front of the first painting, on the right-hand wall as he entered the gallery. He seemed to be sighing at first until Jack realised it was a regular breathing pattern. In fact, there was a touch of Darth Vader to the husky exhalation that didn't seem to be matched by a corresponding intake of air.

Orca leaned in to examine the painting. He'd perched a pair of glasses on the end of his nose, attached to a cord looped over his neck – as much a prop as an optical aid. Then he pulled back and glowered over the glasses at the work. He moved on to the next, and repeated the routine.

Jack's chest tightened; Robert Orca was looking at *his* work, the most influential contemporary-art collector in London (the world?), a man whose imprimatur could make an artist's career. Except it wasn't really Jack's work, it was a scam, a cynical proxy, counterfeit art.

Did the glower mean he knew?

Leaning over the desk, Jack followed Orca's stern sergeant-major routine – inspecting a guard of honour but not impressed by what he saw – until only a paunch was visible, then nothing at all.

Thoroughly unnerved, Jack picked up his phone and called Hugh, but the call rang out, unanswered. He opened the browser on the phone and searched for 'Robert Orca' – a pathetic attempt at exerting control over the situation that was swiftly quashed by the eighty thousand hits it generated. He clicked on Orca's Wikipedia page, fretful eyes flitting between the screen and the entrance to the gallery.

*

Hugh let his phone ring out, knowing better than to interrupt Virgo when he was in full flight. 'We have to crank up production,' he was saying. 'They're queuing round the fuckin' block.'

They sat in the same office building at King George V Dock where Virgo and Luca had first briefed him on the new direction his career would be taking. The workmen had gone but Luca was there again, the building now as dapper as he was.

'I knew this gallery was a runner,' Virgo said, 'but fuck me, I'd no idea just how much of a runner it was. I mean, where to start? The phone's been hopping.' He rolled forward in his chair, elbows resting on the desk. 'I've just got off the blower to an Azeri oil magnate looking for British citizenship for himself and some business associates. He's got a bit of form but we should be able to tidy up his CV. His chums, though, make the Sopranos look like the Nolan Sisters. It's gonna take some serious palm-grease to get British passports for them.'

Luca turned to Hugh. 'Luckily enough, we've persuaded a Home Office minister to dispose of some of his collection through the gallery. The paperwork's all sorted,' he added, turning back to Virgo. 'The cash is coming in through a shell company in the Channel Islands.'

'Or the Funnel Islands, as I like to call them,' Virgo said, rubbing his hands. 'Routine enough, but get this one. Last night, I had the head honcho of a blue-chip multinational crying on my shoulder. He's French – no surprises there. Apparently, there's a video and some photos out there of a transsexual hooker dressed as Little Bo Peep pleasuring him with his, her – whatever – shepherd's crook.'

Hugh couldn't help himself. 'With an *actual* crook?' he asked.

'No,' Virgo deadpanned, 'it was a pre-op Bo Peep. What kind of sick bastards do you think we're dealing with?' He shook his head, sighing. 'Anyhow, this chief-exec chap – let's call him Pepé le Pew, for discretion's sake – cashed in ten million quid in share options last year, so he can well afford to burn through a couple of hundred grand on some hooky modern art. Pepé's taken out a super-injunction, but a courtesy call from Harry and the crew will make anyone think twice about breaking it. Belt and braces, as they say.'

Virgo turned to Luca. 'Which reminds me, we're also sitting on that film of a knight of the realm hyper-asphyxiating with a belt around his neck and a triple-jointed Balinese ladyboy straddling his midriff.' He paused, striking a philosophical pose. 'The Brits like to poke fun at saucy foreigners but if depravity was an Olympic sport we'd be right up there on the medals table.'

Luca paid no heed to his boss's musings. 'The wheels are in motion, Douglas. It's mostly Old Masters in his lordship's collection, but I reckon he'll make space for some contemporary pieces as well.'

'Doctor's orders,' Virgo said. 'But all of that's just for starters. Then we get on to the corporate stuff. That's real meat and drink, ain't it, Luca?'

The accountant pulled out a sheaf of documents, crossed his legs, adjusted the pleat in his tan slacks. 'How long have we got? Top of the pile here is the Lupus hedge fund. They threw a party last week for some of their most valued clients on a yacht off St Tropez.'

'It was like Sodom and Gomorrah on the high seas,' Virgo chimed in, 'a floating fleshpot.'

'We did the event management,' Luca added, 'and there's a two hundred and fifty grand bill they need to run through the books.'

'We're talking a whole exhibition's worth just there,' Virgo said. 'But the list goes on and on.'

'Yeah,' Luca said, 'timing is everything in business, and we couldn't have opened at a more opportune moment.'

It was only as Luca elaborated that Hugh really began to grasp what he'd been dragged into. The gallery wasn't just a front for Virgo's provision of debauched corporate entertainment or a trough full of swill for corrupt politicians and government officials. It was also a septic tank.

No, scratch that. It was a full-on sewage farm.

The financial and corporate elite were being rounded on from all sides. There was the fallout from the financial crash and the consequent frenzy of politicians and regulators to be bought off. There were the 'shareholder springs' and the banking scandals, one after another – rigging interest rates, mis-selling products to clients, setting up Byzantine schemes to circumvent sanctions against Iran or launder money for Mexican drug cartels – all of them making it harder for executives to pay themselves what they felt they were worth. It was so much easier to defend the corporate art budget – call it an investment, or supporting the nation's cultural patrimony (in a tax-efficient way). Play the philistine card if things got really hairy.

Virgo and Luca had it all sussed out.

Hugh's jaw was grinding, his head bowed again, not resigned now so much as pissed off. The idea of helping the super-rich keep their snouts in the trough began to grate in a way it hadn't before.

When he looked up, Virgo's tack-sharp eyes were fixed on him. This wasn't the time or place for a display of conscience, and Hugh did his best to look inscrutable, even though it was an expression he'd never quite mastered, especially under Virgo's knowing glare.

*

Jack's eyes flitted between his phone and the security monitor, showing Orca scowling at the work in the gallery. The collector looked like a farmer tutting at the price being quoted on some mangy low-backed steer.

Jack was racked with self-doubt. What was he thinking? What was he doing here? Come to think of it, what was Orca doing here?

It must have been the ads, Jack concluded, the ones Hugh put in *Art Review* and *Modern Painters* to announce the opening of a new space. He said they'd help create a veneer of legitimacy, in the unlikely event anyone ever got suspicious. But Hugh hadn't banked on Orca showing up. If anyone smelled a rat, surely it would be him.

When the monitor tripped to the street outside, Jack looked at his phone again, at the Wikipedia page that read like a PR puff piece. Robert Orca had made his first fortune producing and directing period English costume dramas: lots of sumptuous outfits, weather-related fevers, love-lorn gazing out of picture-windows, bounders and cads pitted against redoubtable but emotionally constipated bricks. The films were famously described by one critic as David Lean and Laura Ashley's lovechild. The British liked them but the Americans and Japanese *loved* them.

In Britain, Orca was almost as well known as the director of party-political broadcasts that had helped seal four election victories for the Conservative Party from 1979 onwards. You'd think shilling for the Tories would alienate the mostly left-leaning art world, but his influence over it would grow to such an extent that his political endeav-ours were shamelessly ignored.

Orca became disillusioned with the British film industry when Joe Public began to ignore his films too. In the early nineties, he'd turned to crime-caper movies that floundered; he was soon overshadowed by edg-ier filmmakers like Danny Boyle and Guy Ritchie. About the same time, Orca cannily decided that Britain's young contemporary artists were far more interesting – and lucrative.

The Wikipedia entry plied the conventional narrative that – before Orca and the YBAs came along – the British art scene had been mired in a torpid world of ageing Royal Academicians selling staid work to braying, sherry-soaked toffs. Being in the collection of Prince Charles was the height of acceptance. Aside from Francis Bacon raging away on the fringes, the British art scene had barely had a pulse since the sixties, when David Hockney swaggered out of the Royal College of Art in his gold lamé jacket.

It was Orca who held a pillow over the face of this dying scene. A mercy killing – or so the narrative went.

He'd begun by buying up work from graduate shows, sometimes a student artist's entire output (before leaking the news to the press to hike up the value of the work). He'd also bought job-lots of work from the early self-staged shows of the future doyens of the YBA scene – even putting some on a monthly stipend, giving him first refusal on any work they made.

But it was the *In your face* exhibition of a group of his protégés, staged at the Royal Academy in 1997, that really jump-started the new age. The show is rarely cited without the word 'seminal' appearing alongside it. That always sounded liked a *double entendre* to Jack. No matter: the show changed the landscape of the British art scene forever.

Everybody talked about it. Telling a taxi-driver to 'take me to that art exhibition' would get you there without fail. It drew more visitors than any other in Britain that year. The papers called it shock art. It made critic and caterwaul of the old order, Brian Sewell, feel nauseous; the artists' dealers giddy with newfound wealth and influence.

Orca went on to apply the same formula to artists from the US, China and India. In the financial parlance of the collectors who followed in his wake, he became a market-maker: he created a demand where before there had been none. He consolidated his stature by opening the Orca Gallery and publishing a six-volume catalogue of his collection. He was described variously as a visionary, a speculator, a modern-day Medici and an art-world Svengali.

'A Svengali,' Jack muttered to himself, just as Orca emerged from the gallery. 'Don't look into his eyes,' he added, doing his spooky voice.

'I beg your pardon,' Orca said, making his way over to the desk, still exuding a haughty, seen-it-all-before air. (And in fairness, he probably had.)

'Oh gosh, nothing,' Jack said, smiling weakly, slipping his phone into his pocket, 'just gibbering to myself. You don't have to be mad to work here . . .' He cringed, his voice faltering. 'But it certainly helps.'

'Is that so?' Orca said, dryly. He nodded towards the gallery. 'Not an artist I've heard of, this one.'

'Really? That must be because we've just, sort of, rediscovered him. There's a biog on the wall if you're interested.'

'I look at the work, not the CV. I'm not one of these collectors who goes to the wall-text first. I trust my gut. It's served me well in the past.'

Jack nodded, thinking his gut had been well served by him too, as Orca hitched up his jacket and tugged on his belt buckle.

'Mind you,' Orca added, 'this latest crop of collectors don't *even* read the wall-text. They pay somebody else to do it. No doubt you know who I mean?'

'Em . . . yeah, I think so.'

'You must know, these techie squillionaires and the Hamptonite hedge-fundy types, or the Russian oligarchs and Arab *oiligarchs* who pump dollars out of the ground, or those Chinese widget-barons who own factories the size of Greater Manchester. Not to mention all of their assorted hangers-on – barnacles on the hulls of their super-yachts – the bankers, lawyers, accountants that run this city. They're rampant. It's Art Basel first, then on to Venice to hijack the Biennale, then to London for Fresco and the autumn art sales, before Christmas in the beach-house on St Barts. Believe me, there's never been a more vulgar time to collect art.'

'I couldn't agree more,' Jack said, warming to the man.

'The notion of connoisseurship is as alien to them as cleaning their own toilets. They buy what their chums are buying or what their art advisers tell them to – whatever's deemed sophisticated, *de rigueur.* They don't think for themselves. They move in a great school, like tuna fish, all identical. When word gets out that an artist or a gallery is hot, it's just a matter of time before they gather.'

'You're so right,' Jack said, stoking Orca's indignation.

'I am, am I not? What matters is that they be *seen* buying, branded artists to adorn their many houses, floating or otherwise.' Orca sighed, picking up a price-list from the desk. 'Bah, sometimes I wonder if I should've taken up stamp collecting instead.'

Jack gave a consolatory nod.

'But you know what really baffles me?' Orca asked, striking a more reflective tone.

'What's that?'

'Why anyone would hire one of these snake-oil art consultants to build a *portfolio* collection for them?'

'It's beyond me,' Jack said.

'Pay someone to clean your house or walk your dog, if you must, but why on earth would you forego the pleasure of buying your own art? I wouldn't pay someone to eat on my behalf in a Michelin-starred restaurant or to drive me around in my Ferrari, if I owned one – which I don't.'

He gestured to an imaginary crowd of art buyers. 'These people and their art-adviser lackeys are spineless, they only buy the branded artists – and I ought to know, I've created a few in my time. None of them support young, unknown artists, or unrecognised ones. Like this chap.'

He held up the price-list, gazing impassively at it.

There was an excruciating pause. 'Interesting work, this,' he said at last. 'The artist is like the . . . anti-Hirst. It's not slick or commercial but there's a real emotional depth there.'

'I think so much of it is in the execution,' Jack said, fishing for affirmation.

Orca rounded on him, fixed him with gimlet-green eyes. 'You're so right. I'd go as far as to say he's a technical virtuoso, but there's a rare sensibility there too.'

He looked at the list again, skimming over the column of prices. He pursed, then made a clucking noise, his tongue nestling in his cheek. Jack looked at his own hands, still hidden beneath the desk, and began scratching away at the crusted paint on his nails.

Eventually, Orca put the list down in front of Jack and slapped his hand down on top of it. The eyes locked onto Jack's again, and lingered there. The mouth opened but no words came out, until finally he said, 'I'll take them.'

'They're not,' Jack stammered. 'Well . . . which ones?'

'All of them.'

Jack opened his mouth to speak but the words were stillborn.

Orca dropped a card on the desk. 'Call my secretary, she'll sort out the details. You'll give me a discount, of course. I usually get a minimum of 15 percent, but in this case I think 25 would be fair.'

He turned and made for the exit. Jack's jaw hung, twitching, like a man on a noose. He did manage an 'Eh' but Orca was gone, the door clicking shut in his wake.

Jack's breathing became shallow, his hands trembled. *Fuckety fuck fuck fuck. What just happened there?*

He picked up Orca's card; he would call the collector's office now, say there'd been a mix-up, the work was already sold.

But his resolve quickly crumbled. He heard himself mutter 'a rare sensibility', then, louder still, 'a technical virtuoso'. Maybe he should sleep on it, he decided, discuss it with Hugh in the morning.

He leaned back in his chair, swung his legs up on the desk. 'A technical virtuoso,' he said again, sounding almost chipper now. He pulled out his phone and had to quell the urge to log onto Facebook, announce to the world that Robert Orca had just bought out an entire exhibition of his work.

Post a picture of the dog in *Las Meninas* by Velázquez.

Declare that *he* was its bollocks.

CHAPTER 21

Tearing the Envelope

As Ana made her way up the stairs into the loft, her nostrils were scoured by the familiar fumes of the fixative spray that artists use to put a seal over the delicate pigment in a pastel drawing. Her first thought was that Jack must have his crayons out, even though it was only 9PM and he rarely surfaced before midday.

It was only as her head crested the top of the stairwell that she saw her previous day's exertions pinned to the eaves opposite her. (She was loathe to call it *work*; in her mind, it was more the byproduct of an artistic purgative.) Hugh stood a few paces back, arms folded across his chest, with one hand clutching a spray-can and the other reaching up to his chin, as though engaged in an act of connoisseurship.

He turned when he heard a creak on the stairs and attempted one of his disarming smiles. But it was already a code-red transgression for Ana.

She blazed across the room and tore a disfigured drawing of Kolya off the wall – the one with 'cicatrise' and 'scarface' scrawled across the top. The paper gave way at the corners, where it had been held in place by thumbtacks. She did the same with the drawing of her mother next to it, this time tearing it in half as well.

When she turned towards a picture of her father, Hugh stepped in front of her, cracking his head off the eaves as he did so. Even Ana winced.

'Ouch,' he said, rubbing the side of his head. 'Calm down, will you?'

'It serve you right,' she said. 'And don't tell *me* to calm down. Was never good idea for anyone.'

'I can see that,' Hugh said, half grimacing, half smiling, feeling for a cut above his ear.

Ana tutted, frustrated at being upstaged by Hugh's injury. 'Show me,' she said, reaching for his head. Even with his neck crooked, she had to raise herself slightly on her toes. She lifted his hand out of the way and ran her fingers through his hair, looking for a cut. 'You will live,' she said.

When he turned his head towards her, there was a guarded glimmer in his hazel eyes. 'Are you always so quick-tempered?'

'That was not a temper,' she said, her mood abating. 'That was just a little bit annoyed. In a temper, I would have gone for you, not the pictures.'

'Thanks for the heads-up,' he said wryly. 'So what has you annoyed in that case?'

'I put these drawings in garbage bag.'

'I know, I saw one jutting out. Thankfully, you didn't put a match to them instead.'

'Don't worry, I will next time. I not want show them to people.'

'Why not? They're *very* good. Too good for this place.'

'Because they are like the work of a child or – how you say? – an amateur.'

'Believe me, Ana, no amateur could draw like this.'

She threw her hands in the air. 'You cannot sell these, or give them away, or whatever it is you do with our work. Who would want them?'

Hugh was still rubbing his head. 'That's the thing. There's no shortage of takers out there. I got the lowdown yesterday on just how many there are. Some *banker*' – he said it like it was an expletive – 'could get a fat bonus out of these, although he'd be unlikely to appreciate them.'

Ana sighed. 'Maybe I should go back to my old job. At least it was clear who was getting screwed and who was doing screwing.'

'That's not even funny,' Hugh said, touchingly appalled at the idea. 'Look, don't put them through the gallery if you don't want to, but please don't destroy them. Put them away and look at them in a couple of weeks, when you have a bit of distance on them. There really is something in them. The drawing is so strong; the colours are bold and expressive. There's an ironic bite too in the anatomy-book references. I think they're really . . . promising.'

'Promising?' she said, with mock indignation. 'Minute ago you say they are very good.'

Hugh smiled. 'You know what I mean.'

His attempts to mollify her were interrupted by footsteps on the stairs. They turned to see Jack mounting the final flight into the loft at what, for him, was an ungodly hour. He was trailed by a bicycle courier.

'Morning,' Jack said. 'This chap has an envelope for you.'

Jack looked askance at the drawings still hanging from the eaves, then ushered the courier around him, glancing at his Lycra-clad bottom as he did so. 'Could I have a word?' Jack asked, as Hugh was signing for the delivery.

'Sure, in a second,' he said, turning back to Ana. 'When I say promising, I mean there's a powerful, distinctive artist finding her voice in the drawings. You should have more faith in yourself.'

'These are yours, are they?' Jack asked, looking at the work, eyebrows arched.

Ana nodded.

'Gosh, you've certainly loosened up. Hugh didn't slip you a rufie, did he?'

Ana had no idea what Jack meant, and looked to see Hugh's reaction, but he was staring, mouth agape, at whatever he'd pulled out of the envelope.

He looked first at Ana, then with a slight shake of the head turned to Jack. 'There's a cheque here,' he said, 'from Robert Orca.'

'That's what I meant to chat to you about,' Jack said.

'For two hundred and forty thousand pounds.'

'You see, he really liked my . . . eh, *the* . . . he really liked *the* work in the gallery. He reckons it's the work of a technical virtuoso.'

'Two hundred and forty thousand pounds,' Hugh repeated.

Jack hunched his shoulders, his voice faltering. 'With a rare sensibility.'

Hugh just scowled, leaving Jack to dissemble. 'It was just a misunderstanding, really. One minute he was ranting about how crass the art market had become, the next he was buying out the whole show.'

Then he rallied, pointing an accusatory finger at Hugh. 'I did try to phone you.'

'Did you?' Hugh asked, pulling out his phone, checking the call log. 'One missed call,' he said, 'from a blocked number.'

'That'd be me,' Jack said sheepishly. 'I can't be too careful about who has my number.'

Hugh rolled his eyes. 'This isn't good,' he said, making for the stairs. 'I'll be in the gallery. I have to make some calls.' He paused on the top step. 'And don't shred any work while I'm gone.'

When he was out of earshot, Jack shook his head. 'Honestly, you'd think he'd be pleased.' Then he pasted a smile on his face and looked at Ana's drawings. 'These are certainly – what's the word I'm looking for? – *different*.'

CHAPTER 22

Pure Bunce

Hugh stood on the gallery floor with the cheque and a compliments slip from Orca in one hand and his phone in the other. He still had a dull throb at the side of his head, where he'd hit it off the eaves in the loft. As he gazed at the largest piece in the show, the throbbing intensified.

There was a flash of orange and yellow at the centre of the work, surrounded by charred paint and patches of blackened canvas, all of it unified by several coats of glaze and varnish. He knew when he first saw the paintings that Jack had pulled it off, but somehow the work seemed even more *plausible* now than before.

He looked at the blurb – that he'd written – on the wall next to the painting. He winced and gave a low moan. 'The work charts the five-hundred-year evolution of Western easel painting,' he'd waxed. 'The deft contrast of light and dark is an homage to the *chiaroscuro* of an old master, while the scorched surface also marks a new beginning – the birth of modernism, perhaps? – for in the wake of destruction, comes innovation.' Surely Orca couldn't have been taken in by that.

Maybe it was the political subtext to the work? 'The viewer is also reminded how the artist's oeuvre was forged in the creative cauldron of East Germany in the 1970s, its latent violence redolent of the smouldering discontent that would eventually ignite on that fateful night in 1989 when protesters clambered onto the Berlin Wall and began to tear down Europe's most visceral symbol of communist oppression.'

It was shameless bullshit. That said, he'd read far worse.

He looked at the compliments slip, steeled himself and dialled the number at the bottom. His thumb hovered over the call button but, instead of pressing it, he hesitated.

It occurred to him that Orca's interest might be a blessing. He opened the address book on the phone and scrolled down to 'V'. There was only one name listed.

Virgo answered on the first ring. 'Top o' the mornin' to ya,' he said, in a dry monotone.

Hugh was too distracted to rise to Virgo's ethnic baiting. 'There's been a bit of a cock-up,' he said, getting straight to the point. 'Well, more of a gold-standard cock-up, to be honest.'

Other than the jingle of a cup being stirred, there was silence at the end of the line.

'You've heard of Robert Orca?' Hugh asked.

After a slurp, 'Yeah. Fat bloke. Buys art.'

'I suppose that's the potted biography. It's just that he's no ordinary art buyer. When he starts buying, it gets noticed.'

'And you're telling me this because?'

'Orca showed up here yesterday, when I was meeting you, and somehow got his wires crossed with Jack. My fault, I shouldn't have left him in charge. The thing is, Orca took a fancy to the work on the walls and decided to buy it.'

'But it weren't for sale.'

'He somehow got the impression that it was.'

Virgo sighed. 'Fuckin' chimps, the lot of you. How many pieces he buy?'

'All of it. He must be *very* keen. He's just couriered over a cheque.'

Virgo perked up. 'Really, for how much?'

'Two hundred and forty grand. He gave himself a 25 percent discount.'

'Cheeky bastard.'

'So, what should I do? I reckon if I tell him he can't have them, he'll just want them even more. On the other hand, if word gets out that Orca's been buying from us, it'll draw lots of unwanted attention. Either way, the gallery's compromised.'

There was another slurp, the sound of a cup clinking on a saucer, then a clucking noise, as though Virgo was mulling over what he'd just heard, before finally he said, 'The way I see it, that cheque is pure bunce.'

That wasn't the answer Hugh had hoped for; he'd thought Virgo might decide to pull the plug on the gallery. 'You're not planning on taking the sale, are you?'

'Why shouldn't we?'

'Because, for starters, the artist doesn't exist.'

'Thought you said the artist flogged the work?'

'I mean the artist we're saying made the work doesn't exist.'

'But the art does. That's all that matters, ain't it?'

'What if Orca wants to meet the artist?' Hugh asked.

'Tell him he's a recluse. Or we just kill the artist off.' Virgo paused, then added, 'the boys wouldn't even 'ave to dig a lime-pit this time.'

Hugh wasn't laughing. 'Jesus, Douglas, don't lose the plot here. The whole idea was to be discreet. But now you're saying you want to diversify from money-laundering into a full-on confidence trick? Why risk exposure?'

Virgo didn't miss a beat. 'Exactly. Why would Orca risk exposing us? His reputation as the shrewdest collector in London would be up the swanee. I can just imagine him, smudged up in the *Guardian,* a laughing stock.'

'This is insane, Douglas . . . '

'Listen to yourself,' Virgo cut in. 'You woke up this morning skint. Boracic Johnson. Then someone sends you a cheque for two hundred and forty grand and you – potless Paddy – wants to send it back. That's fuckin' vintage, that is.'

Hugh sighed. The throbbing had spread to the other side of his head.

'Just sit tight,' Virgo said. 'I'll give Luca the full SP. He'll handle the cheque, send someone round to pick it up. *You* deal with Orca. Tell him whatever he wants to hear.'

CHAPTER 23

Amuse Bouche

Virgo hung up. After the click came the flat hum of the dial tone, sounding eerily like one of those hospital heart monitors after the patient had croaked.

'Call it,' Hugh said grimly.

He took the phone from his ear, looked at the screen, pressed the red button. He considered calling Virgo back, although chances were, the call wouldn't have been taken. He looked again at Orca's cheque, drawn on an account at Coutt's Private Banking. He hadn't seen too many of these. He ran his thumb over the embossed crest of three gold crowns, held the cheque up to the light, gave a fatalistic shrug when he saw the watermark.

Jack wasn't that type of forger.

Hugh couldn't let the sale stand. That much he knew. He had to call Orca's office, but first he needed to come up with a formula of words to cancel the sale without whetting the collector's appetite even more. Nothing sharpens a rich man's desire like denial, and Orca didn't have the look of a man who'd mastered his appetites.

Telling Orca that someone else had already bought the work would be counterproductive in the extreme. Thy neighbour's wife never seemed so attractive until God decreed that thou shalt not covet her. In this case, thy neighbour probably lives in Cadogan Square and it's his art collec-tion being coveted, not his better half, but the same principle applied.

He could tell Orca that the work wasn't really made in East Germany in the 1970s by an unheralded dissident artist, that it was instead part of an elaborate conceptual project by a young British artist – maybe even introduce Jack as the artist. But whatever about Orca, he couldn't second-guess how Jack would behave, if he'd play along, resist the urge to gloat.

Sod it anyway. He was wasting time. Virgo was sending someone over to pick up the cheque, and once it was lodged there'd be no way back. He'd have to think on the hoof. He dialled the number on Orca's compliments slip and was about to press the call button when the phone at the reception desk rang. His first thought was to let it ring out but then he decided to answer it, on the off-chance it was Virgo calling back, having come to his senses.

Caller ID showed another blocked number. Hugh answered warily. There was a pause, a husky intake of breath, then a sonorous introduction. 'Robert Orca.'

Hugh gathered himself. 'Ah, Robert, I was just about to call you.'

'And you are?'

'Hugh Rhattigan, director of the gallery.'

'Name sounds familiar. Used to work at Frith's, didn't you?'

'Back in the day.'

'Glad to see you got out of auctioneering. A shameless racket.'

Shameless? *You have no idea*, Hugh thought, his eyes skimming over the price-list on the desk. 'About this cheque, Robert.'

'Got it then, did you?'

'First thing. Thanks for the prompt payment. Much appreciated. It's just that . . .'

'Don't mention it,' Orca cut in. 'No doubt cashflow can be a problem with a new gallery. Anyhow, I'm very happy with the work. It has – what's the word? – gravitas. That's why I'm calling. I think we need to raise this chap's profile, get him reviewed.'

'Reviewed?' Hugh said, making no effort to mask the incredulous tone.

'Yes, reviewed. The work deserves it, demands it. Don't fret, though, I'm sending in a critic, a pal of mine, to write up the show for one of the bottom-shelf art magazines. Of course, you might have to take out an ad, help keep the printing presses oiled and all that. But here am I, telling you how to do your job.'

'Look, Robert, that's all very well but . . . '

Hugh hesitated and Orca seized on the dead air. 'Don't worry, I'm happy to keep my end up by gifting the critic one of the pieces I bought yesterday. There's nothing like a vested interest to get the eulogies flowing. A picture to look at over the mantelpiece while the fire's being stoked, so to speak.'

Critics accepting gifts was hardly a revelation. It was ever the way. Hugh remembered hearing stories about the British critic David Sylvester, who took gifts from the likes of Willem de Kooning and Francis Bacon – artists he also wrote about. He later sold the Bacon and bought a house in Notting Hill with the proceeds. Christ knows what the word-rate was on that: maybe a grand a pop?

'Let's attach my name to the artist as well,' Orca continued, not bothering to feign humility. 'Put him on the map. I've already been spreading the word – vicariously, at any rate. Mrs Orca was at a charity auction last night in Kensington Palace. A black-tie banquet affair. Worthy cause, tiresome crowd. The average net worth was going on for half a billion, apparently. Between you and me, I can't help thinking society would've been better served by locking the doors and putting a match to the place. The death duties alone would've kept the NHS in business for ten years.'

Orca gave a hoggish snort. Hugh shook his head, thinking *Christ, not another closet anarchist.*

'Sorry,' Orca said, sounding anything but, 'that was in poor taste. Anyhow, Mrs Orca had barely tucked into her amuse bouche when the interrogation began into what I've been buying. So she pulled up your gallery on her *me*Phone and passed it around. I'd be ready to field some inquiries if I were you.'

'That's great, Robert, but this is all a bit premature. For starters, I have very little work in stock.'

'Make them form an orderly queue then. Take a leaf out of the competition's book. Put a velvet rope across the gallery's main entrance. Tell them they can't come in, and you'll have a scrum on your hands. They'll be sliding their black credit cards under the door.'

Hugh shrugged, his resistance giving way to a creeping sense of how odd it was to be spurning the patronage of Robert Orca.

'Been looking at your website,' Orca continued, 'and I think you've put together a very strong stable of artists. Bold, brave, eclectic. I'd like to work with you, get this work out there. I've been looking for a pet project, and your gallery fits the bill.'

A *pet* project. That felt less like patronage, and more like being patronised, but Hugh went with it, flattery having got the better of him. 'Aren't you worried about having too many pieces by the one artist – or from the same gallery for that matter?'

'Good lord no, I've learned to wade in when I see work I like, then move it on if I tire of it. That's the thing about the art market, you see: there'll always be a richer, greedier fool.'

CHAPTER 24

Kosher

Felix Lazaar left a trail like a man-sized slug.

Kolya could have tracked him down weeks ago. It was just that he'd been in no hurry to slake Vlad's thirst for revenge. It kept his employer distracted, and that suited Kolya just fine.

This morning, though, Vlad had gone off on one, baying for Lazaar's blood, a full-on rage-boner that Kolya knew better than to ignore.

'I'll sort it, boss,' he said, grabbing the keys for one of Vlad's flash motors and bailing, heading north through the park from Knightsbridge.

Ten minutes later, he was pulling into a laneway off Great Portland Street, where the car was less likely to be spotted. That said, it was hard to be discreet in a gold Range Rover with a customised Burberry interior and vanity plates that read 'VL4D NEM' but might as well have said 'Fuck you' to the local constabulary. Rubbing the law's nose in your success like that was not a smart move.

Kolya pulled out a packet of unfiltered Gitanes and lit up as he walked back onto the main street, right across from the Bloomsbury Arts Club. He'd never thought that hunting down art forgers and their crooked dealers would be part of his job spec, but then any illusions he'd had about being a made guy were fading fast. Almost as fast as Vlad's *vor* tattoos.

According to their code, a *vor* shouldn't have any attachments he couldn't walk away from. They even had a saying that the only home he should ever have was prison – not a flash three-storey-over-basement pad in Knightsbridge and a villa in the south of France. But that was par for the course for Vlad, who now only invoked the code when it suited him. Lately, it was all about impressing his rich new friends. That meant collecting stuff: houses, cars, yachts, mistresses and, of course, art – which seemed to be the preferred way to show how big your dick was among London's New Russians without actually whipping it out.

Shaking his head, Kolya dragged on the Gitanes and watched giant four-by-fours pull up outside the school across the street for kids born with a silver spoon up their ass. Asian nannies chaperoned little girls in pinafores, accessorised with cutesy straw hats, leather satchels, violin cases and hockey sticks. There were well-heeled MILFs too. When one of the fitter ones glanced over, he toked hard on his cigarette, nodded at her, then flicked the butt out onto the road between them. She blushed, pulled her shades down from her hair and shooed her daughter into the back of a Porsche Cayenne. Closing the driver's door, she looked over again, either checking him out or concerned that he might be there to snatch her daughter. Possibly both.

His smirk flashed across her tinted windows as she sped away. His eyes trailed the car till it rounded the corner, then returned to the heavy oak door of the Bloomsbury Arts Club, right next to the school for pint-sized rich kids.

Kolya tracked Lazaar down through the porter of another club, a sailing club in Kent. He'd spotted the club's crest once on a blazer the slippery old bastard wore. Lazaar seemed to like jackets and ties with badges on them, unaware that he was leaving a trail for anyone who ever wanted to track him down. He may as well have printed his social diary in one of those bourgeois magazines Vlad left lying around his sitting room. The porter in the sailing club told Kolya that Lazaar – 'Just a bar member, not a proper sailor' – was now using the Bloomsbury Arts Club as his address in London.

Kolya had only met Lazaar a couple of times, but that was enough to get the measure of him. He made it his business to watch people, to really *look*: you learned as much if not more that way than you could by unpicking the lies and half-truths they told you. Of course, some people would never see what was right in front of them, while others chose not to. Like Ana, who used to watch Kolya as she drew him, but never really looked – afraid of what she might see.

As for Lazaar, he wasn't much of a challenge to Kolya's powers of observation: he saw him for what he was straight off. The bluster, the art-wank, the shiftiness, the ass-kissing. It worked on Vlad, who'd even managed to set aside his longstanding distaste for the Jewish race by dealing with Lazaar. (Kolya kept quiet about his own Jewish grandparents – for obvious reasons – although, Jew or gentile, he cared little. Ana would have told him it was the logical flipside of only caring for himself.)

Vlad wasn't mellowing; it was just that he'd developed a blind spot when it came to social climbing. He tolerated Lazaar, who earned him brownie points with his new pals by sourcing bullshit modern art for him at knockdown cash prices. Much to Kolya's amusement, it turned out that the paintings weren't quite as kosher as Lazaar was.

He stubbed out his cigarette on the pavement, crossed the street and took the club's four granite steps in one go. He pulled on the brass door handle and crossed a mosaic-floored lobby. Pushing on the glass internal door, he was hit by a gust of warm, musty air – a blend of mould, bile and stale tobacco. He found himself in a softly lit reception lounge with wooden panels and an assortment of burgundy leather armchairs arranged around low tables. It looked tatty now but may have had a hint of bling – *circa* 1972.

Making his way across the lounge, the deep musty smell was overlaid with high-notes of cologne and alcohol, likely coming from the tweedy old gents in two of the armchairs. One was proclaiming to the other how 'painting like that would be a death for me'. Kolya did a double-take before realising he meant 'a death' in an artistic sense rather than the actual death facing the sly son-of-a-bitch who'd painted the forgeries Vlad had bought.

He turned back towards the entrance, to a porter's cubicle, and knocked on the glass. Without moving his head, the porter lifted his eyes from a tabloid crossword and looked at Kolya over the rim of his glasses. 'Can I help you?'

'I'm looking for a cousin of mine, Felix Lazaar.'

'Cousin?' the porter asked, sceptically.

'Yes, distant cousin. You know, we all Russians Jews, sticking together.'

The porter slid his glasses up the bridge of his nose. 'Is that so? He hasn't been in for a while, I'm afraid. Not here to settle his account, are you?'

In a manner of speaking, Kolya could have said, but didn't. The porter's body language spoke of disaffection, of years of being shat on from on high, of tugging his forelock at obnoxious old goats who, by the looks of this place, still retained their airs and graces, still wore the cloak of entitlement, but no longer had the cash to pay for it.

Kolya put a price on the porter's loyalty to his employers, concluded that it wasn't very steep, then pulled out his wallet and left four crisp fifty-pound notes on the counter. 'Here's down payment. Let me know when he come in next and I pay rest.'

The porter's whole demeanour changed. He leapt out of his chair. All of a sudden it was, yes sir, no sir, three bags full sir.

Kolya took the notepad on the counter and wrote his mobile number on it, without leaving a name. He tore the page off, folded it up with the money and slipped it into the porter's breast pocket. 'No need for receipt. I know you do this for me.'

The porter tapped his breast. 'Think of it done, sir.'

Kolya turned to leave, paused, then caught the porter's eye again. 'Oh, and maybe no say I was here, boss. Felix is little *beet* proud.'

The request was met with a conspiratorial wink. 'Mum's the word, sir.'

CHAPTER 25

Coming into Heat

What's that they say about sharks being able to detect a drop of blood in open ocean from a mile away?

The enquiries began within hours, all fielded by Hugh; he'd never got round to hiring an assistant, loathe to draw anyone else into Virgo's 'circle of trust'. Two art consultants called in the morning, as did the head of the art advisory office of J. P. Morgan and the PA of some Ukrainian mining magnate Hugh had never heard of.

But it wasn't until the afternoon that the gallery hit pay-dirt. Larry Cockburn called, founder and CEO of the Optimus hedge fund. Cockburn managed $20 billion in assets and earned about $400 million a year. He bought art for his mansion in East Hampton and his 7,000-square-foot *pied-à-terre* in Manhattan. He also kept a house on Belgrave Square in London, and had just built another mansion on the island of Martinique with half a mile of empty walls. Put bluntly, Cockburn was an art dealer's wet dream.

Hugh answered the phone to the financier's honeyed Virginian drawl, unfurling down the line and enveloping him as though they were old friends – even though Cockburn didn't seem to recall their only previous encounter, several months before in the gallery in Whitechapel.

'Tell me about this artist you're showing,' Cockburn said. 'Selling like hot cakes, I hear.'

'Even we've been surprised by the response.' Hugh just about managed to purge the sarcasm from his voice.

'I gotta tell ya, I'm kickin' myself. I'd swing by for a look now, only I'm cruising at forty thousand feet, heading back Stateside. I just flew in for the charity auction last night.'

'A long way to come, wasn't it?'

'Happy to put my shoulder to the wheel, sir.'

Cockburn's voice dimmed, like he'd put a hand over the phone, but was still audible. 'Thank you Bianca, that was superb. Can I get a pot of Earl Grey, please?'

Bianca answered with a comely 'Of course, Mr Cockburn'. Whatever kind of a plane he was on, it certainly wasn't Ryanair.

There was a clink of cutlery on a plate, then Cockburn spoke into the phone again. 'Pardon me, Hugh, it's chow-time here. So about this work you're showing: I hear a certain Mr Orca's been in?'

'Word travels fast.'

'In the right circles, yeah. Bought out the whole show, I'm told.'

'Every last one. We're delighted to be able to keep the collection together.' The last time Hugh had used that line to a client, it was because he hadn't sold a single painting.

Cockburn made a clucking sound. 'Every last one, aye? Listen, I won't insult your integrity by asking if I could gazump Bob and pay you a premium to flip a couple of 'em on to me.'

'I appreciate that.'

'I'm sure you wouldn't, even if I did ask.' There was a pause, with just the din of jet engines on the line, before Cockburn added, 'You wouldn't, would you?'

Hugh allowed himself a smile. 'No, Larry, that would be profoundly unethical.'

'I'm only fuckin' with ya, Hugh. That was the right answer. Reputation is everything in your business. How 'bout you keep me in mind when you get more in?'

'Don't know when that'll be, Larry, but we'll do our best for you.'

Hugh was hoping Cockburn would pick up on the noncommittal tone, although the financier's attention seemed divided. His voice became faint again, like he had another conversation on the go, which Hugh could only make out in part. 'Screw 'em, Steve, he ain't backin' out. The small print on that deal is world-class.' There was laughter, more banter: 'Reckon he'll be a mite less rich when we're through with him. Still be a jerkwad, though.'

Then Cockburn came back on the line to Hugh. 'Pardon me, sir, I got the shop on Skype here. Now where were we? Oh yeah, you were doin' your best not to sell me anything. Not used to that, I gotta say. What about your next show? Just pulled it up here on your website. Looks interesting. Bob Orca hasn't bought 'em all yet, has he?'

'Not all of them, no.'

The next show was of the abstract works Jack was making, using gloss paint and multi-coloured string, fixed to panels pins and set under a layer of resin.

'Whataya say you put five of the best aside for me – or do I have to get in line?'

'There has been a lot of interest.'

Cockburn sighed. 'I'll level with ya, Hugh, I'm looking to buy museum-quality work *before* someone puts it in a museum. There's a bigger upside. That crafty old dog Bob always seems to get there first. Don't get me wrong, I like owning beautiful things and all that, but I like making money too and, believe me, there's a ton of money out there to be made. A lotta new buyers in heat. Real skittish.'

There was a slurp. Presumably the Earl Grey had arrived. 'How 'bout I buy a buncha work and get Diedrich Weiss to place a few on loan with some Eur'pean museums? You know, Diedrich, curates my collection for me?'

'We've met.'

'He's got a good eye, even if he does talk a lotta horseshit sometimes. On our side of the pond, my wife's on the board of the Guggenheim and we're trustees, board members, benefactors of, oh, I don't know how many other museums. Let's all work together on this, Hugh.' Cockburn gave an ingratiating chuckle. 'Where I'm from, back in Virginia, we call it the back-scratchin' conga.'

The back-scratching conga. Hugh had to banish a deeply unpleasant image from his mind of a heaving column of collectors, artists, dealers, critics and curators, relieving each other's dorsal itches.

At this point, Hugh could have ended the conversation by telling Cockburn he had another call coming through, with the coda that he'd get back to him, at some unspecified time in the future. He could have thanked him for his interest in the gallery but declined to sell him any work on the grounds that there was a long list of buyers ahead of him in the queue. Or he could have just told Cockburn straight out how breathtakingly crass his approach to buying art was, suggest that he just buy some shares in an auction house if all he wanted was to take a punt on the art market.

But the fact was, Hugh couldn't help himself. It almost seemed immoral *not* to take Cockburn's money.

'Larry,' he said, 'I'm reserving the five best paintings in our next show for you.'

'That's more like it. And while we're at it, how 'bout you give me the heads-up on anything else Bob buys from you?'

'I'll put you on speed-dial.'

'Now you're talkin'. Dollars for doughnuts, we'll all do very nicely. And Hugh?'

'Yes, Larry.'

'Keep up the good work. You're doing a sterling job there, sir.'

With that, Cockburn hung up.

Hugh shook his head, smiling ruefully. It seemed he was finally at the helm of a gallery that was taking off, only for it to be a front for a criminal racket. Two of the more popular strains of irony sprung to mind: 'cruel' and 'delicious'. He couldn't quite decide which was most applicable, so he settled on a combination of the two.

CHAPTER 26

Reduced to Clear

Clarissa Booth held her own gaze in the bathroom mirror, unflinching, certain that her cause was a righteous one.

According to her mother, she was thin-lipped and beady-eyed, but Clarissa saw order in her neat, symmetrical features - an order that she'd always sought to impose on the world around her.

Glancing at the digital alarm clock on the shelf next to the mirror and noting that three minutes had elapsed, she leaned over the washbasin and rinsed the hair-bleaching cream from her upper lip. Then she dried her face and removed the clip from the crown of her head, allowing her hair to re-form into a tidy bob. As a final ablution, she rubbed a pea-sized squirt (as recommended on the bottle) of antibacterial gel onto each of her hands.

She made her way into the sitting room of her one-bedroom flat overlooking Archway Road – just on the right side of the cusp between Archway and Highgate – and picked up the three phonebooks stacked in a pile on the rug in front of the fireplace. She'd used them that morning to exercise, in lieu of the step-aerobics classes she could no longer afford. Her grant application to the Arts Council had been declined (again), and her parents hadn't been able to help out as much financially since their buy-to-let property in Norwich had turned into a 'flipping nightmare'.

She replaced the directories on the bottom shelf of the bookrack and took a firm grip on the handle of the suitcase in the corner of the room. Even with the sinewy arms she'd developed from horse-riding in her adolescence, and had never lost, she was barely able to lift it.

She manoeuvred it out of the corner, pivoted it to one side, then wheeled it into the centre of the room and laid it flat on the floor.

She would have to open it before she left, to check that its contents were in order, but first she needed to eat something, even though all she felt in her stomach was butterflies, not hunger. She went to the fridge and took out the Waitrose couscous and goji berry salad that she'd bought the previous evening. She removed the garish yellow reduced-to-clear sticker first, then peeled back the plastic film, halfway, as she thought it unlikely that she'd be able to finish it.

She sat down in the armchair facing the suitcase. If she got caught, at best she'd be charged with criminal damage or reckless endangerment. There was of course the very real risk that she might injure somebody – most likely herself – but she was prepared to inflict collateral damage if that was what it took.

If she did get caught, chances were she would never come home to her flat again. Her family would have to clear out her belongings – probably after the police had searched it. She wondered if she should leave the flat a little tidier.

She'd lived on her own there since her boyfriend, Clive, had moved into the Occupy camp in front of St Paul's Cathedral. She'd declined to join him, on the grounds that it was all a little too squalid: she saw no trade-off between personal hygiene and principle. When the camp was disbanded, she'd bluntly told Clive that he wasn't welcome back.

Her only regret on the matter was financial. She could use some help to pay the rent, not just because of the failed grant applications and her parent's predicament, but also because the gallery that had been showing her work, however half-heartedly, had given the last of it back to her. The gallery owner told her that both of them were in the 'squeezed middle' and that it was only the very high end of the art market that was thriving.

That merely served to rub salt into the wound. She'd done the rounds of all of the top galleries, but to no avail. She'd started at the top and worked her way down: Alexandra Friedman, the Gagosian, the Marlborough, the White Cube, Hauser & Wirth, and so on down through their ranks, rejected or ignored at every turn, till she came to the Lead White. She held out some hope there. Its owner, Hugh Rhattigan, seemed like a nice man; she liked his soft Irish accent.

She'd bumped into him a few months ago at an opening of a conceptual non-art exhibition in Whitechapel and had just happened to have her portfolio with her. He was too distracted to look at it properly but agreed to meet her a few days later at his gallery. When she showed up for the appointment, though, one of his staff told her that he wouldn't be in today, that things were 'a bit mad around here at the moment'. Clarissa felt her cheeks flushing red. 'Are you people familiar with basic manners?' she'd fumed.

'Look, I'm just the intern,' the girl said.

'Well ...' Clarissa spluttered, stomping towards the exit, '...you're lucky to have an internship.'

It was on the bus ride home that it came to her, the realisation that it was time to take a stand, beyond handing out fliers to visitors to the Turner Prize exhibition, in front of Tate Britain, with a motley group of fellow disaffected artists.

Abandon art all ye who enter Turner Prize Hell, the fliers railed.

Most gallery-goers just ignored them, leaving the picketers with the cold succour of their own chiming indignation.

'Artists who don't paint aren't artists.'

'You're so right.'

'Art that has to be in a gallery to be art isn't art.'

'You said it.'

'You don't win the Booker Prize if you can't write, but you can win the Turner Prize if you can't draw.'

'You've hit the nail on the head.'

'The contemporary-art orthodoxy is being shored up by the philistine wealth of the 1 percent.'

'On the same hymnsheet, mate.'

Grumbling to each other and staging the occasional picket seemed the limit of their imaginative reach. 'Can't we be more original?' Clarissa pleaded one evening, having adjourned to a local pub after a demo. Her eyes then scrolled along a row of blank faces, before recoiling at a bearded mouth, with a scum of ale-froth, and its mucoidal chomping on a pork scratching.

She would have to take matters into her own hands.

She formed a group – a cell, if you will – of like-minded individuals. A cyber-activist Clive knew came to the first meeting, with a laptop stolen from some City type – which made it OK in the view of all present. The lap-top was tethered to a mobile phone bought for cash and apparently untrace-able. He ran the browser with its privacy settings on, via an anonymising service so there was no way of eavesdropping on them. This was a prudent precaution at the best of times, according to Clive's friend, but especially if you planned to look at the myriad of jihadi websites that explained in great detail how to make an improvised explosive device. Frankly, Clarissa was astonished at how much material was out there. It seemed to be an area of interest that had flourished on the internet. Like pornography.

They each brought two cardboard boxes of wine to the next meeting and two tins of brightly coloured gloss paint. Clive and the others had been happy 'to take one for the cause' by drinking the contents of the wine boxes. Fully drained, they removed the bladder-like sacks from the inside and, using funnels, carefully refilled them with the tins of paint. Clarissa insisted on a decent brand, as she could never bring herself to scrimp on materials, no matter how scarce money had become.

Another of Clive's friends, who had a contact at a stone quarry and a diploma in engineering, sourced some explosive and made the detonator using the manuals they'd found online. The cyber-activist-type person built the website and set up the Twitter account linked to it, which they would use to claim responsibility for the attack.

That only left one matter to resolve: who would actually carry out the attack? The question was met with silence at first, which seemed to sharpen the cloying, underlying scent of patchouli oil in the room. Then came the twiddling of beaded hair-braids, the picking of a blackhead and, finally, a rambling excuse about teaching an evening class in sociol-ogy at Surrey University.

Clarissa gave an exasperated sigh and declared that she would do it herself.

She looked around the room they'd all sat in and adjusted the corner of the rug where the suitcase had snagged on it. There was a honk of a car-horn. She looked down onto the street below and saw Clive in his rickety, twenty-year-old Vauxhall Astra: God forbid they might have to outrun the police. She picked up her backpack, with the mask in it, and hauled the suitcase out the door. Half an hour later, Clive dropped her on the pavement, around the corner from the gallery.

CHAPTER 27

Business Boom

Hugh didn't dwell too long on the morality of selling the work to Cockburn, other than asking himself what was worse: defrauding the rich or helping the rich defraud everybody else? It didn't seem like much of a conundrum.

As to the practicalities of pitching the work the gallery exhibited as *real* art by *real* artists, he would only get away with that for so long before he was found out. How long would depend to a large degree on whether or not Orca kept buying. As long as he did, other collectors would happily row in behind. And given Orca's unconventional approach to buying art, that could be quite some time: Orca never went to openings, had little interest in meeting the artists whose work he collected, and bought as much based on intuition as on research or any attempts to divine art-market trends.

The other practical problem was the gallery's beneficial owner. For now, Virgo's attitude was likely to be some variation on 'bleed the rich, gullible [insert relevant epithet]s, dry', but he'd have to see sense eventually, and that could only mean one thing: pulling the plug on the gallery – an outcome which would suit Hugh just fine.

In the meantime, he decided he may as well have some fun. After the call from Cockburn, he'd made his way back up to the first floor, where he'd been laying out the work they had ready for their next exhibition, to show to the growing list of buyers who wanted to see it in advance. Hugh realised he'd have to set Jack and Ana to work replacing the paintings he'd just sold, and was wondering if they could really keep up with the burgeoning demand, when the gallery's buzzer sounded. His next customers maybe – or should that be 'marks'?

He looked down onto the street below and saw a black Mercedes Maybach berthed in front of the gallery, with a chauffeur leaning over the bonnet, polishing it with a shammy cloth. He dashed down the stairs and glanced at an elderly couple in the security monitor before buzzing them in. They emerged from the entrance lobby into the gallery's reception area. Hugh recognised them straight off: Lilian and Eli Beckman.

Like Cockburn, the Beckmans were A-list collectors. Eli had made his first fortune in machine tools, his second in property. Word was that they were laying plans for the billionaire's bauble *du jour*: a private museum to house their massive collection of contemporary art.

'Is this the gallery?' Mrs Beckman asked, in a pinched, nasal New York accent. She had the slightly stooped posture of a lady of seventy-plus, but guessing her age was complicated by the absence of any wrinkles; her face was shot through with enough Botox to paralyse a Jack Russell.

She marched up to Hugh and held out her hand, without removing her black buckskin glove. 'Lilian and Eli Beckman. We heard all about you last night, and the wonderful work you're showing.'

They must have been at the charity auction in Kensington Palace.

Her husband hung back, nodding curtly and casting a wary eye around him. He seemed to be taking an intense interest in the ceiling, as though anxious about something falling on his head. His bald pate was buffed and polished to a high-gloss finish. Hugh wondered if one of the machine tools his company made had been customised for the purpose.

Both wore black suits, Mrs Beckman's with mink lapels, worn over a cream silk blouse, her husband with a purple polka-dot tie and a matching handkerchief in the breast pocket.

'We're not so keen on your current show,' Mrs Beckman said. 'A little dark for our tastes. But we liked the next one, from your website.'

Hugh said it wasn't a problem, that he'd make an exception for them and give them a preview of the next show. He led them up the stairs to the room where the work was laid out.

'Oh my,' Mrs Beckman said, 'these are intriguing, aren't they, honey?' She was struggling to stir any enthusiasm in her husband. 'You know, it says on the website that they're "architectronic".'

She turned to Hugh. 'We love *arkatetcher*, you see. Our home is by Frank Gehry, our beach-house by Richard Meier. And who's doing St Bart's, dear?'

'Rem Koolhaas,' he said tetchily. 'Jeez, poppet, *you* picked him.'

'All right already, I get confused. Don't mind him,' she told Hugh, 'he's just sore 'cause he got outbid on the Murakami last night.'

'I went to two million on it, didn't I?' her husband snipped.

She flapped a hand at him, 'Ya big meanie! It was for *charidee*.' Then she cupped the hand over her mouth, whispering showily to Hugh, 'and for *me*.'

Hard-won experience had taught Hugh never to embroil himself in spousal disputes when there was a prospect of making a sale. He focused instead on honing his pitch. Noticing how rushed some of the paintings seemed, he gave the Beckmans a spiel about the works' improvised nature, about how 'the evidence of their making was never disguised' – as though that was a virtue.

He made a mental note of the line for future use, as it seemed to do the trick. Cutting to the money-shot, he sold them five paintings for a combined total of three hundred thousand pounds. He salved his conscience by telling himself it was the kind of loose change the Beckmans might find down the back of their Eileen Gray sofa.

He took their invoice and shipping details, after a long discussion about which of their houses they'd have the work sent to. In the end, they settled on a free-port storage facility in Geneva.

As they made their way to the exit, there was some polite chit-chat about how they'd almost bought a castle once in Ireland. Then, out of the blue, Mr Beckman asked, 'You must be concerned about security here?'

'Not especially,' Hugh said, thrown by the question. 'Why, should I be?'

'Haven't you seen the news today?'

'Not yet, no.'

'Some kind of artist militia exploded a bomb.'

'A paint-bomb, can you believe that?' Mrs Beckman said, talking over her husband.

'In the Alexandra Friedman Gallery. They're all het up over these one-per-centers' – he said it like he didn't know who they were – 'and the kind of art they're buying.'

Mrs Beckman tutted, clutching at her mink lapels as she stepped outside. 'It's not *their* art folk are buying, honey. That's all that's troubling them.'

CHAPTER 28

The Revolution Will Be Streamed

Hugh closed the door behind the Beckmans and stood with his back against it. The day had been sufficiently surreal for the story about the paint-bomb not to seem all that strange. It was like wandering through a Max Ernst landscape and shrugging casually at a rock shaped like Napoleon in full regalia – bicorne hat, the works – that was pointing imperiously at an elephant with four trunks. Reality had already shifted several degrees left of normal. Far enough that only a drink could restore the natural order of things.

He waited a moment to make sure the Beckmans had been whisked away in their chauffeur-driven Merc (in his surrealist landscape, they'd travel by sedan chair, borne by a troupe of liveried servants, all wearing Tony Blair face-masks).

After a safe interval, he walked out onto the street, crossed over and made for the welcoming embrace of the Bricklayer's Arms. He stopped after a few paces, though, and looked back towards the gallery, at the gable windows of the loft, where the lights were still on. He mulled it over, then turned around and headed for the off-licence a few doors down from the gallery.

He was in and out in under a minute. He'd taken a bottle of Veuve Clicquot from a fridge, paused, reminding himself that they'd sold the guts of a million quid's worth of work that day, then taken out two more.

He made his way back to the gallery, grabbed some glasses and cantered up the six flights of stairs to the loft. Scaling the final few steps, he saw Jack sitting in front of the iMac on the trestle table by the window. Ana was in the opposite corner, by an easel, working up one of the drawings Hugh had salvaged that morning onto a larger canvas. She offered a sympathetic smile, which he reciprocated.

His gaze lingered for a moment. She seemed to have induced a kind of visual amnesia in him: each time he saw her was like the first; each time he was struck again by how beautiful she was. The kicker was that she also seemed to hold up a mirror, presenting Hugh with a craven image of himself as a stooge in a criminal racket – worse still, a racket he was helping Ana to squander her talent on. He'd yet to purge the guilt of how his reckless bloodymindedness had soured, and ultimately ruined, his marriage. Somehow, allowing Ana to embroil herself in Virgo's latest scam pricked his conscience almost as much.

He turned then to Jack, whose equally ample gifts seemed, by contrast, to have found their perfect outlet in the gallery. Jack was pointing a diversionary finger at the screen, looking sheepish, as though he expected a bollocking. They hadn't spoken since the morning.

Hugh just rolled his eyes, set the bottles and the glasses down on the table and said, 'Show me'. Jack had seven or eight windows open in the browser, most of them newspaper articles about the attack. There was a flippant, almost gleeful tone to the headlines:

GOSH WHAT A BLAST! ART WORLD IN A TIZ OVER PAINT BOMBERS

SEND IN THE ART–ILLERY!

'Watch this,' Jack said giddily, clicking on a report from Sky News that someone had posted to YouTube. The camera panned over a large exhibition space. Walls, floors, ceiling were covered in a multi-coloured spattering of paint, as though some strange genetically modified creeper had been left to grow rampant in the space, save for six large white rectangles like window casements – obviously where the paintings had been hung.

The voiceover told how 'The gallery of top London dealer Alexandra Friedman was this afternoon attacked by a group calling itself PSALM – or the Provisional Stuckist Art Liberation Movement. PSALM is a militant offshoot of the Stuckists, a loose collective of artists who have coalesced around their disaffection with the contemporary-art scene.

Dismissed as cranks by the arts establishment, the Stuckists derive their name from a comment by Tracey Emin to her then boyfriend, Billy Childish, that he was 'stuck' in the art of the past. Childish co-founded the collective but has since left.

'In their online manifesto, PSALM say their aim is to reclaim art from the twin tyrannies of conceptualism and a market skewed by the fickle tastes of the super-rich. They aim to reinstate figurative painting to its rightful place at the centre of the visual arts. They say artists like Emin and Damien Hirst are charlatans, that Tate Modern is a cultural house of cards, a celebration of vacuous ego-art on a Barnum-esque scale and, perhaps most ominously, that passive dissent is no longer an option.

'The perpetrator, believed to be a woman, was captured on CCTV, walking in the main entrance of the gallery in a Guy Fawkes mask with an artist's beret sewn on top. She walked to the centre of the space, wheeling a large suitcase behind her, which she then laid flat on the floor before shouting at a gallery assistant and a number of visitors to leave the space. An explosive device in the suitcase – also packed with multiple bags of paint – then detonated, causing what Friedman describes as "unspeakable damage", and leaving the London art world reeling and wondering who might be next.'

Jack made a clenched fist. 'Bloody marvellous. *Viva la revolución.*'

Hugh looked at Ana, who had come to stand at Jack's other shoulder. She glanced at the champagne bottles and gave Hugh a quizzical look. He opened his mouth to speak but was cut off by Jack, who had clutched his forearm.

'Oh, wait till you see this bit,' he said.

'According to the gallery's owner, the attack means the desecration of two years of work by Anu Singh OBE, one of Britain's greatest living artists, with several masterpieces destroyed beyond repair.'

The report cut to Friedman, dressed as usual in a riot of black, standing in front of what she called a 'desecrated painting'. The large canvas – about six by eight feet – was one of Singh's signature works: essentially a giant barcode, with black and white vertical stripes of varying widths, and a row of numbers running along the bottom. The intellectual shtick was that the barcode was actually the stock-listing for the painting in the gallery – some kind of commentary on the commodification of art.

But the austere composition and minimal palette looked great in rich people's houses. This particular painting had a Pollock-like drenching of blues, reds, yellows, greens.

Friedman breathed the righteous fire of a high priestess whose temple had been defiled. 'Sadly,' she intoned, 'philistinism is alive and well in Britain. But our greatest artists will not be bowed. We will stand shoulder to shoulder with them, as we do with China's dissident artists, and indeed with Aung San Suu Kyi, the Dalai Lama and other repressed voices around the world. Freedom of expression *must* be defended. The contemporary artist's voice *must* be heard.'

'Get me a bucket, I'm gonna hurl,' Jack said.

Ana smiled. 'She is, how you say, a piece of work?'

Hugh caught her eye. 'By far the most important in that gallery.'

But Friedman wasn't done. 'Anu Singh has responded to the despoilment of his art the only way he knows how – by making more.' The report cut to a shot of Singh in the gallery, which had taken on the look of a site-specific work, the entire space drizzled in colour apart from the blank spaces stencilled by the paintings. The artist was there in his overalls picking his way through the gaps in the paint-spattered floor with a very expensive-looking camera in hand. The reporter told us how the 'artist planned to document the scene in a series of photographic prints that would feature in his next exhibition. He says 10 percent of the proceeds will go to a hardship fund for struggling conceptual artists.'

'That should really wind up the Stuckists,' Jack said.

Hugh shook his head. 'I think their springs have already snapped.'

The reporter then appeared on screen for the first time. Groomed and composed, she motioned gravely to a computer screen. 'On its website, PSALM draws on the ideologies of the Occupy movement, claiming the arts establishment is in hock to the 1 percent. Also cited as an inspiration are Anonymous, the online activists, or *hack*tivists as they've become known. The major auction houses, in particular, are on high alert against denial-of-service attacks on their online bidding systems. PSALM pledges to continue its guerrilla campaign with more acts of vandalism, real and virtual.'

The reporter waited a beat for effect, then signed off.

Ana looked bemused. 'Why would somebody do this?'

'For publicity,' Hugh said. 'It certainly beats picketing the Turner Prize show. They chose the wrong gallery, though. Alex Friedman is far too clever not to turn a publicity stunt like that to her advantage.'

Ana shook her head. 'I mean, why would they destroy the work of another artist like that, especially when they are claiming to care about art?'

Shit. Hugh was reminded of the paintings Jack had taken a blow-torch to. 'There are lots of frustrated artists out there,' he said, not wanting to dwell on the subject. 'They feel undervalued or just ignored. It's a wonder it didn't happen sooner.'

'Maybe they would prefer Soviet rule,' Ana mused. 'You know, the KGB tore down an exhibition once by artists they called *nonconformist*. Except, they used bulldozers and water-cannons. They even put some of the artists in prison.'

'I can think of a few I'd like to see put away,' Jack said, dryly.

Ana rolled her eyes. 'The KGB also locked up homosexuals.'

Jack gave a fair-cop shrug. '*Touché.*'

'Funny that some of Friedman's best clients are now wealthy Russians,' Hugh said.

Ana sighed. 'Some probably ex–KGB.'

'It's a fucked-up world,' Jack concluded, his tone in no way implying that he was troubled by the fact. 'Come to think of it, one of Felix Lazaar's best clients was a Russian. Bought a lot of my work as well.' His eyes flitted expectantly from Hugh to the champagne and back again. 'I take it we're not celebrating the attack on the Friedman gallery.'

Hugh shook his head and popped the cork of the first bottle. 'I'm not sure we should be celebrating at all, but anyhow . . . .'

CHAPTER 29

Spasibo

Hugh told Jack and Ana about his conversation with Orca, about Cockburn and the Beckmans, about all the other inquiries he'd fielded that day.

'Now *that* calls for a drink,' Jack said.

'One of the great Irish rallying cries,' Hugh said, handing them a glass each.

'Really?' Ana said. 'Russian too.'

Jack drained his glass and held it out for a refill. 'Does this mean I *am* a genius then, after all?'

Hugh shrugged. 'Not sure. I think the cheapening of the word "genius" – like all the other superlatives the art world burns through – is partly to blame for what's happening here. It's not like Van Gogh's time, when a genius could be overlooked. That doesn't happen any more; hence there are lots of brilliant artists doing very well. The trouble with today's art market is that mediocrity too often gets mistaken – or misrepresented – as brilliance.' He paused before offering a conclusion: 'So at the very least, Jack, you have a flair for mediocrity.'

Jack wrinkled his nose, his glass hovering by his chin. 'I'll take that as a compliment then, will I?'

Hugh topped up their glasses. 'Sorry if it sounds a little back-handed.'

'But what about gallery?' Ana asked. 'What happens now.'

'As we were,' Hugh said. 'We'll just have to figure out ways to boost production.'

He glanced at the painting Ana had begun. She smiled, said, 'I think about what you say and I try to make exhibition for you: one painting a day.'

Ana's lambent smile – and the champagne – gave Hugh a rush of optimism, a sense of possibilities beyond the situation they found themselves in. He realised how little he'd seen Rebecca smile in the dying days of their marriage – of how little he'd given her to smile about.

Jack seized on the lapse in conversation. He stood up, gathering a yellow hoodie and a leather satchel in one hand, patted Hugh on the shoulder with the other and smiled, almost fondly, at Ana. 'I'll be off,' he said. 'I was up at eight – middle of the night for me. Too wired to sleep.'

Hugh and Ana watched Jack till he dipped out of view, down the stairwell.

Then it was just the two of them. Hugh was in a chair by the computer, Ana was leaning by the table, the bottles of champagne between them. When she looked back towards the stairwell, Hugh looked up, a sideways, regarding glance. Her hair was tied back, so that he noted again the porcelain skin, the graceful arc of her neck. He held up a bottle, offering a refill, but Ana declined. 'I drink too much already.'

'Of course,' Hugh said, not bothering to top up his own glass either. 'We should probably go.' He turned to face the computer screen, the browser still open. TOP LONDON DEALER SUFFERS *ART* ATTACK.

Sighing, he reached forward and shut the computer down. As he did so, he saw the bottles being pushed into the centre of the table and Ana sliding into the space where they'd been.

'Sorry I not want more champagne,' she said. 'It was nice of you to bring it up to us.' She gave a contrite shrug. 'Believe me, you don't like me when I drink too much. I start out finding way to fix the world but always end up stopping to tell some guy not to be such an asshole.'

'Probably best you stop drinking now, then.'

Ana held his gaze, frowning. 'I don't mean you.'

When they fell into silence again, Ana tilted her head back and held up a red pastel crayon, one eye shut, like she was sizing him up for a drawing. 'Maybe sometime I draw you,' she said, at last.

'I'm expecting to have my portrait done soon, by one of the courtroom artists at the Old Bailey, but I'd much rather you did it.'

Ana's brief smile dissolved as she studied Hugh's face. Then she glanced over towards the canvas she'd been working on, on the far side of the loft. Following her eyeline, he could see now that the painting was based on a sketch of the handsome man, with the muscular torso and the scar on his left cheek. Hugh looked back at Ana, unsure if her expression was tinged with regret.

'We all have our scars,' he said, motioning to stand up, the effects of the champagne already wearing off.

'You are leaving?'

'It's been a long day.'

'I said I want make drawing of you.'

'Some other time.'

'But if you are my model, then is OK to seduce you.'

Hugh paused, turning his head slightly, without looking at Ana. 'Really?'

'Why have men always painted pretty young women?'

'Fair enough,' he said, shrugging, 'but why would you want to seduce me? I'm really not much of a catch at the moment.'

'So, you are vulnerable. Is how men do it, no? Picasso say a woman is only ever goddess or doormat, no in-between. And everyone say he is greatest figure in modern art.'

Hugh raised his hands, surrendering. 'Let's just get some food, talk for a while. And I won't be defending Picasso's sexual predations either. He was a misogynistic bully but that doesn't mean the work wasn't . . .'

Perhaps fearing another lecture, Ana put a hand on Hugh's shoulder and pushed him back into his chair. 'I prefer just to fuck, if that's OK.'

Hugh rocked back into his chair, taking a moment to process what he'd heard. 'You're quite the smooth talker.'

Ana didn't hesitate. She sat astride him, her gaze fixed on his, her fingers raking through his hair from the nape of his neck, sending tendrils of pleasure down his back. 'Sometimes is best not to talk at all,' she said, as her lips nestled on his.

In spite of himself, Hugh still tried to speak, 'Look, Ana, you . . .'

She shushed him, though, with a gentle exhalation. He'd wanted to tell her not to waste her talent on a financial scam, that he might be indentured – for now at any rate – but that she could leave, make her way in the world as a *real* artist. Seeming to know what he was about to say, she didn't want to hear it. She just leaned closer and whispered, '*Spasibo*, but I stay because I want to stay.'

CHAPTER 30

Poets Don't Buy Art

The first time, Ana seemed determined to take control, as though reclaiming the act from the men she'd *been with* in her previous employment. Afterwards, she said it was like getting back on a horse after a fall, so to speak – an analogy that was sufficiently flattering to Hugh for him not to quibble with it.

Second time round, however, back in Hugh's place, neither took control, or rather they both did, taking turns at leading each other in a slow, almost languid release. When they were done, they barely spoke – it didn't feel like there was much left to say. They just slept.

The following morning, Hugh woke to find Ana on the lounge chair in the living room of his flat; he had the top floor of a terraced Victorian house in Camden. She was sketching the stunted, calloused boughs of the pollarded beech trees outside. The drawing was framed by the window and squared off by the individual panes. She said it was nice to draw because she *wanted* to.

She put the drawing on the mantelpiece before they left. They strolled up to Primrose Hill for a coffee and some breakfast. They sat outside a café in the crisp autumn sunshine, opposite a lady in a white fox-fur coat – an old sour-faced lady with a Roman nose and an Afghan hound. Ana fed the dog pieces of bacon under the table while its owner remonstrated with the waitress over the temperature of her tea. When the old lady left, a couple with a toddler in a stroller took her place. Ana pulled faces at the toddler, sparking fits of giggles.

She seemed happier, more relaxed than she'd been before. She talked about her life in Moscow, about how her father had been an official artist, employed by the Soviet state, about how she had ended up in London, and about her wilful naivete in not asking her boyfriend, Kolya, the man in the sketches, why he'd come to London. She spoke of Kolya's boss, Vladimir Nemirovsky, some kind of Russian *mafiya* godfather: it was a name that Hugh recalled from his conversations with Virgo.

When she asked Hugh about his ex-wife, Rebecca, he clammed up at first. When she pressed him, he spoke haltingly, the words snagging on the guilt he still felt. He told her how the marriage had unravelled, how he'd risked pulling his wife down into a mire of debt and criminality with him, how he'd become detached, even cold towards the end, partly to protect her. 'And worst of all,' he said, 'I was too proud, too bloody-minded to say *sorry*.'

Ana shrugged. 'People say sorry all the time, even when they don't mean it – *especially* when they don't mean it.' She put her coffee cup down, her pale-blue eyes settling on Hugh's. 'Kolya never said sorry to anyone. At least he was honest in that way.'

Neither of them were minded to dwell on the past – not that morning, at any rate. Walking back towards Chalk Farm Station, Ana seemed taken by the mottled terraces of townhouses, all a different pastel shade, with Doric porticos and stuccoed balconies, each varying slightly from its neighbour. When they stopped to look in the window of an estate agents' at the end of one block, she did a double-take at the prices. 'They are not *that* pretty,' she said, walking on, and leaving Hugh smiling at his own reflection in the window.

They took the Tube to Old Street and walked the rest of the way to the gallery. It was almost midday when they got there, but after the previous day, Hugh had been in no hurry to open up. Ana went upstairs to the studio, while Hugh sat at the desk in reception and switched on his laptop. His plan for the afternoon was to send off more content to the gallery's web designers: images and whatever biographical and critical blurbs he'd managed to write about the bogus artists they were exhibiting.

The photograph he had open on the screen was one of two hundred he'd taken on a large-format digital camera over the course of an afternoon in Highgate Cemetery a couple of weeks back. He'd whittled the images down to twenty, which he'd initially planned to print in editions of three but had since increased to five, given the demand. He was pricing them at fifteen grand each, adding up to one point five million for the full set.

He was hoping his essay about the work would be even more exhausting to read than it had been to write: 'The artist's latest corpus is testament to her commanding grasp of the history of Western art, stretching from the classical tradition, through the modern and the postmodern. An image of a gravestone wrapped in briar and ivy and lit by an ethereal shaft of light from the tree canopy above, elevates the scene from the mundane to the transmundane, conjuring the elliptical conceit of the German Romantic tradition – in particular the work of Caspar David Friedrich, with its mournful subtext of mortality and decay. Yet the work also appropriates the Duchampian notion of the ready-made and the structurally complex polymaterialism of relational art.'

And so it went on. He mulled over slipping in a spot prize halfway through for any reader intrepid enough to make it that far, like a voucher, say, for a complimentary frontal lobotomy.

It came as something of a relief – however short-lived – when the buzzer sounded.

He glanced at the security monitor and rolled his eyes. Standing at the main entrance were two strays from the Bloomsbury Arts Club. Hugh couldn't put names to the faces but he'd met them there once in the bar, with Felix Lazaar. Even before that, he'd known them as part of the rabble of artists, poets and boho drunkards that he regularly took *off* his invitation list but who still showed up at gallery openings after word got round one of the arts-club bars of that night's free piss-up. No matter how many times they were uninvited, one of them would always make it back onto the mailing list, even if it meant signing the visitors' book under an alias. He'd never been able to shake them off. They would always come back. Like cockroaches.

And here they were again, trying their luck with a new gallery. The shorter one, nearest the door, was combing his hair over a bald patch and looking reproachfully at the camera, no doubt indignant at having to wait for admission. He always did the talking and stood a foot or so in front of the other, who was a couple of inches taller, with thick tortoise-shell glasses and a matted beard. This one rarely spoke, and only ever as a stammering riposte to one of his chum's gambits. Hugh was never sure if they were a couple or not. It really wasn't something that bore thinking about.

Hugh buzzed the door open and turned glumly to face them as they made their way across the lobby. The shorter one led the way. He wore a racing-green wax jacket and a paisley scarf. The oil in his hair looked natural, not from a jar. His stopped in front of the desk, brow furrowed, a pinkie resting on his lower lip. 'Henry, isn't it?' he asked.

'Hugh. The name is Hugh.'

'Ah yes, pal of Felix Lazaar's. Used to run the White Head Gallery, didn't you.'

'*Lead*. The *Lead* White Gallery.'

'Yes, of course, The White Lead Gallery.' He surveyed the lobby, craning to peer into the gallery. 'Hiding under a bushel in Shoreditch, aren't we? But of course, the overheads in the West End must have been a terrible burden for you. Still, moving east brings you a tad closer to the *old sod*.' He made a feeble stab at a brogue Irish accent.

Hugh smiled thinly and looked back at his computer screen

'And to be fair,' Oily continued, raising his voice to regain Hugh's attention, 'you won't have to cast a line very far from here to catch the big fish.'

It didn't feel like fishing, Hugh could have said, more like cage-diving with sharks – or orcas – but he held his council.

Oily persisted. 'I'd be grateful if you'd add us to your invitation list *again*. We seem to have been excised, become *personae non gratae*?'

'Not at all,' Hugh said wearily. 'Must be a computer error.'

Oily then produced a card: *Turtle Stanhope – Fine Artist, Poet, Critic*. 'Perhaps you might vouchsafe this card to one of your assistants. Assuming, of course, you don't do your own data-entry.' A chapped upper lip curled to one side, revealing tobacco-stained teeth.

Hugh took the card and frowned. 'Well, enjoy the exhibition.' He turned to the screen again, but Turtle and his chum didn't move. Sighing, Hugh looked up. 'Yes?'

Turtle was rummaging in a leather man-bag. He pulled out two books. 'I thought I might leave our latest offerings with you – for your perusal. I've just published a book of my poetry, illustrated with some of my own paintings. I've also written the catalogue essay for Matty's latest body of work.' Matty leaned around Turtle and gave a gap-toothed grin, followed by a sharp nod and a pant.

Turtle placed the books on the desk in front of Hugh. 'As it happens, we're considering venues for a joint-exhibition at the minute. Not sure if it's something you might be interested in?'

Hugh shrugged. 'Our programme's full-up, I'm afraid.'

Turtle came over all lofty again, and flapped a hand about him. 'Not sure your gallery's the right fit for us, anyhow.'

Hugh didn't indulge him by asking why.

When, finally, they turned and made for the gallery, Hugh's gaze settled on the books, before he picked them up and leafed through each in turn. The poetry wasn't so bad: Hugh was among that rarefied group of people who actually bought and read poetry collections, and he'd come across far worse. He'd always felt a certain sympathy for the lot of the poet – all but a tiny elite were condemned to chronic penury, unless they had another source of income. Like so many artists, they needed an outsized ego to sustain their motivation to produce new work. Certainly, their sense of self-worth was rarely matched by their net worth.

He put down the poetry collection and picked up the catalogue, skimming over Turtle's essay. Again, it wasn't too bad. At least he could string a sentence together.

Then he looked at the laptop screen and a thought he'd had earlier recurred: he needed to delegate the job of writing essays about the work they were showing. It would give an air of authenticity. Collectors were always reassured by dense reams of text about a show, ideally not written by the artist or dealer. They hardly ever read it, of course; they just liked to know it was there.

He flexed Turtle's card between thumb and forefinger, held it up to his nose, wincing at the dull odour of tobacco. He looked again at the embossed gold inscription: *Fine Artist, Poet, CRITIC*.

Turtle may be a pompous twat, Hugh reasoned, but he was a *verbose* pompous twat – the kind who could write ten thousand words about the inside of a golf ball. Just the skillset for the job he had in mind.

Hugh's deliberations were cut short by Turtle, who sashayed out of the gallery, trailed by Matty and a more acrid stench of tobacco. 'Unusual work,' he said. 'Haven't heard of the artist. Which is, of course, why I liked your old gallery as well. No stellar names, but you do unearth these rough diamonds that so many gallerists would pass over.'

'Glad to hear it,' Hugh said, hesitating before adding, 'As it happens, I need an essay written for our next show. Not sure if it's your kind of work?'

Hugh regretted the idea even as he broached it, but Turtle's face had already lit up, eyes bulging, cheeks flushing. Then he came over all coquettish. 'Would there be a . . . *pour boire*?'

'Sorry?'

'An honorarium.'

'I'm not following you.'

'Would one's palm be crossed with silver?'

Hugh shook his head, smiling blankly.

Turtle spoke slowly this time, carefully mouthing each syllable: 'WOULD YOU BE PAYING ME?'

'Not if you write the way you speak.'

'I beg your pardon?'

'*One jests*. Yes, of course, there'll be a fee. Twenty-five pence a word. I'll leave the content up to you. Unintelligible is fine, just don't get too lyrical. Poets don't buy art. They can't afford it.'

CHAPTER 31

A Vodka Tonic and a Babycham

Felix Lazaar walked into the basement bar of the Bloomsbury Arts Club. He'd been laying low in Tangiers for a couple of months. Moved his base of operations there. Found himself a villa – charming Moorish stylings. And a housegirl, Samira – very biddable.

He was back in London for a fortnight, hoping to close out a couple of deals before he beat a retreat back to the Maghreb. Staying at the Bloomsbury made sense. The rooms were cheap for members and the food in the club restaurant was passable, at the price.

And as for the bar, it was like a home from home. Back in the eighties, someone had decided on a whim to give it a half-arsed Moorish theme. They'd put a lattice screen either side of the entrance, with some black wrought iron above it. They'd also hung a wooden Arabesque relief behind the bar and sectioned off a couple of snugs with coloured-glass blocks. That was it, though. There were no other adornments to the roughly plastered white walls, apart from some pencil sketches of the club's more illustrious former members – a president of the Royal Academy on one wall, a portraitist of the Queen on another. To be fair, the low-vaulted ceiling didn't leave much wall-space.

Most of the banquet seating around the perimeter was empty. At the bar, the same artists – piss artists one and all – sat at the same stools. 'Not that I have any interest in money, of course,' one of them spouted.

'So if you won the Lottery, you'd give it all away?' another asked.

'Dear man, I'd keep making art until the money ran out.'

The punchline was met by jaded laughter.

That windbag Turtle Stanhope sat on the far side of bar with his sidekick, Mikey or Markey or Matty, holding forth about how overrated Lucian Freud was. 'Personally, I find the work clunky, laboured, always reaching for a likeness but never quite getting one. Not wishing to blow my own trumpet,' he intoned, before removing it from its case – buffed and polished – and launching into an overture of self-aggrandisement, 'but my own portraiture eschews physical likeness as an outmoded convention of the genre and strives instead to depict the quintessence of the subject – the very marrow, if you will.' He paused to drain his glass and suck the last tincture of vodka from a lemon slice, before adding, 'Mere representation – to paint with the artistic sensibility of a Polaroid – would be a death for me.'

Felix winked at the barman – 'G&T, old man' – and slipped into one of the snugs, screened by a wall of green and red glass blocks.

As he settled into his chair, Turtle bellowed from across the bar. 'Good lord, if it isn't Felix Lazaar. Back from the dead. Felix *Lazaar–us.*' He guffawed loudly at his own joke. 'No, but seriously, I was just saying the other day, that Lazaar chap, vanished he has, like Lord bloody Lucan.'

'Like Lord Lucan,' the bearded chap chimed in, with an effete warble. '*Vamoooshed.*'

Turtle slid off his stool and flounced past his companion, the stride too long for his short legs. He made straight for Lazaar's table. Other drinkers looked around to see what the fuss was about. Felix nodded at them, his cover blown.

Turtle sat on the low stool opposite him, the chum idling behind.

'What've we been up to, old boy?'

'Oh, this and that. Irons in the fire, pots on the boil. You know the way.' The tone was guarded.

'Been away, though, haven't we? That red nose of yours not just from the gin.'

'Tangiers. Moved the old GHQ there. Damned if I could face another winter in England.' The barman set Lazaar's gin down on the table and glanced at Turtle, who, true to form, had sniffed out a free drink. 'Don't mind if I do,' he said. 'A vodka tonic, and another

Babycham for Matty while you're at it.' Felix rolled his eyes and nodded his assent to the barman.

'Of course, I don't blame you,' Turtle said, turning back to Felix. 'That old bugger Jack Frost does outstay his welcome. I winter in sunnier climes myself. Divide my time between London and Tuscany. Friend there has a villa he lets me use.'

'Good for you,' Lazaar said, reaching for an abandoned copy of the *Telegraph* on the next table.

'Been keeping myself busy, of course,' Turtle said, raising his voice, leaning into Lazaar. 'Just got a major commission the other day to write a catalogue essay for an old mucker of yours, Hugh Rhattigan. Has a new gallery – in Shoreditch, of all places.'

'Is that so?' Lazaar said, putting down the newspaper, interested now but trying not to show it. 'Still exhibiting the same work, is he?'

'Not that I could see. Seems to have turned up a bevy of new artists. Sellers, by the looks of it.'

That piqued Lazaar's interest even more: there were no sellers without buyers, and Felix Lazaar was on the hunt for some new clients. He wangled an address for the gallery, then looked at his watch. 'Good lord, is that the time?'

Knocking back the G&T, he bade farewell to Turtle and Matty.

As the barman ordered him a taxi on his club account, Felix could still make out Turtle's voice. 'Nice chap, Lazaar. Good sport. Does bang on a little, though, and, of course, he doesn't know his art from his elbow. It's all business to him. Might as well be selling . . . oh, I don't know . . . hot-tubs.'

Lucy White

CHAPTER 32

Serpentine

Kolya was double-parked across the street from the Bloomsbury. A Bentley swept up behind him, beeping, headlights flashing. He stuck out a hand, signalling to go around. When the driver finally got the message and overtook, Kolya eyeballed him, gave him the finger – 'Fuck you, limpdick' – then almost smiled. It'd taken a while, but his English was coming along nicely.

He fixed his eyes back on the heavy, dark-wood doors of the club. The porter had called him that morning to say his *cousin*, Felix Lazaar, was back in town. Four more crisp fifty-pound notes, peeled from a wedge Kolya made sure to let the porter see, had kept him keen. He'd just got another text to say Lazaar was in the club's basement bar. Kolya tossed the phone onto the passenger seat of the car – one of Vlad's armoured BMW X5s – and wrapped his torso around the steering wheel. He reached over the dash, flexing his back and shoulder muscles. He'd waited this long, he figured, he could let the old shyster enjoy one last drink.

He was half listening to the radio. There was some mad shit on the news about another paint-bomb, in the Serpentine it sounded like, that oh-so-fucking-hip gallery in the park. As far as he could make out, the nut-jobs who'd done it weren't motivated by money, but by principle – something Kolya did his best not to sweat over.

He'd dropped Vlad off there once, at the Serpentine, for an opening, had a quick scout around – not his scene – then stood outside for a smoke. He didn't tell Ana where he'd been; she might have liked to have gone along too.

It was coming near the end around that time. When he got made, Vlad told him to ditch her, gave him a business card to pass on of a woman who could find her work in the *hospitality* industry. 'No need for a work permit,' Vlad had told him.

Stupidly, Kolya didn't ask at the time exactly what type of hospitality his boss had in mind – Vlad just said it was 'working in hotels and shit like that, all high-class'. Kolya only found out afterwards, when the same woman, Melanie, laid on some complimentary tail for Vlad and his cronies after a Chelsea game. It was his own fault, but he still had a pop at Vlad over it. 'You never told me your contact was queen fucking bee at an escort agency.'

'You didn't ask,' Vlad said, 'and anyhow, I figured you might like to keep in touch with her, this *Anastasia*, in a professional capacity.'

Vlad leered. Kolya scowled, but said nothing – he'd seen Vlad cap a man over a lot less. Luckily enough, though, he'd caught his boss on a good day. Chelsea had put five past Fulham and Vlad had just Greeked some tight-assed novice – what a first night on the job that must've been – probably bringing back fond memories of his time in the clink.

Sprawled on a couch afterwards, in his Armani jocks and vest, he did his *reasonable* psychotic-maniac routine. 'Look kid, the bitch had to go. She was a fine piece of pussy but I didn't want her knowing my shit and, anyhow, it's not such a bad business to be in. You have it, you sell it, you still have it. Sounds OK to me.'

This last part was addressed to his fuckwit cronies, who laughed their fuckwit laughs.

They all deferred to Vlad, respected him. What gave him the edge was not cunning or physical prowess, but meanness. If you're the meanest bastard in the room, no one can take their eyes off you – or, more precisely, no one can risk taking their eyes off you. It was like he gave off waves of static. Spines tingled, flesh goosebumped when he walked in a room. Throw in Vlad's hair-trigger temper for that extra dash of charisma and you're a bona fide rock star among scumbags.

It was the meanness, though, that truly defined him. It wasn't the kind of thing you put on a CV but it seemed to Kolya it was the key to getting what you wanted from life – crook or straight, the distinction was less and less real. The Romanovs, the Soviets, the Whites, the Reds, the New Russians, the *vor*: all were driven by greed and self-preservation; all were sustained by meanness.

Take the New Russians. They got rich by ripping off *sovoks – homo soveticus* – like Kolya's father, who got a voucher to buy shares in the nickel mining company he'd spent twenty years working in. The old man traded in the voucher for a microwave oven in one of the shops set up by the oligarch who eventually took over the company. Kolya heard later that the voucher was probably worth ten thousand dollars.

New Russians, same old shit.

This oligarch was one of Vlad's new chums, one of the people he'd been collecting art to cosy up to – the reason Kolya was stalking a bent art dealer and his pet forger.

He looked back at the doors of the club just as his phone chirped with a new message. He picked it up – 'Laz just leaving now' – then glanced across the street in time to see Lazaar scuttling through the doors, down the steps and into the back of a minicab that had pulled up outside.

Fuck it. Kolya swung into a three-point turn, scowled at the drivers who honked at him. Turning took longer than it should have; the armoured X5 handled like a tank. He had to gun through a red light to catch up with the cab.

The cabbie took a rat-run across the city. Kolya broke a few more lights just to keep up. Twenty minutes later, the cab pulled in by a stone archway, set into a terrace of old buildings – in Shoreditch, Kolya reckoned, half a mile or so from Liverpool Street Station. Lazaar hopped out of the cab, paid the driver, glanced left, right, then craned his neck up and down the building, looking for a sign maybe, or a house number. He flattened down his mullet of grey-blonde hair, patted the lapels of his blazer and scurried under the arch.

Kolya pulled up on the kerb opposite, flicked on the emergency lights and hopped out. He crossed the street, slipped under the arch and stuck his head around the corner into a courtyard, just in time to see Lazaar push open a door under a sign saying 'LW2', and below that another sign saying 'Gallery'. He checked for any other exits. There were none that he could see. He made his way back to the Beamer and climbed into the driver's seat. Sighing, he rubbed a hand over his tightly cropped hair.

Another fucking stakeout: this was getting tedious. But he didn't put on the radio this time. No more distractions.

It was all quiet for five minutes. Then there was movement in the archway. Kolya groaned and buried his face in his hands when he saw who it was: one of Douglas Virgo's toadies, Pavel something or other, a Petersburg face, used to run with the Tambov Gang there till the FSB came down heavy and they scattered like startled rats.

Parting his fingers, Kolya saw Pavel pull a hood over his head, slip an envelope into an inside pocket and head back towards Shoreditch High Street. Kolya's eyes trailed him for a bit, then turned back to the archway.

This wasn't good. He'd met Pavel once, skulking in the background when he'd arranged a meet with Virgo and his crew in a failed attempt to open a diplomatic channel. Vlad was pissing off the local chamber of illicit commerce by expanding too aggressively onto their turf. Kolya could see trouble coming so he took the initiative, without telling Vlad, weighing up his boss's wrath against the likelihood of getting wasted anyway when things got truly medieval. It was also a way of introducing himself, letting them know he was someone they could do business with, if anything were ever to *happen* to Vlad.

It didn't go well. 'Vlad the Inhaler's wing-man,' he was introduced as.

'Nemirovsky is Russian,' Kolya told them. 'Vlad the Impaler was Transylvanian prince.'

'Same difference,' Harry Sykes said. 'You're all fuckin turnip-munching Bolshies.'

It was far from an enlightened cultural exchange. The most Kolya took away from it at the time was that Virgo didn't say much, just watched him, really watched him, eyes boring into his. They had that much in common at least: the watching, forever fucking watching.

There was no more action across the street. Getting edgy, Kolya took a 9mm Beretta out of the glove compartment, lifted up his jacket at the back and stuck it under his belt. He grabbed some plastic ring-ties as well, and shoved them in his pocket.

Then he watched and waited, but not for long. His eyes were drawn to a fit midriff in the passenger wing-mirror, a chest bulging out of a tight denim jacket over a pair of swaying hips that made their way along the pavement before crossing the street behind the Beamer. He turned to check out the rest of her and felt a heaving in his stomach. By the time she stepped onto the pavement and went under the arch, his heart was pounding, like the bolt of an AK on automatic.

It was Ana.

Pavel was bad. This was worse. He had no real reason for believing it, but he was gripped by a nasty feeling that Ana was involved in selling Vlad the fakes. If nothing else, it was a way of getting even.

The worst of it was, she was *still* such 'a fine piece of pussy'.

To use his rat-bag boss's turn of phrase.

CHAPTER 33

A Devious Upgrade

Felix Lazaar pressed on the intercom and took a step back, glancing over his shoulder to make sure no one was following him – force of habit by now – then at the security camera perched above the door. After ten seconds or so, the lock gave a static buzz. He pushed on the door and walked into a reception area. It was big, bright, well appointed. His nose twitched at the scent of money.

He did a double-take when he saw Jack Hastings sitting behind a rather smart *Art Nouveau* desk. Lazaar thumbed through the ledger in his head and pasted a smile on his face, having reassured himself that Jack wasn't on his chronically long list of creditors. 'Of all the art joints in all the world,' he said, with a tad too much *bonhomie*.

Jack was cagey by nature but this time he seemed almost fearful. 'Felix, what . . . ? I mean, how?'

'Just happened to be in the neighbourhood, so I thought I might survey the local galleries. You know me, like to keep abreast of the latest trends.' He clasped his hands together, fixed his eyes on Jack's. 'But tell me about you? Hugh Rhattigan finally found a use for your very particular skill-set, did he?'

Lazaar kept smiling, but inside he was seething that Rhattigan hadn't cut him in. After all, it was him, Felix Lazaar, who'd groomed Jack in the dark art of forgery.

Jack shifted uneasily in his chair. 'Look, Felix, I'm just helping out here on a casual basis. All above board. I *was* relying on you for work, but then you dropped off the face of the earth – again.'

195

'My work has always taken me overseas, Jack, but I concede it's been a while. Truth be told, I've been operating out of Tangiers these past few months.' Lazaar steepled his fingers, rested them on his chin, then pointed them at Jack. 'In fact, now that we've run into each other, you should think about coming down. I've got acres of space. Could set you up in a studio. Wonderful light there, this time of year.'

Lazaar perched on the edge of the desk. 'You wouldn't be the first, either. Lots of artists have sojourned there. Delacroix beat a path. Then, of course, Matisse set up studio at the Grand Hotel Villa de France.' Lazaar winked. 'Might offer inspiration to a man of your talents.'

Jack frowned, looked sceptical.

'If they proved a little too much to live up to,' Lazaar added reassuringly, 'Richard Diebenkorn's Matisse-inspired Moroccan work might be worth exploring. If nothing else, old man, you'll enjoy the general *haute volée* down there. It's a thriving but select little ex-pat scene.'

Jack shrugged and looked back at the screen he'd been reading from. 'Got commitments here at the moment, thanks all the same.'

'Can see that.' Lazaar paused, tugged on the lapels of his blazer, feeling peeved again. 'About at all, is he, your *new* boss?'

'Upstairs, on the phone,' Jack said, pointing at the ceiling.

Lazaar looked up, then at the stairwell, before leaning over the desk, trying his best to seem *blasé*. 'See you have one of those iPad-ma-jigs. Been thinking I should get up to speed on all that interweb malarkey.' He looked at the screen. 'Ah, reading about the Serpentine.'

'Trying to,' Jack said, tersely.

'No harm done, if you ask me. Bloody giftshop with a gallery stuck on the side.'

Jack groaned and pressed a button on the side of the screen that made it go blank. 'I'll go and get Hugh then, will I?'

As Jack spoke, a man about the same age as him came slinking down the stairs with a brown envelope in his hand. Lazaar was sure he recognised him from somewhere, the way he moved – with the grace and cunning of a stoat. The man glanced at Jack, offering only a curt nod.

Jack sat upright and pouted a little when he walked by. Lazaar tracked him too as he made his way to the exit.

Then Lazaar looked at Jack again, while his eyes were still trailing stoat-face. When Jack turned back to Lazaar, he seemed defensive. 'What?' he said, with a bashful tilt of the head.

'Do I know him?' Lazaar said.

Jack tutted, put the tips of his fingers to his temples. 'Em, give me a second . . . it's coming . . . ' Then he sighed, dropping his hands. 'How should I know? What is this? Maybe you're looking for the dementia clinic down the street? That would explain a lot.'

'Not sure I like your tone, young man,' Lazaar said haughtily.

Jack threw his hands in the air. 'How can you just disappear like that, leaving me in the lurch, wondering if it's the Fraud Squad I'll be hearing from next, instead of you?'

'Like I said, my business takes me overseas.'

Jack sighed. 'You should really just go, Felix. This isn't your scene.'

'I keep an open mind, and so should you.' Lazaar stood up. 'Look, I'll just have a quick word with Hugh, then I'll be off.'

'Unbelievable,' Jack grumbled, as he came out from behind the desk. He pointed at the floor in front of Lazaar. 'Stay there.'

Left alone in the reception area, Lazaar clucked, then whistled a few bars of *Für Elise* to himself as he peeked into the gallery. He wrinkled his nose at the work, mumbled, 'Dear me, some people will buy any old tat', and turned to look at the desk again. It was super-smart, nicest thing there, definitely *Art Nouveau* – not unlike one he'd bought for Douglas Virgo about five years back. In fact, it *was* the one he'd bought for Virgo. He could tell by the gilt-bronze mounts he'd had commissioned to pass the desk off as a Louis Majorelle. A devious upgrade, but Virgo had been none the wiser.

'That's odd,' he thought.

Then a chill came over him when he remembered where he'd seen stoat-face before: he was one of Virgo's rent-a-thugs. He'd stood on the fringes, cracking his knuckles, tweaking his crotch, when Virgo issued his ultimatum to Lazaar to pay up what he owed him. That was a few years back. He'd been avoiding Virgo and his lowlife henchmen ever since.

Lazaar decided it might be prudent to weigh anchor. He glanced up the stairs. No sign of Jack or Hugh, so he made for the exit. As he did so, an attractive young lady, clad in denim, was coming in. She smiled, held

197

the door open for him. 'Please, after you,' she said. The Russian accent set his nerves on edge even more.

He walked out onto the street, heading back towards the City, cursing the waste of a taxi fare. The path took him under a railway bridge with 'Scary' written along one wall in angular black and white letters. He veered out towards the kerb, muttering 'Bloody vandals', and picked up his pace. It was then that a big black SUV lurched up on the pavement in front of him. The edge of the bumper on the passenger side raked along the wall. Lazaar tried an about-turn but a young man, far more agile than him, had jumped out of the driver's side and come around behind.

'We can do this easy way or I can crack some of your *reebs*,' the man said, almost casually. He opened the passenger door. 'Get in.'

Lazaar did as he was told. The man shut the door and snapped on the central-locking. Lazaar fumbled with the door-lock but couldn't figure out how it opened. It was no use in any case: the man unlocked the doors and climbed into the driver's seat. He frowned when he saw Felix clutching at the lock, then shook his head gently, rolling his steely-blue eyes, his tongue wedged in a scarred left cheek. He looked like he had little appetite for the job.

'Put your hands like this,' he said, holding his wrists together.

'Look,' Felix said. 'I can explain everything to Mr Virgo. I've been let down by people I placed my trust in as well.'

The man shook his head, more firmly this time, and sighed. 'I don't work for Douglas *Veergo*. I work for Vladimir Nemirovsky.'

Lazaar felt the blood draining from his cheeks, a tightness in his chest, a tremor in his bowels. The man bound his wrists in plastic ring-ties, did the same with his ankles.

Ever resourceful, though, Felix Lazaar gathered himself. 'Well, that is a relief,' he said, with a gusty sigh. 'Douglas Virgo and *his associates* will have Mr Nemirovsky and me to answer to now.'

CHAPTER 34

The Clicking Stops

Hugh held a hand on the window-pane, fingers drumming. He gazed out at a black BMW parked up on the kerb across the street, then turned back to a room steadily filling with *manufactured* artworks. He was on the phone to Thea Cappellini, an Italian art consultant calling on behalf of a big-ticket Chinese collector.

She was about to take the bait.

'The work is whispering "Maurizio" to me,' she purred.

'Yeah, for sure,' Hugh said, 'you can see the influence of Maurizio Cattelan, but I think the artist's vision is ultimately her own.'

'You're right. It's A-plus, A-plus. Can feel it now. Put me down for the five.'

'Will do,' Hugh said.

'And give my love to Roberto. He will be calling in again soon, won't he?'

'Robert Orca is his own man, Thea, I think we both know that. But he has thrown his ample weight behind the gallery.'

'Great, great, darling. I'm sold. I *believe*. Will wait to hear. *Ciao.*'

Cappellini hung up. She'd just bought five of Hugh's stuffed animals – each with their own glibly ironic twist – for a grand total of two hundred and fifty grand. He'd have to get back on to his taxidermist.

He looked uneasily towards the stairwell. He'd been loathe to leave Jack in charge of the gallery after last time, but the phone had been ringing off the hook. He also had other business to attend to. Pavel was prowling in front of him, there to pick up an envelope with a bundle of cheques in it.

'Hang on,' Hugh said, as the phone rang again.

He answered to a man's voice. 'Great, yeah, I'm looking for Hugh Rhattigan?'

'Speaking.'

'Fielding your own calls. Hands-on. Sweet.' The man spoke briskly, with a touch of mockney. 'How's tricks? All good, I 'ope.'

'All good. Who is this?'

'Jamie Holloway, from Fresco. We've met.'

Fresco was the art-fair that colonised a corner of Regent's Park for four days every October. In just ten years, it had established itself as a fixture in the diaries of the jet-setting plutocrats who fuel the high end of the art market. Galleries from all over the world clamoured to get in.

Hugh was surprised by the call all the same. The fair was opening in six days' time, and he certainly hadn't applied. His old gallery had been rejected four years in a row. Maybe Holloway was phoning to say LW2 wouldn't have got in anyway.

'Listen, we've always been big fans of the work you show.' Holloway sounded remote now, like he'd put Hugh on speaker-phone. 'It's just unfortunate there hasn't been room for you in the fair. We've been five, six times oversubscribed, so some really top galleries get left out. But as it happens, this year, a gallery from Athens we offered a booth to hasn't come up with the funds. Very sad, the whole Greek situation.'

'I'm sure the Greeks would be touched by your concern.'

'Yeah,' Holloway said, unfazed by the sarcasm. 'Anyhow, Hugh, the show must go on, and it is *the* show – not that you'll need reminding. Let's talk about your latest venture. We've been hearing good things. Robert Orca called us, made a very strong pitch for your inclusion.'

'Well that was . . . *kind* of him.'

'Not sure "kind" is the word. "Astute", maybe. We have tremendous respect for his opinion. Hence my call. We'd like to offer you the vacant booth. It's four hundred square feet, in a nice spot too, near the VIP lounge. Now, it *will* be full price; we don't negotiate on booth charges. With a waiting list as long as ours, we don't nee to. But how about we throw in a few extra invites for the champagne private view?'

After four straight years of rejection, Hugh should have snatched at the offer, but he suspected Holloway wanted LW2 in his fair more than he let on. The absence of Orca's new pet gallery would be a grievous sin of omission.

As Hugh mulled it over, a pen clicked at the end of the line.

'Sorry, Jamie,' he said, 'I'll have to put you on hold.' He put the phone down on the windowsill, said 'Wait there' to Pavel, and walked up the stairs to the studio to get the envelope with the cheques in it. He made his way back down, ambling this time, handed the envelope to Pavel and gave him an off-you-go nod.

He picked the phone up off the windowsill and noticed the BMW again, hitched up on the kerb across the street. There was a man sitting in the driver's seat. When he held the phone to his ear, the pen was still clicking. 'Jamie,' he said, 'this is all very short notice, and I'll be honest, we're looking at doing some other fairs, not to mention the museum collaborations we have pencilled in. But what can I say? I don't want to let you down either.'

There was silence for a moment, save for the clicking. 'I appreciate that,' Holloway said.

'I suppose if you cut us a deal, we might consider it.'

The clicking stopped. Fresco didn't entertain haggling. They didn't need to. Holloway stalled, then said, 'Well, I suppose we could shave off 5 percent, in view of the short notice.'

'I think 25 would be fair, given you have an empty booth to fill.'

'I have five hundred rejected galleries to cherry-pick from,' Holloway said, getting tetchy.

'Off you go, then.' Hugh stared across the street and tried to make out the face of the man in the BMW. The glass was tinted, but the driver's window was half-open.

'Listen, Hugh, let's not fall out over this. I want you on board, and so do the selection committee. How about 15 percent?'

'Twenty-five,' Hugh said again.

Holloway sighed. 'Christ, hold a gun to my head, why don't you?'

'I don't own a gun,' Hugh said. 'But I might have to consider getting one.' He watched the man in the BMW reach into the glove compartment, lift up his jacket at the back and shove what looked like a pistol under his belt.

'Right, whatever,' Holloway said, grudgingly, 'twenty-five it is, then. I'll get the contracts couriered over.'

Hugh hung up without another word, still gazing out onto the street. He saw Ana walk along the pavement on the far side and cross behind the BMW. Then he turned to see Jack standing in the middle of the room, looking agitated. 'You'll never guess who's downstairs,' he said.

Hugh strode past him. 'Tell me on the way down.'

They met Ana in the downstairs lobby but there was no sign of Lazaar. She looked at Jack, then at Hugh, a little perplexed. 'Everything is OK?'

'Fine,' Hugh said. 'Maybe go on up to the studio. We'll be up in a minute. I'm calling a staff meeting: we have a busy few days ahead of us.'

Hugh walked out the door, under the arch and onto the street. The BMW was receding out of view, towards the railway bridge.

When he turned, Jack was behind him again. 'I didn't tell Lazaar anything,' he said, 'Scout's honour.'

'I know,' Hugh said, ushering him back into the courtyard. He ran a hand through his hair, gazing through Jack, his mind ticking over. 'We're missing something here. There was a man parked across the street in a BMW. Don't think it was one of Virgo's boneheads – didn't recognise the car, anyway. I couldn't make out his face but I'm pretty sure he had a piece on him.'

Jack gave him a sideways look. 'What, some sculpture?'

Hugh rolled his eyes. 'No, a *gun*. I saw him take it out of the dash.'

'A gun? Shit.'

'We need to be careful. It's not just Lazaar, or the goon with the gun, but why has Robert Orca *really* taken such a keen interest in the gallery? You know he's lined up a booth for us at Fresco?'

'Maybe he just likes my . . . *the* . . . whatever . . . work,' Jack said.

Hugh shrugged, unconvinced. 'Yeah, sure, that must be it.'

By the time they'd climbed the stairs to the studio, Ana had her artist's apron on and was about to start work on a large canvas.

'So Ana,' Hugh said, sheepishly. 'I've just been telling Jack about Fresco. They've offered us a booth, and I accepted. A little rash, maybe.'

'Isn't the opening on Thursday?'

'Yeah,' Hugh said. 'Doesn't leave much time, does it? Especially given most of the finished work we have is already vouched for.'

As he spoke, though, a plan was germinating in his mind. 'Here's what we could do. I've ordered a batch of neon signs; I could get the delivery speeded up. And you know I mentioned getting high-res images of those Old Master paintings: how are we doing with that?'

'Got most of them,' Jack said.

'Good, we'll need to get them blown up and printed onto canvases. If we do it digitally, we should have them back in a couple of days. I want you to varnish them and age them as best you can. We'll need exact measurements for the canvases by this evening to give to the framer. That should leave us enough time to wire up the signs and mount them over the pictures.'

Jack caught Ana's eye, then turned back to Hugh. 'Christ, it's getting more and more like the A-Team around here – one of those scenes where they lock themselves in a barn and emerge three hours later in a tank made from oil-drums and some old lead pipe. Except we're supposed to produce an exhibition's worth of new artworks. Can't you at least tell us what it is we're making?'

Hugh turned to the window. 'What, and ruin the surprise?'

He gazed down onto the street, at the spot where the BMW had parked. He'd done his best to sound casual, but his temples pulsed and his fists were clenched, the nails scoring his palms.

CHAPTER 35

Crouch, Touch, Pause, Engage

Hugh was tense, strung out, even before the Russians showed up at the gallery.

He'd woken up early from a shallow sleep, with a sense of unease welling up from the pit of his stomach. Ana had spent the night at his place again, but he hadn't told her about the man in the BMW with the gun who he'd seen the day before. It seemed obvious in hindsight that the man had been watching the gallery. First came the reconnaissance, then the infantry.

They looked like the buffed-up bodyguards he'd seen before at exhibition openings, mostly flanking wealthy Russians. They wore black suits, open-collared black shirts, earpieces and black trainers – the trainers in case they needed to chase down anyone rash enough to take a pop at their employers.

They slipped in behind Ana, on her way back with a cardboard tray of coffees from the café around the corner. They caught the door behind her before it clicked shut.

Hugh turned to the door and straightened his back when he saw them, a chill coursing through his veins. For starters, he knew that two men rarely looked around a gallery together, unless they were a couple – and this pair didn't look like love's young dream. One was about six foot, the other just under. The taller one was the more chiselled, lantern-jawed, with an aquiline nose that kinked to the left halfway down the bridge. He was missing part of an ear; the bottom half was a jagged stump of cartilage, the edges like a bite-mark.

The shorter one's nose was pummelled flat. He had bulbous lips and flushed, pockmarked cheeks. His lugubrious, melancholic eyes would take little pleasure in his work.

They looked at Hugh first, checking out his size and condition, then at Ana, before throwing each other a knowing glance. They spoke to her in Russian. Hugh picked out the word 'Nemirovsky'. When they turned to Hugh, the shorter one did the talking. 'Our boss, he want meet you.'

Hugh fixed his gaze on him. 'I don't do blind dates,' he said. 'Tell him there are websites for that sort of thing.'

The bravado was a little too self-conscious: the Russians just rolled their eyes. The taller one wandered into the gallery; the other scoped out the lobby.

Ana shook her head at Hugh, mouthing 'No'.

The shorter one stopped and turned, about two feet in front of him. 'I think you will coming with us now.' He nodded towards Ana. 'And she is artist, no? She will coming too.'

'We're not going anywhere,' Hugh said, then gestured towards the door. 'Now, if you wouldn't mind leaving before . . . '

The Russian cut him off. 'Before what? You will calling police.' He smiled at his sidekick.

Hugh glanced at Ana, his chest tightening, just as the shorter one lunged forward and drove a fist into his stomach. The impact made him stagger backwards, his head recoiling. The pain radiated through his midriff, up and down his spine. He folded over, his hands settling on his knees.

Looking up, he could see the suits exchange smirks. He breathed deeply. He was still bent over, but a wave of adrenalin soon numbed the pain, leaving only his wounded pride. He fixed his eyes on the one who'd punched him, then on the taller one.

Hugh had never looked for a fight in his adult life but every rugby player gets dragged into a brawl now and then. He'd spent twenty-five years playing as a lock – a second row in the scrum – at school first, then at Trinity College, Dublin, and over the past fifteen years for the London Irish Amateurs. He still had muscles in all the right places.

He sized up the Russians. Both had the classic physique of a prop – front row of the scrum, not as tall as the lock but broader, with a stout, muscular neck that sloped down to the shoulders, like the tendrils at the base of an oak tree. The front row has three players, with a Tighthead and a Loosehead prop at either side. The former's head is tucked inside and is usually the one with the mashed-up ears and, funnily enough, even the odd bite-mark.

The prop has a lower centre of gravity and is generally stockier, but the lock has a height advantage and a longer reach. Hugh had a good three or four inches on each of them, but he knew he'd have to get down low with the first one. At the very least, he had the element of surprise. The Russians wouldn't have expected an art dealer to put up much of a struggle.

He charged at Loosehead – the shorter one, who'd punched him – with his arms spread. The Russian crouched into a kind of martial-arts pose, then tried to sidestep and deflect Hugh with a fist to the side of the head, but Hugh's momentum took him through the blow. His shoulder crashed into the Russian's chest. He wrapped one arm around a squat neck, stuck the other between his legs, and slammed him into the wall. Then he twisted him past the horizontal and drove him down, head-first, in what is known as a spear tackle. It was a citable offence under International Rugby Board rules, likely to cause serious neck or head injuries, but Hugh was happy to take his chances with any disciplinary panel.

With his partner down, the other prop, Tighthead, the one with the mangled ear, grabbed Hugh by the shoulders and tried to drag him back. Hugh swung an elbow – another citable offence – and hammered it into Tighthead's temple. By this stage, Loosehead had clambered onto all fours. Hugh swung a foot at him but only clipped his forehead: unfortunately, locks are not noted for their kicking skills.

He was slightly off balance when Tighthead caught him again from behind, this time in a bear-grip. Hugh tried a reverse headbutt, twice, but each blow was parried. So, making use of his longer reach, he wedged a hand in between them, grabbed hold of his assailant's crotch and twisted: the modern lock is expected to have strong ball-handling skills. There was howl from behind that began at a tenor and rose almost to a falsetto before Hugh shook himself free.

As Tighthead reeled away, Ana threw her coffee in his face, picked up a laptop off the desk and cracked it over the side of his head.

It was then that Loosehead, back on his feet, sprayed something in Hugh's eyes – pepper spray, or ammonia maybe – before sinking another pile-driver fist into his solar plexus. This time it *really* hurt. Hugh folded over again but straight away turned his head up, squinting, eyes burning, as another fist hammered into the side of his head.

He collapsed on all fours.

He was struggling back to his feet when something cold and hard was pressed into the base of his skull, driving into the soft-flesh lacuna beneath the ear. 'Mr Nemirovsky wanted do *thees* himself but we can do it here now, if you liking.'

Hugh managed to peel one lid open, the light searing his eyes, and focus on the door. It was ajar. Ana was gone.

As Loosehead made for the door, going after her, Tighthead hauled Hugh up off the floor, with the gun barrel stuck into the nape of his neck. After a minute or so, he heard a car pull into the courtyard and park by the door. His eyes burned when he opened them, as if scalded by steam. He could see that the car was big and black, with tinted glass. A BMW, maybe?

They shoved him into the back seat and pulled a cloth sack over his head. Then the gun barrel was pressed into his ear. 'Put your wrists together,' one of them said. He did as he was told, while a plastic ring-tie was wrapped around the wrists and yanked tight, biting into flesh. 'Your girlfriend getting away,' the other said. 'We deal with her later.'

As they drove, the adrenalin abated and the pain intensified, but Hugh felt strangely calm, resigned even. He wondered whether Ana would try to contact Virgo, or even the police. And also why the Russian's had come after *him*? The obvious answer was that the gallery had been dragged into a turf war between Virgo and Nemirovsky.

But simmering away beneath his conjecture was the sense that this was a crisis of his own making – that he'd gone from being coerced into fronting a criminal racket to throwing himself into a life of crime with the gusto of a man who had finally found his calling. He thought of Rebecca's admonition to him that he couldn't make his own set of rules for living without breaking everyone else's. And of what she couldn't have realised at the time: there are different sets of rules for different sets of people, and that Hugh would end up breaking all of them.

After twenty minutes of self-flagellation, it was time for someone else to have a go. They took a sharp right turn and dropped down a ramp into an underground car-park, fast enough for Hugh to feel he'd left his stomach up on the street. They screeched to a stop. The driver jumped out first. The back door opened and a hand grabbed the top of the sack, along with a clump of hair, dragging Hugh out onto a concrete floor overlaid with a strip of red carpet. The gun prodded him, directing him into a lift. At the very least, his eyes were working again: he could see a hessian carpet and a smoked-glass fascia around the floor.

When the lift doors opened, the gun barrel was driven into his lower back, this time catching a vertebra, making him wince. He walked across a hallway, through a door and across an expanse of lush white carpet into a brightly lit room with a polished-marble floor. He was pushed into a chair with enough force that he barely regained his balance before toppling backwards.

The bag was pulled from his head.

CHAPTER 36

The Credit Crunch

Hugh blinked, his eyes adjusting to the light, still stinging from whatever had been sprayed in them. He squinted up at a ceiling dotted with recessed halogen lights.

The scene slowly came into focus. He was sitting in a chair, in a bathroom – an enormous one, as big as most people's living rooms. A stout, ruddy-faced man stood in front of him, shoulders rolling, hips swaying, like he was hearing music in his head. He was wearing the trousers and waistcoat of a Harris tweed three-piece.

The man arced his neck to the side till it cracked, then fixed his gaze on Hugh and snarled, his full, fleshy lips curling to one side. The eyes remained vacant, though, the pupils like lead shot.

He turned to the Props, who were standing behind him. They spoke in Russian but Hugh was sure he heard the words 'Anastasia Ivanova Zaitseva' before all three of them turned to the figure in the corner, by the door. Hugh turned as well: it was Kolya, easily recognisable from Ana's drawings. Kolya held Hugh's gaze and offered a barely perceptible shake of the head.

Hugh looked to his left, where Felix Lazaar sat in the chair next to him. 'Fancy meeting you here, old boy,' Lazaar said, a tremor in his voice. He was unshaven, his pelt of grey-blonde hair matted and straggly.

Hugh sighed, then looked around, still getting his bearings.

'I know, we're in a lavatory,' Lazaar said, babbling nervously. 'Lord knows why. I for one don't need to go. Truth be told, went in the boot of the car on the way here.'

209

Hugh glanced down at Lazaar's lap. A dark stain had spread from his crotch over the left hip of his olive slacks.

'What we talking 'bout?' the man in tweeds asked, turning back to them. He couldn't have looked any more ridiculous in a matching deer-stalker hat. 'Is private chitty-chat, or can anyone joining in?'

Lazaar waved his bound hands in front of him. 'Just saying, Vlad – I mean *Vladimir* – what a nice lavatory it is.'

'Is not fucking lavatory,' Vlad hissed, covering them in a mist of spittle. 'Is *wet-room*.' He pointed at the floor, the walls, 'Open eyes, man, is marble tiles everywheres. That shit is Italian.' He shook his head derisively, said 'Lavatory' again, then pointed at one of the sinks. 'I spend more on those taps than they will spending on your cockbag fucking funerals.' He turned a tap on and off to demonstrate how smooth an action it had. 'See that? That is *Sweden*, man.'

Loosehead stuck out his lower lip and nodded in approval.

His boss took a deep breath, as though trying to regulate his temper. 'Wet-room is useful in my business, you see. If not want stainings everywhere.'

Tighthead brought a chair in and put it down, facing Hugh and Lazaar, then walked around and stood behind them. Vlad sat in the chair, raising his arms as he did so, gesturing towards the open door. 'Is very nice here. Is apartment yes, but are no riff-raff in building, and anyways, am having private lift. I like because is *pentyhouse*. On summer evenings, can sipping beer on balcony and looking down at shitkickers in park.'

He sighed, glancing about him, admiring his well-appointed wet-room. 'Is pity, though, am spending lot of cake on place but not really using it. Maybe just bringing bitches here sometimes.' He fixed his eyes on Hugh. 'And sacks of shit like you.'

Hugh gazed back impassively as the Russian puffed his ruddy cheeks out, then exhaled. 'Is also sound . . . what is words? . . . No sounds getting in. Or out.'

'Proof,' Hugh said, still holding his gaze. 'Soundproof.'

'Yes, is that. Could land Apache helicopter on roof, not hearing it inside. And in here, can use power tools, not even knowing it downstairs.'

There was silence then as Vlad studied Hugh, leaden eyes running him up and down, taking in every detail. The eyes broke away when he addressed the others. 'Ah mans, why are we here?'

Hugh doubted this was an existential crisis. He looked at Lazaar, who averted his eyes, his cheek twitching, his gaze dropping to the floor.

'I mean, I'm having open mind,' Vlad said. 'Lot of things are not what they seem in this town. Everywheres are women with fake titties.'

Loosehead smiled knowingly.

'But when I buy famous modern artist,' his boss continued, 'I at least expect paint to be dry.'

Lazaar looked up, tried to open his palms out, grimaced as the ring-ties cut into his wrists. 'Like I said, Vladimir, it was an Auerbach, heavy impasto. Could have taken years to dry fully.' He turned to Hugh with an arched eyebrow that said 'Back me up here'.

'Leave me out of this,' Hugh said.

Vlad looked at Hugh, sighed, then turned back to Lazaar. 'Are you having the piss. Label on back say "1961".' He shook his head, holding a fist over his chest. 'This is hurting me here, man.'

'Understand completely,' Lazaar wittered. 'Fool me once, shame on you. Fool me twice, shame on *him*.' He nodded at Hugh. 'Won't happen again, though. I'm sure he'll learn his lesson.'

'No, it won't be happening again,' Vlad said flatly, then turned to Hugh, 'He tell me paintings come from your gallery and that you working for Douglas *Veergo*.'

Hugh looked to Lazaar, who gave an apologetic shrug.

'He thinks this make it OK for him,' Vlad said. 'That he maybe even doing me favour.'

Lazaar tried an ah-shucks-don't-mention-it face.

Vlad rolled his eyes. 'Some favour, huh? It remind me of bull faggots in Lgov Prison. They would fuck you up the ass without asking you first, but sometimes if they think maybe you start to like, they would give you . . . em . . . what is English?'

He looked at Kolya, who shrugged.

'Is a reach-around, maybe,' Vlad said, answering his own question. 'Yes, a reach-around.'

He gestured with his hand to leave little doubt as to what he meant, then glowered at Lazaar. 'You think you can fuck me . . . ' – he emphasised the 'me', stabbing a finger into his own chest. 'You think you can fuck *me* up the ass, then give me reach-around like you do me favour, like I some kind of faggot *peellow*-biter?'

Lazaar was trembling now.

'Answer fucking question,' Vlad roared, veins rippling in his temples.

Lazaar tried to speak but his cheeks just flapped like a fish gasping on a harbour wall. He gave Vlad a sideways look before his eyes flitted to Kolya. He was desperate to work out the right answer. He shook his head: 'Yeah . . .' Then nodded: 'No . . . oh . . .'

Calmer now, Vlad said, 'Maybe you are saying I am a homo . . . a homo . . . what is word?'

They both looked to Kolya. 'Em . . . sexual?' he said, hesitantly. 'Homosexual?'

'No, no,' Vlad said, irritably. 'Is like but different.'

'Oh,' Kolya said. 'Phobic, maybe.'

'Yes, is word.' Vlad turned back to Lazaar. 'Are you saying I am a homosexual-phobic?'

'I would say you are a man of . . . em . . . how to put it? . . . a man of conviction.' Lazaar hedged as best he could.

Vlad nodded, seeming to approve of the answer. The calm held this time, bar a slight sneer, which was, Hugh realised, more of a permanent facial feature than an expression. He put a hand over his shoulder for Loosehead to hand him a pair of secateurs, then leaned forward and snipped the ring-tie, freeing Lazaar's hands.

Lazaar slumped over, sighing, then pulled his cuffs back gingerly, blowing on his bloodied wrists.

'Today you give me reach-around,' Vlad said, handing back the secateurs to his grunt, 'so I give you second chance. But you getting my money back. Plus 200 percent – interest and penalties.'

Lazaar nodded, a little too vigorously, and motioned to stand up from his chair, but two enormous hands clasped his shoulders and forced him down again. He looked up at the pitiless, boney crags of Tighthead's face.

Vlad wagged a finger. 'Not *feeneeshed*. We was still talking, man, shooting the shit, about life in Lgov Prison. I'm spending four years there, you know. It was hard, mans. Not same as like prison in this country. Is like fucking Four Seasons here. In Lgov, the *zeks* – is "prisoners", I think – they would cut themselves with razors to protesting about *feelthy* cells, beatings and everythings.

'I'm not minding all that so much. Is more just borings for me. There was nothing to do, man: no TV, no games. Just fighting – and fucking – is all. Prison library was full of bullshit communist propaganda. But it have some books in English, so I say, "Vladimir, you teach yourself, you go to America when you're getting out." After while, I find some shit not written by Marx or Lenin: story-book by *Jeelie* Cooper – maybe is to show rotting Western ways – and book of nursery rhymes. Anyways, I'm starting with last one. Some other *zek* write in translation in Russian, so I teach myself few words.'

Lazaar leaned forward as though he was genuinely interested, gave an empathetic nod.

'You know which little kiddie rhyme I like best?' Vlad asked.

Lazaar shook his head.

Vlad smiled, caught the eye of Tighthead. 'Give me your hand, Felix,' he said.

Lazaar offered it – far too readily. For one brief instant, perhaps, he thought they were about to shake on it, reason having prevailed.

Vlad stretched out his hand as if to shake, but it moved swiftly past the one offered and instead gripped Lazaar by the wrist. At the same time, Tighthead bent over and wrapped his arms around Lazaar's chest, pinning him to the chair.

'I want tell you favourite kiddie rhyme,' Vlad said. 'Is good for you, I think, but you must holding out fingers.'

Lazaar looked confused. 'Like this,' Vlad said firmly, splaying his own fingers.

Lazaar tentatively did as he was told, his breaths short and shallow. Vlad reached over his shoulder with his other hand for Loosehead to hand him the secateurs again. He slid the blades around Lazaar's little finger. 'How is going?' he said. 'Let me thinking.' He mumbled to himself, smiled, then said, 'Yes, first was "This little *peegie* go market."'

He squeezed a little on the secateurs but pulled away the blades, leaving only a red line on the skin.

Hugh looked anxiously at Kolya, who had his eyes fixed on the ceiling. Vlad moved on to the second finger. 'This little *peegie* stay home.' He squeezed till a bead of blood formed on the blade.

Lazaar was gasping now, like the air was being sucked from the room. He shifted in his chair, the metal legs scraping on the marble tiles.

'This little *peegie* have roast beef.'

The blades sliced cleanly into flesh on the index finger, then stopped. Lazaar's face was bleached by fear. Staccato breaths turned to an apoplectic wheeze as Vlad positioned the blades on the fourth finger.

'This little *peegie* have none.'

The blades sliced through skin, then flesh, and crunched through bone, stopping before they cut clean through. 'That must be what they calling the *credit crunch,* boys,' Vlad said, smirking at his lackeys.

Lazaar was howling, more piss trickling onto the floor from the front edge of his seat. Hugh could hear blood coursing through his own eardrums, as a wave of nausea passed over him.

Vlad loosened the secateurs and moved them to the thumb, below the knuckle. 'This little *peegie* go wee. All of way home.'

He cut clean through this time. Blood sprayed onto his tweed waistcoat and flecked his face. The thumb tapped on the floor.

Lazaar rasped, his voice cracking before it reached the pitch of scream. Then he folded over, panting and sobbing at the same time.

Vlad looked down at the crown of his head. 'Fool me once, I cut your fingers off. Fool me twice, I *reep* your bastard kike head off.'

Hugh's breaths quickened as he saw Tighthead move into position behind him. He glanced over at the corner, but Kolya was slipping out the door, without his boss noticing.

Vlad nodded at Tighthead, who reached down and pinned back Hugh's arms. The ring-ties cut into his wrists as he tried to pull them apart. Vlad reached for Hugh's crotch and began to undo his belt buckle, talking all the while. 'I'm also liking other kiddie rhymes: *London Bridges Falling Down; Jack and Jeel; Mary Having Little Lamb*. And what is calling again?'

He looked up at the ceiling, squeezing rhythmically on the secateurs, as if to jog his memory, then stopped. '*Who Killed Cock Robin?* Yes, that is very good one.' The buckle open, he ripped Hugh's belt out and threw it in a corner. Then he leaned back in his chair. 'How is going again? Let me thinking. Is somethings like:

All of birds of the air
Fell a-sighin' and a-sobbin'
When they *heared* the bell toll
For poor Cock Robin.'

Seeming to know the routine, Loosehead leaned over, grabbed Hugh's trousers and boxer shorts at the hips and reefed them down onto his thighs. Hugh tried to headbutt him but Tighthead must have seen it coming and caught his temple with a right hook.

Dazed, and struggling to catch his breath, Hugh's eyes settled on Vlad, who was gazing down at the exposed crotch. The Russian nodded, adjusted his own crotch, gave a not-bad shrug, then looked at the secateurs, mulling it over. 'What the fuck, I try it anyway. Will not be clean cut, but I not need telling you, man' – he fixed his eyes on Hugh's – 'this is *not* a perfect world.'

Hugh tried to kick at Vlad but Loosehead gripped his legs while Vlad swiped a back-hand across the side of his face.

Vlad grabbed hold of Hugh's penis, squeezing it, stretching it tight. Hugh clenched, straining every sinew to free himself, but the Props weren't going to let him get the better of them this time either.

Vlad moved the secateurs into position, his jaw set, teeth bared, a man relishing the task at hand. All Hugh could do was suck in the air he would need to sustain a howl of agony; he was beaten, spent, impotent – or about to be.

Just as he felt the sharp pinch of steel, though, music rang out. At first he thought it was his imagination – some kind of surreal psychological displacement in the face of trauma – but Vlad seemed to hear it too. It was the chorus of *Please Release Me, Let Me Go* by Engelbert Humperdinck. Hugh lifted his eyes from his crotch at the same time Vlad did. They held one another's gaze for an instant before they both looked down again. '*Please release me, let me go*' rang out a second time.

Then Vlad shook his head. 'Always when I'm in *meedle* of something,' he grumbled, leaving the secateurs in place but reaching into his pocket with his other hand. He pulled out a phone and answered it.

Hugh's breath quivered; his chest throbbed. Vlad listened to the caller, his lip curling again. '*Veergo*,' he spat, 'how you getting my number?' Then, after a pause, said, 'Well, I'm having useful friends too, you know.'

Vlad gave a Slavic shrug. 'Yes, is here.' There was more nodding, then, '*Da . . . da . . . .* OK, I *theenk* about it.'

He hung up, looked at Hugh. 'Was your cockbag boss. He says let you go now and he settle up with me. Wants meet me in your gallery.'

Vlad put the phone back in his pocket and dabbed at his forehead with the tips of his fingers, where Lazaar's blood had spattered. He gazed at the blood, then licked his lips. For a moment, it looked like he was about to taste it. Instead, though, he dragged his fingers slowly across the inside of Hugh's thigh and gazed blankly at him.

The blades still bit into flesh. Vlad's grip twitched, making Hugh flinch, then the Russian smiled a truly malignant smile.

'You tell him OK, but that I want *fresh meet.*'

He pulled away the secateurs, slicing only the skin, stood up and tossed them in a sink. He looked at Hugh, who was slumped in the chair, then at Lazaar, who was still bent over double, emitting a low moan. Then his eyes drifted back to Hugh's crotch, his tongue resting on his lower lip.

'Put that thing away, man, before you're having someone's eye out.'

CHAPTER 37

The Care of the Faithful

'I'm in the Raphael room.' Ana pressed 'send' and put the phone back in her bag.

Hugh had called her when they'd let him go. They'd bundled him back into a car and dropped him in a laneway, on the edge of Hampstead Heath. He made sure Ana wasn't hurt, then told her briefly what had happened to him – including the bizarre manner of his reprieve. He said he was getting a taxi, and arranged to meet her at the V&A Museum.

A few minutes after she'd sent the text, Hugh hobbled down the steps into the cavernous, vaulted room. His eyes were bloodshot and raw, with a cut over the left one, the brow swollen. The other side of his face was flushed red and grazed, the first traces of a bruise leeching through.

Wincing, he eased himself onto the bench next to her. She rubbed a hand up and down his back, then rested her head on his shoulder. His head was bowed. She put her other hand on his thigh, looking up at him. 'How's Engelbert?'

Hugh's smile broke into a grimace. 'Hilarious,' he said, without meeting her eye. He was still breathing heavily, trying to compose himself. 'How did you get Virgo's number?' he asked.

'I didn't. I call the police, gave them number-plate of the car. I hid in a doorway down the street and see you leave.'

'Who did call Virgo, then?'

'You must have angel watching over you.' She paused before adding, 'But it means police will want speak to you.'

217

'That's the least of my worries. I can pretend it was a hoax call or a prank gone wrong.' He looked down. 'Almost horribly wrong.'

Ana smiled awkwardly, studying him at the same time. He seemed reluctant to meet her eye. When she ran a hand gently over his temple, he tensed up.

'You like men with scars, don't you?' There was an edge to his voice.

She gazed down at the mosaic floor.

'He was there, you know,' Hugh said.

'Who?' Ana asked.

She knew full well who he meant, and he knew it too. When she looked up, his eyes settled on hers, like he was trying to see inside her head, probing for the seam between what she said and what she felt. Then he looked away, either afraid of what he might find, or withdrawing to protect himself.

His eyes scrolled from one end of the room to the other. 'I haven't been in here in a long time,' he said, as much to himself as Ana.

They sat at the centre of the room that housed the seven surviving cartoons – or template drawings – Raphael made for his tapestries in the Sistine Chapel. The room was dimly lit, save for a skylight in the domed ceiling at one end, illuminating a sixteenth-century altarpiece, adding to the sepulchral air. The light was carefully regulated to protect the work, which had always been fragile; it was no more than sheets of paper pasted together, with charcoal underdrawings and a distemper or a wash of colour pigments, mixed with lead white, animal glue and water.

Ana turned to him. 'It is one of my favourite places in London. I came here a lot when I worked as a . . . you know. It reminded me of better side of human nature.'

Hugh had closed his eyes, lost in thought. He had withdrawn from her – like Kolya, ironically – unable or unwilling to convey how he felt. This didn't necessarily trouble her. She had withdrawn from people for most of her adult life as well, with a sense that the only person she could truly rely on was herself. The one constant in her life was art. It sounded glib, pretentious even, and it wasn't a feeling she had ever shared with anyone, but for her, art was an objectification of something good in the human psyche. A testimony: drawn, sculpted, filmed.

Maybe it was a feeling Hugh had shared once, but he seemed to have long since objectified art as a commodity to be traded – or counterfeited.

She sighed, looking around the room. People drifted through, barely pausing to look at the work. There was a malingering group of Spanish students on the next bench, flirting with each other, their interest in the human form unmediated by Raphael. The sour-faced porter sitting opposite watched them with hooded eyes. When a camera flashed, he turned and barked 'No photographs!' at a startled-looking Japanese man, who bowed his head by way of apology.

A posse of American students were next to file past the porter. A gangly boy in a UCLA baseball cap squinted at one of the wall-notes. 'Raphael, wasn't he one of the Mutant Ninja Turtles?'

'Check out the deltoids, man,' another said, pointing at the axe-wielding figure in *The Sacrifice at Lystra*. 'Man, he is ripped.'

A wavy-haired blonde girl turned to him. 'You're so lame, Brett. This is art.' Still, even she barely glanced at the work.

'Can we go?' another girl said. 'It's so gloomy in here. Seriously, I'm like, creeped-out.'

The one in the baseball cap shouted, 'Yo, Brett, we're gonna bounce.'

The porter sprang out of his chair and shushed them, but the homies were already meandering towards the exit.

It struck Ana that most people spent no more time in front of the Raphaels then they would in front of a Damien Hirst spot painting. This was the kind of thing Jack would rant about in a rapture of indignation but Ana had seen beautiful Hirst paintings: there were thousands of them, so they couldn't all be bad. She had also seen a few dud Old Masters.

The Raphael Room didn't have the pulling power of Tate Modern or whatever 'blockbuster' exhibition had just been hyped in the media. This wasn't to denigrate more modern work because of its popularity. It was irrelevant to her when a work of art was made, as was who had made it, how many there were, or who went to see it in a gallery.

It was equally absurd to her to judge a piece of art by the price paid for it, or by the people who bought it or wrote about it. It was like judging a flower by the person whose garden it was in, or a book by the person reading it. The Nazis looted works of art – many of them masterpieces – and hung them in their own houses. That didn't diminish the art; maybe it even showed a flicker of humanity in the evil people who coveted it.

She raised her eyes from the floor and fixed them on the Raphael in front of them: *Christ's Charge to Peter.* She knew the scene well. Her father had often made her copy it from a book when she was a child, telling her the Raphael cartoons were the finest expression of the drawn form ever created. In this scene, Peter crouches before a resurrected Jesus with a small band of apostles behind him. There was a flock of sheep on the left of the composition. Ana read from the wall-text next to it: 'Christ charges Peter with the care of the faithful, symbolised by the sheep.'

'And my, aren't those sheep faithful,' Hugh said, alert again, reading a message on his phone.

Ana read some more and turned back to him. 'It is *unbelieve*, no, that Raphael do all seven of these in one year with just few helpers. It say he got one hundred ducats each for them. It not seem like very much?'

'See, that's what happens when artists act as their own agents.' Hugh had put his phone away and was staring straight ahead of him. 'That was Virgo. He wants me to come and meet him.'

There was a moment's silence between them. Ana studied him again, mulling over a question that had been troubling her. It had never seemed like the right time to ask – then, least of all – but she asked it anyway. 'Hugh, why are you an art dealer?'

'What?' he said, perplexed, as though he hadn't thought about it in a long time.

He gazed blankly at the Raphael, before turning to her, mouth open, waiting for the words to form. 'To be honest,' he said, 'I can't remember.'

Then he leaned over, as if to kiss her on the forehead, but changed his mind at the last moment. He hoisted himself off the bench and hobbled back the way he'd come.

CHAPTER 38

A Richer, Greedier Fool

Hugh arranged to meet Virgo in a pub off Haymarket: the aptly named Captain's Carbuncle. It had a threadbare carpet, flaking burgundy wallpaper and a musty smell cut through with piss and detergent. The nautical theme began and ended with a ship's wheel hung behind the bar.

Hugh bought a double Jameson and eased himself into a seat by a fireplace that hadn't seen a fire in a long time. The flickering lights of the fruit machines needled his eyes, still smarting from whatever Loosehead had sprayed in them.

A few minutes later, Virgo rolled in the door with Harry, who peeled off towards the bar. Virgo made straight for Hugh, undid the buttons of a black cashmere overcoat and took a seat opposite, looking about, unimpressed. Then he fixed his eyes on Hugh, a smile gnawing at the corners of his mouth.

'How's it hangin'?' he asked. '*Or is it?*'

'Very funny,' Hugh said. 'I'm glad everyone finds the travails of my manhood so amusing.'

Virgo was looking around the bar again, checking out the other drinkers.

'Why meet here?' Hugh asked.

Virgo shrugged. 'I own it.'

Hugh rolled his eyes. '*Of course* you do.'

'You wouldn't believe how much this place turns over.'

'It's a good location, I suppose,' Hugh said, indifferent.

'No seriously, you *wouldn't* believe it,' Virgo said again. 'Must have a word with Luca. He'll get me fuckin' nicked.'

Virgo was smiling but the menace still bled through the banter; it always felt like the wrong soundtrack on a film.

Hugh spoke up, before he lost his nerve. 'Look, Douglas, I'm through. That business this morning was . . . '

Virgo cut in. 'Got you out, didn't I, chopper an' all?'

'What do you want, a box of fucking *Roses*?' Hugh tapped a finger on his temple. 'Nemirovsky is out of his mind, totally fucking loolah.'

'Tell me about it,' Virgo said. 'Even his crew know it.'

'It was one of them who called you, wasn't it?'

'Never you mind who called me.'

Harry's gristled mug loomed over them. He handed a gin and tonic to Virgo and put another double Jemmie down in front of Hugh, catching his eye, smirking, making a snipping gesture with his fingers. 'The dirty little 'erbert,' he said, turning back towards the bar.

Virgo took a sip, sighed. 'The way it is, Hugh, things have been coming to a head with Vlad for a long time. He's been pissing all over my manor like a tomcat with a dickie prostate. But the last thing I expected him to do was start a barney over some snide modern art.'

Hugh slammed a fist down at the centre of the table. 'He. Tried. To. Cut. My. Penis. Off.' The two suits on the next bench along turned to look, mouths agape. 'Is there a problem?' Hugh said, rounding on them, with more than a hint of his own menace.

'Take it easy,' Virgo said, then turned to the suits, shrugging. 'Stag parties, aye, they can really get outta hand.'

The suits drained their glasses, got up and left. Hugh shook his head, took a slug of whiskey. 'Vlad seemed to know all about your little hobbyhorse in Shoreditch, by the way.'

'Bought from you, did he? No discounts for that Cossack cunt. He's ironing out more loot than I am.'

'It seems he's been dabbling all right, but from an even less reputable source than us. Felix Lazaar put together a collection for him.'

Virgo's cheek gave a barely perceptible flinch, his eyes the slightest twitch. 'Not pukka?' he said.

'Not pukka,' Hugh said.

'What's it got to do with us, then? Vlad's not the only one who's been rumped by Lazaar.'

'Lazaar told him we were behind the fakes, said they came from the gallery. Don't ask me how he knew about it.'

Virgo put down his glass, gimlet eyes boring into Hugh.

There was nothing as charismatic as menace.

'Someone been mouthin' off, have they?' Virgo asked.

Hugh didn't blink. 'As far as I can see, Lazaar just walked in off the street and worked it out.'

'Yeah,' Virgo deadpanned, 'or maybe he's just boning Mystic Meg.'

Hugh wasn't amused. 'So what you gonna do about Vlad, pay him off?'

'Like I said, it's not about the money. He's minted.'

There was silence for a moment. Virgo caught Harry's eye, pointed at the drinks on the table and gestured for two more.

Hugh swirled the ice at the bottom of his glass, then looked up, remembering something Vlad had said. 'Oh, and by the way, he wants a *fresh meet*, whatever that means.'

Virgo sighed. 'Fuck me. It's like being stalked by Jimmy Cagney. He means *fresh* as opposed to *packed*.' He made a stab at a Cagney-esque drawl. '*No shooters.*'

They fell into silence again. Thinking about it, Hugh realised how well this could work out for Lazaar – missing or mashed digits notwith-standing. Having the Russians take out Virgo, or vice versa, would mean one less bilked client for him to fend off.

Harry dropped over the drinks, grumbling – 'Do I look like a fuckin' lounge girl?' – then turned back for the bar.

Virgo ignored him, took a swig. 'We'll meet Vlad and his crew at the gallery on Wednesday evening. You might wanna make yourself scarce.'

'I think I can manage that,' Hugh said, draining his second glass. 'Make sure to give Vlad my best.' The whiskey burned the back of his throat, cauterising his wounds – and his nerves. 'There's something else I need to discuss with you. Fresco called. They offered us a booth.'

'What, you mean the art circus in a big-top in Regent's Park?'

Hugh rolled his eyes again. 'Not how they'd describe it. But anyhow, I didn't know if I should accept.'

'Why not? I feel it's important we bring our artists to as wide an audience as possible. These rich fuckers *deserve* an opportunity to buy from us, and like I said before, why would they risk exposing us?'

'Just as well I said yes then, isn't it?'

'Bit of initiative, that's more like it. Who we gonna show, then? Dug up a good-un, 'ave you?'

'Haven't made the work yet, to be honest.'

Unfazed by minor details, Virgo puffed his chest out. 'I'm quite liking this whole gentleman-art-dealer thing. It's almost as lucrative as me other rackets.'

'I wouldn't give up the day job just yet,' Hugh said. 'We'll run out of rich mugs to sell to eventually.'

'Nah, it's like an old friend of mine says: there'll always be a richer, greedier fool. '

Hugh's glass hovered by his mouth. 'What did you say?'

'There'll always be a richer, greedier fool. Hardly a revelation to an art dealer, is it?' Virgo stood up, closed the buttons of his overcoat, offering another mirthless smile. 'Try and keep your pecker out of mischief.' He turned and made for the exit, trailed by Harry.

Hugh put his glass down, still trying to process what he'd just heard. *There'll always be a richer, greedier fool.* The exact same words Robert Orca had used the first time he'd called Hugh.

Robert Orca: *an old friend.*

Hugh thumped his forehead with the ball of his palm. How could he have been so stupid not to have worked it out before now?

He pulled out his phone, opened the browser, googled Robert Orca. There were thousands of hits: galleries, arts blogs, newspaper articles – so many stories about Orca, the dark lord of the contemporary art world, the Svengali-like figure who could make an artist's career by buying work as easily as wreck it by offloading the very same work. Half the stories were clearly placed by his PR people because, of course, Orca didn't talk to the press. Hugh opened one of them. ARTIST SAYS ORCA DESTROYED HIS CAREER. He skimmed over it: 'Orca claimed through a spokesperson that the artist had a pathological need to be rejected in public.'

How much easier it would be to cut the artists out altogether?

Hugh stalled before adding 'Douglas Virgo' to the search bar. Scrolling through Google Images instead, his eyes lit on a twenty-year-old photo someone had posted of Orca leaving the Groucho Club on Dean Street with the then Tory Party treasurer, Timothy something-or-other. But it was the man in the background who caught Hugh's eye. He was slimmer than now – no jowls – but had the same slicked-back hair and steely watchfulness.

Finally, Hugh added the name to the search-bar. A story came up from the mid-nineties about how 'the convicted drug dealer and former City trader, Douglas Virgo, has been hired as a script consultant on a London gangster film being produced by Robert Orca'.

It had been staring Hugh in the face all along – that Virgo's motives were more complicated than laundering money. If the starting premise for the gallery was that the art market was a dumb beast, actually selling the work wasn't much of a leap. Then there was the almost spiteful disdain towards the wealthy that shaped Virgo's worldview. The gallery was just one more way of getting his own back.

It was hardly about the money for Orca either, unless there was a wager involved. More likely, it was an experiment to see how fickle and gullible the growing legions of super-rich collectors truly were. The art was incidental. What mattered was who bought it, and where it was sold. It was as though Orca saw himself as the Henry Higgins of the art world. Unfortunately, that would make Hugh its Eliza Doolitle.

He almost smiled at the notion, just as his phone rang. He didn't recognise the number; the prefix was foreign – Swiss or Austrian. He answered it.

'*Güten tag.* Is that Hugh?'

'It is.'

'Deidrich Weiss here. I am calling on behalf of Larry Cockburn. As you may know, I curate his collection. I was wondering if I might make an appointment to visit the gallery for a sneaking preview of the work you will be showing at Fresco.'

'That might be tricky,' Hugh said.

'Oh, I'm sorry, Mr Cockburn indicated he had an arrangement with you.'

'No, of course, I'm happy to let you have a preview. It's just that, well... the shippers – yes, the shippers – have let us down, and we won't have the work in the gallery till Thursday morning. Cutting it fine, I know.'

'Well, these things can happen,' Weiss said. 'How about we grab some breakfast on Thursday before we go and look at the work?'

Hugh paused, mulled it over, but couldn't help himself. 'Oh wouldn't that be *loverly*,' he said, with a slight lilt in his voice.

'I beg your pardon?'

'Never mind. It's complicated. See you Thursday.'

CHAPTER 39

(Just) A Flicker of Remorse

Kolya tapped out a rhythm on the window with his signet ring, then gave the car in front a blast of the horn. Wednesday evening was a dumb time to drive across central London.

It didn't help that his temples ached, his sinuses burned. Vlad had doused himself in half a bottle of aftershave, while one of the ex-military meatheads in the back had overdone it on the borscht and was trumping like the regimental bugle.

Kolya was at the wheel of an armoured X5 again, the blue one this time. The black one was in the garage for a new bumper and a re-spray. The boss wasn't pleased about that.

But it was Lazaar's story about Douglas Virgo that really got Vlad fired up, properly fucking torqued.

He said it was time to sort Virgo once and for all. Kolya tried to talk him out of starting a war – for lots of reasons. But Vlad told him to cork it, stood him down. The next morning he sent in the meatheads, Yuri and Kirill, to haul Rhattigan in for interrogation. One of them must have clocked Ana there and remembered meeting her once with Kolya. Somehow – maybe thanks to Rhattigan – she got away.

The next part was truly hilarious. Yuri and Kirill were hard-asses and liked to crow about it. They were ex-special forces, trained in close pro-tection, black belts in Sambo, experts in marksmanship and emergency medical treatment – although Kolya had only ever seen them pronounce someone dead. Hardened to extreme violence by three tours of duty in

227

Chechnya, there were only so many separatist heads they could crack open before the time seemed ripe for a better-paid career move. Who would have thought a pair of bone-crunchers like that would barely have got the better of an *art dealer*?

Kolya would still be grinning about it if they weren't with him on the crew for this meet. Having to help Vlad settle his scores was bad enough.

He pulled into a laneway, a few doors down from the gallery. They all climbed out. Kolya led the way. Vlad was behind him, with Yuri and Kirill dragging their knuckles at the back. They walked under the arch. Kolya pressed the intercom and peered over his shades at the camera above the door. The lock buzzed. He pushed on the door and led the others into a reception lobby.

The four men already there turned to face them. Virgo had brought Pavel, Harry and another bloke – not as tall as Harry but even stockier, with cropped salt-and-pepper hair and a nose like heavily worked putty. Virgo nodded at the latter. 'Do the honours, Terry, would you?'

The protocol with a 'fresh meet' is that one member of each crew frisks all the members of the other.

Terry stepped forward. 'Spread your legs, arms out,' he said. The voice was a sluggish monotone, East End through and through. He patted down Kolya first, then the meatheads.

When it was his turn, Vlad started grinding his hips. 'Oh yes, you are liking that, *Ingliesh* faggot.'

Virgo caught Kolya's eye, nodded towards Vlad. 'Can't take him anywhere, can you?'

Terry didn't know where to look. He had the air of a man who would rather be at home, dunking biscuits in his tea, watching this kind of shit on his giant plasma TV, rather than in the middle of it.

When Terry was done, Yuri stepped up to do Virgo's crew. They might have been tempted to offer some innuendo of their own, but Vlad was a tough act to follow.

Formalities seen to, all eight of them moved into the gallery: a big white box, the walls bare. Vlad nodded his approval, turned to Virgo. 'Maybe I'm taking this place too as part of my compensation. 'Cause I'm liking art and all that shit. But of course, you're knowing that already, aren't you?'

Virgo rolled his eyes.

'Or maybe I let you keep gallery,' Vlad said, mulling it over. 'You sell your hookie *peectures*. Leave real crime to professionals.'

The look that Virgo gave Vlad must have taken a lifetime to refine. It was a look of disdain condensed to its purest, uncut form. 'Let's just get this over with,' he said.

'Down to business,' Vlad said, 'I'm liking that. Here is deal. I *geeve* you account number. You *geeve* me ten million quids. We do it here, right now, on computer. Then we all going home.'

If Virgo had said yes, chances were Vlad would have changed his mind, asked for twenty. 'How about a longer-term fix?' Virgo asked instead, pausing to think it over. 'Let's carve up some territory.'

Vlad eyeballed him, said nothing.

'You take Slough,' the Englishman said, 'leave the rest of Greater London to me.'

Virgo must have known the reaction he would get: Vlad's temper was legendary. 'You think this is fucking joke,' Vlad said, his breathing becoming heavier. 'If you want opening can of whoop-ass, let's do it, man.'

There was a moment's standoff. Four men facing one another on either side of the gallery – it was like one of those spaghetti westerns Kolya was so fond of. Ennio Morricone could have scored the scene.

Then Yuri and Kirill took a step forward.

Vlad caught Kirill's eye, yanking his chain, nodding towards Harry. Kirill kept moving, twisted, and launched a roundhouse kick at Harry's head which only made it as far as his chest. Harry was driven back towards the wall, pursued by Kirill. Harry stuck out an arm, clamped a hand under Kirill's chin, swivelled him around and pinned him against the wall. The back of Harry's supersized camel-hair coat stiffened then as a fist was driven into his midriff. Harry's head rolled back to dodge the hooked punch that followed, before lunging forwards onto the bridge of Kirill's nose. There was a crunching sound as the nose gave way like an egg with a chick inside. Blood spattered onto the white walls on either side. Harry followed up with a knee to the groin and a battering-ram fist to the side of the ribcage. As Kirill slumped to the floor, the steel-tipped heel of Harry's black brogue hammered into the side of his head.

'*Fack* off out of it, you Ruskie cunt.' He turned around, wiping blood from his forehead with a cashmere cuff. The pastry-coloured overcoat was flecked with blood – an English beef Wellington with a Russian dressing.

Harry's expression said *Who's next?*

Kolya paused for a moment of professional regard. The idea of an unarmed meet with Harry's forehead in the room seemed a little dumb now. But Kolya's lapse in concentration almost proved fatal.

Pavel had hunkered down and was rummaging in his shoe. He pulled out a flick-knife and released the blade. The malevolent raze of metal on metal cut through the clamour of grunts and cracking knuckles. He turned to Kolya and launched himself forward. Kolya deflected the blade with his left forearm but it still ripped into his leather jacket, slashing skin. In the same motion, Kolya swung his right elbow across Pavel's face, slamming it into the bridge of his nose. As Pavel reeled away, Kolya glanced at Yuri, who was lunging towards Terry. It was then that Kolya felt a searing pain just above his right hip. Pavel had twisted 180 degrees and stabbed him on his blindside.

As Yuri caught Terry on the side of the head with a flying kick, Kolya drove at Pavel, who was staggering backwards now, clutching his nose. Kolya caught him with a right hook, flinching himself when he felt the tearing in his gut. Pavel twisted till he was side-on, so Kolya delivered a scything kick across the back of his knees, making him crumple onto the floor. He put one foot on Pavel's wrist, till the knife rolled away, and pinned his head down with the other. Kolya picked up the knife, wincing with pain as he bent over, then fixed his eyes on Pavel's. The prone man's eyebrows and lashes were matted with blood, his pupils dilated. He looked up at Kolya, sideways on, with the despair of a man who was about to die a long way from home – a despair he would only ever get to share with his killer.

But Kolya didn't kill him.

He grabbed hold of Pavel's outstretched arm, twisted it and stamped down on it, popping the elbow-joint. Then he turned around to see Yuri, striding towards Harry, coiling into the stance of a six-dan black-belt. A kick aimed at Harry's head only made it as far as the shoulder. Harry stepped into the kick, grabbed Yuri by the ears and hit him with another lump-hammer blow from the forehead. There was a crack like a piece of timber snapping. Yuri pitched backwards into the corner, then slid onto the floor. This time, even Harry was reeling.

Kolya looked down at Yuri and Kirill. They'd be even uglier when they came round. Brain damage wasn't an issue. Someone had beaten Harry to that.

By this stage, Harry was staggering like a drunk, clutching his temples, all of his dulled strength channelled into staying on his feet. Terry was listing as well, with only the wall propping him up.

When Kolya turned to Vlad and Virgo, they stopped their bitch-slapping and fixed their eyes on the knife. Vlad bore an expression of almost manic delirium. Virgo looked like he knew what was coming, the eyes saying, *Do it, get it over with.*

The knife tore into the lower intestine. Kolya yanked the blade up towards the ribcage, slicing through gut, liver, stomach and spleen.

He felt a flicker of remorse.

Just a flicker.

CHAPTER 40

The Cutting Edge

Deidrich Weiss picked up the knife and cut his Danish pastry down the middle. Then he twisted the plate by ninety degrees and sliced the pastry a second time.

He glanced up at Hugh Rhattigan, who was on his phone again, getting ever more agitated. He'd been making calls all through breakfast, leaving a variation on the same message: 'Douglas, call me back.' These frantic calls, combined with his scratched and bruised face, gave him a slightly deranged air. He'd excused his appearance by claiming that a large, wall-mounted installation had fallen on him in his gallery.

Perhaps the blow to the head also explained his downright rudeness. It was bad enough that Deidrich had been coerced into this meeting by Larry Cockburn. Frankly, most of what Deidrich had seen so far of the work in LW2 was derivative. But Mr Cockburn evidently had his reasons – most of which were the byproduct of Robert Orca's malign influences.

No matter – he who pays the piper, and all that. Galleries, artists, even curators have always pandered to the unrefined tastes of collectors. Take a look at the altarpieces in the medieval wing of any museum and at the donor portraits in the side panels. Like it or not, collectors and benefactors keep gallery doors open, they keep artists and curators clothed and sheltered, and in Deidrich's case, they pay for his daughter's exorbitant tuition fees.

But the fact that it may ever have been the way made it no less galling. The notion of that diva Mrs Cockburn passing off Deidrich's insights as her own truly rankled, as did her taking a seat on the boards of so many museums. Sitting on the board of the Guggenheim in particular had inflated her hubris to ghastly proportions, although truth be told, she hadn't been doing much in the way of *sitting* these past few weeks since she'd had her 'Brazilian butt-lift'. At least, Deidrich believed that was the proper idiom.

His musings were disturbed by Rhattigan. 'We should go,' he said, without having touched his *pain au chocolat*. He left a twenty-pound note on the table, stood up and made for the exit. Deidrich gazed at the untouched pastry and, with unashamed Teutonic frugality, wrapped it in a napkin and slipped it into his briefcase, before following Rhattigan out onto the street.

They walked in silence down Bishopsgate, Rhattigan seeming to quicken his pace with each step. Deidrich had to scurry just to keep up.

They arrived at the gallery, an unprepossessing building, a few hundred metres off Shoreditch High Street. Deidrich trailed Rhattigan as he unlocked the doors. Rhattigan turned on the lights in a reception area first, then in the exhibition space.

Deidrich gasped when he saw the work. Now this, *this* was something special. A mutilated corpse, the face a fleshy pulp, its tailored suit saturated in blood. The blood also dripped onto the floor, pooling before being smeared on all sides, even across the walls. The dull but rank odour was a wonderful touch, challenging the olfactory as well as the visual sensibilities.

'I love it,' Deidrich said, with a frankness uncommon in a seasoned curator.

Even Rhattigan seemed stunned; when a work still had the power to move a dealer, it must be remarkable.

'I love it,' Deidrich said again. 'I love it.'

He knew instantly that he had a duty to showcase the work at the Yokohama Triennial, which he was co-curating. All the more so, when he heard it was the work of an unheralded Russian talent. So be it if the work's inclusion would also help cement Deidrich's standing as a cutting-edge curator. Had he not discovered the artist?

After a brief discussion on the installation, Rhattigan apologised, saying the shippers must have brought the work for Fresco directly to

Regent's Park. But Deidrich was unperturbed: his journey across London had not been in vain.

As he ushered Deidrich to the exit, Rhattigan was back on his phone, even more agitated than before, angry perhaps at the mix-up over the work for the fair. 'What the fuck happened . . . ?' His voice trailed off, his eyes settling on Deidrich's. 'You'll find your own way back, won't you?'

'*Natürlich*,' Deidrich said, turning his face towards the City, with the brio of aesthetic discovery in his heart.

CHAPTER 41

Go, Get the Butter

Still only halfway through the opening night of Fresco and Jack already felt like a Guantánamo Bay inmate. The chemical burn in his nostrils of expensive perfumes and aftershaves relayed itself to his stomach as a dull nausea. The unforgiving spotlights scorched his retinas, while the plastic chairs the fair organisers rented to exhibitors at fifty quid a pop caused him to shift his weight from one cramping buttock to another. His arse hadn't ached like this since the night he'd gone home with that Latvian couple who'd run out of lubricant and had made do with a self-tanning lotion. Adding insult to injury, he'd also had an arse like a baboon for the next month.

Strangely enough, it never occurred to them to use butter.

He looked again at the pink neon sign mounted over an Old Master print on the wall beside him: 'Go, get the butter', it read. He thought it was funny when he first saw it, but it was getting funnier and funnier as the evening wore on. It almost made the whole bun-fight bearable.

It was one of seven pieces they were showing at the fair. Hugh had drawn up a list of famous movie quotes to juxtapose with Old Master paintings. Then he had Jack and Ana source high-res digital images of the paintings, which were all out of copyright, so it was just a matter of contacting the museums where the work was held. They had the images printed onto large canvases, which they coated with *Vernis craqueleur*, a varnish favoured by forgers of Old Masters, as it formed a fine filigree of cracks upon drying. They put the canvases into reproduction swept frames – similar to the frames on the original paintings, distressed to make them look old. Hugh had already ordered the neon signs, for about six hundred quid each. The signs were mounted over the framed, varnished prints. The finished work had the edgy mix of high-concept and shoddy DIY that fitted right in at the fair.

They used the Marsellus Wallace line from *Pulp Fiction:* 'I'm gonna get medieval on your ass', over a painting by Ingres of Joan of Arc in full battle armour.

They used 'Look how she moves, that's just like Jell-O on springs' from *Some Like it Hot,* over Botticelli's *Birth of Venus.*

'I'll have what she's having' from *When Harry met Sally* over *The Ecstasy of Saint Teresa* by Rubens.

'You're gonna need a bigger boat' from *Jaws* over *The Raft of the Medusa* by Géricault.

'You talking to me?' over Vermeer's *Girl with a Pearl Earring.*

'I'll be back' over a Crucifixion scene by Michelangelo.

And of course, Jack's favourite, 'Go, get the butter' from *Last Tango in Paris* over the Archangel Gabriel appearing to the Virgin Mary in *The Annunciation* by El Greco.

The artist who'd supposedly made the work was also Hugh's creation – another publicity-shy misanthrope, from Serbia this time. Each of the seven pieces was the first in an edition of three, and each was priced at eighty grand. That might have sounded steep, but once word got round that Robert Orca had bought a full set, the booth came under siege from people desperate to buy one or more.

Go, get the butter was by far the most popular. Hugh reckoned he could have sold it a hundred times over. The irony was almost too exquisite.

Hugh could have been forgiven some triumphalism over the demand for the work but he had been too strung out to celebrate, and border-line gruff with prospective buyers. The art consultant, Thea Cappellini, hung around the booth for half an hour with the client she'd brought, teasing out the work's many nuances. 'For me, cultural dislocation is the leitmotif here,' she'd waxed.

Hugh just rolled his eyes, told her to get on with it before he sold the work to someone else. Put on the spot, Cappellini's client couldn't choose between the three pieces he liked best, so he took all of them.

Hugh dropped the client's business card on the table – 'Sir Jeremy Jiggins, Chairman of Iniquus Asset Management' – and told Jack that their employer 'would have been especially pleased about that sale'.

Would have been. All very odd. Was he not planning on telling Virgo? And as to why Hugh was so tense, Jack could only reason that art fairs must be nerve-racking for dealers. He also suspected that Hugh might be suffering from post-traumatic stress, after that business last week with the Russians. (Jack was vague on the details but he'd reassured himself that it was nothing to do with him.)

After Hugh had closed the sale with Cappellini and her client, he slipped out to make another phone call. But before leaving, he told Jack not to sell anything else, that the work was fully vouched for – all three from each of the seven editions. 'Someone even tried to reserve the fire extinguisher on the side of the booth,' he said, 'so really, there's no need to engage anyone in conversation. Just nod, smile vacantly, tell them I'll be back in five minutes if they're really pushy.' The subtext was clear: things never seemed to turn out well when Jack was left in charge.

Unfortunately, Hugh had no alternatives. Ana left just as things got going, saying she was nervous about running into anyone who might have recognised her from her previous employment. And hiring someone else to staff the booth never seemed to be a runner.

That just left Jack – and his meagre customer-care skill-set. He turned his gaze on the crowds that flowed by like a river swollen with rain, a piece of flotsam occasionally snagging in a booth before being swept away again.

There was much to gawp at for any rubber-neckers who'd managed to get an invite, or had somehow ended up working there, like Jack. He'd seen a familiar cast of celebrities: he wasn't sure what the collective noun was, a 'conceit' maybe? He'd also seen lots of art-world grandees: Nicholas Scrota, director of the Tate, chatting to Charles Saatchi; and of course Orca, who was being fawned over by artists and dealers, stalked by art consultants and portfolio managers, anxious to see what he was buying.

Jack took a keen interest too in the array of plastic surgery on view, the quality as uneven as the artwork. Some of the fair-goers seemed to have stopped ageing at about thirty five – money clearly the elixir. Others looked like escaped exhibits from Madame Tussauds.

In fact, the fair was far more conducive to people-watching than art-appreciation. The booths were wobbly, cramped, patchily lit, and too shallow to give a proper perspective on the work. The rat-run layout of the aisles – more shopping mall than white cube – was made worse still by the disorientating effects of the crowds and the champagne. The whole spectacle reminded Jack of one of the pick-up bars he had frequented over the years, at 3am, when the lights had come back on. What had seemed so desirable quickly lost its allure.

He checked the time on his phone. Only 8PM. Still another hour to go till closing time. As he slipped the phone back in his pocket, a woman striding towards the VIP lounge veered into the LW2 booth.

'I've just got to have one of these,' she gushed, hands raised, fingers flailing, like she was singing a show-tune.

Jack looked up at a blonde lady, dressed head to toe in Prada. Her expensively coiffed locks bobbed between tanned, body-sculpted shoulders.

'I'm afraid I can't sell you any of them,' Jack said.

'Why not?' she asked, still smiling. The laughter lines dated her close to fifty, although if she had been more carefully lit, she could have passed for thirty five.

'It's complicated,' Jack said. 'You wouldn't understand.'

There was an indignant pause. 'I beg your pardon?'

His eyes scrolled over her. 'You just look like the kind of person who wouldn't understand.'

She pulled a face like she'd just found a turd in her six-grand Hermes handbag. 'Don't treat *me* like I'm some kind of blonde airhead,' she sniffed.

Languidly, Jack fixed his eyes on hers. 'Wouldn't dream of it, madam. You're clearly not a real blonde.'

She inhaled so sharply she snorted. 'You little toe-rag!' – her voice acquired a rasping edge – 'We could buy and sell this gallery fifty times over.'

'That may very well be true, but you can't buy any of these. So kindly fuck off. Madam.'

Jack sat back then – observing – as the woman's veneer of sophistication peeled away like one of her expensive exfoliation treatments. She stormed out of the booth, fumbling in her bag for her gold iPhone, clattering into Hugh as he made his way back down the aisle. 'What's up with her?' Hugh asked, eyes narrowing.

Jack shifted his weight again, his aching bottom mildly relieved. 'Beats me,' he said.

CHAPTER 42

Not All Scars Fade

Hugh turned and began to prowl up and down the booth, feeling more and more like an exhibit himself – as though he was being watched.

In the hours before the fair's opening party, he had all the usual concerns of a dealer: moving and installing the work, doubting its quality, and sizing up the competition. But the usual concerns seemed trivial compared to the scene that had confronted him at the gallery that morning – a scene that still cloyed at his senses, clinging to his nostrils in a rash of tiny lesions, searing the inside of his eyelids, like an etcher's copper plate scored in acid.

The explanation, however, still eluded him. He had been trying to contact Virgo all day, but the calls went straight to voicemail. These calls were made more in hope than expectation. The body must have been Virgo's. It wasn't just the unanswered calls. The face was mutilated beyond recognition but the physique was right – although a little bloated – while the suit was a Paul Smith and the shoes had a Cleverley's logo on the sole, both favoured brands of his.

He had tried calling Harry and Luca, also to no avail. If the Russians had seen to them too, would they come after Hugh next? Or Jack?

Or Ana?

The cooling of relations with Ana was also troubling him, more than he would ever have expected. He felt guilty over his insinuation that she was somehow still involved with Kolya. Yet he also knew that her feelings for her ex were more complicated than she would admit to, or even realised. Hugh didn't know if he should feel jealous or betrayed.

She'd seemed uneasy at LW2's especially flagrant display of dishonesty at the fair, so Hugh told her to take a few days to mull things over, that he would call her on Monday. He certainly didn't want her, or Jack, going anywhere near the gallery for the next few days. They knew nothing of Nemirovsky's *installation,* but he had no idea who did know about it, or who he should tell. Virgo had an estranged wife and one child that he knew of.

There was also the question of what to do with the body. Someone had made a start of disposing of it – disfiguring the face, extracting the teeth, cutting off the fingertips – but had left the rest behind. Wondering if he should finish the job himself only served to remind Hugh how out of his depth he was.

The grisly scene flashed before his mind's eye again as he nodded limply at a WPC who strolled past the booth. He was at once reassured and unnerved by the police presence at the fair. There was an officer patrolling each of the aisles. There was also a crowd-control unit corralling a wretched band of Stuckists and Occupy protesters into a pen – outside the tent, of course, set back fifty yards from the main entrance. The police were keeping a weather eye on things, not taking any chances after the paint-bomb attacks at Alexandra Friedman's and the Serpentine.

Hugh watched the WPC merge into the crowd and turned just as the artist Craig Charlton slunk up behind him. Charlton's mouth twitched into a smile. 'Great to see you again, Hugh.'

'And you, Craig.' Hugh sighed, pulling his phone from his pocket, in no mood to be drawn into conversation. He hadn't seen Charlton since the opening in Whitchapel four months before, when the artist had blown him out.

'This work is . . . em . . . interesting.' Charlton gave a cursory glance around the booth. 'Been hearing great things about your new gallery. LW2 is the hot ticket, apparently.'

'Is that so?' Hugh was scrolling through his contacts again, settling on Luca's number.

There was an awkward pause. 'You know I left the Alexandra Friedman Gallery?'

Hugh looked up. The artist bore the expectant face of someone who had just dropped a momentous piece of news. 'Did you?'

'Yeah, I just didn't feel she was committed enough to the work. The final straw was the paint-bomb at the gallery. My work was on view too. Granted it was upstairs, away from the blast, but I wasn't even mentioned in any of the interviews she did. Frankly, it was insulting.'

Hugh had to suppress a smile. 'That's truly shocking,' he said.

'It is, isn't it? I'm glad you think so.' The artist bit on his lower lip. 'Maybe I should reconsider your offer to show my work?'

'That's not such a good idea . . . .' Hugh's voice trailed off when, from the corner of his eye, he saw a familiar figure, brooding and intense, hovering at the far end of the booth. The face was drained of colour so that the scar seemed to stand out even more. Hugh turned back to Charlton. 'If you want my advice, Craig, stick with Alex Friedman. Now if you'll excuse me . . . .'

He sidestepped Charlton and pressed through the crowd, Kolya's eyes following him all the way. Maybe Hugh should have approached more warily, but whatever was coming, he was resigned to facing it. He stopped in front of the Russian, who looked shorter than his full six feet, hunched over, a hand pressed against his lower abdomen, just above the hip. He had a hunted look about him, his grey-blue eyes – paler even than Ana's – flitting left and right. 'Where is she?' he asked.

'Who?'

'Ana.'

'She's not here.'

The eyes grew dimmer still. He lowered his head. Hugh noticed a bloodstain on the hip of his jeans. 'Are you all right?' he asked. 'What happened to you?'

Kolya looked up. 'Why is she not here? I need speak to her.'

'Don't you have her number?'

'She changed it.' The tone was accusatory.

'I can call her, tell her you're here. Or you could leave a message?'

Kolya glanced up and down the aisle, as though checking whether he'd been followed, before gazing absently at one of the works on the wall. Finally, his eyes settled on a bare patch next to it. He lifted up the rim of his jacket, exposing a makeshift bandage. He peeled it off, along with a clump of gauze, matted with blood. Fresh blood oozed out from a crudely stitched gash – more like a piece of meat bound in twine than a properly sutured wound. His eyes narrowed and his breathing quickened as he gouged at the stitches with his fingers, till the blood formed a trickle.

'I will leave a message,' he said.

He mopped up the blood with the bandage and turned to the bare patch of wall. He held up the blood-sodden cloth and began to smear it across the white surface, forming letters: an 'S' first, then an 'O'.

He paused to mop up more blood.

Rivulets of crimson dribbled down the wall.

He added an 'R', fixed on the task, oblivious to the gathering onlookers, to the gasping, to one woman's muffled scream and another's nervy appeal for reassurance: 'This is a performance piece, right?' He soaked up more of the blood, which was now forming a fresh stain on the hip of his jeans, glistening in the spotlights. He added another 'R' and a 'Y', then turned to Hugh.

'Tell her I came.' The eyes were glassy, gazing through him without really looking. He turned to leave.

'Wait,' Hugh said. 'What happened at the gallery last night?'

Kolya paused, this time meeting Hugh's eye. 'I didn't do it for you.'

As they held one another's gaze, Hugh saw more than one scar that wouldn't fade with time. He saw remorse, cauterised by resignation, not redemption.

There was a shout above the din. 'Over here!' Hugh turned to see a security guard beckoning a policeman into the booth. They must have been searching for Kolya. The policeman pushed through the crowd and grabbed hold of Kolya's arm, ushering him towards the aisle. Kolya shrugged him off, pausing till the policeman backed away. The Russian looked at the crowd gathered around him, as if aware for the first time that he was being watched. He seemed to steel himself – his emotions sinking back into the still pools of his eyes – before he walked towards the exit without looking back.

Hugh's gaze tracked him as the crowds parted to let him pass. Then he turned back to the inscription on the wall. The letters were crimson in patches, fading into red ochre where the blood was smeared more thinly and beginning to dry. He struggled to grasp what he had just seen, his shock tempered by a grudging respect – a sense that Ana's taste in men may not be so bad after all.

His efforts to process what he'd seen were cut short by a shrill voice from behind: 'Now this, I like.' He turned to see a raven-haired woman in a grey opera coat marching into the booth, pointing flamboyantly at Kolya's inscription. She looked about her, settling on Hugh's exhibitor ID tag.

Thinking about it in hindsight, he could have told her what a good eye she had, that the piece was one of a number of *interventions* the gallery would be staging along with their programmed work for the fair, that it was by a young Russian artist, part of a new wave from that country who didn't shy away from the visceral, the shocking, the macabre. But the faculty for bullshit that had carried him this far, finally deserted him. He looked for inspiration to an ashen-faced Jack, who had come to stand by his shoulder, mouth agape. Jack promptly took a step backwards.

Luckily for both of them, however, the woman was the kind of person who liked to *tell* the gallery or the artist about the work and her response to it, rather than be told about it. 'I think I like the sentiment even more than the execution,' she proclaimed. 'The work of a man, I take it?'

Hugh nodded.

'Knew it,' she said. 'The word "sorry" never trips easily off the tongue for you men.'

The best Hugh could manage was a *mea culpa* shrug.

CHAPTER 43

Haiti, Not Hades

Hugh was home by 11PM. He double-locked the front door and put on the security chain that he'd fitted himself a few days before. He slumped on the couch in his living room, throwing his legs up on the ottoman in front of him. He looked down at the exhibitor ID tag from the fair, still dangling from a cord around his neck.

Hugh Rhattigan, Director, LW2 Gallery.

When Jack had first seen the tag that morning, he had suggested that Hugh add 'Auteur' to the job title.

'I'm not an auteur, I'm a fraudster,' Hugh told him.

'Not the way I see it,' Jack said. 'Making art under an alias is hardly illegal. How many successful conceptual artists actually make their own work anyway? Does it even matter any more? When Jeff Koons signs the work of a studio assistant, is this a confidence trick, the validation of a forgery?'

Hugh had just rolled his eyes, in no mood to kick it around. Even thinking about it now seemed like so much intellectual spit and polish – too complicated to unravel.

In fairness to Jack, he had no idea how Hugh really felt: numb, spent, his chest weighted down so that he could barely catch his breath. Hugh took no relief in Virgo's death, even though he had been under the man's thumb for so long. Maybe it was because he'd actually been fond of Virgo, or, more likely, it was because he wasn't shot of him yet. Virgo's corpse was still decomposing – in the gallery of which Hugh was director. The laminate badge around his neck was a millstone too.

Then there was Ana, the real cause of his melancholy. He'd tried phoning her, to tell her what had happened at the fair. but the calls rang out unanswered. There was a bitter irony in her frostiness towards him. He'd seen her incandescent with rage – or passion – but it was her coolness, her self-containment, that he'd first found so alluring. Now, the very qualities that he had been drawn to were being marshalled *against* him.

His breathing grew heavy, his eyes panning over the room, settling on the paintings stacked on the floor in the corner – paintings he'd never got around to hanging. Ana had promised to call over some evening and hang them herself. He doubted now that she ever would.

The only artwork on display was her drawing, propped up on the mantelpiece under the mirror. ('What kind of art dealer hangs a mirror over his fireplace?' she'd teased him once.) She left the drawing there the first time she stayed over: it was of the stunted boughs of the pollarded beech tree on the street outside. The tree was pruned every autumn, with that year's growth cut away, leaving only the gnarled stumps reaching out towards, but never touching, the trees alongside.

He looked from the drawing to his phone. He knew what the right thing to do was. He opened the photo he had taken of the bloody inscription on the wall of the booth. Its artistry, however intuitive, was undeniable. There was a directness about it, an absence of guile or knowingness, that bypassed the cerebral contortions of most of the work at the fair.

He sent the image to Ana with a message saying that the inscription was meant for her and that she should contact Kolya.

He must have dozed off shortly afterwards. He dreamed about the gruesome scene that had confronted him at the gallery that morning. In the dream, he was about to turn the lights on – with his old Jesuit headmaster by his side, rather than Diedrich Weiss. Just before he flicked the switch though, he was woken by the ringing of his phone, which lay next to him on the couch. He hoped it might be Ana, but the caller ID said 'Luca Ambrosini'. He checked the time. It was almost midnight.

The Australian sounded groggy, like he'd overdone it on the pills. He had to shush some girlish titters in the background. 'No doubt you've heard already, mate, but Douglas has departed these shores.'

Hugh sighed, remembering his Greek mythology. 'Not sure he'll make it very far, Luca, there were no coins left on the eyes to pay the ferryman.' (There were no eyes to leave them on, he could have added, but didn't.)

'What was that?' Luca said, shushing his playmates again, his reedy voice becoming muffled. 'I'm on a call here, babes.'

'No coins,' Hugh said wearily, rubbing his temples, 'for the journey, to Hades.'

This time Luca yelled into the receiver, 'Not *Haiti*, mate, but close enough.'

'Haiti?' Hugh said, presuming he had misheard. 'Did you say *Haiti*?'

But Luca was talking over him, rambling on about how he'd been busy all day, tidying up Virgo's affairs – Jersey first, on the red-eye out of City Airport, then on to Luxembourg. He apologised for the bloody mess in the gallery and promised to get someone in overnight to clean things up. His voice trailed off mid-sentence, replaced by the sound of petting, and a Hispanic girl grumbling that her 'baggy' was empty. 'No worries, sweetheart,' Luca said, sounding less and less like a man grieving his employer, 'plenty more where that came from.'

Hugh hung up. 'Not Haiti, but close enough,' he muttered, shaking his head, hauling himself off the couch.

He went to bed replaying the conversation with Luca in his head, prompting one question over and over: if it wasn't Virgo's corpse, whose was it?

He did sleep – eventually – but was jolted awake every couple of hours at the same point in the same dream, just as he turned on the lights in the gallery. Each time he was accompanied by a different person: his mother, his ex-father-in-law, Rebecca, *Ana*.

But each time, the corpse was the same: his own.

CHAPTER 44

An Arm and a Leg

Hugh was up and out by 8am the following morning. He'd skipped breakfast, thinking himself unlikely to be able to keep it down.

He brought a bag, with a change of clothes in it and a pair of old shoes. He was resigned to disposing of the corpse himself. He may not have been the gallery's beneficial owner but he was its public face, the one who would have to explain the fetid stench of death emanating from the building. He reckoned a cocktail of barbiturates, Viagra and booze – not to mention a harem of coked-up hookers – would have scuppered any chance of Luca organising a clean-up crew, while Virgo seemed to have fled the country after his showdown with the Russians and was out of radio cover. Likewise Harry.

Hugh stopped at the Starbucks in Camden, ordered a double espresso and sipped it as he skimmed over the results of a web search on the disposal of human corpses. His predicament was far more common than he would ever have suspected; the prescribed solutions were grisly and absurd in equal measure.

Bury the body in a lime pit. Dissolve it in acid and pour it down the drain. Dismember it and find an agreeable pig farmer. Bribe a hospital porter and burn it in an incinerator. Dump it at sea, wrapped in chains, or stuffed into an oil-drum, weighed down with concrete.

One thing was sure: no one had thought to exhibit their problem corpse as an artwork, not even with some maggots in a glass vitrine. like Hirst had done with the cow's head. Hugh got lucky when that clown,

Deidrich Weiss, presumed the body was waxwork, part of an installation, but it couldn't stay where it was. That much he knew.

He took the Northern Line to Old Street and walked the rest of the way. He stopped at a hardware shop on Shoreditch High Street and bought some heavy-duty refuse sacks, a pair of work gloves, an eighteen-inch hacksaw, a face-mask with a charcoal filter, and a gallon of industrial-grade disinfectant.

As he turned onto Rivington Street, he felt strangely detached from himself, as though he was trailing ten paces back, watching an alter ego walk along the pavement. He was like a voyeur of his own slide into criminality – which was about to get a lot steeper.

It was as he emerged from under the railway bridge that he saw the flashing blue lights. At first, he thought that someone must have complained about the stench. Then, that the Russians had called the police as an act of revenge. The trouble was, as he conjectured on why the police were outside the gallery, his criminal avatar kept walking.

The archway was cordoned off with yellow police tape that stretched out into the middle of the street. Hitched up on the kerb were two panda cars, a police transit van with 'Forensic Science Service' printed on the side and an unmarked car with a blue light on top. There was a man in a mud-coloured suit leaning against the back of the van. He dragged hard on a cigarette before dropping it into a paper cup.

Hugh stopped in front of him, suddenly reunited with his disembodied, criminal self. He almost held out his wrists – to be cuffed this time, not bound with plastic ring-ties.

'Can I help you, sir?' the man said, glancing down at the bags Hugh was carrying. The man looked profoundly unhealthy – bug-eyed, with a bloom of broken veins over yellow, waxy, almost cadaverous skin.

'I'm Hugh Rhattigan, the owner of the gallery.'

'Ah, so you do exist.' The man swirled the cigarette butt in the dregs of his milky tea.

'I need to explain what happened . . . .'

The man cut in, held up his warrant card. 'Inspector John Bates. No need, you're here now.'

He handed his cup to a uniformed officer and gestured for Hugh to follow him. 'Left a right bloody mess,' he said. Hugh sighed. So much for Luca getting a crew in. 'But funnily enough, not a lot for forensics to go on,' the inspector added.

That threw him. Hugh had never been a fan of police-procedural novels, but even his scant knowledge told him that the evidential trail in this case shouldn't be too hard to follow.

He'd opened his mouth to speak but hesitated when he noticed the jimmied lock. Then the smell hit him: oil-paint mixed with cordite. Walking into the lobby, he saw the tendrils of colour bursting from the mouth of the gallery. He followed Bates, picking his way through the paint.

The gallery was like a cave. The blast had smashed most of the light-bulbs. Stalactites of paint dripped from the ceiling. The walls were layered with waves of brown and grey, breaking into colour here and there, where the paints hadn't mixed.

'Sorry for not letting you know sooner,' Bates said. 'Our boys should have contact details for all the local businesses.'

Hugh barely managed a nod of the head.

'Fire brigade have been and gone. Not a lot for them to do, really.' Bates turned to Hugh, his brow furrowed. 'You all right? Must be an awful shock for you. Let me take those bags.'

Bates glanced into the bag from the hardware shop. 'Planning on doing some DIY, were you? Got your work cut out for you now. Wouldn't blame you for doing it yourself, though. Tradesmen in this city, charge a bloody arm and a leg.'

'What was that?' Hugh said, startled, having tuned out for moment.

'Just saying, tradesmen in this city, take a bloody arm and a leg.'

'Yeah,' Hugh mumbled, 'arms, legs, and the rest too.'

'Right . . . ,' Bates said, a little bemused. 'Now, unless I'm missing something, there doesn't seem to have been any art on display.'

Hugh was looking at the corner where the corpse had been. There were so signs of it, none that he could see at any rate. Luca must actually have got it together. As his eyes surveyed the space, Hugh had to suppress a wry smile. If only the paint-bombers knew the truth – that the gallery's owner was an ideological fellow traveller.

'Funny thing is,' Bates said, 'one of the trainee forensics bods ran a test for blood. Bit too keen, I would have thought, but he's only gone and found some, albeit trace amounts.' The inspector shook his head, the discovery seeming to compound an already weary outlook on life. 'Sick bastards. Call themselves artists, apparently. Will have to run a DNA test on it, I suppose. More sodding paperwork.'

Bates turned, as though he felt the need to unburden himself, eyes fixed on Hugh's, ruddy jowls bulging over his shirt collar. 'You know what really gets my goat.'

'What's that?' Hugh asked, wary again.

'I mean here you are, running your own business, trying to earn an honest living, and these idiots come along, hell-bent on wrecking it. Probably all on the scratcher too.'

'Yeah,' Hugh said absently, eyes panning over the gallery again. 'I didn't expect to see a mess like this when I showed up for work this morning.'

CHAPTER 45

If the Shoe Fits

Hugh called a locksmith, asked him to fix the locks and courier over a new set of keys. Then he left them at it – CSI Shoreditch – telling them to pull the door shut behind them when they were done. He was heading back across town to Regent's Park, to Fresco.

A queue for admission had already formed by the time he got there, coiling away into the park. Hugh flashed his exhibitor ID and made his way through a maze of booths patrolled by dealers and their surly assistants. They occasionally snatched a passing fair-goer, spitting the indigestible ones – artists looking for representation or punters insufficiently rich for the dealer's palate – back out into the aisles. Hugh made it to the LW2 booth without being drawn into conversation; word had yet to spread of the latest paint-bomb attack. He sat at the table on the edge of the booth, bowed his head and exhaled for what felt like the first time in days. He was unlikely to be arrested or abducted – not this morning, at any rate.

The relief was only partial, though. He still felt the cloying regret that his relationship with Ana was ending the way it was, and worse still, that it may never have been the relationship he thought it was to begin with. In spite of himself, he pulled out his phone and selected *Ana* from the contacts. His thumb hovered over the call button but he didn't press it. He told himself again to let *them* be.

He was still gazing at the phone when a black-clad figure sauntered up beside him, trailed by the scent of a subtly expensive perfume. 'Rough night?' It was Alexandra Friedman, looking down on him, smiling wryly. 'We were beginning to think you weren't coming.' Hugh glanced either side of the dealer – the 'we' referred only to her. 'Maybe there was no point in you coming at all?' she added. 'Word is, you've already sold everything.'

Hugh shrugged. 'We've been on a good run. Mostly word-of-mouth sales.'

Friedman wore a tight, knee-length dress – low-cut, accentuating a bust that hovered just above his eye-level. She gazed at the bloody inscription on the wall. 'This is the new piece, I presume. Have you sold that too?'

'I'm waiting to hear back from a client.'

She arched an eyebrow. 'Even we'd struggle to sell that. Still, what it lacks in technique, it makes up for in spontaneity – so I'm told, anyway.'

She perched on the edge of the desk. Her eyes – dark brown, verging on black – settled on his. She leaned over the table, one hand resting in front of him, the other flicking her hair back over her shoulder. She had always seemed daunting to Hugh, austere even, but now she was warm, almost flirtatious. 'I'm fascinated by this artist,' she said, pointing at the neon works, 'but rather annoyingly, they're all sold.'

'Every last one,' Hugh said.

'That's such a pity. I have a client who's *very* keen.' She mulled it over, then asked, 'What about the artist's copies?' The artist's copy – or proof – was traditionally the first, unnumbered piece in an editioned work that the artist kept. But in recent years, it had become a way for the artist to make more pieces in a sold-out edition. 'Maybe you' – she pointed at Hugh, a knowing glint in her eye – 'maybe *you* can sell me the artist's copies?'

It was only when he thought about it afterwards that he was unnerved – could she really have guessed there was no artist, apart from him? – but at the time he just smiled. She seemed more teasing than threatening.

'We could discuss it over a drink this evening?' She posed the question casually as she waved at another dealer walking past the booth. Waiting for an answer, her eyes browsed over his torso.

She *was* flirting with him. Hugh was usually wise to women who flirted with him even when they had no interest in sleeping with him, but he was having trouble calling this one. More so since he was feeling his first amorous stirrings since his ordeal in Nemirovsky's wet-room.

Why not? he thought. If Ana – and Rebecca – had moved on, why shouldn't he? Friedman was ten years older than him, but all the more attractive for it. She was also the queen-pin of the London art world. It was hard not to be flattered.

He was about to accept the invitation for a drink, when he saw *her*, standing on the edge of the booth, shoulders hunched, smiling awkwardly. His gaze lingered; her navy jeans and a pale blue T-shirt were a pleasant contrast to the ubiquity of black at the fair. He turned back to Friedman, shifted in his seat and sighed. 'I can't tonight, Alex, but why don't I pick the artist's brains, see if he's open to the idea?'

Friedman looked over her shoulder, eyes running Ana up and down, before turning back to Hugh with a playful pout. 'I'll leave you to it,' she said, seemingly unfazed by the brush-off. She swaggered into the opposite booth, hips swaying, arms outstretched, ready to greet a couple – clearly clients of hers – who looked like they'd just stepped out of a Burberry catalogue.

Hugh stood up as Ana edged cautiously towards him. They stopped a few paces apart. Ana's eyes trailed Friedman before turning back to Hugh. 'I hope I not interrupt.'

'No, she was just, em . . . sizing up . . . the competition.'

'Oh,' Ana said, nodding. 'I got your message.' She glanced at the inscription on the wall and grimaced. 'You are not cleaning it off?'

'I kinda like it,' Hugh said. 'Not sure I could have put it any more eloquently myself.'

When Ana smiled, the pale-blue lustre in her eyes made Hugh catch his breath. 'I spoke to Kolya,' she said. 'We sorted out some things.'

He gave a fatalistic shrug. 'I'm glad.'

'I made sure he go to hospital too.'

'Good.'

After an uneasy, almost bashful pause, Ana slid her bag off her shoulder and put it on the table. 'You like some help here today?'

'That'd be great,' Hugh said. 'I'm not expecting to see Jack for a while. Reckon he might be suffering from post-traumatic stress after last night.'

'So are some of people he dealt with, I would say.' Ana smiled again. It might have been wishful thinking on Hugh's part, but the smile seemed more than just fond.

Hugh watched Ana as she turned to a woman who had been hovering nervily on the edge of the booth, with an inquiry about the work, more than likely. Ana set the woman at ease, asking if she could help.

Hugh turned away, looking up and down the aisle, at the gathering swell of the crowd. The queue outside had begun to sluice through the turnstiles. It would be a long day.

As he gazed towards the main entrance, an outsized head bobbed into the crowd, floating above it, with the same totemic face that Hugh had seen at the opening in Whitechapel four months before, looking even more incongruous now – the forehead bandaged, the nose like a bruised plum. But this time, the face drew a different response from Hugh: curiosity rather than dread.

Harry rolled up to Hugh; their eyes were on the level. He checked out the cuts and bruises on Hugh's face, and stuck out his chin as a mark of approval.

Hugh did likewise. 'You look even worse than I do, Harry.'

'There was a bit of a tear-up the other night. You mighta worked it out.'

'Well, I'd guessed the meeting didn't end with a handshake and a glass of Pimm's. To be honest, I thought you would've skipped the country as well.'

'Nah,' Harry said, squaring his shoulders. 'Let 'em come after me. We'll fight 'em on the beaches and all that.'

'Right,' Hugh said, unconvinced by the Churchillian defiance. 'Speaking of *all that*, aren't you gonna tell me what happened?'

'A little hazy meself, to be honest. I was off me bonce, seeing stars. Pavel was out of it too, with a bust nose and a forearm swingin' like a ragdoll's. It was the boss who gave me the SP. One of the Russians turned on Vlad, knifed him in the gut.'

Hugh knew instantly which one. Kolya's words to Hugh the night before began to make sense: *I didn't do it for you.*

Who did he do it for, then?

Himself?

For Ana – to protect her?

Or for everyone Vlad had ever murdered or maimed, or was likely to? Kolya didn't have the look of a man who'd mastered his own conscience – surely a weakness in his line of work.

The questions were still tripping over themselves in Hugh's mind as Harry explained the mess in the gallery. Virgo's other henchman at the meet, Terry, was told to process the body. He was still compos mentis – as much as he ever had been, at any rate – but the task required a degree of know-how and, as it turned out, Terry was no craft butcher. He tried to hack the head off, with the flick-knife Kolya had used on Vlad, but surrendered to the stubborn resistance of tendons, Adam's apple and vertebrae. He did make it as far as the main blood vessel in the neck, the carotid artery. Hugh knew that from his own research on the subject. Hence the pools of blood around the corpse.

Terry ducked out then to get a secateurs and a pliers from the car – indispensable tools for the criminal mortician. When he came back, he snipped off the fingertips and pulled out the teeth: fingerprints and dental records were still the easiest ways to identify a body if it wasn't on the Old Bill's DNA database.

It was while he was hacking away at the face that he retched up the chicken vindaloo he'd had earlier that evening. He gave way to frustration then, stood up and began stomping on the face with the steel-tipped heel of his brogues. Virgo snapped, told Terry to leave it, that he'd send a crew in later to clean the place up and dispose of the body.

But Virgo had also decided it might be prudent to skip the country, in case the *mafiya* got all tribal, looking for payback. In the confusion, the plan to get a removal crew in got waylaid. It was the following night before they made it in to pick up the body and clean up the mess.

Ever the opportunist, Virgo also hit on the idea of swapping shoes with Vlad before they left. Virgo had been wearing his hand-made brogues from Cleverley's, the ones he'd crowed to Hugh about, made from eighteenth-century reindeer hide salvaged from a Danish brigantine that had sunk off the coast of Plymouth. Each pair was numbered, and the shop had a record of who bought them. As it happened, Virgo and Vlad were both a size ten. Virgo left in Vlad's Gucci loafers.

'The cozzers aren't always the sharpest tools in the box,' Harry said, 'but even they should be able to follow a lead like that. The boys dumped

Vlad's body off a jetty at Battersea power station this morning. It'll wash up handily enough for the law to find it.'

Virgo's criminal conviction predated the setting up of the National DNA Database, so unless any of his relations consented to a DNA test – which was unlikely – the death should be recorded as his.

Why fake his own demise? Every crim reaches a point where dying is a good career move, and Virgo reckoned now was as good a time as any.

'This is privileged information,' Harry said. 'I'm tellin you 'cos I know you'll keep shtum. Kolya knows, but he's not likely to talk. No one else does, apart from Pavel and Terry. The two bodyguards Vlad brought to the meet have been *retired*.' Harry shook his head, the hard-man façade slipping momentarily. 'They almost retired me first. Right fuckin' bruisers they were.'

'I think I might have run into them,' Hugh said.

'So I heard. Gave 'em a bittova goin over an' all.'

'Did my best – no one's ever pulled a gun or a can of pepper spray on me on a rugby field.'

Harry looked around the booth. 'This art palaver's lost on me, but a bloke who can handle himself in a scrap, that I can appreciate.' His flinty eyes settled on Hugh's. 'The boss might even have been right about you.'

'How's that?'

'Maybe you was born with some balls after all.'

'Maybe,' Hugh said, looking over the crowd, 'or else I've just been breaking in a new pair.'

Not the End...
To be continued in Vermil£ion